OVER THE UNDERWORLD

Also by Adam Shaughnessy

The Unbelievable FIB 1:
The Trickster's Tale

OVER THE UNDERWORLD

by
ADAM SHAUGHNESSY

Algonquin Young Readers   2017

Published by
Algonquin Young Readers
an imprint of Algonquin Books of Chapel Hill
Post Office Box 2225
Chapel Hill, North Carolina 27515-2225

a division of
Workman Publishing
225 Varick Street
New York, New York 10014

First paperback edition, Algonquin Young Readers, October 2017. Originally
published in hardcover by Algonquin Young Readers in September 2016.
Printed in the United States of America.
Published simultaneously in Canada by Thomas Allen & Son Limited.
Design by Carla Weise.

Library of Congress Cataloging-in-Publication Data

Names: Shaughnessy, Adam, [date]– author. | Shaughnessy, Adam, [date]–
Unbelievable FIB ; bk. 2.
Title: Over the underworld / by Adam Shaughnessy.
Description: First edition. | Chapel Hill, North Carolina : Algonquin
Young Readers, 2016. | Series: The unbelievable FIB ; book 2 | Summary:
"It's been a year since friends ABE and Pru joined Mister Fox's Fantasy
Investigation Bureau—otherwise known as the Unbelievable FIB. In their
next adventure, they must outrun trolls, explore Asgard and the Viking
underworld, and try to outsmart the Queen of the Dead herself to change
fate, save the world—and survive seventh grade"—Provided by publisher. |
"Published simultaneously in Canada by Thomas Allen & Son Limited."
Identifiers: LCCN 2016018798 | ISBN 9781616204990 (HC)
Subjects: LCSH: Fantasy—Juvenile fiction. | Gods, Norse—Juvenile fiction. |
Mythology, Norse—Juvenile fiction. | Magic—Juvenile fiction. | CYAC:
Gods, Norse—Fiction. | Mythology, Norse—Fiction. | Magic—Fiction.
Classification: LCC PZ7.1.S49 Ov 2016 | DDC [Fic]—dc23
LC record available at https://lccn.loc.gov/2016018798

ISBN 978-1-61620-747-2 (PB)

10 9 8 7 6 5 4 3 2 1
First Paperback Edition

For my mother, always.

And for Jane, forevermore.

OVER THE UNDERWORLD

CHAPTER
1

THE OLD MAN SAT IN HIS CHAIR AND WATCHED THE FIRE WITH HIS ONE GOOD eye. Two ravens perched nearby, Thought and Memory. He ignored them the way one ignores familiar companions or unwanted guests.

Sometimes he wondered which they were.

As he gazed into the fire before him, he imagined he could see images of gods, giants, and mortals in the dancing flames. They acted out the events of their lives like performers in a show, each playing her or his role.

Now events were occurring that forced him to think about the performance's conclusion.

Sitting there, alone, the old man thought about the days to come.

He thought about the future.

So far, it was going just the way he remembered it.

CHAPTER
2

"MISTER FOX IS A JERK!"

ABE looked around to see if anybody was close enough to have heard Pru's shout. Fortunately, he and Pru stood in a remote section of Middleton Cemetery. The only bodies nearby lay six feet under the ground and probably weren't very interested in Pru's frustration with their former mentor. They stayed quiet.

ABE did, too.

He'd learned that there were two things you didn't talk to Pru about when she was in this kind of mood: One, Mister Fox. Two, everything else.

It was best to just let her work through things on her own.

"He said we'd see him again," Pru complained.

"Well, *technically*, he said it was true we wouldn't see him." The words were out before ABE could stop them. So much for staying quiet.

Pru put her hands on her hips. "You know, ABE, one of these days I'm going to teach you that honesty isn't *always* the best policy."

"Sorry."

"It's okay," Pru said, letting her arms fall to her sides. She sat down on a tree stump and flashed ABE a smile. "It's not you I'm mad at. Not really. Seriously, though. Didn't you think we'd see him again?"

"Yeah, I did. I mean, especially since you thought we would. You always understood him better than I did. Well, except for the time you thought he was Loki and tried to set fire to his house . . ."

"Not helping, ABE. Don't make me change my mind about not being mad at you."

"Right."

Pru sighed. "It's been almost a year."

"Almost," ABE agreed. Mister Fox had arrived in Middleton in his magical Henhouse, headquarters of the Fantasy Investigation Bureau—or, as Mister Fox called it, the Unbelievable FIB—in October of the year before. He'd come to investigate an invasion of gods and giants from Norse mythology.

That's what Mister Fox did. He investigated mysteries that involved magic and myth. But he didn't do it alone. He couldn't. He needed the help of kids. They had a talent for seeing magic where others couldn't. So Mister Fox had recruited ABE and Pru to become Fibbers, junior members of his detective agency. Together, they'd vanquished giants and foiled the attempts of Loki, the Norse trickster, to recover a magical artifact called the Eye of Odin.

But that had all happened last year. Now it was the end of August and school was about to start. Pru and ABE had spent the better part of a year waiting for Mister Fox's return, hiking the wooded trails around Middleton at least once a week. Pru called it patrolling and insisted they do it just to be on the safe side. Their patrols almost always ended in the cemetery, where they could check to see if the Henhouse had returned.

It never had.

Neither had Ratatosk the Insult Squirrel. That's what Pru called him, anyway. Really, Ratatosk was the messenger of the Norse gods. But since so many of the messages he carried were insults, he had developed a rather . . . unique . . . way of speaking to people. Despite that, Ratatosk had become their friend, and ABE missed his company as much as Pru did.

In fact, all the Mythics (Mister Fox's term for beings from Worlds of Myth) who had been in Middleton had left after their battle over the Eye. Even the town patriarch, Old Man Grimnir, who was really Odin in disguise, had left. According to the people who ran the museum wing of his mansion, he'd "gone traveling." No one knew when he'd be back.

"Mister Fox could still show up," ABE said, slipping his looking glass, a gift from the detective, back into his belt.

The looking glass resembled a normal magnifying glass. It had a wooden handle with a brass raven's head at its base and a brass frame around the glass itself. But the device was anything but normal. One side of the glass was actually a mirror that had the power to banish Mythics back to their own world. The other side functioned like a regular magnifying glass, except it could also identify and track Mythics that appeared on Earth.

"I know he *could* still show up. But will he?" Pru glanced at ABE out of the corner of her eye. "I still think we should try my idea to catch his attention in case the Henhouse goes by overhead."

"Pru . . . I figured it out. It would take about fifty-two fallen trees to spell out *MISTER FOX, COME BACK*. And that's assuming all the logs were the same size. I'm not sure we could cut down that many trees. I definitely don't think we should be setting dozens of dead trees on fire."

"Fine." Pru stuck her tongue out. "I'll come up with a new plan."

Pru stood up on the tree stump and pulled her own

looking glass from her messenger bag. It looked a lot like ABE's, only it had a squirrel's head at the base of its handle. She held the glass to her eye and spun in a slow circle. When she'd completed one rotation, she sighed again and slipped her glass back into her bag.

"What if this is it, ABE? What if he doesn't come back and this is it? Just this . . . every day, forever?"

ABE didn't know what to say. A part of him did want to see Mister Fox again. Another part of him wasn't sure. He still had nightmares about when Loki and his chief frost giant, Gristling, had abducted him and taken him to Asgard, the world of the Norse gods.

Silence filled the space between them as the late afternoon sun warmed their skin. Finally, Pru glanced at her watch. "I guess we should be getting back. To-night's the open house. I can't believe it's time to go back to school already."

"Yeah," ABE agreed. He found himself thinking of fresh school supplies and crisp new textbooks with spines that crackled when you opened them for the first time.

"What do you look so happy about?" Pru asked, eying him suspiciously.

"Me? Oh, nothing." Pru was coming out of her mood about Mister Fox. ABE didn't want to push her buttons by admitting that he was actually excited about the start of a new school year.

"I was just looking at the bright side of school start-ing," he said instead.

"Which is?"

"Well, we may have to go back to school. But at least you—*we*—won't have to see Mrs. Edleman anymore."

CHAPTER 3

AS HE AND HIS DAD DROVE TO THE SCHOOL THAT NIGHT, ABE WONDERED IF HE had been too optimistic earlier.

It was true that, as seventh graders, he and Pru wouldn't be in Mrs. Edleman's class—or Cell Block E, as Pru called it—anymore. Unfortunately, Middleton was so small that the junior high school was just an addition to the elementary school. It didn't even have its own entrance. So while he and Pru would no longer have to endure Mrs. Edleman's tyrannical approach to public education, they were still likely to see their former teacher every once in a while.

"So," his dad said, "I bet you're disappointed about school starting, huh?"

"Me? Oh . . . yeah." ABE folded up the class schedule he'd been studying and stuffed it in his pocket.

"Right? I know I always hated the end of summer vacation when I was a kid. No more pickup games of Wiffle ball or touch football . . ."

ABE fiddled with his seat belt as his dad's voice trailed off. He tried to think of something he and his dad had in common that they could talk about to fill the sudden quiet. He was still thinking when they pulled into the school's parking lot.

"Well, here we are," his dad said. "And look, there's Pru and her mom."

"ABE, over here!" Pru said, waving, as he and his dad got out of the car. "Hey, Mr. Evans. Catch the game last night?"

"Sure did, sport!"

ABE walked around the back of the car and greeted Pru's mom. "Hi, Mrs. Potts."

"Hi, ABE." She ruffled his hair. She kind of had a fascination with his curly hair. He didn't mind. "Hi, Gavin. No Maddie tonight?"

"Working, unfortunately."

"That's too bad. Well, shall we head inside?" Pru's mom said. "Ready for a new year, Pru?"

"If I say no can I have another month of summer vacation?"

"Nice try, kiddo."

They joined the flow of people walking from the parking lot to the school buildings. The first fallen leaves of the season blew across the pavement in front of them as they approached the entrance.

"What room are we looking for?" Pru's mom asked as they stepped inside.

"Thirteen," Pru answered. "I can't believe our home-room is number thirteen. Like that's not an omen."

"There are no such things as omens," Pru's mother said. "Don't read anything into a room number. There's no predicting the future."

Pru looked back at ABE and raised her eyebrows dramatically. He hid a grin.

"Looks like this is us," ABE's dad said when they found the right room.

ABE let Pru, her mom, and his dad go in first. He followed them but stopped short just inside the doorway, surprised by the appearance of their new homeroom.

Mrs. Edleman's classroom had been set up with neat rows of desks all facing the front of the room. The walls had been covered with rules.

The desks in this new classroom had been clustered together into makeshift tables with four or five chairs around each. Posters of book covers and pictures of authors lined the walls. ABE beamed when he saw his favorite book, *The Phantom Tollbooth*, among them.

He pulled out his folded schedule. It said what his classes were, and when. It also listed his teachers. He hadn't paid too much attention to his teachers at first—he hadn't recognized any of their names. Now he looked more closely and saw that he had the same teacher for homeroom and language arts, Mr. Jeffries.

"Hey. Who's that?" Pru asked as the four of them settled into seats around a table near the back and a young man with neatly trimmed stubble stepped to the front of the room.

"The adult standing at the front of your homeroom?" Pru's mother asked. "Well, if I was going to go out on a limb, I would guess that's your homeroom teacher. Said the mother to her would-be-detective daughter."

"Funny, Mom. Seriously, though. You think? But he's wearing sneakers. Do teachers wear sneakers? Do they even own them? Weird. Imagine Mrs. Edleman in sneakers." Pru shivered in her seat. "Ouch. I think I just broke my brain."

"Shush," her mom said, giving Pru a playful nudge with her elbow. "You'll get me in trouble. There's no talking in class."

ABE smiled. Pru had said she and her mom hadn't always gotten along so well. But they seemed to have a great relationship from what ABE had seen over the past year. He glanced at his dad, who directed a glassy-eyed stare to the front of the room.

"Hi, everyone, and welcome to Middleton Junior High School," the man with the stubble and sneakers said. He gestured to a poster on the wall beside the whiteboard. "One of my favorite poets, Jean Inglelow, once wrote:

Children, ay, forsooth,
They bring their own love with them when they come,
But if they come not there is peace and rest . . .

"Since you've all been good enough to show up tonight, I suppose I can say good-bye to peace and rest."

Chuckles and snorts of laughter filled the room. ABE was surprised that some of the laughter came from Pru.

Not everyone was amused, though. A boy at the table next to theirs whispered to his friend, "*Forsooth?* Who says that? What does it even mean?"

"Actually," ABE said, turning in his seat, "*sooth* is another word for *truth*, so *forsooth* basically means 'in truth.' It's an old English word and—"

Beside him, Pru groaned. ABE turned back to look at her and saw his dad studying the table, red-faced.

"I did the whole ABE-the-walking-dictionary thing again, didn't I?" he whispered to Pru. She nodded. ABE heard snorts of laughter from the table next to theirs. He sank into his chair as his teacher continued speaking.

"I'm kidding, of course. I'm thrilled to see everyone here tonight. I'm Mr. Jeffries. Everyone who's too young to drive a car, I'm going to be your homeroom teacher and your language arts teacher. For everyone else in the room, I'm one of the people your child will likely be complaining about for the next nine months or so. Sorry for that."

More laughter.

"Careful, kiddo," Pru's mother said, leaning in to whisper to Pru. "Someone might actually think you're enjoying yourself at school."

Mr. Jeffries kept them a little longer. He explained the school's website and gave out his e-mail address. Then he invited all the students (and their families) to walk around and meet the rest of their teachers in other classrooms.

"Well, I guess that wasn't *too* painful," Pru admitted to ABE later in the evening as they left the gym. She'd checked first to make sure their parents were out of earshot behind them.

"Yeah. Mr. Jeffries seems nice. And funny."

"A little, I guess. He's an improvement over you-know-who at least." Pru stopped short, her eyes suddenly narrowed. "Oh, man. Speak of the devil."

ABE followed Pru's gaze. Mr. Jeffries was walking

down the hall toward them, but he wasn't alone. Mrs. Edleman walked by his side.

"Abe," Mrs. Edleman said, looking down over her glasses as they approached. "How nice to see you. And Prudence, of course."

"Hi, Mrs. Edleman," ABE said.

"Mrs. Edleman," Pru said. ABE imagined he could hear western showdown music in the background.

"Are these former students of yours, Mrs. Edleman?" Mr. Jeffries said. "How nice! I believe I have the pleasure of having them both in my homeroom. ABE and Prudence, isn't it? Sorry. I'm still learning names."

"It's *Pru*."

ABE didn't think Pru realized how snappish she sounded. Mrs. Edleman sort of had that effect on her.

"So, um, did you have a nice summer, Mrs. Edleman?" he said to change the subject.

"I did, Abraham, thank you for asking."

"It's . . . uh . . . I'm not . . ." That wasn't his name. ABE was an acronym, a nickname made from the initials of his real name, Aloysius Bartholomew Evans. Should he correct Mrs. Edleman? Before he could decide if it was okay to correct a teacher, his dad and Pru's mom stepped up behind them.

"Mrs. Edleman," Pru's mom said with a nod as she placed a hand on Pru's shoulder. Mrs. Edleman returned the nod.

"Mrs. Potts. Mr. Evans. A pleasure to see you both. Did you enjoy the open house?"

"We did," Pru's mom said. "In fact, we'd just finished up and were about to go get some ice cream. Gavin and ABE, would you like to join us?"

"Sounds good," ABE's dad said.

"Yeah," ABE agreed, admiring how quickly Pru's mom had managed to get them out of the chance encounter with Mrs. Edleman.

It just wasn't quick enough.

"Prudence," Mrs. Edleman said before they could make their escape, "just remember, this is a new year. That means a fresh start. I'm sure you will make the most of it. There's no need to repeat past mistakes and problem behaviors."

Pru's face turned bright red. ABE followed her gaze from Mrs. Edleman to Mr. Jeffries, and he saw their new teacher watching the exchange with raised eyebrows.

Pru was about to lose it. ABE needed to say something to distract her. What? He could ask Mr. Jeffries how he liked Middleton, since he was new to the school. Or was that a weird question to ask a teacher? He needed to say *something*.

"Let's go, Pru," her mother said, instead, rescuing Pru (and ABE).

ABE breathed a sigh of relief. Realizing that he was shifting his weight from foot to foot, he forced himself to stop. His mom always laughed when he did that, but in a nice way. She said it reminded her of when he was a toddler and just learning to walk. She said he would walk in place, like he couldn't decide which way to go.

"Mom, did you hear her?" Pru said when they'd walked a little way down the hall. "That was so embarrassing."

"I heard, honey. And I don't like it, either. But there's nothing to be done about it now. I'm sure it will blow over once the year starts."

Pru didn't say anything. She just looked back. ABE did, too. Mr. Jeffries and Mrs. Edleman were standing close together, talking. He saw Mrs. Edleman point in their direction—he was sure she had pointed at Pru. Mr. Jeffries frowned.

When ABE looked back at Pru, her face was still as red as her hair. He sighed.

Cell Block E might not be as easy to escape as they had hoped.

The air outside the ice-cream parlor smelled of a delicious combination of pine trees and the shop's special homemade hot fudge. ABE, his dad, and Pru's mom settled into a picnic table behind the store. Pru had gone back inside for napkins.

ABE looked up at the colored pennants that lined the picnic area. They flapped in the evening breeze. Gazing beyond the flags, ABE was disappointed to see clouds rolling in. He had hoped for a view of the stars.

"Why does the air always seem to smell so much better in the summer?" Pru's mother asked, inhaling deeply.

"Actually, it doesn't just seem to," ABE said. "It really does. I read an article about how odor molecules don't travel so well when it's cold, so there's not as much to smell."

"ABE, you are a marvel!" Pru's mother pointed her spoon at him. "You have so much knowledge floating around in that head of yours. Gavin, you must be so proud."

ABE looked at his dad, who blinked. "Yeah, he's a smart kid all right. Certainly doesn't get it from me. When I was his age all I cared about were sports and cars."

"He's been a good influence on Pru, that's for sure. I think she read more this summer than she has in the past . . . well, eleven years. Who'd have guessed she'd like mythology so much? Speaking of Pru . . ." Her mother paused to look around. "Where's she gotten to? How hard is it to find napkins?"

"I'm sure she'll be right out," ABE said.

"Yeah. It's an ice-cream parlor. How much trouble could she get into?" Pru's mother's eyes crinkled in a smile. "Then again, this *is* Pru we're talking about. We might want to have the National Guard standing by."

She and his dad laughed. Even ABE smiled.

"Maybe I should go check on her," Pru's mom said, setting her cup of ice cream on the table.

"I'll go," ABE said, glancing at his dad. "I, uh, want to use the bathroom anyway."

As he walked around the building to the front entrance, he wondered if he should he have said *restroom* instead. Was the word *bathroom* impolite? What was proper etiquette when it came to lavatory terminology? *Lavatory!* Maybe he should have said that.

He was so lost in thought that he nearly walked right into Pru as she barreled around the corner.

"ABE," she said, pulling him aside. "You'll never guess what I just overheard! I was eavesdropping on a couple of teenagers—"

"You were eavesdropping on teenagers?"

Pru rolled her eyes. "Fine. I wasn't *actually* eavesdropping. I was just interested in what they were talking about, so I stood someplace where I could be sure to accidentally overhear what they said. Okay?"

ABE wanted to point out that he hadn't been objecting to eavesdropping. He'd just been surprised. But Pru seemed excited, so he stayed quiet.

"The point is, one of the teenagers has been working at Winterhaven House this summer. He was saying how crazy today had been up at the mansion because . . ."

Pru took a deep breath. She gripped his shoulders.

"Because they're getting ready for Old Man Grimnir's return tomorrow. ABE, *Odin is coming back*!"

CHAPTER 4

ABE WOKE UP THE NEXT DAY TO A SKY THE COLOR OF MOURNING. THE BOOK he'd been reading when he fell asleep—a collection of Norse myths—lay closed on his bedside table. He guessed that his mom had placed it there after she came home. She always checked in on him when she worked a late shift.

He dressed and paused outside his parents' room on his way downstairs, wondering if they were up and if he had time to say hi to his mom before going to meet Pru. He was about to knock when he heard his father's voice on the other side of the door.

"It was fine, I guess. A little dull. What can you expect? It's school. But I'll tell you, Maddie, I'm worried about the boy. Last night, one kid laughed at him and his old teacher called him the wrong name. ABE didn't say or do anything. It's like the kid doesn't even know how to stand up for himself. It was painful to watch."

ABE pulled his hand back from the door. It hung in the air a moment before he lowered it to his side and went downstairs. He'd leave them a note. They were used to him and Pru spending the day together.

As ABE passed the front door, he heard an urgent rapping that announced Pru's early arrival.

"Are you ready?" she asked when he opened the door.

"Just about." He sat on the bottom step of the staircase and wiggled one foot into a sneaker, pulling on the heel flap when it got squished into the shoe. He had new sneakers in a box in his bedroom. But those were for the first day of school. He didn't feel right about wearing them before then.

Pru paced back and forth outside the screen door. She rubbed her hands together with glee.

"Can you believe it, ABE? Odin is here in Middleton again! I wonder what brought him back."

"You don't think he wants the Eye of Odin back, do you? It was his actual eye, after all. Maybe he's mad we hid it."

Pru paused. She chewed her lower lip. It was a new habit. Her hair had grown in the past year. It no longer fell in a bob around her chin, so it wasn't as easily accessible for chewing.

"No," she said, resuming her pacing. "He went centuries without his eye. I bet he doesn't even miss it anymore. And besides, *we* didn't hide the Eye. Mister Fox did. If Odin wants to be mad at Mister Fox, then that's fine with me. He can get in line."

After a quick dash to grab a granola bar from the kitchen, ABE opened the door to join Pru on the porch. Glancing at the leaden sky, he went back in to grab an umbrella.

"Anything *else* you want to do before we go?" Pru asked.

"Ah, no. I'm good," he said, following Pru as she set off. He tried to match her brisk pace. "Um, Pru, what do you think is going to happen when we get there? I mean, it's exciting that Odin is back. But we don't even know if he'll want to see us."

Pru didn't say anything at first. Instead, she chewed her lip again.

"I know," she said. "But at least his being back is *something*. You know? He *has* to see us."

Pru quickened their pace even more as the sky began a slow leak. ABE opened his umbrella. Around them, tear-shaped drops of rain fell from the clouds above, completing ABE's sense of foreboding about what they might find when they finally reached Winterhaven House.

✳

They needn't have worried about getting in to see Odin. Two sights greeted them at the mansion's iron gates. The first was a sign announcing that the building and grounds were temporarily closed while the museum underwent renovations.

That might have presented a problem if not for the second sight. A broad-shouldered woman with a long blonde braid stood on the other side of the gate. She appeared to be waiting for them, unbothered by the rain.

"Hilde!" Pru called as she broke into a run.

Odin's assistant reached down and unlocked the gate. She swung it open to admit Pru and ABE.

"Hello, children."

"Hi, Hilde," ABE said, catching up and holding his umbrella up higher to try to cover everyone. "Why are you standing out in the rain?"

"I'm waiting for you, of course." A hint of a smile showed on Hilde's usually stern face.

"Waiting for us?" Pru repeated. "Why? How? Wait! Don't tell me. Is 'Mr. Grimnir' *expecting* us again?"

Hilde's smile slipped from her face as though washed off by the falling rain.

"This is not a time for jokes, children. Come with

me. Odin *is* expecting you. But he does not wait with good news."

"What's wrong?" ABE asked.

"That is for Odin to say."

They walked in silence across the gravel drive and through Winterhaven's halls, where ABE's eyes followed the frozen march of the Viking warriors carved into the towering stone walls of the mansion. He watched them disappear down corridors not taken.

Hilde led them to the same room where they'd had their first audience with Odin. It was empty this time, though. Hilde said she would return with "the others" shortly and left them with instructions to wait as she exited through a different door.

Pru threw her arms out wide as soon as Hilde had closed the door behind her. "We're back!" she exclaimed, clearly not fazed by Hilde's somber mood.

"Six chairs," ABE said, walking around the long table that ran the length of the room.

"What?" Pru asked.

"There are six chairs." ABE gestured to the setup. He recognized one of the chairs, a high-backed and intricately carved wooden seat at the head of the table. It was the chair Odin had sat in on their last visit.

"There's the two of us plus Odin and Hilde," Pru said, considering. "That's four."

"Hilde said she'd be back with 'the others.' I wonder who the last two chairs are for."

"Maybe Thor's back, too."

"Maybe. I kind of hope not, though."

"What? Are you crazy? Thor's awesome!"

"No, I know. It's not that I don't want to see him. I do. Thor saved our lives. He's great!"

"Then what's wrong?"

ABE turned to one of the narrow windows that lined the wall. "It's the rain. Last night, I noticed that clouds had rolled in. I didn't think anything of it at first. Then you found out Odin was back."

"And you wondered if maybe Thor was back, too." Pru frowned. She'd been practically dancing through the room. Now she slowed down. ABE guessed she was arriving at the same conclusion he'd reached.

"We know that the weather can reflect Thor's mood, right?" he said. "We got all those clouds last year because Thor was mad about being locked up. But, even with everything that happened then, it never rained. The clouds today remind me of the clouds last time. With the rain, though, and Hilde's mood . . . everything seems . . . I don't know. Sad."

Pru opened her mouth as if to argue. But she closed it again without saying anything and joined ABE at the window. A chill filled the room, despite the fire that burned in the hearth and the flaming torches that lined the walls.

ABE had wondered about the torches last time. Now, knowing what he did about Mythics and their incompatibility with technology, he supposed that torches made sense for a room where gods gathered and held council.

"What do you think has happened?" Pru asked. She drew her finger across the glass of the window. Beads of moisture gathered on her fingertip.

"I don't know . . . but I think we might be about to find out," he said as Thor's booming voice reached them from behind the door through which Hilde had left.

"And so they must carry the weight of our inaction?" Thor demanded of someone.

The door burst open and the god of thunder stormed into the room. His presence charged the air with a current of anger and tension that raised the hairs on ABE's arms.

"Thor!" Pru exclaimed, taking a step toward him. She stopped in her tracks as Thor turned his fierce glare in their direction.

Seeing them, the god's brow smoothed a bit.

"Children, forgive me. Hilde mentioned you had arrived. It is good to see you again." Thor's mustache and beard parted in what looked like an attempt at a smile. He took a deep breath. The atmosphere in the room lightened a little, but Thor's clenched fists and the corded muscles of his arms betrayed his tense emotion.

"What's wrong?" Pru asked.

"A great many things." Thor glanced back at the door. The wood along the upper hinge had splintered, and the door hung limply in its frame. Thor closed his eyes and took another deep breath. "All of which we shall discuss, and soon. First, though, I have yet to greet the brave lad who recovered the Eye of Odin from the field of battle during our last meeting."

Thor approached ABE and gripped his shoulder. ABE's eyes widened and he clenched his jaw shut to keep from crying out. Thor's grip was iron! Why did he even bother carrying a hammer around? His pinkie could probably drive a railroad stake through the ground!

"Yup. He's the brave lad, all right," Pru said, her eyes dancing. Thor's arrival had restored at least some of her good humor. "Did you know his name— *Aloysius*—means 'famous warrior'?"

"A fine name for such a . . . strapping young lad!"

ABE looked down at his scrawny frame. "That's, ah, very nice, sir. But ABE's fine. Really."

"But your true name has such strong meaning, lad!

And it fits someone with the courage to charge into a field of frost giants. You should embrace your fierce nature!"

Pru started nodding vigorously.

"*Yes.* Yes, ABE, that is exactly what you should be doing. I am *always* telling him to embrace his fierce nature," she confided to Thor.

ABE cast a sidelong glance at Pru. She responded with a look of innocence. At least ABE assumed she was trying to look innocent. Not having had a lot of practice actually *being* innocent, she wasn't pulling it off too well.

"Blustering oaf," a voice muttered, interrupting the exchange.

A bent old man entered the room, carefully navigating through the damaged door. ABE turned to Pru in amazement when he recognized the newcomer. Her dropped jaw reflected the surprise he knew must show on his own face.

Odin, Allfather of the gods of the North, god of wisdom and war, shuffled into the room. He leaned heavily on a long wooden walking stick. A blue cloak lay across his stooped shoulders. Every few steps, Odin reached out with one hand to gather the cloak at his neck as if it were a shawl. The wide, broad-brimmed hat atop his head bobbed up and down as unsteady steps carried him across the room.

"Go, children," Thor whispered. "Stand behind your seats. Sit after he does. Speak when addressed and do not test my father's patience. I have already lost my temper with him once this morning and I should not have done so. These are troubled times."

ABE followed Thor's directions. Odin hadn't seemed this weak and old the last time he and Pru saw him. What had happened?

The Allfather made his way to the seat at the head of the table, and Thor moved to stand behind the chair to his father's right. Hilde returned to the room and stood across from ABE and next to Thor. ABE glanced at the empty seat at the foot of the table.

Odin's chair slid across the floor and the god dropped into it, muttering. He removed his hat and hung it off the back of his throne-like seat.

ABE, Pru, and the others also sat.

"We are here because of betrayal," Odin wheezed, looking at everyone around the table. "We are here because of trickery! We are here . . . because of death."

ABE's stomach sank with dread.

"My son is dead!" Odin's declaration came in a hoarse gasp. "Baldur, the best of us, is dead."

ABE clutched the table to steady himself. The room swayed in the flickering torchlight. Everything seemed suddenly less stable and less sure.

"Oh no!" Pru said. "I'm so sorry."

ABE heard empathy in her voice, the empathy of someone who had also lost a loved one. But she didn't really understand. She hadn't read and reread the Norse myths like he had. If she had, she wouldn't be sad.

She'd be terrified.

"That's it, then?" ABE said, forgetting Thor's instructions not to speak. "It's started?"

"What's started?" Pru asked.

"Ragnarok," ABE said, looking at her. "Ragnarok has started, Pru. It's the end of the world."

CHAPTER
5

"WHAT ARE YOU TALKING ABOUT?" PRU DEMANDED OF ABE. SHE TURNED TO Odin. "What's he talking about? What does he mean, Ragnarok has started?"

"Let your friend tell you," Odin said. "Like you, he seems unable to hold his tongue, even when instructed to do so."

ABE flinched at the reprimand, but he didn't let that stop him from answering. He spoke quickly as his words tried to keep pace with the fear building inside him.

"You know how the Norse myths work," he began. "Some of them are stories about things that have happened. But because Odin drank from the Well of Wisdom and gained the ability to see the future, some

Norse myths are stories about things that haven't happened yet but will. They're stories that came from what Odin saw in his visions. One of those myths is of Ragnarok, the end of all things."

"I *know* all that. But what makes you think Ragnarok has started?"

"Because Ragnarok doesn't just end in death. It *starts* with death, too. Baldur's death. Loki kills Baldur, the favorite of the gods. Then Loki runs away from Asgard. Thor finds him and brings him back to be judged and imprisoned. Loki eventually breaks free and all the giants join him to fight the gods. And everyone on Asgard and on our world dies in that war. *Everyone!* That's how the stories go."

Pru nodded, her lower lip tucked under her front teeth. "I remember now. But can't we do something? I mean, I knew Ragnarok was coming . . . someday—but not now! Can't we change what's going to happen?"

"The fates hold us tight, child," Thor said. "But—"

"Change what is going to happen?" Odin interrupted. He leaned forward. "We cannot *change* the future. We should not want to! Your clever friend is wrong. Not *everyone* dies. Tell the story true, boy."

ABE frowned. "He's right, I guess. There are supposed to be a *few* survivors among people and gods. But hardly any—"

"Yes," Odin said, interrupting again. "And in time

those survivors will rebuild Asgard and Midgard. But they will make better worlds, untouched by evil. Because through the sacrifice of the gods, all giants and monsters will be destroyed during Ragnarok. Imagine that, boy! A world without evil! It will be a most terrible triumph."

"Triumph? But so many will die," Pru said.

"All things die, even gods. What matters is *how* we die. And, more, how we are remembered. The gods of Asgard will not be remembered as cowards who hid from their fate."

"So there's nothing we can do?" ABE asked. "No hope?"

"There has never been hope. Only fate and duty and death."

A long stretch of silence followed Odin's words, during which the dim stone room felt like a tomb.

A soft rumble in the sky above broke the silence. Thor shifted in his seat.

"My father is right, of course. Our fate is set. And yet . . . while there may not be hope, there may yet be time."

Odin snorted. Thor did not look in his direction but continued.

"The lad was right in his accounting of events. Loki has killed Baldur and now he has fled. He must be found and imprisoned. Honor and justice demand it. But that imprisonment will take place in Asgard. Remember that time passes differently there. Loki's imprisonment may last hundreds or thousands of your years."

Thor's words offered a little comfort. But ABE still felt the weight of Ragnarok—of all that death—pressing down on him.

"Listen to Thor, the hero of Asgard," Odin mocked in his withered and withering voice. "He whose mighty hands wield Mjolnir would hide behind the hands of a clock. What does it matter if Ragnarok comes in a day or a thousand days? My son is dead! I will have his killer brought to justice. And you—*all of you*—will help me!"

"Us?" Pru asked.

"Yes. I have seen the moment of Loki's capture. All of you in this room will be present for it. All of you . . . and one other," Odin said a moment before someone knocked.

The sound came from the door through which ABE and Pru had entered (the one still on its hinges).

"Who?" ABE asked, but he was interrupted by the sound of Pru's gasp.

"*I knew it!*" she said.

"Knew what?" ABE looked from Pru to the door as the handle began to turn.

"ABE, think about it! Middleton is filled with Mythics again. That can only mean one thing!"

The door opened and light spilled in, revealing the silhouette of a single figure. As ABE's eyes adjusted to the brightness, he made out the shape of a tall man. The twin peaks of his hat stood up almost like ears, and the tail of his long coat hung below his knees.

"Mister Fox!"

The detective strode into the room. He looked exactly as he had the last time they'd seen him. *Exactly*. ABE wondered if Mister Fox had just the one hat and coat or a bunch of identical ones.

"Sorry to interrupt. I assume my invitation to this little get-together got lost in the mail. Don't worry, it happens. Here's a tip. Use *domovye* for all your future postal needs, especially where invitations are concerned," Mister Fox said, referring to the Russian household spirits that also lived in the Henhouse. "That's what I do."

Pru grabbed ABE's sleeve. He didn't need to look at her to know she was smiling. He was, too!

Any misgivings he might have once had about seeing Mister Fox again vanished. Considering what they faced—the literal end of the world—there was no one he would have rather had walk through that door and start rambling. And, boy, was he rambling!

"Of course, you can run into a small problem with *domovye*," Mister Fox continued. "Every once in a while, your message will end up in someone's shoe.

But that's the *domovye* for you. *Weird* fascination with shoes." Reaching the table and resting his elbows on the back of the empty chair, Mister Fox leaned forward and said, "Hello, Pru. Hi, ABE."

"Hi, Mister Fox," ABE said.

Pru grunted.

ABE looked at her, eyebrows raised.

Oh right.

This was Pru. She wasn't going to let Mister Fox off the hook *that* easily for staying away so long.

"Who is this?" Hilde asked.

"Excellent!" Mister Fox exclaimed, snapping his fingers. "Names. It's usually a good idea to begin with names. That's what I always say. You can avoid so much trouble if you just figure out names right from the start. Isn't that true, Pru?"

"*I'm* not talking to you, Mister Stay-Away-for-a-Whole-Year."

Mister Fox sucked his breath in between his teeth. "Ooh, close. Very close. But, no. It's Mister *Fox* not Mister Stay-Away-for-a-Whole-Year. You were half right, though. Well done, Pru. Excellent memory, almost."

Pru squeaked in protest.

ABE wanted to laugh. Mister Fox was in top form. How was he always so confident? It didn't matter. *He was back.* Just when they needed him most, Mister Fox was back! If anyone could find Loki and help imprison him in Asgard, Mister Fox could.

"I'd be glad to finish introductions," Mister Fox said as ABE relaxed into his seat, "but I'm afraid I'm on a tight schedule and can't stay."

"*What?*" ABE sat up straight again.

"I'm leaving. And you two are coming with me."

"We can't leave," Pru said. "You don't understand! Baldur is dead. Ragnarok is coming."

"I know," Mister Fox said. He removed his hat and spoke to Odin. "For what it's worth, I'm sorry for your loss. I truly am. I met Baldur once in my youth. He was kind to me."

"Then you should want his murderer captured!" Thor said, slapping the table.

"And you're so sure that's Loki?" Mister Fox said, turning his gaze on Thor.

Thor froze, stunned. "What?"

"You sound sure that Loki killed Baldur. Why? Did you see him do it?"

Thor's face turned red and he scratched his beard. "I was, ah, distracted."

"Very distracted from what I heard. According to my source, the circumstances around Baldur's death were fairly chaotic. It happened in the middle of a wild celebration."

Thor said nothing. Instead, he cast a guilty look at

Odin. The Allfather, however, kept his one eye on Mister Fox.

"What 'source'?" Hilde asked. "How do you know this?"

"Good question," Mister Fox said. "I like that. Let's just say a little bird told me. Well . . . a furry little bird. Kind of ratty looking. No wings, but a long, bushy tail and a worrisome penchant for inappropriate language. That kind of little bird."

"Ratatosk!" ABE said.

"We've kept in touch," Mister Fox agreed with a shrug.

"My father saw my brother's death!" Thor said, recovering from his embarrassment. "He saw long ago that Loki would kill Baldur."

Mister Fox stood up straight and slipped his hands into his pockets. "Yes. Your father had a vision of the future. In that vision, Loki kills Baldur. Now, because of that vision, we're supposed to condemn Loki. But here's the problem. Nobody saw Loki commit the act in the present. And the last time we crossed paths with him, Loki was trying to get the Eye of Odin so he could see a way to *change* his future. So I have to ask . . . what if Odin's vision was wrong?"

Thor also stood. A low, threatening peal of thunder rolled outside. "My father's visions have never been wrong."

"There's a first time for everything."

ABE looked from Thor to Mister Fox. What was happening? Why were they arguing? They were supposed to be on the same side!

"You think Loki is *innocent*?" Hilde said, eyes wide with disbelief.

"I don't know," Mister Fox said with another shrug. "Not for sure. But that's the point. None of us know anything for sure. You're all making assumptions based on a vision. That's not justice. That's a witch hunt. I have a particular objection to witch hunts, by the way."

"This is madness!" Thor roared, banging his fist on the table. "You would stand there and defend Loki when we have all witnessed his mischief and evildoing? He was my friend once. But even I see that time has passed. He must be caught and brought to justice. He *will* be! My father has seen it!"

"Well, good luck with that. We're leaving. Let's go, Pru and ABE."

"You will *not* leave this council!" Thor commanded. Thunder rumbled outside, like a drumroll's call to battle.

"Sit down, boy," Odin said, waving Thor back into his seat.

Thor pressed his eyes closed. The cords in his neck tightened as if his head wanted to blast off from his

40

body and soar into orbit. After a moment, though, he collapsed into his seat, arms folded.

All eyes turned to the Allfather, who had kept otherwise silent through the exchange. Though Odin continued to address his words to Thor, his eye remained fixed on Mister Fox.

"The witch's foundling's words do not matter. He is a child who is frightened of his fate and hides in his religion of uncertainty and disbelief. Let him go. Let them all go."

Odin flicked his hands in a gesture of dismissal.

"But, Father . . ." Thor said.

"Hush, boy. It does not matter. Nothing they do matters."

ABE rose as Mister Fox jerked his thumb in the direction of the door. Pru followed a moment later after muttering "Sorry" to Thor. It wasn't until she and ABE had covered half the distance to the exit that Mister Fox also turned to leave. Odin called out to them one last time before they reached the door.

"This changes nothing. You—all of you—will be there at the moment of Loki's discovery and you will assist in his capture. I have seen it," Odin said, straining his voice until it broke into either a cough or a laugh, ABE wasn't sure which. "You cannot change the future!"

"Don't be so sure," Mister Fox said, closing the door on the gods.

Pru burst through the front doors of Winterhaven House, leaving ABE and Mister Fox in her wake.

"Is it me or does Pru seem upset about something?" the detective asked ABE in a near whisper.

"Yes, she's upset about something. And, yes, it's you." That was all the warning ABE could give Mister Fox before Pru spun around.

"*Where have you been?*" she demanded.

"I thought you weren't talking to me?"

"I'm not. I'm yelling at you. It's completely different."

"Ah."

"No, seriously! Where were you? You said we'd see you again."

"And now you have!" Mister Fox said with a bow and a flourish of his hat. "You see? I always keep my word—eventually."

Pru muttered something impolite that made it clear she'd spent far too much time in Ratatosk's company.

Mister Fox relented. "I know I've been gone a long time. I'm sorry for that. But it couldn't be avoided. It's a big world, and there were other problems that had to be dealt with, other mysteries that had to be solved. My job keeps me hopping."

ABE laughed.

Pru and Mister Fox turned to him.

"Uh . . . sorry. I thought that was a joke. 'Hopping'?

You know, because the Henhouse hops around on a giant chicken foot."

Pru groaned while Mister Fox grinned at ABE.

"Sorry," ABE said again. "Yelling makes me a little nervous."

"Anyway," Pru continued, "you've been gone a year. Then you come back just when things are getting interesting, and you say we can't be part of the adventure. It's not fair!"

"I said nothing of the sort. Just because Odin and I don't see eye to eye—"

ABE gave another nervous laugh, and Pru looked at him with an exasperated expression.

"Eye to eye?" ABE repeated. "Because of the Eye of Odin? Never mind."

Pru shook her head. "Seriously, ABE. *Timing.*"

"Sorry," he said. Clearly, Pru didn't appreciate a good pun.

"As I was saying," Mr. Fox went on, "just because Odin and I don't . . . agree . . . on what needs to happen next doesn't mean there isn't work for us to do. Let Thor and Hilde try to find and punish Loki. We three have another task."

"What?" Pru asked.

"Visit me tomorrow at the Henhouse. We'll discuss it then."

CHAPTER
6

LYING IN BED THAT NIGHT, ABE COULDN'T TURN HIS MIND OFF. HE WENT BACK and forth between worrying about Ragnarok and wondering what Mister Fox had planned for them. His thoughts kept him awake late into the night. He'd only just drifted off when a knock woke him.

"Mom?" he mumbled, rolling over.

He sat up when he heard the knock again. He rubbed his eyes. Weird. The sound hadn't come from his bedroom door. Had he dreamt it?

Knock, knock.

Pulling his covers up to his chin, ABE swallowed. The sound was *inside* his room. It had come from the foot of his bed.

It was at that unfortunate moment in the darkness

of his bedroom on a cloudy, starless night that a thought occurred to ABE: if Mythics were real, then were monsters under the bed real, too?

And did they knock?

ABE crept to the bottom of his bed and peered over the footboard.

Sitting among a pile of recently finished books was the box shaped like a miniature Henhouse he had received from Mister Fox. It shone with a pale blue glow. The light seeped through the cracks between the house's siding and through the small window above the door.

The knocking came again. It came, without question, from the miniature Henhouse.

"Okay. This is new. You never glowed before. Or knocked. So I should probably open you, right? When a box starts making knocking noises that's probably what it wants, I guess. Okay. So I'll open you. Because this isn't creepy or weird at all."

ABE lifted the Henhouse onto his bed and reached toward the clasp that held the box shut. It had been designed so that the Henhouse could swing open on hinges along a break that split the front half of the house from the back half, like a dollhouse. His hands paused a moment on the metal. It felt warm. Taking a deep breath, ABE undid the clasp and opened the box.

"ABE! It's about time! How soundly do you sleep?"

ABE scrambled back in shock, his blankets bunching beneath him.

The looking glass he'd received from Mister Fox hung suspended inside, as expected. Unexpectedly, however, the detective's face looked up at him from the enchanted mirror. A nimbus of orange light surrounded him.

"Mister Fox?"

"Were you expecting someone else?"

"What? No! I wasn't expecting anyone at all. You can talk to me through this?"

"Yes. It's a variation on scrying, like I showed you at the Henhouse last year. It's one of the enchantments worked into the looking glass. Listen, there's not much time—"

"Does Pru know?"

At the mention of her name, the image of Mister Fox in the looking glass wavered. An image of Pru replaced it.

"ABE! How cool is this? We can talk to each other through these and . . . wait." Pru covered her mouth with her hands. ABE could tell she was trying (unsuccessfully) to hide a smile. "ABE, are those tie-dyed pajamas?"

"Oh! Ah . . . yeah. Sorry. Um . . . are those unicorns on yours?"

Pru yelped and dove out of sight just as Mister Fox's image reasserted itself.

"We don't have time for this. If I didn't have my hands full right now, we'd be having a very serious conversation about the misuse of magical artifacts. Well, first we'd talk about Pru's surprising fascination with unicorns. But *then* we'd have a serious conversation about artifacts."

"Is something wrong?" ABE asked.

"You could say that. Trolls are attacking Winterhaven House."

Only then did ABE understand the whole meaning of the image in the looking glass. The orange glow behind Mister Fox was not part of the enchantment that allowed them to communicate. It was fire.

"Are you okay?"

"Of course. It's not my time. It's you two I'm worried about. I want you both someplace safe. Go to the Henhouse. I'm on my way, but I don't want you to wait. Pru, you know the way in."

"But what about our parents?" ABE asked.

"Your parents should be fine. In fact, I think they'll be safer without you two there. Trolls are attracted to treasure, especially magical treasure. Your looking glasses are two of the most powerful objects in this town right now. Your families should be safe once you leave. But I've convinced some of the *domovye* to keep an eye on your houses, just to be sure. The rest will escort you to the cemetery. Now go, and take your looking glasses with you!"

The connection broke, and Mister Fox's image faded from the glass.

ABE leapt off his bed and dressed. He grabbed his phone just as it rang.

"You're there!" Pru's relief was clear. "Are you okay?"

"Yeah. I was about to leave. I'll see you at the Henhouse?"

"Let's meet at the Earth Center. It's on the way for both of us. We can go to the Henhouse together from there."

"Good idea," ABE said before hanging up. He hadn't liked the idea of walking to the cemetery alone.

Looking glass in hand, ABE grabbed his windbreaker from his closet and slipped downstairs. Goose bumps rose on the back of his neck as he stepped out into the night air. He zipped up his jacket. At the end of his walkway, he hesitated, still anxious about his parents' safety.

Mister Fox had said he'd send *domovye*. But they were mostly invisible. ABE wondered how he would know when they got there. Should he wait?

He caught himself shifting his weight from foot to foot and forced himself to stop. Instead, he tightened his grip on his looking glass. The familiar polished wood of the handle comforted him. He had never admitted it to Pru, but he felt like a wizard whenever he held it.

The looking glass, of course!

Kicking himself for not thinking of it right away, ABE lifted the glass to his eye and peered through the magnifying side. After all, the *domovye* were household spirits. That made them Mythics. They should be visible through the enchanted glass.

Light flared as ABE looked through the device and dozens of figures appeared, lit by the golden glow that surrounded Mythics when viewed through the glass.

ABE had read about *domovye* after meeting Mister Fox, so he was somewhat prepared for their bizarre appearance. Despite being called spirits, there was nothing ghostlike about the creatures around him. They looked like small men (just a little taller than ABE) with thick walrus moustaches that blended into even thicker gray beards.

ABE had learned that *domovye* often adopted the look of the master or mistress of their house. Sure enough, the *domovye* all wore the same coat and hat that Mister Fox wore—only their clothing was almost cartoonishly big. The oversized brims of their hats and their buttoned coats and upturned collars hid most of their bodies.

The *domovye* avoided open spaces. They crouched in patches of darkness between buildings and seemed to have a fondness for climbing. ABE saw one *domovoi* scale the side of a house to perch beside a chimney. It moved with the skill of a jungle ape. Another one had crouched beneath a tree close to ABE. He approached it.

"So . . . you guys will stay and watch over my mom and dad?" he asked.

The figure nodded.

"Okay. Thanks."

ABE took one last look at his house before hurrying off to meet Pru, a dozen *domovye* following closely behind. He tried very hard not to think about the trolls out there, somewhere in the night.

CHAPTER
7

ABE WAS GLAD FOR THE COMPANY OF THE *DOMOVYE* AS HE MADE HIS WAY through the deserted streets of Middleton. The night seemed particularly quiet. Granted, he was not used to walking the town's streets in the hours after midnight. But he had expected to see *some* signs of life. An occasional car. A light in a window.

Instead, Middleton appeared deserted.

A ghost town.

ABE smiled despite his discomfort as the phrase sprang to mind. After all, his companions were actual spirits—in name, anyway. He lifted his looking glass to his eye to reassure himself that the *domovye* were still there.

Strange. Were there fewer of them than the last time he'd checked?

He hurried on.

He found Pru waiting for him at the Earth Center. It was weird being there with her again. They had both avoided the place for months after their adventure with the Eye of Odin. It had reminded them too much of Loki. But ABE believed in the center's environmental mission, so he had gone back to volunteering after a while. Pru had stayed away.

"It's about time," Pru said as ABE approached.

"Sorry. I wanted to make sure the *domovye* showed up before I left my parents alone."

"Are they cool, or what?" A quick smile lit Pru's face. "I'd only seen their hands before. The way they look and move—it's like someone crossed Mister Fox and a monkey!"

"That's a mental image that will stick with me."

"Glad I could help." Pru's shoulders relaxed a little. "I'm glad you're here. It was creepy waiting by myself. Come on. Let's go."

They set off for Main Street, which ran all the way from Winterhaven House through town and down to the cemetery. They'd only traveled a couple of blocks when Pru paused. She held her looking glass to her eye.

"ABE, I thought you said you waited for the *domovye* before you left your house."

"I did."

"Didn't any come with you?"

"Yeah. About a dozen. Why?"

"That's not possible. I had about that many with me, too. But now I can only see a handful."

"What?" ABE lifted his own glass. He counted six, maybe seven, *domovye* in the area. What had happened to the rest?

"ABE," Pru hissed. "Look!"

ABE turned in the direction she pointed. The looking glass framed a shadow in the distance. His stomach lurched as the enchanted lens zoomed in on the shadow. It magnified and sharpened the image in the glass.

A troll!

ABE shuddered. Trolls were *awful* looking. They were worse than giants. Giants at least looked like people (even if they were really big). Trolls were something else. The brute before them had two heads—*two heads!*—and at least four arms. Though not as tall as a giant, the troll still stood a couple of feet taller than the biggest person ABE had ever met. Hair (or was it fur?) covered its massively wide chest and a loincloth hung from its waist.

As ABE watched, two *domovye* launched themselves at the troll. The creature howled and reached for a nearby stop sign. It tore the sign—and a good bit of sidewalk—from the ground with a shrug of its massive shoulders. Swinging the makeshift club, it struck one of its attackers and sent it tumbling hat over coattail across the ground. As it rolled, the *domovoi* grew increasingly less solid until it vanished from sight completely.

"Did that *domovoi* just die?" Pru said. "*Can* domovye *die?*"

"I don't know. But we sure can! Come on, let's get to the Henhouse!"

Pru nodded. ABE took one last glance at the troll through the looking glass. The remaining *domovye* had taken their fallen companion's place and were swarming the beast.

"ABE, come on!"

He forced himself to look away and followed Pru. They turned onto Main Street, and ABE wondered how much time the remaining *domovye* could buy them.

A popping sound behind him soon offered the first hint.

"The streetlights are going out!" Pru said. "Why?"

"The troll must have defeated the *domovye*," ABE said, struggling to keep up with Pru. "Mister Fox said Mythics and technology don't mix. I think the troll is chasing us and the lights are going out as he passes them!"

He looked back—and immediately wished he

hadn't. The troll was using its multiple arms as additional legs and was closing in on them fast!

Beside ABE, Pru stopped short.

"What's wrong?" he asked, turning back to tug on her arm. "We have to go!"

"No," Pru said, standing up straight. "We can't keep running."

"Yes, we can! It's easy. I'll show you!"

"We won't make it, ABE. The troll is too fast. Besides, we're Fibbers! These looking glasses can send the troll back to wherever it comes from, right? So let's send it on its way."

ABE stared at her. She was serious. And insane.

And kind of amazing.

"I think this is a terrible idea," he said, moving to stand beside her.

"You think *all* my ideas are terrible," she said. He knew she was trying to sound brave, but her voice shook.

The troll had slowed when its prey stopped moving, perhaps sensing a trap. Or maybe it was just stunned by what it considered to be a truly astounding display of stupidity. It stood in the middle of Main Street, about a dozen yards away. The Laundromat was to its left, and the barbershop ABE went to get his hair cut was on its right. He would *never* look at those places the same way again.

Assuming he and Pru survived.

The troll snorted. It resumed its bizarre loping movement—slowly at first, but it soon picked up speed.

Pru raised her arm and pointed the looking glass toward the troll.

The troll continued to move closer. ABE felt the muscles of his neck tighten. Why hadn't it vanished? How close did it need to be?

"Pru . . . it's not working!"

"It *has* to work!" She wiggled her looking glass the way one might shake a TV remote with failing batteries.

The troll leapt at them with all four arms outstretched.

"ABE, run!" Pru shouted.

Pru dodged to the right as ABE dodged left.

One of the troll's heads turned to follow ABE's movement, and the other followed Pru. Its attention split, the troll landed clumsily on the ground and tumbled over itself, its limbs instantly entangled. Pru ducked into a narrow alley as ABE scrambled to hide behind the florist's delivery van, parked on the side of the road.

He peeked around the back of the van just in time to see the troll stand back up and, after a moment of indecision, chase after Pru.

He had to do something! But what? Their looking glasses hadn't worked.

Well, Pru's hadn't. He hadn't tried his. But why would his work if Pru's didn't?

The troll reached the opening of the alley, but its massive frame proved too wide for the narrow space. Luckily, the creature seemed too dumb to try to turn sideways. Apparently, two heads *weren't* better than one.

ABE groaned. Pru was right. He really needed to work on the appropriateness of his timing with puns.

Wait! Two heads!

The troll had two heads. The looking glasses worked by magnifying a Mythic's sense that it didn't belong on Earth. But maybe to work, *both* of the troll's heads would have to look into the enchanted mirrors. Two heads probably meant two brains.

He peeked at the troll again. It tore at the brick-work at the mouth of the alley with terrifying efficiency. Chunks of masonry and dust flew from its four jack-hammer-like hands as it beat at the opening of Pru's safe haven.

The troll still hadn't tried turning sideways.

Two *very small* brains, ABE decided. But his idea still made sense.

He rounded the van and tiptoed into the street. Somehow, he had to get Pru's attention without letting the troll see him. He had to be as quiet as a—

Clank!

ABE froze as the metallic clang filled the air. He looked at his feet. A steel road plate lay on the ground beneath him. The road crew that had put it there (probably to cover an area of construction) must have placed it poorly, because it had shifted under the weight of ABE's step and banged against the concrete.

Swallowing past the lump in his throat, ABE looked up just in time to see one of the troll's heads turn toward him. A large blob of drool pooled on the beast's lower lip as it curled in a snarl. The drop fell, and before it could even hit the ground, the troll lunged in ABE's direction. ABE retreated until his back pressed against the florist's van.

"Hey, ugly!" Pru called, stepping out from the alley. "Leave him alone!"

One of the troll's heads stayed oriented on ABE while the other head turned toward Pru. Torn by conflicting desires, the troll stalled in the middle of the street.

"Pru!" ABE called. "Two heads! I think we both have to use our looking glasses!"

"Right!" she agreed as the troll howled in frustration. The muscles in its legs coiled, signaling that it was ready to pounce.

ABE lifted his looking glass at the same moment Pru did. There was a flash of light. When it faded, the troll had vanished into a cloud of shimmering gold sparks.

ABE and Pru lowered their glasses. Walking slowly, they met in the middle of the street. They stopped in the exact spot where the troll had stood, moments before.

ABE couldn't believe it. The plan had worked.

"We're safe," he said. Relief spread over him in a wave of soothing warmth.

That's when a truck screeched around the corner and, catching their startled faces in its high beams, barreled directly at them.

CHAPTER
8

A ROOSTER CROWED.

ABE's eyes fluttered open.

He floated in a cloud of softness, embraced by cool linens. His head rested on a pillow so fluffed with down that someone could have put a whole bag of frozen peas beneath it and no princess would ever have known.

He spread his arms and legs wide, sinking deeper into the marshmallow mattress that held him, basking in the comforts of his home and bed.

Except his bed wasn't that soft.

Or that big.

He sat up in a flash as the events of the night before came back to him. He remembered his flight from home and the troll and then, just when he had thought they were safe, the headlights that had borne down on him and Pru and . . .

His head sank back into the pillow. He sighed in relief as the rest of the evening came back in a rush.

The truck that had nearly hit them had been driven by Mister Fox. He'd swerved at the last moment, and the truck had spun into a streetlight. Mister Fox had escaped unharmed. Rather than send them home, he'd brought them back to the Henhouse.

The Henhouse.

ABE sat up once more. A smile spread across his face. He pulled himself out of bed, surprised by how smooth the wooden floor felt beneath his bare feet. Light streamed in through a large stained-glass window that displayed an image of Stonehenge.

He pressed his hand to the glass, wondering if it would feel warm. Was it real sunlight? He couldn't be sure. The Henhouse was an impossibility. Mister Fox described it as a series of houses all occupying the same space.

That would have made some sense if each house were a little smaller than the one that contained it. But the witch Baba Yaga had built the Henhouse. She had used her magic to put the larger versions of the Henhouse *inside* the smaller ones. That meant the Henhouse grew in size the deeper one went.

Considering the size of his room, ABE had to be

pretty far inside the Henhouse. So how could the light be actual sunlight? But the window was, indeed, warm. ABE shook his head in wonder.

He *loved* this place. It was a giant riddle.

Someone knocked. Expecting Pru or Mister Fox, he opened the door.

No one was there.

That's what ABE thought at first, anyway. A slight disturbance in the air alerted him to the presence of a *domovoi*. Squinting, ABE could barely make out the blurred shape of the telltale coat and hat. Apparently, the spirits were somewhat visible inside the Henhouse even without the looking glass.

The *domovoi* gestured, and its hands slipped out from beneath the sleeves of its coat. Unlike the rest of it, the *domovoi*'s hands showed clearly. Was it because they were the only part of its body not covered by clothing? Whether that was the case or not, ABE could see why Pru had seen nothing but the floating hands she had described on her first visit.

The spirit gestured again. Nodding his understanding, ABE exited his room. He closed the door and followed the seemingly disembodied hands. They traveled up through the Henhouse all the way to the attic, where a forest of branches reached from the floor to the top of the vaulted ceiling.

The effect gave the Henhouse a sort of visual logic

among its otherwise impossible architecture. It was as if all the tree trunk columns that separated the Henhouse's many levels crested in the attic, and he was walking through the canopy layer of that petrified forest.

As ABE ducked beneath a low-hanging branch, Pru's voice drifted back to him from somewhere up ahead.

"So he's okay?"

"He's fine. The *domovye* can't be killed," Mister Fox's voice answered.

They had to be talking about the *domovoi* ABE and Pru had seen vanish during its fight with the troll.

"They can, however, be weakened to the point where they disappear temporarily," Mister Fox added. "See, the *domovye* draw their strength from the Henhouse. The farther from it they roam, the weaker and less solid they become. If they go too far, or if they are injured, they lose their solid form and their essence returns to the Henhouse to regain its strength."

ABE rounded a branch and reached his destination. The *domovye* had set up a rectangular table in the middle of the Henhouse's forested interior. It was richly set with an assortment of silver platters and dishes. Mister Fox sat at one end and Pru sat at the other. Beyond them and through the trees, ABE could see the Henhouse's large circular window. Even in the distance, it seemed larger than he remembered.

ABE had read books about fairylands where mystical

beings spirited children away for magical feasts and celebrations. Looking around, he felt like he was a character in one of those stories.

In a way, he supposed he was.

"ABE," Pru greeted him. "It's about time. Come sit down. We're having pancakes."

An empty chair sat between her and Mister Fox. Up close, ABE saw that the place settings were all finely crafted and carved with intricate patterns. Smaller dishes of cream, assorted jams, and sliced salmon surrounded a large covered platter in the center of the table. There was also a bowl filled with what looked like small black beads.

A pained expression crossed Mister Fox's face. "We're not . . . Pru, I told you. They're not pancakes. They're blini, a traditional Russian breakfast."

"Whatever," Pru said as ABE took his seat. "But watch out for the black things, ABE. They're *fish eggs*. Gross, right?"

"It's called caviar, Pru. And I'll have you know it's considered a . . ." Mister Fox paused and tilted his head to one side.

Squinting, ABE saw a *domovoi* standing beside the detective, whispering in his ear.

"Excuse me a moment, you two. Let me deal with this." Mister Fox rose and walked a few feet away from the table to talk with the household spirit.

Pru leaned in toward ABE and whispered, "I actually knew they were called blini. He's said it like a dozen times already. He can be *such* a know-it-all. No offense."

"None taken—wait, what?" ABE stammered. He wasn't a know-it-all!

Was he?

No. He'd definitely know it if he was a know-it-all.

Mister Fox returned to the table. Before he could speak, Pru said, "Hey, ABE, remember how Mister Fox almost ran us over last night? You want to know why he did that? *Because he doesn't know how to drive!* Can you believe it?"

Mister Fox grimaced. "I've been traveling around in the Henhouse since I was younger than you are now. I'm sorry if I never learned how to drive a car. I'll tell you what. When *you* learn how to operate a magical house that travels about on a giant chicken foot, *then* you can be critical."

Pru stuck her tongue out at the detective. Since she had a mouth full of pancakes—or, rather, blini—the sight wasn't pretty.

"Very mature," Mister Fox said. He kind of gave up the moral high ground, though, because his mouth was also full as he spoke. Pru snickered.

"Let's get down to business. We have a lot on our plate," the detective said (after he'd swallowed). He held up a finger as ABE opened his mouth. "Just a figure of speech, ABE. I wasn't making a pun about breakfast."

Too bad. It would have been a good one.

"As I was about to say before Pru decided to comment on my driving, that *domovoi* was reporting back on things at Winterhaven House. In case you were wondering, everyone there is okay. Thor and Hilde fought off the trolls. Though apparently they did a fair amount of damage to the mansion."

"Do you know why they attacked?" Pru asked.

"No. But I don't like it. Their appearance on Midgard couldn't have been an accident. Someone must have sent them."

"Loki?" ABE asked.

Mister Fox frowned. "Possibly. But before we get into a conversation about Loki, I'd like to hear what you thought about yesterday's meeting."

"Well, I'm not excited about the whole end of the world thing," Pru said. "I kind of think we should do something about *that*."

"Fair point. But first, what were your impressions of the people there?"

"I was surprised by Odin," ABE said. "He seemed so . . . frail. I don't remember him being like that last year."

"Yeah," Pru agreed. "Me neither."

"That surprised me as well. I've heard things over the years suggesting that Odin had weakened since his visions of the future. The word is he sits on his high seat, alone, and watches events in the three worlds unfold. He doesn't participate. He doesn't interfere. He just sits and watches."

"It's kind of sad," ABE said. "He wasn't always like that. I mean, according to the stories, there was a time when Odin was almost like Prometheus."

"Who?" Pru asked.

"Sorry," ABE said. "Different set of myths. According to Greek myth, Prometheus was a Titan who stole fire from the gods and gave it to mortals."

"Odin gave fire to people?" Pru asked. "What was the point if this Prometheus guy had already done it?"

"No," Mister Fox said, taking up the story (which didn't seem *entirely* fair to ABE, who thought he'd been doing a fine job of telling it). "But there is an old story about how Odin snaked his way into a giant's stronghold and, taking the form of an eagle, flew off with something called the Mead of Poetry. He shared *that* with humankind. According to the story, the mead was a magical elixir that gave people the power of storytelling. Which, if you ask me, is at least as useful as fire."

"Odin changed into an eagle?" Pru asked. "He can shape-shift like Loki?"

"He can. It's a rare talent, but one that he and Loki

share. In fact, the two have a fair amount in common. They both have curious minds and prize intellect and knowledge. That's also uncommon among the Norse gods. You know that. You've met Thor. The point is, there was a time before Odin had his visions of the future when he and Loki were the best of friends. One of the tragedies of Ragnarok is that, according to the stories, they're destined to be generals on opposite sides.

"It was kind of hard to see him so weak yesterday," ABE said.

"Baldur's death really seems to have pushed him over the edge," Pru agreed.

"If so," Mister Fox said, "we might be able to make that work to our advantage. Given Odin's foreknowledge of events, he probably knows exactly where Loki is hiding. Odin could send Thor and Hilde right to him if he wanted to. But he seems inclined to let fate take its course and let the thunder god find Loki on his own. That gives us time to do our thing."

"Finally," Pru said. "Are you going to tell us now what 'our thing' is? What do we get to do?"

"Simple. While Thor and Hilde go on their quest to find Loki so they can punish him for killing Baldur, the three of us are going to launch an investigation into whether the trickster is actually guilty of the crime."

CHAPTER
9

"WAIT." ABE SHOOK HIS HEAD IN DISBELIEF. "YOU WERE SERIOUS AT WINTER-haven House? You think Loki is *innocent*?"

"I never said that. All I said—all I'm *saying*—is that we don't know for sure whether he is innocent or guilty."

"You do remember Loki tried to kill ABE and me last year, right?" Pru asked.

"I'm not saying he's perfect," Mr. Fox admitted. "The question before us whether he committed *this* particular crime. If you—if *anyone*—can provide me with evidence that he did, then fine. Great. I will jump aboard the let's-catch-and-punish-Loki train. I'll even be the conductor. I'll wear a funny hat and everything."

"Another one?" Pru asked, smiling sweetly.

Mister Fox ignored her.

"The point is that there *isn't* any evidence. This is what we know. Baldur was killed during a feast at his home in Asgard. It was chaos. I had Ratatosk ask around. None of the gods saw what happened. There are even mixed reports on whether Loki was there. There's nothing to tie him to the murder except Odin's vision. The gods expect us to believe that vision without question. You two know my opinions on belief."

They did. One of the first things Mister Fox had said to them was that they shouldn't believe him. People believed too easily, according to him. Belief and certainty were what blinded people to magic. ABE suspected that one of the reasons Mister Fox nicknamed his detective agency the Unbelievable FIB—besides an understandable fondness for acronyms—was that a fib was something you shouldn't believe.

It made perfect sense that Mister Fox would want them to investigate Baldur's death and not just believe what they'd been told. Or, it *would* have made perfect sense if they were talking about anyone other than Loki.

It was easy for Mister Fox to try to be fair. He hadn't been kidnapped by Loki and handed over to Gristling. ABE had. And Gristling had threatened to do terrible things to him.

Terrible things.

There had been talk of bone grinding. And devouring.

That made it hard for ABE to be fair, or to give Loki the benefit of the doubt. He was sure Pru felt the same way. She would never agree with Mister Fox's plan.

"Okay," Pru said.

What?

"*Okay?*" ABE repeated, his voice rising in pitch. He cleared his throat and tried to speak normally. "You agree that Loki's innocent? Even after all he did to us last year? How come you're letting him off the hook so easy?"

"What can I say," Pru said, shrugging. "I have a forgiving nature."

"Since when?"

Pru narrowed her eyes and glared. "Careful, buddy, or I'll—"

"There!" ABE said, pointing at her. "See?"

Pru blushed and quickly recovered. She lifted her chin in the air primly. "I'm just *trying* to keep an open mind."

"That's all I ask," Mister Fox said. He had watched the exchange with his chin resting in one palm and his fingers covering his mouth. His hand didn't quite hide his smile.

ABE wasn't buying Pru's act. She was being far too reasonable. There had to be something else.

"So what are we looking for?" she continued.

"Motive and opportunity, right? We need to find out who had reason to kill Baldur, and who was in the right place at the right time to commit the crime. We'll need witnesses."

Of course. Pru loved being a detective. Investigating a murder mystery would be the holy grail of detective work to her.

Mister Fox nodded approvingly. "I couldn't have said it better myself. The gods are useless as witnesses. They were too distracted by their celebrations. But there were other people there at the scene of the crime—household servants. One of them must have seen something. You'll start there, with them."

ABE slumped in his chair. It looked like they'd be going on a mission to try to clear Loki's name, after all. He wished he felt better about the idea.

"I don't get it, though," he said with a sigh. "Wouldn't the easiest way to find out what happened to Baldur be to find Loki and ask him if he did it?"

"No," Mister Fox said. "Listen to me, both of you—this is important. We are *not* joining the search for Loki. I need you two to understand that. No matter what happens, no matter who tries to persuade you otherwise, you are *not* to go looking for Loki. Leave that quest to Thor and Hilde. Do you understand?"

"Fine with me," Pru said. She had a distant look in her eyes.

"ABE?" Mister Fox said.

ABE thought about it. Did he understand? He wasn't sure. Mister Fox was oddly insistent about them not joining the search for Loki. Why was that?

"If you say so," ABE said halfheartedly.

"Good," Mister Fox said. "Then tomorrow we'll start our investigation."

"Why tomorrow?" Pru asked. "Why not now?"

"I want Ratatosk to join you. He'll arrive tomorrow." Mister Fox grinned. He leaned back in his chair and clasped his hands behind his head. "It will be just like old times. What do you think? Are you both ready to become Fibbers again?"

"Please," Pru scoffed. "Like we ever stopped."

A short time later, ABE stood with Pru in front of the large circular window. While they waited for something—Mister Fox wouldn't say what—the detective explained the passage of time when traveling to and from Worlds of Myth. Behind them, back among the trees, dishes rattled as the *domovye* cleared the remains of breakfast from the table.

"Basically, time passes more slowly on Worlds of Myth than it does on Earth," Mister Fox said. "I could get into the mechanics of it more and talk about how Worlds of Myth are eternal realms where time, size, and distance are as much matters of perception as physics. But that complicates things. All you really need to know is that it doesn't matter how much time you spend on a World of Myth. The Henhouse will always be able to bring you home to the moment after you leave Earth."

Mister Fox was reassuring ABE, who had noticed during breakfast that the sky outside the Henhouse seemed to be getting darker—not brighter, as one would expect if it were morning. The detective had explained that they were on Asgard, not Earth, and that it was evening.

"So we don't have to worry about our parents missing us?" Pru asked.

"It shouldn't be an issue. ABE, the only reason you were gone overnight last year is because it took Pru and me a day to figure out where Loki had taken you."

They grew quiet after Mister Fox finished his explanation. ABE passed the time studying the window itself. It definitely seemed bigger. He asked Mister Fox about it.

"I might have misrepresented things a bit on your last visit when I described the Henhouse," the detective answered. "It's true that the Henhouse is a series of identical houses all occupying the same space. It's also true that each house is a slightly larger version of the one outside it. However, it's not true that the smallest version is the one you see on the outside or that this version we're standing in now is the largest. There are both smaller and larger versions. The Henhouse shows whatever side of her suits her mood."

"You fibbed," Pru said. "How surprising."

"I simplified things. You two had a lot to absorb."

Mister Fox's explanation seemed to confirm something ABE had been wondering about ever since the Henhouse in his room had started to glow. "The houses you gave us to hold our looking glasses aren't just models or copies of the Henhouse, are they?"

Mister Fox arched an eyebrow. "Very good. You're right. Those are smaller versions of the actual Henhouse that have been separated from the main building."

"So they're magic?" Pru asked.

"They are. How else do you think the *domovye* got to your houses so fast?"

"They came out of the Henhouses in our rooms?" ABE asked. But they were so small! Then again, size didn't seem to matter where the Henhouse was concerned.

"Of course," Mister Fox said. "All the versions of the Henhouse are connected. If necessary, the *domovye* can travel between them. Otherwise, they would have been too far from home to get to you two in time. As it was, their strength was diminished. Your Henhouses lost most of their magic when they were separated from the main one. Not all, but most. So the *domovye* were

75

only operating at a fraction of their strength when they fought the troll. Usually, they're very strong."

"So how big is the Henhouse, really?" Pru asked.

"Honestly? I'm not sure. Sometimes at night I hear sounds that make me wonder if the *domovye* are still building. So I don't know how big . . . or how small . . . the Henhouse really is. Now shush. It's starting."

ABE turned to the window, curious about what Mister Fox had brought them to Asgard to see.

Outside, a line of figures carrying torches snaked its way through the darkness. Some of the figures broke off from the main group and lit a row of additional torches that must have been set out in preparation for whatever event was now taking place.

As the growing firelight brightened the scene, it revealed that the figures stood in a small bay framed by a rocky stretch of sand at one end and a high cliff at the other. The water reflected some of the torchlight, which also revealed a large, beached Viking longboat.

"How close are we?" ABE asked, surprised by how clearly he could see the people on the beach.

"Not as close as you'd think," Mister Fox said. "The oculus is magnifying the image."

"Oculus?" Pru asked.

"It's a word for an eye," ABE said. "Sometimes they call round openings in architecture an oculus, too."

"So it's the window? You could have just said it's the window, ABE."

"Sorry."

Mister Fox shushed them, and they resumed their observation of the events outside.

More figures moved into view below. They were carrying something. With a start, ABE realized it was a body. There were nine bearers. One was Thor. Odin trailed slightly behind the procession, stooped with exhaustion, age, or sorrow.

A phantom chill swept over ABE as he realized they were watching the funeral of the god Baldur.

The nine bearers and Odin continued to the edge of the water, where a long plank led up to the longboat. Still carrying Baldur's corpse, they climbed aboard. They laid Baldur on the deck and placed his shield and sword on top of him. Thor and the others stepped aside while Odin leaned down and lowered his head beside that of his dead son.

"What's he doing?" Pru asked.

"He's whispering something. No one knows what," Mister Fox said. "It's an odd detail that's survived in the myth about Baldur's death. The story clearly records that Odin whispers something into Baldur's ear. But nowhere is it written what Odin says. I've always wondered about that."

Odin rose and, taking a torch from Thor, touched it to Baldur's shroud. As the fire took hold, Thor held his hammer, Mjolnir, over the body of Baldur in a final salute or blessing. Then he and the others climbed off the boat.

Back on the shore, Thor and another figure ABE didn't recognize stepped forward and placed their shoulders against the stern of the vessel. Together, they pushed the ship into the water. As the lapping waves carried the longboat farther from shore, the fire of the funeral pyre burned higher and brighter. It became a pillar of light that illuminated the cliff face and revealed a host of figures perched atop the bluff. All bore silent witness to the final voyage of Baldur.

As the ship left the bay, the image in the oculus grew smaller, as though the window were a camera being pulled back. The pillar of light, bright though it had been, shrank to insignificance compared to the vast blackness of the open sea. The firelight no longer defied the darkness. All it did now was provide some scale to the overwhelming emptiness of the night. Soon the fire would burn out, and—with the death of Baldur's light—the dark would overwhelm the world.

CHAPTER
10

MISTER FOX PROVED AS GOOD AS HIS WORD. THE HENHOUSE RETURNED THE three travelers to Middleton at a time not long after they'd left. ABE and Pru walked home along the empty streets. Neither of them spoke much. The stark and solemn images of Baldur's funeral had touched them both, though ABE thought it had been harder for Pru. It must have reminded her of her dad's funeral. He tried to think of something to say, but nothing seemed enough. He hadn't lost anyone, not like she had. The difference in their experiences wasn't a gap—it was a chasm, and he had no idea how to cross it. So he just walked along beside her.

It was still dark out as ABE slipped back inside his house and climbed the stairs to his room. He didn't think he would sleep. After all, he'd already eaten breakfast. But his trips to the Henhouse and to Asgard had messed with his sense of the day, and the darkness outside his window whispered to him that it was still time to doze. He lay on his bed and, before he knew it, drifted off.

The dream came quickly.

He stood in a forest. Only, it wasn't a proper forest. The trees that rose up around him weren't trees at all but a complex network of roots that stretched down from the sky. The roots belonged to Yggdrasil, the giant ash tree that connected the three worlds of Norse mythology. ABE was in Asgard, the place where Loki had brought him to recover the Eye of Odin.

He had read an article once that there was no such thing as a recurring dream. According to the article, the notion of a repeated dream was a trick of memory, like déjà vu. ABE didn't think he believed that. He *knew* this dream. It had haunted him for a year.

Usually, the events of the dream followed what he remembered from his abduction. In it, he relived his trip to Asgard with Pru and Ratatosk. Only he was never as lucky in his dream as they had been in real life. The dream always ended with Gristling reaching for him, a wicked leer on his face.

This time, though, the familiar dream took an unexpected turn.

A wall of mist rolled through the dreamscape like a tidal wave. It erased the familiar surroundings and replaced everything with a sea of undulating gray. Only the roots remained visible—except they no longer resembled trees. They looked more like bars that imprisoned him.

Panic gripped him. He tried to run to the tree line so he could escape the bars that now formed a circle around him, like a cage. But the mist was cold and unnaturally thick. Moving through it was like swimming through jelly.

A flicker of movement to his left drew his attention. He tried to turn to get a better look at the disturbance, but the mist slowed his movements. By the time he'd turned, whatever had been there was gone.

Another flash of motion caught his eye, this time to his right and a little bit closer. He struggled to turn more quickly. He managed to get a quick glimpse of a woman before she disappeared into a thicker patch of rising mist. She wore a black cowl with the hood pulled up over her head.

The temperature plummeted. ABE pulled his hands up into his sleeves and hugged his arms to his chest in an effort to stay warm as the cold stabbed at his skin like tiny needles.

The woman appeared again. ABE didn't have to turn to see her. She strode into view directly ahead of him on the other side of the roots, and this time he saw her clearly.

Hair the color of a freshly dug grave spilled over her left shoulder in long tendrils that curled like worms on the pavement after a storm. She held the right side of her hood tightly in one hand, concealing that half of her face. Her one visible eye bore into him.

ABE opened his mouth to ask who she was. Before he could speak, though, she turned quickly and began to walk away from him. The mist rose up once more and stole her from his sight.

Nothing happened for what seemed like a long time. Just as ABE began to worry that he would be stuck there in the limbo of his dream forever, a voice drifted through the mist. It was a woman's voice. It came from everywhere and nowhere at once.

"I carry a riddle for you, young hero, a message from another. Listen. *When is a truth-teller not telling the truth?*"

ABE blinked in surprise.

A riddle?

Young hero?

Before he could answer (not that he even had an answer!), the mist retreated. It fled as if someone had hit a rewind button and reversed the tidal wave that had brought the fog in the first place.

Within seconds, ABE found his dream had returned

him once more to the roots of Yggdrasil in Asgard. But he wasn't alone. He staggered back as he found himself face-to-face with the giant Gristling. The monster grinned and reached for him.

ABE woke up screaming. He sat up and fumbled for his light. A flurry of movement by his window temporarily distracted him. When he managed to switch on his bedside lamp, though, he found his room empty. The curtains billowed slightly in a breeze. He hadn't realized he'd left his window open.

ABE collapsed back onto his bed. Afterimages of the nightmare drifted though his mind. He saw the hauntingly beautiful woman when he closed his eyes. Her voice—he assumed it was her voice, anyway—echoed through his thoughts: *When is a truth-teller not telling the truth?*

It was a strange sort of question.

Even stranger was the answer that occurred to ABE.

He repeated the question out loud. "When is a truth-teller not telling the truth?"

He couldn't quite bring himself to say the answer out loud, though. It made him uncomfortable, as if he was being disloyal to a friend. So he whispered the answer in his head: *When he's a Fibber.*

"I CAN'T BELIEVE IT'S THE FIRST DAY OF SCHOOL ALREADY," PRU SAID TO ABE the next morning in homeroom. "You wouldn't believe the nightmare I had last night after we got home."

A wave of relief washed over ABE. He'd been worrying about his own nightmare ever since he woke up. The whole thing had seemed so weird and vivid and alien that it had almost felt like a dream that someone else had imagined and then stuck in his head.

That sounded crazy. He knew it. But if Pru had dreamt something similar, then maybe there *had* been something unnatural about the dream after all.

"Really?" he said. "I'm kind of glad to hear that."

"I dreamt that Mr. Jeffries got up in front of the

class and then reached under the collar of his shirt and *pulled off his face*—except it wasn't his face. It was a mask! And underneath was Mrs. Edleman! She just looked at me and said, 'I'm ba-aaack.'"

"Oh."

"I *know*. Pretty awful, right?"

"Uh, yeah. That does sound pretty bad."

"Tell me about it. I bet you didn't have any nightmares about the first day of school."

"Um, no," ABE said. "Not about that."

"Of course not. You love school. You're the only kid I know who looks forward to the school year starting."

"I never said I was looking forward to school."

"ABE, come on. You're sniffing your notebook as we speak."

"What? I am not . . . Oh." ABE lowered his notebook with its fresh, soothing bouquet of newly opened loose-leaf paper. Changing the subject, he said, "You're in a good mood, all things considered."

"I *am* bummed about summer vacation being over, obviously."

"Right. But, no . . . I kind of meant the possible end of the world."

Pru glanced around to make sure no one was paying attention to their conversation. She needn't have worried. The other kids in homeroom were fist-bumping and high-fiving as though they hadn't seen each other

85

for months, which was odd since Middleton was so small you couldn't turn around without seeing someone you knew.

"Well, there's that," Pru said. "But I guess I'm *not* too worried about Ragnarok. I know I should be. Maybe part of me is. But, ABE, Mister Fox is *back*. He'll fix things. I know he will."

"You really believe in him, don't you?"

"Of course I do. But don't you dare tell him that!"

ABE looked down at his feet. His new shoes had brought him very little comfort so far that morning.

Obviously, Pru believed in Mister Fox. She *should* believe in him. ABE should, too. There had been a time after they'd first met the detective that ABE hadn't believed in him. But he had moved past that. Hadn't he?

So how come his dreams told him that Mister Fox was lying to them?

"Are you okay?" Pru asked, studying him. "You're being quieter than usual."

"Yeah. I guess . . . I guess I'm just having trouble with this whole idea of thinking about Loki as innocent."

"Oh," Pru said, sounding satisfied with ABE's response. "That. Well, I understand that. But an investigation is an investigation. As long as it means we get to go on another adventure, I'm willing to play along.

And imagine if we get to prove Mister Fox is wrong. Think about how much fun *that* could be."

ABE couldn't help smiling at her as Mr. Jeffries stepped to the front of the room.

"So. First day of school," he said, "Always a strange thing, am I right? New room. New teachers. I'm sure you're all wondering what to make of me. I'll tell you what I make of myself. I like to think that I'm fair. Which means that if you try your best and treat each other—and me—with respect, then there's a good chance you'll survive homeroom and language arts. After that, no promises. Junior high is its own world, am I right?"

A few of the kids chuckled. Even Pru smiled a bit. ABE couldn't remember her ever laughing at one of Mrs. Edleman's jokes.

Then again, he couldn't remember Mrs. Edleman ever actually making a joke. So maybe it wasn't a fair comparison.

"Let's get things started," Mr. Jeffries continued. "First of all, in just a moment I'm going to ask everyone to walk over to the carpeted area in the front of the room and sit down in a circle.

"No, seriously?"

ABE looked over at the boy who had spoken. He recognized the kid as the same one who had laughed at him the night of the open house. According to Pru, his name was Danny. He'd been in the other sixth-grade class last year. Pru described him as one of those kids who was nice to your face—but only to your face.

"Seriously," Mr. Jeffries said. He addressed the whole room with his next words. "I get it. Sitting together in a circle to start the day sounds babyish, right? I know it will take some getting used to. If it makes you feel any better, classes all the way through twelfth grade started their day this way at the school where I used to teach. The idea is that it builds a sense of community. You'll all be going from one class to the next this year. It can get kind of hectic. Call me corny, but I want you to think of this as your *home*room, not just in name."

It did sound corny. It also sounded kind of nice.

Pru seemed to think so, too. She sat up straighter, and ABE could tell she was making an effort to look interested in what Mr. Jeffries was saying.

"I'd call it corny, all right," Danny said, quietly enough that his voice wouldn't carry to the front of the room. "And lame."

"Be quiet, Danny," Pru said. "It's his first day, too."

ABE wiggled a finger in his ear. Had he heard that right? Had Pru just defended a teacher?

At the front of the room, Mr. Jeffries cleared his throat. His tone was friendly but firm as he said, "One of the things that you'll all quickly learn about me is that I'm a fan of courtesy. When it's your turn to talk, I'll listen. I promise. Just keep in mind that I expect the same in return."

Though his words were addressed to the whole class, his eyes settled on Pru as he finished talking. A slight frown crossed his face. It was quick. ABE wanted to think he'd imagined it. But as Pru sank red-faced into her chair, it was clear that she had noticed it, too.

CHAPTER

12

PRU AND ABE WENT TO THE HENHOUSE AS SOON AS SCHOOL ENDED. As so often seemed the case with first days of school, the afternoon felt particularly fall-like. The first stains of yellow and orange showed among the green leaves.

"Little house, little house, hear my plea. Turn from the woods and look at me," Pru said as they reached the ramshackle hut that served as the headquarters of the Unbelievable FIB.

ABE took a step back as the Henhouse stood up. With an ease that one might not normally expect from a house balanced on a single chicken leg, the Henhouse made a full rotation. Planks of wood shifted and the sound of feathers rustling filled the air.

When the Henhouse settled again, an arched double door stood in front of them atop rickety steps. The oculus looked out at them from above.

"Here we go!" Pru said as she pushed open the doors.

Again thinking about his dream, ABE wasn't paying attention to his surroundings as he entered. So he nearly ran right into Pru where she'd stopped, just a few yards in.

The hallway had ended. Before them was a small but cozy sitting room. Dark wood paneling covered the walls, but the space was brightened by art that hung in frames throughout the small room. The paintings and drawings depicted fantastic landscapes and impossible creatures. They all appeared to have been done by the same artist.

Mister Fox sat in one of three overstuffed chairs in the center of the room. He looked up to greet them as they entered. "Welcome."

"What happened?" Pru asked. Then, in an accusing voice, she added, "Where's the rest of the Henhouse? Did you break it?"

"Don't be ridiculous. You can't *break* the Henhouse." Mister Fox hesitated, then added, "Well, okay, technically you can. And I did. Once. But that was a long time ago. Everything is fine now. No, I just convinced the *domovye* to rearrange things a bit for your visit. You won't be staying long, so I figured I'd save you a climb to the oculus and meet you here, in one of the smaller versions of the Henhouse. That way, we can chat briefly and then have you off on your investigation."

"What do you want to talk about?" Pru asked, sitting in one of the two remaining chairs.

"Assumptions."

"What about them?" ABE asked, also taking a seat.

"I'll tell you one of the hardest parts about being a Fibber and investigating mysteries that involve mythical beings. We tend to think we know the individuals we're dealing with because we know the myths. That's a dangerous assumption."

"Does this have something to do with what you said once about stories changing over time?" Pru asked.

"In part. Stories exist at the whim of the teller. Myths have been told over and over again. So, yes, we have to take the details in them with a grain of salt. But there's more to think about than that."

"Like what?" ABE asked.

"The Mythics themselves. The temptation is to see them through the lens of the stories you know. But the thing about stories, especially old ones—and most especially myths—is that they reduce characters to their most basic elements. That's where archetypes come from."

"What's an archetype?" Pru asked. She squeezed her eyes shut as soon as the question was out, perhaps realizing she'd opened the door to another visit from ABE-the-walking-dictionary.

ABE didn't disappoint. *Not* because he was a know-it-all. It was just good information to have.

"It's a type of character that you see over and over again in stories. The trickster figure is a good example. Loki is the trickster in the Norse myths, but there are tricksters in other myths from around the world, too. They're all kind of different, but also kind of the same."

"How so?" Pru asked. She sounded reluctantly interested.

"Well, trickster figures all share some common traits. They're usually able to change their shape, for example. They're also usually greedy. That greed can drive them to cause trouble, but sometimes their actions can bring about good things and be a boon to people, too. Like Thor wouldn't have a hammer if it wasn't for one of Loki's pranks."

"The funny part," Mister Fox added, "is that Mythics have taken a liking to humankind's terms, like *trickster*. Mythics use those words, too. But the point is that archetypes can be misleading. If we think we know a Mythic because we know the myth, then we risk overlooking important truths.

"Mythics are just like us. They're complicated.

They have desires and fears and hopes. That's why I wanted you to see Baldur's funeral. I want you to remember that these are real people. The myths don't always capture that."

"So basically you want us to keep an open mind when we're talking to people in Asgard," ABE said.

"Interrogating witnesses," Pru corrected.

"Exactly," Mister Fox agreed. "In the past, I've told you that Fibbers ask questions and seek answers. In other words, I've told you to be suspicious of other people's truths. Now I'm telling you that you should be suspicious of your *own* truths—or things you think are true. In short, avoid assumptions. They're just beliefs in different clothes."

"This is about you still thinking that Loki is innocent, isn't it?" ABE asked. He couldn't quite keep the resentment from his voice.

"This is about me thinking that we should go into this investigation without assuming we know how it will end," Mister Fox said. He peered at ABE. "I thought we were on the same page with that."

ABE ducked his head. "I know. It's just . . . never mind."

"Just what, ABE?" Mister Fox asked.

ABE couldn't bring himself to look at the detective. He couldn't just ignore the question, though.

"It's nothing. Forget it. I just had a weird dream last night. It really shook me up. I'll get over it."

"Is that all?" Pru asked. She rolled her eyes.

But Mister Fox leaned forward in his chair, his full attention on ABE.

"Dream? What kind of dream?"

"A nightmare, really," ABE said.

"Is that right?" Mister Fox sat back. His nose twitched. "I think you'd better tell us about it, ABE. Try not to leave anything out."

ABE took a deep breath. He told them about the woman and her riddle. He tried to convey what a *strange* dream it had been.

"Okay," Pru said when he finished. "I admit that sounds like a weird nightmare. But I don't see why it's got you so shook up. It's just a dream."

"He's shook up because he doesn't really think it *was* just a dream. He thinks it was a message, like it claimed. Isn't that right, ABE?"

"That sounds crazy, doesn't it?"

"Pretty much," Pru said.

The detective shushed her. "No, ABE. It doesn't sound crazy. Well, I don't think so, anyway. And I'm the one you should be listening to just now."

ABE looked away again.

"Ah . . . I see." Understanding dawned on the

detective's face. "That's the problem, isn't it? You're not sure you *can* trust me at the moment, are you?"

"Why wouldn't he trust you?" Pru asked, as ABE slouched deeper into his chair. "That's nuts."

"Easy, Pru. There was a time you doubted me, too. I seem to remember a particular incident involving you trying to set my house on fire."

"Why does everyone keep bringing that up?" Pru demanded. "*Once.* I tried to set your house on fire once. *People make mistakes.* Seriously, you guys have to get over it. Besides, we're talking about ABE. Why doesn't he trust you?"

"He thinks the riddle might be about me. Is that it, ABE? Are you worried I'm lying to you about something?"

ABE wished he could disappear into his chair. Mister Fox's sympathetic tone only made him feel worse. The detective was defending him!

"No . . . Maybe. I don't know. Loki did so many terrible things last year. And you seem so eager to let him off the hook! Then I had that dream: 'When is a truth-teller not telling the truth?' I thought . . ."

"You thought the answer was 'When he's a Fibber,'" Mister Fox said. "You thought the dream was warning you about me. I understand, ABE. It makes sense."

"No," Pru said. She looked at ABE. "It doesn't.

First of all, Mister Fox *isn't* a Fibber. That's what he calls the kids he works with. Which means even if your solution *is* right, it's more likely the riddle is talking about one of us. And how do you know the answer is a *he*? Maybe it's 'When *she's* a Fibber.'"

"Oh!" ABE said. "I . . . I hadn't thought about it like that."

"So," Pru added, arching her eyebrows, "are *you* lying about anything, ABE?"

"No!"

"Good. Because I'm not, either." Pru tilted her head to the side. "Well, not about anything I can think of at the moment, anyway."

ABE buried his face in his hands. What had he been thinking? He'd let a dream make him doubt a friend. He forced himself to look the detective in the eye.

"Mister Fox, I'm so sorry. Really. I shouldn't have doubted you. I guess I really am just having a hard time keeping an open mind about Loki. I was kind of upset that you were willing to forgive him for all he did and—"

"ABE, stop. You have nothing to apologize for. You only did what I've always encouraged you to do. You questioned things. And, for all we know, the riddle could still be about me."

"Wait," Pru said. "You mean you *are* lying to us?"

"Not about anything big," the detective said with

a wink. "But that's not the point. The riddle doesn't directly suggest *lying*. Someone could not be telling the truth because they don't know what the truth is. They could be wrong, and therefore what they're saying *wouldn't* be true. But the meaning of the message doesn't concern me much at the moment. I'm more curious about who sent it."

"Any ideas?" Pru asked.

"One or two. But I want to do some research. We'll discuss it when you get back. One last thing before you go, though." The detective reached out and put a hand on ABE's shoulder. "You're wrong, ABE. I haven't forgiven Loki for what he did to you or Pru last year. Not by a long shot. But this investigation is bigger than that. If Loki *is* innocent and we can prove it, then maybe Ragnarok doesn't have to happen, ever. Maybe all those people don't have to die. I think that's worth exploring. Don't you?"

"Yeah," ABE said with a grateful nod. "I do."

CHAPTER
13

MISTER FOX HAD A GIFT FOR THEM BEFORE THEY LEFT.

"Clothes?" Pru said, examining the pile of items a *domovoi* handed to her. "Clothes are the worst kind of gift."

"These are special clothes. They'll help you fit in on Asgard."

"I didn't have special clothes last year when I rescued ABE."

"You were trying to remain unnoticeable last time. This time is different. This time we want people in Asgard to notice you. We want them to talk to you. These will help."

ABE looked down at the folded clothes Mister Fox

had provided. There was a pair of sturdy brown pants and a blue long-sleeved shirt. Both items looked like something that might have been worn in a Viking village hundreds of years ago.

"Where did you get them?" he asked.

"The *domovye* made them. They have many talents, but domestic magic is their specialty. They're particularly good with fabric. They make their own clothes, which render them almost invisible. Your clothes will do the opposite. The *domovye* have enchanted them, so they'll make you *more* visible. People will be able to see and interact with you."

Mister Fox and Pru stepped out into the hallway while ABE changed. Then ABE and Pru switched. Pru came out wearing clothes that looked a lot like ABE's, only her shirt was green, with a different pattern embroidered around the neck. She also carried a satchel over her shoulder, presumably provided to replace her messenger bag. Mister Fox had been smart to include it. Pru kept her dad's detective badge in her messenger bag. She'd carried the badge with her ever since his death. She'd told ABE that carrying the badge was like carrying a piece of her dad with her. She didn't go *anywhere* without it. ABE guessed the badge and her looking glass had already been transferred to the satchel.

The detective walked them down the hall but held back as they approached the exit.

"This is as far as I go. The rest is up to you two. Go to Baldur's house and find out what you can. Then come back. Hurry, now. There's someone outside who's been waiting to see you both."

The Henhouse had settled on a hilltop. A short distance away, beyond a massive wall, stood the city of Asgard. Magnificent buildings rose from the ground, monuments of timber and stone. Their multilayered and peaked roofs stretched toward the sky and glistened in the sun.

ABE had read that the dwarves that lived in the nearby mountains provided the gods with a wealth of jewels and precious stones. He suspected those gems decorated the buildings and were catching the light, causing the sparkle.

"So that's Asgard," ABE said from the steps. "It's . . . amazing."

Before Pru could answer, a small, furry projectile launched itself at her from the roof of the Henhouse. Her cries of "What is it?" and "Get it off!" quickly stopped when she realized the newcomer's identity.

"Ratatosk!" she exclaimed

"Shortwits!" Ratatosk answered.

ABE wasn't offended by the greeting—well, not too much. It was the squirrel's way. He'd spent a lifetime carrying insults back and forth between the eagle that lived at the top of Yggdrasil and the dragon, Nidhogg, who lived at the bottom. They'd sort of been a bad influence on Ratatosk's language development. And his social development. Still, Ratatosk did seem very pleased to see them, despite his greeting. He scampered up to Pru's shoulder and nuzzled her cheek before head-butting ABE's shoulder.

"It's so good to see you," ABE said.

"Yeah," Pru agreed. "But how come you never came to visit us?"

"Has it been long? It's so hard to tell with you mortals. You hurry through days so fast! Rush, rush, rush! It can't have been *that* long, no. You're still relatively *short* shortwits."

"What? Look who's talking!" Pru said. "You don't even come up to my knee."

Ratatosk sniffed. "I'm very big for a squirrel, yes! Tall. Stately. Statuesque!"

"So," ABE said, clearing his throat, "this is Asgard, huh? We were just saying how fantastic it is."

"Yes, yes, yes. Splendid Asgard, home of the apotheosized gods and their overblown egos."

"Apo . . . theo . . . sized?" Pru repeated.

"Glorified," ABE said.

Ratatosk huffed, as though he had wanted to explain.

"Sorry," ABE said.

Pru shook her head at the both of them. "If you two could stop trying to impress each other with your *apotheosized* vocabularies for a second, that would be great. This is my first Mythic city. I'm trying to have a moment."

"Sorry," ABE said as Ratatosk snorted.

Pru laughed and ABE did, too, struck by the pleasure of the reunion and familiar roles. Ratatosk soon joined the laughter. ABE assumed Ratatosk's quick breathing was what passed as laughter for the squirrel, anyway.

"We should get going," Pru said as they quieted. "Ratatosk, can you take us to Baldur's house?"

The squirrel nodded, and the three of them set off down the hill toward the gates of Asgard. Pru glanced back at the Henhouse.

"He'll be okay," ABE said. He hoped that was true. "I'm sure he's used to this by now."

"I know. But . . . this place, ABE. Breathe it in. Like you said, it's *amazing*. We're in a whole other world. Imagine being able to travel to places like this all your life . . . and then suddenly not being able to go anymore."

ABE nodded, not knowing what to say. He hadn't been sure how he would react to a return to Asgard. His first trip had been terrifying. This time, though, ABE felt an excited quiver in his belly as he approached the fabled city.

In a way, visiting Asgard was like traveling back in time. The view of the city from the hilltop had revealed a metropolis that resembled drawings ABE had seen of a Viking village, though on a much, much grander scale. He might as well have been stepping into one of his favorite books as they approached the gates and the smell of fish and smoked meat filled the air while the clanging of metal rang in the distance.

Ratatosk slipped into Pru's bag as they passed through the gates, huge wooden doors tall enough to give even the giant Gristling pause.

"I have a bit of a reputation," the squirrel explained. "Best if I stay out of sight, yes."

"Maybe if you didn't insult people so often, you'd have a better reputation," Pru said.

Ratatosk snorted.

"Where did all the people come from?" ABE asked as they walked the crowded streets. The stories mostly talked about Asgard as the home of the gods and goddesses. But Asgard was filled with people.

"There are three classes in Asgard," Ratatosk explained from Pru's bag. "The gods and goddesses are one. Haughty. Imperious. Warriors are next. Most are mortals that Odin and the Valkyries brought here to live in Valhalla and train, waiting for Ragnarok. They fight and eat, eat and fight. An army of barbarous gluttons. They die each night to rise the next day and fight some more."

"Some life," Pru said.

"Who said they were alive? Not alive, no. Not dead. Something in between."

"What's the last group?" ABE asked, shivering at the thought of the undead warriors.

"Serfs. When the worlds started to drift apart, the gods allowed some mortals to come here to live and serve them. Why be a god if there is no one to worship you?"

"Those must be the people Mister Fox wants us to talk to at Baldur's house."

Ahead, a large timber building loomed over them. ABE couldn't quite figure out how many stories it was. It seemed to be a mass of sloping roofs that intersected with each other at various stages. Braided carvings trimmed the wood.

A strange feeling settled over ABE as they approached the building.

"It feels so . . ." he struggled for the right word.

"Peaceful," Pru said, finishing his thought.

"That is Breidablik," another voice said.

ABE turned to see a girl in a long dress approach from around a corner of the building. She appeared to be a few years younger than them.

"What is?" Pru said, looking around.

"That feeling." The girl laughed. "That sense of peace you feel. It comes from Breidablik, home of Baldur, fairest of the gods. Welcome."

CHAPTER 14

"IS THIS YOUR FIRST TIME IN THE SHINING CITY?" THE GIRL ASKED. "HAVE you come from far away?"

"You could say that," Pru said.

"I have heard of other villages, but I have not been to any! I am Eira." The girl ducked her head in a greeting. "My mother is Alva. She is . . . *was* a weaver here at Breidablik. She left after . . . what happened. She couldn't stand to be here anymore."

"Eira!" a voice called from inside the building. "Quickly, now! No dawdling."

"I must go!" Eira said.

"Wait," Pru said. "We want to ask you about . . ." Her voice trailed off as Eira rushed off and disappeared into the building.

"Well, at least we know we're in the right place," ABE said as they followed the girl into Breidablik.

Baldur's home welcomed them with its vast halls, open courtyards, and sprawling gardens. They wandered aimlessly, not sure where to start or whom they should ask about Baldur's death. In the end, because they encountered so few people after Eira, they asked anyone they could.

The first person they met was a gray-bearded old man. He walked with a stoop and a head turned slightly to one side, as though he had spent a good deal of time bent over things and never quite got the hang of straightening back up again.

"Hello, children," he said cheerfully. He introduced himself as Harald and explained he was a tanner.

"I'm Pru. This is my friend ABE. Nice to meet you. You know, we were starting to think we were the only ones here. You're only the second person we've seen. Where is everyone?"

"Oh, there are few enough of us left here now— that's a fact," Harald said, scratching his beard with calloused fingers. "Since our poor master died, there's little call for work."

"Yeah, we heard about Baldur," Pru said, jumping at the opening. She shook her head. "Terrible news. Did you . . . by any chance see what happened?"

"No, no. I was on an errand and away."

"But you must have heard about it, right?" Pru pressed.

"Who would talk about such a thing? Who would bring such bad fortune on themselves?" Harald asked, blinking. Then, perhaps realizing that he himself was talking about it, he looked around anxiously. "I must be off. Good day, children. Be well. Enjoy the peace of Breidablik."

Harald hurried off.

"That didn't go so well," ABE observed.

"You think?"

Their luck didn't change as the day went on. The few cooks and groundskeepers they met were friendly enough at first. But everyone ran off as soon as ABE or Pru mentioned Baldur or Loki.

"This is getting us nowhere!" Pru complained. "What's wrong with these people? How am I supposed to interrogate anyone if they won't answer my questions?"

"Serfs are a superstitious lot," Ratatosk said. "*Over*-credulous, yes. *Un*skeptical. They know Baldur's death heralds dark days ahead."

"At least people are friendly," ABE said.

"Yeah," Pru said. "Why is that? I mean, we're just wandering around in here. How come nobody is throwing us out?"

"I've been wondering about that, too. Remember what the girl said about Breidablik being peaceful?

That kind of fits with some of the things I read about the place. The stories say nothing unclean can enter its walls. It's supposed to be a safe haven. I think the people here are used to an open-door policy."

"Yes, yes," Ratatosk said from inside the bag. "Odin placed a charm on Breidablik to keep anyone with evil intent from entering. Guests are allowed to walk freely."

"Speaking of evil intent," Pru said, gesturing down the hall in which they stood. "I think we're being watched."

ABE looked. Eira's head poked out from around a corner a short distance away. Discovered, the girl approached them, blushing.

"I'm sorry. I did not mean to listen in," she said.

"No harm in a little eavesdropping," Pru said with a shrug.

"In that case, may I ask a question? Did your bag just talk a moment ago?"

ABE exchanged a look with Pru. She raised her eyebrows. He shrugged. What did they have to lose? They weren't getting anywhere on their own. Maybe Ratatosk could help.

"Okay, I'll show you," Pru said. "But it's a secret. Okay?"

Eira nodded eagerly and Pru opened her bag. The girl peered inside. Ratatosk winked at her and waved. Eira jumped back, clapping a hand over her mouth.

"The Messenger!" she said, her fingers muffling her voice. "Who *are* you that you travel with the Messenger?"

ABE didn't want to lie to Eira. He also knew they couldn't tell her the truth. He and Pru had to fit in by appearing as though they belonged, the way Odin did when he masqueraded as Old Man Grimnir.

"Pru and I are, um, apprenticed to a storyteller." That was sort of true, he supposed. They were kind of apprenticed to Mister Fox. And a fibber was someone who told stories, after all.

"You're skalds? But why are you here? And how is it you travel with the Messenger? Are you friends of the gods?"

"We are," Pru said. "Totally. They sent us to gather information for a new story about Baldur's death."

ABE nodded, impressed with how quickly Pru had adapted to his story and improved on it. They hadn't had any luck just asking people about Baldur's death. But maybe Eira would be more talkative if she thought they were creating a story for the gods.

"Were you here when it happened . . . when Baldur died?" Pru asked. ABE held his breath as he waited for an answer.

"No," Eira said, and ABE's shoulders drooped. "But my mother was here that day. You could come with me to my house tonight! My mother would be so pleased to have skalds who know the gods under her roof. I'm sure she will do whatever she can to help you!"

✳

The sun hung low in the sky as ABE and Pru arrived at Eira's village just outside the walls of Asgard. It consisted of a collection of about twenty long, rectangular houses. The walls of the houses were made with stacked logs. They reminded ABE of building toys he'd had when he was little.

They followed Eira along the worn paths that marked the roads of the village. Around them, people lit torches and lanterns as the dark began to gather. Everyone ABE saw cast frequent looks over their shoulders and spoke in hushed tones.

Eira's home looked like all the other buildings. The door stood in the center of one of the long walls of the house. Tears welled in ABE's eyes as he entered the smoke-filled interior. At first, he worried the house had caught fire. But as his eyes stopped watering, he realized the space just lacked ventilation for the long, open hearth located in the center of the structure's only room.

A woman sat beside the fire, tending a large iron cauldron that hung on a chain from a roof beam. Eira introduced her as her mother, Alva.

"Mother, this is ABE and, er, Pru," Eira said, stumbling a bit over their names. "I met them at Breidablik. They're skalds!"

Eira's mother snorted and said, "A bit young for skalds."

"But, Mother," Eira said, "they travel with—"

"Apprentice skalds," Pru interrupted, elbowing Eira. ABE leaned in to remind the girl that Ratatosk was a secret.

"We're gathering information about the death of Baldur for a story—" Pru continued.

"Hush, child! We do not speak of that in this house," Alva said, rising to her feet and wiping her hands on her apron. "Eira, go fetch your brother. Your friends may stay for dinner, but we will have no gossip under this roof."

"Okay. Not a promising start," Pru whispered to ABE as Eira followed her mother's directions. "But I'll wear her down. Adults are easy. Watch. It's just a matter of coming at it from the right angle."

Eira returned with her brother, Sten, and the family sat down for a meal of fish and some drink that ABE was pretty sure his mom wouldn't have let him try at home. Pru began her interrogation as soon as dinner started.

"Beautiful weather, wouldn't you say? I bet it was a dark day when Baldur died."

"Weather?" Alva said. "Who can attend to the weather when there is work to be done? Most days I don't know if the sun shines or the snow falls."

Pru chewed her lip. ABE made a note to slip the definition of *subtle* into a conversation with Pru. Soon.

"That's a beautiful dress, though," Pru said later. "Was that what you wore the day Baldur died?"

"Clothes! Don't talk to me about clothes. I have baskets of clothing to mend for my own children and others in the village. I hardly notice my own clothes. For all I know, I might have gone naked to Breidablik that day."

Sten and Eira giggled. Pru's bottom lip was beginning to chap from all the lip-chewing Alva's evasions had inspired.

When the meal was done, Sten asked ABE and Pru for a story. Alva sat back expectantly. Apparently, being an apprentice skald—even a pretend one—came with certain obligations.

ABE figured the task would fall to him. Pru surprised him, though, by rising to her feet first.

"Listen now to the story of the Eye of Odin," she said. "It begins in the land of Midgard, across the Rainbow Bridge. There, in a small town, there lived a brave young girl who was not at all small for her age. Her name was Prudence the Red. Prudence had a loyal friend named Aloysius the Fierce and a magical pet fox who she called Mister Fox."

ABE groaned. Pru ignored him and continued.

"Now, it just so happened that, long ago, Odin, Allfather of the gods, had hidden a very special stone in

Prudence's town. On that stone was written the secret location of the Eye of Odin, a magical talisman that had the power to see into the very future."

"Ooh," exclaimed Sten and Eira at once. Even Alva appeared caught up in Pru's telling.

Just then, a different voice reached ABE's ears. It came from Pru's bag. But it wasn't Ratatosk's voice. It was Mister Fox, trying to reach them through the looking glass.

Before ABE could react, Ratatosk peeked out, unnoticed, and grabbed a nearby piece of cloth. He pulled it into the bag and must have wrapped the glass in it because Mister Fox's voice became muffled and then fell silent. ABE followed Ratatosk's lead and quietly wrapped his own glass with a napkin, then stuffed it in the bag.

Pru went on to tell how the brave band of heroes journeyed to Asgard and temporarily recovered the Eye of Odin, only to lose it once again to Loki. ABE had to admit that Pru was a talented storyteller. Even having lived through the events, ABE found himself caught up in her telling as they reached the moment when Prudence the Red, Aloysius the Fierce, and Ratatosk were cornered by Gristling and Loki and about to meet their end.

"But Prudence the Red knew just what to do," Pru said. "Do you know why?"

"Because she was very brave and very smart?" Eira asked, her eyes wide.

"Well, yes. That. Definitely that. But also because when she had held the Eye, even though it was only for a short time, *she had seen the future*. She knew just what to do to save herself and her friends. She took a deep breath and called for her close, personal friend, Thor. *BOOM!* He arrived in an explosion of thunder, and there was a huge battle. Thor polished off the giants, and then they hid the Eye of Odin once again so Loki would never, ever find it!"

Eira and Sten cheered. And, a bit to ABE's surprise, Alva joined in.

"I have a question, though," Sten said. "What did Mister Fox do?"

"Surprisingly little," Pru said. She was really enjoying the authority of being the storyteller. "Mostly, he got in the way and made sarcastic remarks. But Prudence the Red was generous and kept him around anyway."

"Oh."

"It was a fine story," Alva said. "You more than earned your meal and a night's lodging."

"A night's lodging?" ABE said. "That's nice. But we can't stay."

"You certainly can't go!" Alva said.

"Oh, no, you mustn't go out at night!" Eira said.

"Why?" Pru asked.

"Trolls! They've become more and more bold since . . . "—Eira glanced at her mother—"well, lately. They've been seen in the fields at night."

"You can sleep on the floor," Alva said. "There's plenty of room. You can be off on your way tomorrow."

"What do you think?" Pru asked ABE.

"It doesn't look like we have much choice. We're no match for trolls here." Their looking glasses could only banish Mythics from Earth, where they didn't belong. They'd be useless on Asgard.

"Okay," Pru said. "Thank you. Now, since you enjoyed the story so much, perhaps you'd like to pass the time by answering some questions about Baldur's death?"

"No," Alva said. "I would not. I must get these two to bed and get some sleep myself. Tomorrow will be a busy day. I have those four baskets of clothes to mend. That is how I earn *my* keep. Stories are fine, but they will not feed my family."

"That woman is so *stubborn*," Pru said to ABE when they stepped aside to discuss the situation.

"Yeah. But I've been thinking. Maybe we've been approaching this the wrong way. Have you noticed how she keeps mentioning how much work she has to do? Maybe if we could somehow help her with that, we could get her to talk to us."

"ABE, that's it! You're a genius!"

"I am?"

"Totally. And so am I. Because I have a brilliant plan."

"Ah, how brilliant exactly? And how much mortal danger does it involve?"

"Be quiet. Even you will like this one. Trust me."

CHAPTER
15

THE FIRE HAD FALLEN TO EMBERS AND SHADOWS FILLED THE SMALL HOME when Pru called out to Alva in a soft voice, so as not to wake up Sten or Eira.

"What is it, girl?" Alva said, also whispering.

"I have a secret to tell you. My friend and I haven't been completely honest with you."

"Oh?" Alva shuffled over to the corner of the room where Pru and ABE sat on blankets that had been placed over piles of hay.

"We are not who we told you. My friend here is Aloysius the Fierce. And I . . ." Pru passed for what ABE could only assume was dramatic effect, "I am Prudence the Red."

"Are you now?" Alva's tone suggested she did not properly appreciate dramatic effect.

"Yes. We're not just skalds. We're great heroes of Midgard, too, and friends of the gods. As such, we have access to great powers and magic."

"Is that so?"

"*Yes*. And because you've been so kind to us, we are going to give you a boom."

"*Boon*," ABE corrected, assuming she meant a favor and not an explosion. Though with Pru you could never quite be sure.

"Right. *Boon*. When you wake up in the morning, you will find all your clothes mended. You will also find new clothes for you and your family to help you through the winter."

Wait. What? ABE tried to catch Pru's eye, but she ignored him.

"Of course, in return, it *would* be nice if you were to take some time and tell us about the events on the day Baldur died."

Alva stared at her while ABE held his breath. Finally, the woman snorted. It might have been a sound of amusement or disgust. "Child, you may the boldest liar I have ever met."

"I prefer Fibber," Pru said. "But I'm telling you the truth about this."

"Very well. You have a bargain. In return for your . . .

boon . . . I will answer any questions you have about the day the Fair One died. *But* I will do so in the morning. After you have delivered on your promise."

"Deal."

Alva snorted again, then walked off to her rest.

"Pru," ABE whispered, "what are you doing? Where are we supposed to come up with all those clothes? And where's Ratatosk gone?"

"Don't worry," Pru said. "It's all part of the plan."

"Thor's hammer!"

ABE sat up, instantly awake. He brushed hay from his hair and squinted in the bright glow of morning. "What is it? Where are we?"

Alva stood in the center of the room. Her hands were clasped to her cheeks. In front of her, where there had been four baskets the night before, sat no fewer than *ten* baskets. Neatly folded clothing filled every one. Eira and Sten knelt among the baskets and explored their contents with excitement.

"Mother, look at the weave on this dress! It's the finest I've ever seen!" Eira said, holding up a garment.

"*How?*" Alva said, turning to Pru. "How did you do this?"

"Sorry," Pru said, sitting on her pile of hay. "Explanations weren't part of the deal."

Alva said nothing for a moment. Her eyes went

from Pru to the baskets. ABE crossed his fingers and watched to see how the woman would react.

"No. No, they were not. Very well. A bargain is a bargain, girl. Sten and Eira, go outside until I call for you. I have things to discuss with our guests."

Alva's two children said their good-byes, and Alva seated herself on a chair near the hearth.

"Go on, then, children. Ask your questions."

Pru blinked. She seemed too surprised that her plan had worked to think of a question.

"Were you there when Loki . . . when Baldur was killed?" ABE asked, jumping in.

"I was. I was cleaning blankets in a corner of the yard where the gods had gathered."

"So you saw what happened?" Pru asked, recovering.

"I did." Alva lifted her chin. There was a quivering about her lips that seemed out of place on her strong, confident face.

"I'm sorry," ABE said. "I am. It must have been awful. But . . . we have to ask. Can you tell us what you saw?"

"Why, boy?" Alva snapped. "Why must you make me relive it? You *know* the story. We all do. The Allfather told it long before it happened."

"Yes, but now that it *has* happened, we need the details," Pru said. "So . . . so we can tell the story better."

"The old story has been around so long," ABE said. "And stories change."

"So be it." Alva took a deep breath and began. "It was a feast day. A celebration. The gods gathered at Breidablik as they often did. Baldur was the fairest and most beloved of all, and his home the most beautiful. The celebration became boisterous. And, as was so often the case, the gods fell to their favorite sport, throwing weapons at Baldur."

"Some sport," Pru muttered.

ABE shushed her. He didn't want to interrupt Alva. The gods' choice of games did seem odd. But he had expected it from the myth of Baldur's death. The story described how Odin had used his power as Allfather to magically protect his beloved son from almost everything on the three worlds. Only mistletoe had escaped Odin's notice, but it was considered too small a plant to cause any harm. Baldur's near invulnerability had given rise to the peculiar sport Alva had witnessed.

"As had always happened before, the weapons they threw bounced off Baldur. No blade or bow could pierce the charms of protection Odin had placed on his son. Until . . ."

Alva hung her head. ABE waited silently for her to continue, as did Pru.

"Until the spear struck him and pierced his chest.

Wooden, and worked through with oil from the mistletoe plant it was. Everything stopped when that spear struck. There was no movement. No sound. Even Baldur did not cry out. He just stood there, run through by the spear, the dew of slaughter spilling from the wound in his chest."

Alva dabbed her eyes with her apron before continuing.

"The first sound came from Thor. No thunder, no rage. The cry that came from his throat was too powerful to be contained by any storm. He ran to the Shining One's side and caught him as he fell. Thor wept as his brother died in his arms. They all wept, all the gods, all the goddesses, all of us. Everything and everyone wept as Baldur's light died. All but one."

"Loki?" ABE guessed.

"Father of wolves and worms! Trickster to the gods! Bringer of death! He had no tears to shed for the fairest of the gods."

"He was there?" Pru asked. "Loki? You're sure?"

"Of course I'm sure. I know the liar's face. It haunts my dreams!"

"Did you see Loki throw the spear?" ABE asked.

"No. Blind Hod threw the spear. Poor fool. He threw what had been given to him. He meant no harm. He only wanted to be part of the game."

"So it was whoever gave Hod the spear laced with mistletoe that wanted Baldur dead," ABE said.

"Did you see who gave Hod the spear?" Pru pressed. "Was it Loki?"

Alva frowned. "I did not see. I was distracted by my work. I did not look up until after the deed was done. But I *did* see the trickster slither away after the fact, snake that he is!"

"You're *sure*?" Pru asked. "You're sure you saw Loki slipping away?"

"I'm sure," Alva said. "He went right past me as he fled."

ABE broke the silence that filled the room after Alva's pronouncement. "Thank you, Alva. I'm sorry you had to relive all that. I guess we should go."

"One last thing," Pru burst out. "I have to ask. Why did the gods do it? Why did they make sport out of throwing weapons at Baldur? They *knew* what would happen. Couldn't anyone have stopped Hod from throwing the spear?"

"Can you stop the will of the Fates, child?" Alva said, sounding shocked. "Are the gods such cowards that they would try? No! Each played their role, as they were and are fated to do."

As her initial wave of outrage passed, Alva's voice took on a softer tone.

"Besides, no one expected the fateful throw to come that day. Hod had thrown a thousand spears over the years. No one attended to that throw. It was such a shock. Even knowing it would happen one day. No one thought it would be *that* day. I suppose no one ever thinks it is their day. We all hope for more time. The end should always come tomorrow, never today."

✳

"How *did* you do it?" ABE asked Pru as they left the village behind. "How did you get all those clothes?"

"Simple! Last night, I sent Ratatosk back to the Henhouse with a message for Mister Fox. Ratatosk told him that I needed the clothes, and why."

"Of course!" ABE said. "So Mister Fox had the *domovye* mend and make the clothes."

"Right. And apparently it worked. The clothes were there before I woke up this morning. The *domovye* must have slipped in and out while everyone was asleep. They're good at that, too."

"Pru . . . that plan was *brilliant!*"

"I told you so," Pru said. She grinned and added, "But thanks."

They reached the Henhouse in short order and found Mister Fox waiting in the same sitting room they'd encountered on their last visit. He paced the small room, stopping only when they both entered.

"It's about time," he said.

"Well, excuse us for being late," Pru answered. "We were busy out there getting the job done."

"You're right. I'm sorry." Mister Fox pinched the

bridge of his nose. "And I'm eager to hear what you've learned. Sit. Tell me what happened."

ABE and Pru each took a chair. Mister Fox remained standing, leaning on the back of his seat. His foot tapped lightly on the floor.

"Well, it took some work," Pru began, "but I think we found out everything we could."

She recited the events of the morning and previous day. ABE supplied details as needed. Otherwise, he let Pru have her moment. After all, it had been her clever idea that had earned them the information they'd been looking for.

Mister Fox scratched his nose while he processed everything he'd heard. When they finished, he said, "Well done, you two. The trick with the clothing was inspired. So what do we know?"

"We know now that Loki *was* there when Baldur died," ABE said.

"And he ran off when Baldur got killed. Not a good sign," Pru added.

"No," Mister Fox agreed. "It's not. But it's not proof, either. Your witness, Alva, didn't see him give the spear to Hod."

The detective pressed a hand to his temples, massaging them with his thumb and index finger for a moment before pulling the hand down his long face. He looked . . . worried. ABE couldn't remember Mister

Fox ever looking worried before. He felt a pang of sympathy for the detective and lingering guilt for doubting him earlier.

"Like you said, though, we don't have proof. I mean, we don't know for sure that Loki gave Hod the spear to throw."

"Wait," Pru said, swiveling in her seat to look at him. "Now you're defending Loki? Do you really think he's innocent?"

ABE ran a hand through his hair. "No. Not really."

"I appreciate the thought, though, ABE," Mister Fox said. "Bottom line? You two accomplished a lot, but our investigation isn't done. We'll discuss next steps when you come back tomorrow."

"You're sending us home?" ABE asked.

"But we're in the zone!" Pru said. "And you said you'd tell us your theory about ABE's dream when we got back."

"Things have changed. I didn't expect you to spend the night. I don't want to keep you in Agsard any longer than I have to."

"What's the big deal?" Pru asked. "You can still get us back to the moment after we left, right?"

"Yes. But that's not the point."

"So what *is* the point?"

"Well, in part, Ratatosk had to go tend to some of his own business for a bit. Delivering messages. Or gathering acorns. I don't know. Whatever mischievous squirrels do for their day job. I'd like him to be here when we pick things up again. We're going to need him."

"You could still tell us what you think about who sent my dream," ABE said.

"I could, yes. I *could*. But I'm not going to."

"How come?" Pru demanded.

"Because it won't change anything if you wait a day, and I think it will drive you both a little crazy to *have* to wait. It's petty, I know, but I think a little retaliation is in order."

"Retaliation? For what?" Pru said as the Henhouse launched itself into the air.

"*Surprisingly little. Mostly, he got in the way and made sarcastic remarks,*" Mister Fox quoted, repeating Pru's words about him from the night before.

Pru sank into her chair with a groan as ABE remembered Mister Fox's attempt to contact them through the looking glass. He must have heard Pru's story before closing the connection. ABE considered pointing out that Pru had told the story, not him, but it occurred to him that he hadn't spoken in the detective's defense.

"So, uh, I guess we'll just get going then," Pru said as the henhouse landed.

Mister Fox smiled sweetly and waved good-bye.

CHAPTER
16

ABE AND PRU PARTED WAYS WHEN THEY RETURNED TO MIDDLETON. IT WAS weird to think that even though they'd spent the night in Asgard, it was still the same afternoon they'd left Earth. ABE saw kids with their backpacks on, heading home from the first day of school.

He was just a couple of doors down from his house—he could see his dad stretching on the front steps for a run—when he heard the sound of kids on bikes behind him. He stepped onto his neighbor's lawn to make room for them to pass.

As they rode by, ABE recognized the riders as Danny and another boy from his homeroom whose name he didn't know.

"Hey, look," Danny called, turning his bike onto

the empty street to make a slow loop beside ABE. "It's forsooth boy. I wish you good day, forsooth boy!"

ABE hung his head as Danny completed his loop and rode off, laughing with his friend.

Walking up to his house, he greeted his dad without meeting his eyes and went inside. He hoped that would be the end of it—but he knew it wouldn't be. His dad followed him into the kitchen.

"ABE, what just happened?"

"It's nothing, Dad," ABE said as he opened the fridge. He'd been starving during the walk home. Now he'd lost his appetite. "It's just a kid from school being a jerk."

"Yeah, I can see he's a jerk. I couldn't miss it. But I'm not talking about him. I'm talking about you. ABE, you can't just let that kind of thing happen. You *have* to learn how to stick up for yourself. Even if it means getting knocked down a time or two. Otherwise, people are going to walk all over you for the rest of your life."

"I know, Dad. I just . . . I've got a lot on my mind right now. Is it okay if I grab a snack and head up to my room?"

His dad looked like he was about to say something more but shrugged. "Okay. If that's what you have to do."

ABE watched him go. Then he closed the fridge

and climbed the stairs to his room, empty-handed. Danny's laughter echoed in his head.

So did something else, though.

Forsooth.

Something about the word nagged at him.

But he wasn't in the mood for riddles at the moment. Reaching his room, he knelt by his bookshelf and looked for another world to escape into.

The next day at school, ABE sat with the other kids in his homeroom in a circle on the carpet in the front of the room. So far as he knew, their class was the only one that had what Mr. Jeffries called a Morning Meeting.

Each meeting began with everyone in the circle greeting someone else. After that, three kids could share something that was on their minds or going on in their lives. Then, if there was time, they would play a quick game before heading off to their first class.

Most teachers wouldn't have been able to pull off something like that. A few kids made jokes about how ridiculous they thought Morning Meetings were. Danny was the most outspoken—though of course he only said something when he was sure Mr. Jeffries wouldn't hear.

But most of the conversations ABE overheard suggested that the other kids really liked Mr. Jeffries so far.

ABE did. He was pretty sure Pru did, too, even though she wouldn't admit it. So most of them were willing to give him the benefit of the doubt when it came to Morning Meetings.

That morning they finished up early, and Mr. Jeffries asked if everyone knew how to play Telephone.

Most of the kids did. Mr. Jeffries would whisper a sentence into the ear of the person sitting next to him. That person would whisper the same sentence, as she or he had heard it, into the ear of the next person, and so on. The idea was that, by the end, the sentence would usually break down into an absurd series of words because one person would mishear something—and that misunderstanding would get passed on and added to.

It reminded ABE of how myths changed over time.

Sure enough, by the time the girl next to him, Isabella, whispered the sentence to ABE it was: "Blue chickens eat pimply avocados." Isabella could barely say it with a straight face and shrugged to suggest she'd done her best.

ABE whispered the message to Pru, who passed it on to Danny, who sat at about the midpoint of the circle.

As soon as she finished, Danny leaned away and threw up his hands.

"Whoa, Mr. Jeffries. I don't know what you said, but

I'm pretty sure you wouldn't want me to repeat what Pru just said to me. That was totally inappropriate."

"What? I didn't say anything bad!" Pru insisted, turning red in the face. That started a domino effect, with everyone in the circle quickly denying that *they* had been the one to say anything wrong. The room quickly exploded into chaos.

"STOP!"

It was the first time Mr. Jeffries had raised his voice. Everyone immediately quieted.

"I'm disappointed," he said. His voice returned to a regular volume but his face was slightly red. "We don't have to do this. We could have a homeroom where everyone sits silently until the day starts. I happen to think that school can and should be fun, though. And I think that one of the best ways to build a community is to play games together. But that doesn't work if you all can't handle it."

Most kids in the class wore sheepish expressions and avoided looking Mr. Jeffries in the eye. ABE glanced at Danny. His head was ducked and he was hiding a smile.

"Tomorrow, we're going to try a different game. I hope it goes better. I would hate for us to have to stop because of the actions of one person, whoever that one person was." Mr. Jeffries's eyes settled on Pru.

"It wasn't me!" she said.

"I didn't say it was."

"So why are you looking at me like that, then?" Pru stood up.

ABE winced at the hurt in Pru's voice.

"I have to go to the restroom," she said. She stormed out of the room without waiting for Mr. Jeffries's response.

Mr. Jeffries watched her go, his mouth set in a firm line. Turning back to the class, he said, "Everyone can take a book out until the bell rings."

ABE reached into his backpack. For once, though, he didn't feel like reading. He wanted to go check on Pru, but he had a feeling that Mr. Jeffries wouldn't let anyone else leave the room at that point.

ABE let his eyes wander. By chance, they happened to land on the poster with the poem that Mr. Jeffries had read on the night of the open house:

Children, ay, forsooth . . .

Danny's mockery from the day before came back to him. The sting of it had lessened overnight. ABE considered why the word had caught his attention. *Forsooth.*

Of course!

He straightened in his seat. At least something good had come of the day.

ABE had just figured out the riddle from his dream. And it wasn't about Mister Fox at all!

CHAPTER
17

PRU HADN'T RETURNED TO HOMEROOM BEFORE THE BELL RANG, SO ABE caught up with her at lunch, eager to share his discovery. She had other things on her mind, though.

"I have to stay after school today to talk to Mr. Jeffries."

"Oh. Sorry. That wasn't fair at all."

"Tell me about it." Pru shoved the food around on her cafeteria tray.

"I'll wait for you."

"No, you go on to the Henhouse. I'll meet you there. I have a feeling I'm going to need some space after Mr. Jeffries and I *talk*."

The Henhouse's ribbed hallway opened to the vast inner courtyard ABE had grown used to during his first visits to the magical structure. A *domovoi* met him there and gestured with floating hands for him to follow.

ABE expected the *domovoi* to take him to the oculus room. Instead, they entered an unfamiliar section of the Henhouse. The *domovoi* paused in front of a set of arched double doors at the end of a long hallway. ABE breathed in the familiar heavy scent of the forest, but it seemed stronger there. Opening the doors and stepping through, he instantly understood why.

The room beyond the double doors was, without question, the most wonderful place ABE had ever seen.

It was a library.

It was a forest.

It was *both.*

At first, the interior of the room looked normal enough. In fact, it looked a lot like the Henhouse's inner courtyard. Columns rose up on either side of the door, carved like trees. The pattern of columns repeated itself for about ten feet in every direction.

Then, gradually, they changed. The columns began to look more realistic. After about twenty feet they no longer *looked* like trees, they *were* trees. Actual trees! Massive branches, heavy with leaves, stretched out above him as ABE walked along. The branches hid the ceiling and offered refuge to the many birds that flew overhead. ABE even glimpsed something that flew like a bird but seemed reptilian and had bat wings. Could it have been a tiny dragon?

Lost in his study of the treetops, ABE tripped. Looking down, he saw that the polished planks of the floorboards had all but vanished beneath a mossy scrub. The walls of the library had also given way to the forest and disappeared. He could only make out the door, in the distance, through which he'd entered, lightly lit by the oil lamps that hung on either side.

ABE clambered up an embankment, turning his head in every direction to take in the splendor around him. As astonishing as the living forest was, the books were what made the space truly spectacular.

There were books *everywhere*. They sat on bookshelves that seemed to grow out of the landscape. Some shelves stretched between trees while others appeared to have been carved into boulders. ABE even found a collection of Arthurian legends stacked within a hollowed-out tree trunk.

Crossing a quaint wooden bridge over a creek, ABE discovered an area ahead that appeared to be an oasis of ordered architecture among the wilds of the living library. Tables stood together on a surface that was more floor than ground, in front of a fireplace whose chimney disappeared into the thick branches overhead.

To the left of the fireplace, a two-story section of wall stood independent of any other structure. A walkway, supported by tree branches that gradually morphed into support timbers, separated the two stories.

Mister Fox stood on the walkway, examining the shelves. He removed a book and turned as ABE approached. "Just you today?"

"What? No, Pru's coming. Mister Fox—what *is* this place?"

"It's the library, of course. I thought you of all people would recognize that."

"No, I see that. It's just . . . wow. So many books." ABE shook his head and tried to focus his thoughts. *So many books!* "But how come it's like this?"

The detective climbed down a ladder from the walkway and joined him. He placed the leather-bound book he'd selected on a nearby table.

"It's like this *because* it's the library," Mister Fox explained. "Magic is all about possibility. What is magic, after all, if not the possibility of something *more*, something fantastic, beyond our everyday experience? Well, books are possibility made real. Think about it. Every page turn, every new chapter represents the possibility of something new. A single book is magic. Now, imagine a room full of books, or a building. Libraries are focal points for wild magic. Not just here. Everywhere."

"Wait. Really?"

"Of course. Think back to libraries you've visited. You've felt it. Walking down the aisles among the shelves—a prickling of energy. A tingling just on the edge of your senses, teasing you. Just out of reach. Why do you think libraries are such ordered places? Alphabetization. Dewey decimal system. Card catalogs. Enforced whispering."

"Card catalogs? Mister Fox, when's the last time you were actually *in* a library?"

"Doesn't matter. The point still stands. All those things, all those orderly systems, they've evolved over time to keep the wild magic in check. And it works out there in the world. But here? In the Henhouse? Oh, no. That's different. Here the wild library magic changes things. It takes the Henhouse's essence and makes it . . . *more* somehow."

"More what?"

"More Henhousey. You know what I mean. Columns that look like trees *become* trees. The *domovye* tend it. They keep it from spreading too much."

"It's beautiful."

Mister Fox closed his eyes and inhaled deeply. "Oh yes. It is, isn't it?"

The detective took one more breath. Then he opened his eyes. "So while we wait for your partner in crime, shall I tell you my theory about your dream?

It will drive Pru crazy if we both know something she doesn't."

"Actually, I think we should wait for Pru. She's had kind of a rough day. Anyway, there's something else I'd like to talk to you about."

"Be my guest." Mister Fox gestured to the table where he'd placed the book and invited ABE to join him there. "What's on your mind?"

"I've been thinking about Pru and me and our time yesterday in Asgard. And I've been thinking about how eager you were to get us home once we returned to the Henhouse."

"Oh?"

"Yeah. See, I was thinking about when Loki and Gristling kidnapped me last year. I was so scared. I still have nightmares, actually. But looking back, I don't really remember feeling very homesick. A little. I wanted to get away. And I wanted to go home. But I only remember wanting to go home because it was somewhere safe. I don't remember thinking a lot about my mom or dad after a while. And the thing is . . . I kind of felt the same way this time. I hardly thought of home at all while we were gone."

ABE paused, hoping Mister Fox would say something. He pushed on when the detective remained quiet.

"You said we slip from the minds of people on Earth

when we travel to Worlds of Myth. So I was wondering . . . does it work both ways? Do people on Earth slip from *our* minds when we go traveling?"

"You're a very clever young man," Mister Fox said with a tip of his hat. "Yes, ABE. That's exactly what happens."

"So if we spent enough time on a World of Myth . . ."

"You could forget your homes, forget your families. And you could be forgotten in turn. And the potential danger is greater than you realize. The effect is cumulative. The more often you travel to a World of Myth, the harder it can be to reconnect with the people you left behind. And the more time you spend there, the quicker you forget."

"Why didn't you tell us?"

"Because you're nowhere close to the threshold of danger. You could spend weeks, maybe months, traveling back and forth before suffering any ill effects. But I'm always conservative about how much time I keep Fibbers away from their homes. You just never know what could happen."

ABE paused to let that sink in. He still couldn't help feeling like the detective should have told them. But that wasn't the only thing that bothered him, or even the thing that bothered him most.

"Mister Fox . . . would we have seen you again if the Mythics hadn't come back to Middleton?"

The detective stared into the flames blazing in the nearby fireplace for a long time before answering.

"No, ABE. Probably not. Earth and Worlds of Myth have grown too far apart. You can't live in both. Not for long, anyway. Not anymore. If you or Pru or any of the children who have worked with me as Fibbers over the years were to spend too much time in the Henhouse or in Worlds of Myth, then eventually you'd grow estranged from your home and your families. It's better if, when I go, I stay gone."

Mister Fox paused, and ABE realized he wasn't staring into the fire anymore. He was gazing at a painting hanging over the fireplace mantle. It showed an elderly woman dressed in traditional Russian garb, with a babushka tied under her chin. She had a wise face and a kind smile.

"That's Baba Yaga, isn't it?" ABE asked softly.

"Yes. It's how she looked when I last saw her."

"Is she still alive?" ABE blushed. "Sorry. I just . . . I remember the story you told us last year of how you met . . . I couldn't tell . . ."

"It's okay, ABE. The truth is that I don't know if she's still alive. If she is, she's somewhere in the thrice-tenth kingdom, the Russian World of Myth. It's a beautiful place, with soaring palaces, flocks of magical birds, and wish-granting fish. But there's no way for me to know if Baba Yaga is still there. It's someplace I can't go anymore."

Mister Fox fell silent. ABE wasn't sure what to say.

Well, he was sure. It just wasn't going to be easy.

"You have to tell Pru. You have to tell her she won't see you again once you're done here."

"Do I?" Mister Fox's question sounded sincere. "Is that kinder, do you think?"

When ABE didn't answer immediately, Mister Fox leaned back in his chair.

"You're a good friend, ABE. Pru is lucky to have you. It took courage for you to come here and confront me about this."

"Courage? Me?"

"You sound surprised."

"Well, yeah. I mean, that's not really my thing. Pru's the brave one. I'm the one that's always scared."

"Is that what you think? Do you really think that's what your story is about, ABE? Finding courage?"

"I don't know. Maybe. My dad doesn't think I stand up for myself enough."

"Ah. What do you think?"

"I guess he's right."

"And you think that's because you're scared?" Mister Fox tapped his chin with his long index finger. "No. No, I don't see it."

"You don't?"

"No. Ever since I met you, ABE, I've seen you stand up for and stand by your friends, no matter what. Whether it means going back to face the giants who kidnapped you or confronting an eccentric detective about emotionally abandoning your best friend, I have never seen you back down from doing what's right for the people you care about. Not once. If you think that isn't *courage*, then you don't know the meaning of the word. And between you and me, Aloysius, the likelihood of you not knowing the meaning of the word is very small indeed."

"Maybe," ABE said, shrugging.

"You don't sound convinced."

"I don't know. I'd like to be courageous. I feel like I'm supposed to be. You say I'm brave. My parents gave me a name that means 'famous warrior.' Thor thinks I should embrace my fierce nature. Even the lady from my dream called me 'young hero.' But none of those things feel like me."

"Good."

"Good?"

"Yes. Good. Don't get me wrong. I'm sorry that struggling with other people's expectations of you is causing you pain. But it's good you're struggling. Consider the other option. You could surrender to others' expectations. But I think that would just cause you more pain in the long run."

Mister Fox leaned forward and folded his hands on the table.

"ABE, there are always going to be people in life who want to tell you who you're supposed to be. Parents. Teachers. Friends. Enemies. It doesn't matter how old you get. There are always going to be roles you're expected to play. The important thing to remember is that it's *your* life. You'll get to the *you* that you're meant to be. I know the possibilities seem overwhelming, like—well, like books in a library. But you'll get there. Until then, remember that there's nothing worse than having to play a role that someone else gives you. There's nothing worse than letting someone else define who you are. That way lies misery."

ABE didn't know what to say. He couldn't remember anyone talking to him in such an honest way ever before. Before ABE could think of a response, Pru stormed into view.

"Mister Fox! We need to take the Henhouse somewhere—*fast!*"

CHAPTER
18

MISTER FOX ROSE FROM HIS CHAIR, INSTANTLY ALERT.

"What is it?" ABE asked. "What's happened? Where do we need to go?"

"We need to take the Henhouse to school and drop it on our teacher, Mr. Jeffries."

The detective sat back down.

"I can't do that, Pru," he said.

"Why? You dropped it on Gristling last year. Now when I need a *tiny* favor, you're suddenly all moral about dropping your house on people?"

"A little bit, yes. But just to save some time, let me be clearer. I literally *can't* do that. I told you last year that the Henhouse is very limited in where it can set foot." The detective turned to ABE. "And no, ABE, I'm not making a pun on the word *foot.*"

ABE closed his mouth, disappointed.

"The point," Mister Fox continued, "is that when it's on Earth, the Henhouse can only land in places where Earth and Worlds of Myth intersect, what I call the Borderlands. That's true of all witch's houses. The Henhouse, however, has the added limitation that it can only set down on grounds that border the living and the dead. Graveyards, cemeteries, and the like."

"Right. You think it's because you're mortal and not a witch," ABE said, remembering.

"Precisely. Which is why we can't use the Henhouse to squash your teacher, Pru. Sorry."

"Fine. Then I want a hammer. Thor has a hammer. *I* want a hammer," Pru said, throwing herself into a chair next to ABE's. She glanced around and added, grudgingly, "Nice library, by the way. What happened to the old one?"

"The room you saw last year? That was just a work-shop, a space I use for a specific project. I set that one up during our last investigation specifically to study the Middleton Stone. And while we're on the subject of Thor's hammer and things related to Norse mythology, perhaps we can return to our navigation?"

While Mister Fox collected the leather-bound book

he'd taken from the shelves earlier and paged through it, ABE whispered to Pru, "Things didn't go well with Mr. Jeffries?"

"I don't want to talk about it."

ABE leaned back, frowning.

"Okay," Mister Fox said, turning the book to show ABE and Pru the page he'd been seeking. "ABE, have you ever seen this woman before?"

ABE gasped.

"That's the woman from my dream!" The book was a handwritten journal and the image was a pencil drawing, but it was unquestionably of the woman from his dream. The likeness was uncanny, even if half of the woman's face was so heavily shaded that it looked like a black shadow.

"Not a dream, ABE," Mister Fox corrected. "A nightmare."

"Well, yeah. Technically, I guess."

"The distinction is actually important in this case. Do either of you know what a mare is?"

"It's a horse!" Pru blurted. "Sorry, ABE. Beat you to that one. Not that I have a thing about horses!"

ABE decided that was the perfect time to not bring up her unicorn pajamas.

"Well, yes," Mister Fox said. "But in this case, that's not the answer I was looking for. A mare is also the name for a creature from Norse mythology. It's a spirit that visits people when they're sleeping. They deliver bad dreams and, sometimes, messages. The two meanings are connected, actually. The spirit is said to sit on the sleeper's chest, riding him, in a sense."

"So you're saying one of those things—those mares—was in my room with me?" ABE shivered, remembering the flurry of movement by his window.

"But who sent it?" Pru asked. "And who's the woman in the dream—the woman in that book?"

"Well, that's where things get interesting. The woman in ABE's dream is Hel, though she prefers to go by her title as ruler of Niflheim—the Queen of the Dead."

"Whoa," Pru said.

"And I'm guessing she's the one who sent the mare in the first place. Mares are creatures of Niflheim. They go where the queen sends them."

"So the queen sent the mare to carry a message to ABE," Pru said. "But in his dream, the woman said the message came from someone else. Who gave her the message in the first place?"

"I think I might know," ABE said.

"Who, ABE?" Mister Fox asked.

"I think maybe Loki sent the message."

"What?" Pru exclaimed.

"Why do you think that?" Mister Fox pressed, his nose twitching.

"Well, I was thinking about the riddle today. Our teacher, Mr. Jeffries, has a quote on his wall. One of the words in it is *forsooth*."

"So?" Pru asked.

"It got me thinking. Remember what *sooth* means? It's another word for *truth*. The riddle talks about a truth-teller. But if we turn that phrase around a little bit, it becomes *sooth-teller* . . . or *soothsayer*. A soothsayer is someone who can see the future. Like Odin."

ABE took a deep breath, and forced himself to slow down. He always got excited when explaining riddles.

"Remember what Mister Fox said about the riddle's meaning? He said someone could not be telling the truth if they didn't know what the truth was. So what if the riddle really means Odin's wrong? *When is a truth-teller not telling the truth?*"

"When he's wrong," Pru said. "So the Queen of the Dead sent ABE a message from Loki saying that Odin's vision is wrong? But why send the message to ABE?"

"That makes sense, if you think about it," ABE said. "Loki knows I like riddles and word games. That's how I figured out he was disguised as Fay Loningtime last year. He saw me change the letters around to spell 'I am often lying.'"

"But why use a riddle? Why not just say he's innocent?" Pru asked.

"I've been wondering that myself," Mister Fox said, at last chiming in. "It's the one bit I haven't been able to figure out."

"So you think we're right," Pru said.

"I do. I figured out that the phrase *truth-teller* was a reference to Odin, a soothsayer, almost immediately."

"Why didn't you say anything?" ABE asked. "You let me think the riddle was about you!"

"Because I didn't trust my judgment." Mister Fox rose and walked to the fire. "You were right yesterday, ABE. I do want Loki to be innocent. But I only told you both part of the reason why. It's true that I want to avoid Ragnarok. But I also want Odin to be *wrong*."

"Why?" Pru asked, taking the word out of ABE's mouth. "Why is it so important to you that Odin is wrong."

The detective turned to face them.

"Because if Loki *is* guilty, if Odin's visions are right, then I'm as good as—"

"As good as what?" Pru asked when he didn't finish.

"As good as useless," Mister Fox said, pinching the bridge of his nose. "Don't you see? What am I always telling you two? 'Don't believe it. Don't be so sure.' Odin was right. Uncertainty *is* my religion. But if Odin's visions are always accurate, then the future is set. There *is* no uncertainty. It doesn't exist! I don't know how I fit into that world. I'm not sure I do."

ABE and Pru looked at each other. Neither knew what to say. Finally, ABE took a deep breath.

"Okay," he said. "But this is good news, isn't it? If we're right about the riddle, then Loki is trying to tell us he's innocent. That would mean that Mister Fox is right and Odin is wrong."

"But how do we know Loki is telling the truth?" Pru asked. "Just because he says he's innocent doesn't mean it's true."

"I'm afraid Pru's right," Mister Fox said. "We need proof."

"But we've run out of witnesses," ABE said. "The gods didn't see anything. Alva didn't see anything. There's no one left who can tell us who gave Hod the spear that killed Baldur."

"That's not entirely true," Mister Fox said, returning to the table.

"It's not?" Pru asked. "Who else is left?"

"Isn't it obvious? We have to talk to Baldur."

"Baldur?" Pru and ABE said at the exact same time.

"But he's dead!" ABE added.

"Exactly," Mister Fox said. "Which means we know just where to find him."

"You mean . . . you want us to go to Niflheim?" Pru asked. "You want us to go to the world of the dead?"

"That's a terrible idea! *The world of the dead?*" ABE tried to come up with a way to explain to Mister Fox just how bad an idea it was. "But that's, like, a world . . . full of dead people!"

"Very articulate, ABE, but—"

"How will we avoid the zombies?" Pru asked. She sounded both frightened and curious.

"Zombies? What? No. Wait, you two. Listen. Niflheim is the world of the dead, yes. But there aren't zombies or walking skeletons there. Many mythologies include an underworld. There's a reason for that. Mythics are magical beings. When their corporeal forms die, their magical essence abides for a time in their version of the underworld. The people in Niflheim will look like people . . . for the most part."

"No zombies?" Pru asked.

"None."

"I still think this is a terrible idea," ABE said, pressing his forehead to the table.

"Don't worry," he heard Pru say to Mister Fox. "He says that a lot."

"You should be happy, ABE," Mister Fox said.

ABE looked up. "I should? Why?"

"Because you're about to go meet the girl of your dreams."

ABE waited for Pru and Mister Fox on the other end of the library's bridge. The detective had asked for a moment alone with Pru before she and ABE left for

Niflheim. ABE assumed he wanted to tell Pru that he would be leaving for good once their investigation was over.

Sure enough, Pru's eyes were red when she crossed the bridge a short time later. Mister Fox wasn't with her.

"Are you okay?" ABE asked.

"Yeah," Pru said.

"Really? I thought you'd be more upset."

"I guess I'm not really surprised."

"You're not?"

"No. I didn't really expect him to be in Niflheim."

"Wow. You're taking this better than I thought you would. Wait . . . what? You didn't expect who to be in Niflheim?"

"My dad."

"What?"

"That's what Mister Fox wanted to talk to me about. He wanted to make sure I understood that Niflheim was only a place where Mythics from Norse mythology went, not people from Earth. He didn't want me to be disappointed when my dad wasn't there."

"Oh!" ABE said, surprised. "That's ridiculous, though! Of course your dad wouldn't be there."

"Thanks, ABE," Pru said, charging past him and shoving his shoulder as she went. "You don't have to rub it in that I was being silly."

"No! Pru, wait! That's not what I meant at all. It's just . . . according to the myths, heroes don't go to Niflheim when they die. Your dad would never have been there. He was a hero."

Pru stopped and turned. He had thought that Pru couldn't surprise him anymore, but the hug she gave him then—fierce and honest—surprised him more than almost anything in his life.

"So, um, where's Mister Fox?" ABE asked, rubbing the back of his neck as Pru stepped away.

"He's going to meet us in the entryway. First, the *domovye* will take us somewhere to change into special clothes for Niflheim. I guess it's pretty cold there. So are you ready for the world of the dead?"

"Absolutely not. But let's get going, anyway."

CHAPTER
19

ABE, PRU, AND MISTER FOX GATHERED IN THE ENTRYWAY OF THE HENHOUSE. ABE tugged at the collar of the shirt Mister Fox had given him. It was similar to the one he'd worn for the trip to Asgard but much thicker, as were his new pants. He also had a *domovoi*-crafted coat, hat, and gloves to protect him against Niflheim's cold.

"There are rules in Niflheim," Mister Fox was saying. "Some of them were made by the queen, some of them bind her. She has no dominion over living things, for example. That includes both of you. But two things can change that, so *don't* do either of those two things."

"What two things?" Pru asked.

"You can't take anything while you're in Niflheim.

Take no souvenirs, accept no gifts. Do not put your-self in debt to her. The Queen of the Dead keeps what is hers. If you take something from the queen, you become part of her horde. *Forever.* So take nothing. Nothing precious, nothing prized. Understand?"

"Got it," Pru said.

"What's the other thing we should avoid?" ABE asked.

"Dying," Mister Fox said. "Definitely avoid dying."

"*Very* helpful," Pru said.

"I try." Mister Fox stepped forward and opened the door. "You should be fine. The queen sent ABE that message. That doesn't mean she sees you as friends. But at least it means she's not openly hostile to you. Still, don't take anything for granted. The queen is the Norse personification of death. She's impossible to predict and harder to understand. Be careful."

"We will!" ABE said.

"Good. For what it's worth, the journey should be straightforward. Ratatosk will lead you due south through the landscape of Niflheim, right to the City of the Dead at the base of the Mountains of Mist. Time and distance will blur, just like it did on Asgard. You'll be at the city before you know it."

"That's what I'm afraid of," ABE said.

"You won't find anything to worry about in the bulk of the city itself. It was built to house those who die during Ragnarok. You'll find it mostly empty at this point. The Palace of the Dead sits at the southernmost edge of the city. That's where the queen lives and that's where things will get tricky. Be on your guard and remember what I told you."

ABE followed Pru onto the steps of the Henhouse. She paused there and looked back at the detective.

"You're sure about the no zombies thing, right?"

"Absolutely," Mister Fox said.

"Good," she said.

"Just be sure to watch out for the dragon," Mister Fox added with a wink. Then he closed the door.

"*Dragon?*" ABE squeaked.

An odd snorting came from above. ABE thought it might even be that of a dragon, until Ratatosk dropped onto his shoulder and he recognized the squirrel's laughter.

"Nidhogg's nowhere near—no, no. Big Nose is joking."

"You're sure?" ABE asked, and Ratatosk nodded confidently.

"So which way?" Pru asked after greeting Ratatosk with an affectionate scratch on his nose.

Ratatosk chittered happily at the attention and then nodded in the direction they should go. He did not abandon his perch on ABE's shoulder. Apparently, he intended to hitch a ride.

As he looked around Niflheim, ABE's chest tightened in panic. For a minute, he was sure that he was back in his dream! Bars rose up from the mist, trapping him. Gristling would appear any second and—

"ABE? *ABE!*" Pru gripped his shoulder. "Are you okay? You're white as a ghost."

"I . . . yeah. I'm okay." ABE shook off the panic as understanding settled in. He wasn't in his nightmare version of Asgard. Yggdrasil, the World Tree, had roots in all three worlds of Norse mythology. The Henhouse had simply landed at Yggdrasil's roots in Niflheim. Those roots were what he had mistaken for bars.

"It's like a haunted-house version of Asgard," Pru said, looking around.

ABE nodded. He had always enjoyed hikes in the woods in winter, when the leaves had all fallen and the branches were empty. But even in the coldest, darkest heart of winter, life survived in the forests on Earth. It could be hard to see, but it was there. The promise of renewal and rebirth lay just beneath the surface.

Not in Niflheim. The world of the dead stretched before them, a bleak alien landscape of mist and ice. Almost nothing lived there other than Yggdrasil's roots, and even they looked sick. ABE huddled in his coat and thought of cozy fires, hot chocolate, and his mother's vegetable soup. He thought of all the warmth of home and was comforted by not just the memories but also his ability to remember.

They had not walked far through the haunted tangles of Yggdrasil's roots when Ratatosk dug his claws into ABE's shoulder and hissed at Pru and him to stop.

"Wait here," the squirrel said. "Be still, be silent. Constrained. Composed. Closemouthed!"

"What is it?" Pru asked, but Ratatosk shushed her and jumped from ABE's shoulder. All but his tail disappeared into the fog. It cut through the mist like a submarine's periscope moving through a sea of vapor.

Ratatosk made his way toward a huge mound in the distance. It was about the size of a barn. ABE squinted. On second thought, maybe it was the size of *two* barns.

"Hey, Pru?" ABE whispered. "Does it look to you like that mound up ahead is getting bigger?

Pru's eyes widened and she grabbed ABE, pulling him behind the nearest root as a deep, booming voice echoed through the forest.

"RATATOSK! I THOUGHT I SMELLED SOMETHING UNPLEASANTLY ALIVE."

"Hello, Nidhogg," Ratatosk answered.

"Nidhogg?" ABE squeaked. "Nidhogg, *the dragon*?"

Pru clasped a hand over ABE's mouth as Ratatosk continued.

"I have a message for you," the squirrel said, clearing his throat.

ABE wiggled a finger in his ear. Had he heard that right? He knew that Ratatosk carried messages back and forth between Nidhogg and the eagle at the top of Yggdrasil. But did he have to do it *then*?

"Let's see," Ratatosk continued. "Ah yes! Eagle wants you to know that you 'are a cow-footed snake whose breath smells like the dung pile of a drove of a thousand swine.' Hmm! Eagle went for a focus on smells this time, yes, that I think was a nice departure."

Nidhogg roared and a crashing sound of wood splintering filled the air.

"Whurf's hahning?" ABE asked through Pru's fingers.

"What?" Pru asked, lowering her hand.

"What's happening?"

Pru peered around the edge of the root. She pulled back quickly. "Nidhogg is having a tantrum. He's biting through the roots and smashing them with his tail."

"You can see him? Is he big? What does he look like?"

Pru peeked again. She swallowed.

"You don't want to know."

ABE scrunched his eyes shut.

"TELL THAT LOATHSOME, OVERGROWN CHICKEN THAT HE FLIES ON THE UPDRAFTS OF HIS OWN FLATULENCE!"

"Yes, yes. Will do. I'm sure he'll be delighted to hear it."

Nidhogg roared. The sound of cracking wood filled

163

the air again. It grew gradually quieter, as though the dragon was moving away. Soon afterward, Ratatosk returned.

"I thought you said Nidhogg was nowhere near us when we got out of the Henhouse!" Pru said.

"He wasn't. No, no, no. It took some work to find him."

"*You mean we came looking for him?*" ABE asked.

"Of course! I have a job to do, after all! I can't play with you shortwits *all* the time!"

ABE and Pru eventually broke free of Yggdrasil's roots and found themselves on a vast plain that looked like the set of an old science fiction film for which most of the budget had been spent on fog machines and dried ice. Mist pooled along the ground as far as the eye could see. A few trees, withered and bare, rose from the mist, as did some rocks. Nearby mountains stabbed at the sky like jagged teeth.

The City of the Dead lay at the base of one of those mountains. ABE and Pru never would have reached it without Ratatosk's help. Three times they came to great chasms hidden in the fog. Ratatosk led them unfailingly to bridges that crossed each abyss. ABE felt sure that without him, they would have lost their footing and tumbled over the edge of an unseen chasm and down to the frozen river below.

They met their first nondragon resident of Niflheim at the final bridge, just before the city. An old woman who leaned heavily on a staff halted them with an upraised hand.

"What have we here, hmm?" the bent and bedraggled woman said. Matted hair hung over her face, and it was sometimes hard to tell where it ended and the animal skin rags that covered her body began. "Messenger, you are off your path. And who have you brought with you? Mortals! Still alive? A feast for Nidhogg, then."

"We're not a feast for anyone," Pru said, shivering. "Who are you?"

"I am Modgud, guardian of the bridge. Who are you, child, and what is your purpose?"

Ratatosk leaned in and whispered something in Pru's ear.

"I'm Pru. My friend ABE and I are here to talk to Baldur."

That was direct. Had Ratatosk told Pru to be honest? He'd clearly had dealings with Modgud before.

"Oh? Have you come to seek his release from the misty realm? You have traveled far for naught, then. It has been decided. The Queen of the Dead will keep what she has."

"We just want to talk to him," Pru said.

Modgud studied them a moment then turned back

to Pru. "Be warned, child. This path is not meant for mortal feet. I can see things in the mist, shapes of things to come. If you go this way, you will not return."

"What's she talking about?" ABE asked Ratatosk.

Ratatosk peered at Modgud.

"You have no authority to keep them," the squirrel said.

"I will not bar your way, Messenger, or the way of these children. I just tell you what will be."

"Can she really see the future?" Pru asked.

"The seeress of Niflheim knows strange things," Ratatosk said. "Not good, not good."

"What should we do?" ABE asked.

"We don't have any choice," Pru said. "We need answers. We have to talk to Baldur."

Pru stepped past Modgud and onto the bridge. ABE followed. They were halfway across when Modgud called out, "Farewell, children of Midgard. Give Modgud's greetings to the Queen of the Dead. We will not meet again on this journey."

Her cackling echoed through the chasm below, following them across the bridge and all the way to the gates of the City of the Dead.

"Who are they trying to keep out?" ABE asked, looking up at the gates. They hung on walls that rose even higher than the walls around Asgard.

"Not out, no, no, no. *In*," Ratatosk replied. "Like Modgud said, *The Queen of the Dead keeps what is hers.*"

Ratatosk was right about the walls not being there to keep anyone out of the city. Neither of the guards that stood on either side of the city's gates challenged ABE and Pru as they passed through.

The City of the Dead resembled Asgard in some respects. The basic architecture was about the same. But the timber in Niflheim was rotted. So was the stone somehow. And while Asgard had sparkled with gems and precious stones, the City of the Dead sparkled with ice and snow. Perhaps the greatest difference, though, was the absence of people.

"It really is empty," Pru said.

"The halls of the City of the Dead will overflow when Ragnarok comes," Ratatosk said. "Mostly empty now. Desolate. Untenanted."

Sure enough, they continued all the way to the palace without passing another soul.

Most of the city's buildings had been constructed from wood. The palace, however, was made from stone. It reminded ABE a little of Winterhaven House. The massive hall seemed to grow out of the mountain itself, just as solid—and somehow far more imposing. Bracing himself, he crossed the threshold and prepared to come face-to-face with the specter from his dream, the Queen of the Dead.

CHAPTER
20

THE QUEEN OF THE DEAD SAT IN THE HALL OF HER PALACE. SHE WAS beautiful.

And she was terrible.

Her left side was lovely. The queen's black hair and ripe, red lips were just as beautiful as ABE remembered them from his dream. But that was only half of her.

The right side of the queen's face was a withered husk of flesh the purplish-blue color of a well-aged bruise. An eldritch fire burned in the hollow socket where her right eye should have been.

The two aspects of the queen's appearance were in perfect balance, divided equally down the center of her body.

"Kneel," Ratatosk hissed at ABE and Pru.

They did. ABE was grateful for the excuse to drop his gaze, though some part of him longed to look at the queen again.

"Ah, guests. What a pleasant surprise." The queen's honeyed voice reached out from the throne and caressed his ears. "Two mortal children and the Allfather's pet rat. And look! One of the mortals is my young hero. I bid you welcome. You may rise."

ABE stood, whispering reassurances to Ratatosk, who had not appreciated the rat comment at all. Beside him, Pru rose, too.

"Tell me," the queen went on. "What brings you to my hall?"

"We, ah, were hoping to see Baldur," Pru said.

"I see." The queen considered. "Of course you may see him, then. First, though, you must be hungry. It's been such a long journey. Come. Eat from my plate."

The queen pointed to a table beside ABE. Had it been there when they entered? He hadn't noticed it.

On the table sat a plate covered with succulent meats and fruits so plump and fresh looking that ABE's mouth watered.

Suddenly, he was *famished*. How had he not realized it until that moment? His stomach was empty. He felt like he'd never eaten before! Even the meats looked irresistible—and he was a vegetarian. He reached toward the plate.

"ABE, no!" Pru hissed.

At the same time, Ratatosk dug his claws into ABE's shoulder and whispered. "No! Her plate is hunger. Take nothing. Look away!"

ABE froze, his fingers inches from a juicy-looking apple. He'd come so close to disaster! He lowered his hand to his side.

"No?" the queen said. "Pity. Shall I send for Baldur, then? Nothing would please me more than to give you the gift of an audience with the fallen god."

"Wait," ABE said, interrupting Pru before she could answer. "That's . . . very kind of you. But we aren't looking for a gift . . . as generous as that is. Is there any other way we could speak with Baldur?"

"Such a clever lad." The queen smiled. "And so polite. Very well, young hero. You have pleased me with your good manners. Not a gift, then. We shall make a trade. Truths for truths. I will ask you three questions, which you will answer truly. In return, you may ask Baldur three questions, which he will answer truly. Nothing is taken, nothing is lost. Agreed?"

"Ratatosk?" Pru said.

The squirrel hesitated. "And we may go when we are done?" he asked the queen.

"So long as you abide by the terms of the bargain, yes. I swear on my throne."

Ratatosk nodded.

"Okay," Pru said. "Ask away."

The queen turned to ABE and said, "I think you will find my questions easy. Recently, I delivered a riddle to you. I only wish to see that you showed me honor by giving my words due consideration. Here, then, is my first question. To whom do I refer in my riddle?"

ABE frowned. That wasn't the kind of question he had expected. He glanced at Pru, who nodded encouragement.

"Odin," ABE said. "The truth-teller is Odin, the soothsayer."

"Oh, *very* good," the queen said. "Next. My riddle posed a question. What is the answer to that question?"

"'When is a truth-teller not telling the truth?'" Pru said, repeating the riddle's question. "When he's wrong," she answered.

The queen looked at the two of them, considering. ABE held his breath. Finally, the queen said, "Acceptable. Not the answer I expected, but a valid one."

"What was the answer she expected?" Pru whispered. ABE wondered, too. But he didn't have time to give it any more thought before the queen asked her third question.

"The riddle was a message and I was the messenger. But for whom did I deliver the message?"

"Your father, Loki," ABE said, pleased that he had figured out the true meaning of the riddle.

"Ah," the queen said. She sounded disappointed.

But was that a good thing or a bad thing?

"Very well," she continued, and ABE breathed a sigh of relief. "A bargain is a bargain."

The queen waved her arm, and a column of mist rose from the undulating ground cover. The mist parted and revealed a new seat to the queen's right. In it sat a man. A halo of blond hair framed the noble features of his face, but his eyes had a faraway look, as though he wasn't aware that anyone else was present.

"What's wrong with him?" Pru asked.

"Death is a new state for Baldur. He is still adjusting. He will be able to answer your questions, though, and he will answer them all truly. Such is his nature, and such are the terms of our bargain. Ask."

"Well, we might as well start with what we came for," Pru said, looking at ABE. When he nodded, she addressed Baldur. "Do you know who killed you?"

Baldur opened his mouth to speak. Before he could, the queen reached over and lightly rested her hand on Baldur's arm.

"Answer only the question they asked," she counseled, "but answer it truly."

Baldur's lips thinned—a quick flash of emotion on his otherwise placid face. But he nodded, then said, "Yes."

ABE waited for more.

172

"He has to tell us who!" Pru blurted.

"Most certainly not," the queen said calmly—pleasantly, even. "That is not the question you asked. I hope you would not try to cheat me by expecting two answers for one question. Such behavior does not become friends."

"She's right, Pru," ABE said. "We have to be careful—"

"Fine," Pru blurted, "Baldur, *who* killed you?"

"Okay," ABE muttered, "That should work."

The queen's hand remained on Baldur's arm. "Answer her question truly," she said again. Her pinkie finger caressed the fallen god's arm. ABE shivered, thinking about the touch of her rotten flesh.

Baldur closed his eyes and said, "I was killed by my brother Hod, who threw the spear that pierced my heart."

"No!" Pru exclaimed. "We *knew* that. We need to know who gave Hod the spear. Do you—"

"Pru, *wait!*" ABE covered Pru's mouth with his hand and looked at the queen. "That didn't count. She didn't ask a question."

The queen nodded in acknowledgment. The left side of her mouth curled in the smallest of smiles.

"We have to word this question right," ABE said to Pru. "It's our last one."

Pru nodded, and ABE removed his hand from her mouth.

"You'd better ask," Pru said. "You're better with words."

"Baldur, I'm sorry for what happened to you. I hope . . . I hope you're at peace. But we need to know— who gave Hod the spear that took your life?"

ABE hoped that would do it. If Baldur didn't know the answer to the question, he could say so. But if he did know, he would be compelled to tell them who it was.

The fallen god opened his mouth—then closed it again. Strain showed on his face. He looked to the queen.

"You *must* answer their question. And you must speak the truth."

Baldur nodded.

The hall fell silent in anticipation. It was a pure silence, a quiet more still and lifeless than any ABE had ever experienced—the silence of the grave. When Baldur finally spoke, his voice seemed to boom. In truth, though, he spoke softly, a whisper from the dead.

"The trickster."

CHAPTER
21

"INTERESTING," THE QUEEN SAID SOFTLY.

ABE barely heard her.

That was it.

They were done.

They'd solved the mystery.

Throughout most of their investigation, ABE had not just believed that Loki was guilty—he had *wanted* Loki to be guilty. The trickster had caused so much trouble. And so, he had wanted to believe Loki was capable of the worst of crimes.

Now that Loki's guilt had been confirmed, though, ABE felt an emptiness in his belly. Partly, he felt bad for Mister Fox. He'd be so disappointed. Mostly, though, ABE felt bad for everyone else, including himself. Loki had killed Baldur. Odin's visions were true. Ragnarok was coming.

Their only hope now was that it would happen in Earth's distant future. Alva's words came back to him: *The end should always come tomorrow, never today.*

"We must go," Ratatosk whispered in his ear, bringing him back to the moment. "It is not wise to linger too long in the company of death. No."

"Pru," ABE said, touching her shoulder. She looked as lost in thought as he had been. "We need to go."

She nodded and addressed the queen. "Thanks for your help. We're going to get on our way."

They bowed, turned, and started for the door.

The Queen of the Dead cleared her throat. ABE and Pru froze.

"I think . . . I think perhaps not." The queen's voice changed as she spoke. It began sweetly but became something that scratched and crackled. It crawled up from behind them, like a thousand spiders scuttling over each other to get from one place to the next. Even as ABE winced at the sound, he realized it made sense that the queen would have two voices, one for each of her aspects.

"What? Explain!" Ratatosk said as all three of them spun back to face the queen.

"You may go, Messenger," the queen said, her voice once again soft as silk. "I would not keep Odin's pet from his work. But I think the mortal children will stay. They belong to me now."

"No way!" Pru said. "We had a deal!"

"We did," the queen agreed. "One you broke."

"How?" ABE asked, running through their interview with Baldur in his head. What had they done wrong? "We made a trade. We gave you three answers in return for three answers."

"Ah," the queen said. "I see the confusion. It is a simple misunderstanding on your part. Our bargain was not for answers. It was for *truths*. I gave you three. You gave me only two."

"What are you talking about?" Pru said.

But ABE saw it. Too late, he saw how cleanly they'd been trapped. He faced the queen.

"Loki didn't give you the message for me, did he?" he asked.

The queen bowed her head.

"What? Who did, then?" Pru asked ABE.

"I don't know, but it's the only question we could have gotten wrong."

"So we got it wrong! That's not the same as lying!"

ABE shook his head. "Don't you see? It doesn't matter. Not to her. It's like Mister Fox said. Someone can say something thinking that it's right. But if it's not—if it's wrong—then it's not technically *true*. They haven't told the truth."

177

"A fact you acknowledged yourselves when you answered my second question," the queen reminded them.

"We said a truth-teller isn't telling a truth when he's wrong," Pru said, recalling their answer. Her face paled.

"And I accepted your answer."

"No, no, no!" Ratatosk leapt from ABE's shoulder to Pru's and stuck his head out at the queen. "You're cheating. Deceiving! Defrauding!"

"Watch your tongue, *rat*," the queen said, leaning forward in her throne and showing her first sign of anger. "My bargain was true. *I* am the injured party here. These children gave me two truths and tried to escape with three, in turn. That final truth is a gem of knowledge they did not have when they entered my hall. I cannot allow them to take such a treasure from me. The Queen of the Dead keeps what is hers!"

The queen settled back in her throne. As she did, a low growling sound came from the shadows behind her. An enormous black hound, roughly the size of a small horse, stepped out of those shadows and into the gray light of Niflheim.

"If you disagree," the queen continued, her fractured mouth twisting in a crooked smile, "you may take it up with Garm. Such a precious creature. He *so* hates to see his mistress wronged."

Garm, the hound of the dead. ABE had read about

him. The beast sat beside the queen's throne, his black eyes lost in the deeper night of his fur.

"You can't do this." Ratatosk shook with anger—and also, probably, fear of Garm.

"It is done. Leave now, Messenger, while you can."

"What about ABE and me?" Pru said. "What are you going to do with us?"

"*Do?*" The queen's voice registered surprise. The hostility of the tone she'd used with Ratatosk disappeared. "Nothing, child. You are my guests. You have my permission to roam my palace as you wish. If you try to leave, however, you will be at Garm's mercy."

"Garm knows no mercy. None! Zero! Null!" Ratatosk said.

"True." The queen folded her hands on her lap, apparently content to sit back and let the two of them decide their own fate.

"What are we going to do?" ABE asked after he, Pru, and Ratatosk stepped away from the queen to talk things over.

"What choice do we have?" Pru said. "We have to stay here for now. Ratatosk, go to Mister Fox and tell him what's happened. He'll figure something out."

"But what can he do?" ABE asked. "He can't leave the Henhouse."

"No. But he's smart, ABE. And he won't abandon us here. You know he won't."

"Yeah. You're right."

"I don't like this, no. Not at all!" Ratatosk said, pulling on his tail. "Death should not be so bold."

"We'll be fine," Pru said.

ABE marveled at her confidence. She had to be scared, too, but she was doing a much better job than he was at appearing calm.

Then again, she didn't know everything he did. His conversation with Mister Fox returned to him, and a fresh worry struck him: how long could they stay in Niflheim before they started forgetting home?

Ratatosk muttered something about the queen that ABE couldn't quite hear. It seemed to have something to do with odor and personal hygiene. He had muttered it *very* softly.

"Fine!" the squirrel said in a louder voice. "I'll be back."

With that, Ratatosk leapt to the ground and fled the room. ABE watched the squirrel go, abandoning Pru and him to Death.

ABE groaned, wishing he hadn't thought of it in quite those terms.

CHAPTER
22

ABE AND PRU WANDERED THROUGH THE TOMB-LIKE PASSAGES OF THE PALACE
of the Dead for what felt like hours. ABE couldn't really
judge the passage of time in Niflheim. The world
of the dead was still, unmoving and unchanging.

Somehow, that stillness was the worst part. ABE
felt like he was already a ghost haunting the silent,
empty halls of the palace. Only Pru's company and the
knowledge that Ratatosk and Mister Fox were working on an escape plan made it possible for him to fight
down the panic that built with every step.

Early on, Pru had insisted they scout the gates—just
in case. As soon as the palace's exit came into view,
however, Garm had seeped out of the shadows.

"Going somewhere?" he'd asked in a low growl.

"You can talk?" ABE had asked.

Saliva had spilled from Garm's mouth, where his red, raw tongue hung over jagged teeth. "Talk. Stalk. Hunt. I do many things, few of them pleasant. Care to learn more?"

They'd left immediately.

Eventually, they found what appeared to be an empty banquet hall and sat in two of the chairs that surrounded the long table.

"Pru, what if we never get out of here?" ABE said, no longer able to hold in his worry. He raked his hands through his hair. "What if we're stuck here forever? What will we do? What will we eat? We don't even know where the bathrooms—sorry, *lavatories*—are and—"

"*ABE*," Pru said, sharply. "Stop it. You're panicking. We can't panic. Mister Fox *will* get us out of here. Then we'll join the search for Loki. We'll see to it that he gets caught and imprisoned for a long, long time."

"You don't know that. You can't!" ABE sucked in his breath, ready to launch into a new list of worries. He was interrupted, though, by another voice.

"Pru? ABE? Are you there?"

ABE bolted to his feet, looking for the source of Mister Fox's voice. Pru was quicker. She dug into her bag and retrieved her looking glass.

"Mister Fox," Pru said. "It's about time!"

"Sorry. I didn't want to reach out until we had a plan for getting you out of there."

"Do you? Have a plan, I mean?" ABE asked.

"I think so."

"I *told you*," Pru said to ABE. "Okay, let's hear it."

"Absolutely. But first—did you talk to Baldur? I have to know! Did he tell you who gave Hod the spear?"

"He did," Pru said. "I'm sorry, Mister Fox. It was Loki."

The detective disappeared behind his hat as he ducked his head. In a way, ABE was glad to be spared the look of disappointment he knew must be showing on Mister Fox's face.

"Okay," Mister Fox said when he finally looked up. "We'll deal with that later. Right now, let's get you two out of there. The plan Ratatosk and I came up with isn't ideal, but it will have to do. I've been searching through the Henhouse for information on Niflheim and the queen's palace. I never spent much time there myself when I was younger. But between my research and Ratatosk's impressive knowledge of the three worlds, I think we've come up with a way to get you out."

"I hope it's not through the front gate," ABE said. "Because, trust us, that's pretty well guarded."

"I heard that you met Garm. Is he as big and mean looking as I remember?"

"Yes!" ABE and Pru said together.

"Well, then I have good news and bad news. Good news first. I have maps here at the Henhouse that suggest that the queen's palace abuts a series of caverns and tunnels that were once mined by dwarves. According to what Ratatosk and I have pieced together, these caverns and tunnels link the three worlds."

"How is that possible?" ABE asked. "I thought Yggdrasil was the only thing that connected the three worlds."

"Yes and no. Yggdrasil is the axis that binds them all together. But Asgard and Niflheim are planes of existence. All Worlds of Myth are, really. And there are places where they touch and overlap. Theoretically, you should be able to escape Niflheim and return to Earth through the caves."

"*Theoretically?*" Pru said.

"Ratatosk knows the entrance, but he isn't familiar with the tunnels themselves. He's clever, though. He'll find the way. He's already on his way back to you. You'll escape together."

"You mentioned bad news," ABE said.

"Right. From what we can tell, the dwarves called the entrance to the caverns Gnipa Cave."

"What's so bad about that?" Pru asked.

"Norse myths associate Garm with two specific

locations. One location is the gate at the entrance to the Palace of the Dead."

"What's the other location?" ABE asked, though he knew what the detective was going to say before he said it.

"Gnipa Cave."

✳

Ratatosk returned a short time later. ABE had never in his life been so happy to see a squirrel.

"Are we glad to see you!" he said. He had to put his hands behind his back to keep from wrapping Ratatosk up in a bear hug—or squirrel hug.

"Yes, yes. Now shush, shortwits, and follow me. We must be quick."

ABE waited for Ratatosk to offer other words for *quick*, as was his usual style. But he didn't say anything else. Instead, he led them from the room. The squirrel's restraint spoke volumes about how dangerous their situation was.

The palace walls proved no match for Niflheim's mist. The vapor had conquered the palace's defenses and infiltrated the corridors as they crept through the darkened halls.

ABE felt better now that Ratatosk had returned and they had a plan. He also felt better knowing that Mister Fox could contact them through their looking glasses. He'd forgotten all about that in his panic about being trapped. Now he walked with the polished handle clenched tightly in his fist. He noticed Pru had her glass out, too.

Every time they came to a set of stairs, they went down. The corridors were increasingly timeworn and decrepit the further they went. The topmost levels of the queen's palace had been made of carefully chiseled stone. The bottommost corridors, though, appeared to have been carved into and through the rock of the mountain itself.

Ratatosk picked up his pace as they approached an intersection of two hallways. "We go left here. Then straight on to the cave entrance. Then up, up, up."

ABE felt his pulse quicken. They were so close!

They turned left where Ratatosk had indicated. The corridor extended straight, its end lost in shadows. ABE squinted and tried to make out the cave's entrance.

Instead, he saw something move in the darkness.

Jagged white teeth flashed into view as Garm emerged from the shadows and said, "Going somewhere?"

No! They'd almost made it. It wasn't fair!

Ratatosk sucked in his breath. His tail ballooned to twice its size as hair stuck out in all directions.

"Let us pass," Ratatosk said. His voice sounded feeble, even to ABE.

"Be careful, Ratatosk," Pru cautioned.

"Oh, I don't think so, rat," Garm said. "I think you've had your freedom for too long while I've been bound to this realm. I think your running days are done. I think *all* your days are done. You first, rat. *An appetizer before the main course!*"

With a vicious bark, Garm lunged toward Ratatosk, knocking ABE to the ground as he raced past him. Ratatosk scampered up the nearest wall and buried himself in a shallow crack in the stone, just out of Garm's reach.

"Leave him alone!" Pru shouted. She ran at Garm and swung her looking glass at the hound's head. Garm saw her coming, though, and ducked the blow. He launched himself forward with his hind legs, crashing into Pru's chest and sending her tumbling to the ground. Her looking glass flew from her hand and skidded into the shadows.

ABE regained his feet in time to see Garm glowering down at Pru.

"Pru, get up!" he called. But she lay on her back looking dazed. Before ABE could think of what to do, Ratatosk leapt from his perch and landed on Garm's haunch. Grabbing the massive hound's tail he bit down—hard!

Garm yelped in pain as Ratatosk jumped to the ground. The hound spun on him, his head held low and a wicked growl rumbling from deep in his throat.

"I will make you suffer for that, rat. Your death will be long and slow and oh-so-very-*very* painful."

"Catch me first," Ratatosk said, and he took off down the hall—away from the entrance to Gnipa Cave.

Garm crouched, preparing to give chase. But just before he launched himself at Ratatosk, he stopped. His muscles relaxed and he turned back—slowly—to face ABE and Pru.

"Do you think I am such a fool as to let my mistress's prizes escape? The rat will get his due in time. First, I shall deal with both of you."

Garm moved toward them, malice in his eyes. ABE had managed to get Pru to her feet, but she was still dazed.

He backed away from Garm, pulling Pru along with him. What could they *do*? They could run for the cave, but what was the point? Garm was playing with them now, a cat stalking a mouse. Or maybe a dog stalking a cat. Or, given Garm's size, a horse stalking a . . .

What did horses stalk?

ABE shook his head. It didn't matter! They'd never make it to the cave. Garm would be on them in a second, and then . . .

ABE didn't want to think about what would happen then. He knew it would involve those teeth—those awful, sharp teeth and his and Pru's soft flesh and—

The sound of a small throat clearing halted both

Garm's attack and ABE's rambling inner monologue. The hound looked back, and as he did, ABE saw that Ratatosk had returned.

The squirrel sat calmly on his back legs in the middle of the tunnel. He looked Garm squarely in the eye. Then that insane, rude, wonderful squirrel did what he did best—he started talking.

Ratatosk had spent his entire life carrying messages. ABE didn't know how old Ratatosk was, but the squirrel had to be at least a thousand years old if he'd been around during the days of the Vikings. ABE suspected he was much, much older than that. Most of the messages Ratatosk had delivered had been insults passed back and forth between Nidhogg and the eagle that lived at the top of Yggdrasil. That meant that Ratatosk had been collecting insults over hundreds, probably thousands, of years.

Nothing else could have prepared Ratatosk to unleash the extraordinary verbal assault he delivered at that moment. The astonishing litany of scathing brickbats that emerged from the squirrel's mouth was of such an awe-inspiring and prodigious caliber that even frost giants from the coldest realms of Jotunheim would have felt the heat of embarrassment and blushed. After about a minute, ABE had to cover his ears. Pru lasted a few seconds longer, then she slapped her hands to her head, too. Garm's own ears shot up and a low whine escaped his throat as Ratatosk released a torrent of insults the likes of which had never been heard in the three worlds before and never would be heard again.

A moment of silence followed Ratatosk's tirade. Then Garm's ears curled back against his head and, with a rabid howl, the hound of Niflheim charged the squirrel.

Ratatosk was already on the move, though. He raced down the hall away from ABE and Pru and once more away from the mouth of Gnipa Gave. This time, Garm followed the squirrel, his only thought to retaliate against the abuse he'd received at Ratatosk's hand . . . or, rather, *mouth*.

Two words echoed back through the halls as Ratatosk and Garm disappeared. They were spoken by Ratatosk, his voice hoarse from exertion.

"Run, shortwits!"

CHAPTER 23

ABE HAD THE FORETHOUGHT TO GRAB A TORCH FROM THE WALL BEFORE HE and Pru ran into the darkness of Gnipa Cave. Pru was still a little dazed from Garm's attack. Just how dazed wasn't clear until they'd gone a good ways into the cave and Pru suddenly stopped them.

"My looking glass! I left it back in the palace!"

"Pru . . . we can't go back. I don't know how much time Ratatosk bought us. But I don't think we'll get this chance to escape again."

"I know!" Pru bit down fiercely on her lip, clearly torn. "But do we even know where we're going? We were supposed to escape *with* Ratatosk. He was going to lead the way."

She had a point. ABE craned his neck to look in both directions, unsure what to do. Should they go forward and away from Garm? Or should they go back and find Ratatosk?

In the end, they decided to go on a little ways. So far, the tunnel had been straight, with no side passages. They reasoned they could safely continue for a while. That way, they could put a little more distance between themselves and Garm, but Ratatosk would still be able to find them without any trouble if he doubled back.

The tunnel continued fairly straight, with a slightly upward slope, for a good distance. Eventually, though, their luck ended as the tunnel forked.

"Which way?" ABE asked. "Or do we wait?"

"I think we have another problem." Pru pointed at their sputtering torch.

He'd noticed the dimming light a while ago and had been trying to convince himself that it was his imagination. The thought of the torch going out filled him with uncontrollable fear. They would be entombed in the pitch-dark caverns of Niflheim and left to wander in an endless, empty void for the rest of their lives with no hope for—

Suddenly, ABE's looking glass lit up and an image appeared.

"ABE! ABE, can you hear me?"

"Mister Fox!" Pru exclaimed.

ABE held up his looking glass. Mister Fox's image looked out at them. "Good! You're both there! I worried when Pru didn't respond."

"Things went sour," Pru said. She went on to explain their encounter with Garm, their separation from Ratatosk, and the loss of Pru's looking glass.

"Okay. I agree. Things could be better," Mister Fox said. "But let's not worry too much about Ratatosk yet. He's fast and clever. I'm sure he's a match for Garm."

"We have one more problem," ABE said. "Our torch is about to die."

Mister Fox considered that for a moment. "I think I can help with that. I can teach you how to use some of the looking glass's enchantments to capture the light of the torch. But there's a catch. I won't be able to call you again. If I do, it will break the charm and you'll be left in the dark."

ABE hated the idea of being cut off from the detective. He was sure Pru felt the same way. But the thought of being left alone in the dark was even more terrifying. As it was, ABE was already beginning to imagine he could hear things in the emptiness around them. He'd become aware of a rhythmic tapping sound in the distance, for example. He knew it was probably something natural, like dripping water, but his imagination had partnered with his fear and given birth to all kinds of unpleasant alternatives. Many of those alternatives involved things with very big and very sharp teeth.

"Teach us how to capture the torch's light," Pru said. She looked ABE. "Agree?"

"Yeah," he said.

"All right. But since this might be our last chance to talk for a while, we need to establish a plan. Listen. It's possible Ratatosk won't make it back."

"But you said—" ABE began.

"I know what I said. And I still hope he'll find you. Wait a little while. According to the lore, Garm is bound to the Palace of the Dead. He can't go beyond the palace gate or the mouth of Gnipa Cave. So he won't be able to reach you where you are. But you can't stay forever. If Ratatosk doesn't return—"

"But you still think he will, right?" ABE interrupted.

"If Ratatosk doesn't return," Mister Fox repeated, "you'll have to go on without him."

"How are we supposed to do that?" Pru said, her confidence cracking. ABE felt a fresh burst of worry. "This cave system could be huge. We might never find our way out."

"You don't need to find your way out. You just need to cross the border from Niflheim to Midgard. The Henhouse will note your crossing and take me as close to you as it can. I can use my looking glass for the rest. I *will* find you. Just keep going up."

"Okay," Pru said, sounding a little reassured.

"But you *do* still think Ratatosk is coming, right?" ABE said quickly. "Right?"

"I hope so, ABE. But your torch is dimming. We can't put this off any longer. I'm going to break the connection. When I do, ABE, I want you to hold your looking glass up to the torch so that the mirror is reflecting its light. Then say *zapomni*. Repeat that."

ABE did, and when Mister Fox was satisfied he'd said it right, he continued.

"Good. Then say *pokazhi*."

Mister Fox had ABE practice that word, too.

"Good," the detective said. "Those words will allow you to use some of the looking glass's most basic enchantments. The first incantation will tell the looking glass to capture the image in the mirror. The next incantation will allow you to summon the image. When you don't need the light anymore, say *khvatit*. That will stop the spell."

"Wait," Pru said. "I just thought of something. Why don't we just keep the connection open with you. There's light coming from the Henhouse. That way, we can have light *and* be able to talk to you."

"I considered that. But the looking glasses only work so long before they need to be recharged. That's another purpose of the miniature Henhouses I gave you. Capturing the light will use much less magical energy than keeping this connection open. I'm going to go now before the torch dies. Good luck."

"Wait," ABE said, though he didn't have any good reason other than not wanting to lose the lifeline to the detective.

It was too late. The image in the looking glass faded to black.

They were alone.

Pru nudged him. "ABE, quick!"

"Right," ABE said. He handed the torch to Pru and turned the mirrored side of his looking glass to the torchlight and said, "*Zapomni.*"

"Cross your fingers," Pru said.

ABE did so. His hand shook as he repeated the second incantation they'd been taught. "*Pokazhi.*"

Immediately, his looking glass began to glow with a golden light.

"Cool!" Pru said. "Instant flashlight."

"Okay," ABE said, taking a deep breath. He felt oddly reassured by the glowing light of his looking glass. Had he just done magic? Despite their circumstances, a shiver of excitement ran up his spine. He really *did* feel like a wizard.

"So now we wait," Pru said.

They waited.

And waited.

Long after their torch died and they were left with only the faint glow from ABE's looking glass, they waited. Long after they reached the terrible point of certainty that no help was coming, they waited, unwilling to admit to each other that something must have happened to Ratatosk.

As they waited, ABE paced in circles while Pru sat in front of his looking glass where it lay faceup on the ground, like a dim campfire.

What should they do? Part of ABE wanted to still wait for Ratatosk, both because he wanted the squirrel to be okay and because he didn't want to risk finding their way through the caverns without him.

Another part of him, though, was desperate to get moving. How long before they started to forget about their lives on Earth? He kept testing himself to see if he remembered everything about his home and family. But how could he tell if he had forgotten something he didn't remember if he couldn't remember what he'd forgotten?

That thought sounded crazy even to him.

"ABE," Pru said finally, rising, "we have to face it. Ratatosk isn't coming."

"Yeah. I know." ABE stood still. "Do you think he's okay?"

"I hope so. But even if something did happen to him, I think our best chance of helping him is getting to Mister Fox."

ABE nodded.

"ABE, do you hear that tapping sound?"

"I do. It's been going on for a while. I thought maybe it was just in my head."

"No. I hear it, too. It seems to be coming from the left path. I think we should go that way. It goes up at least."

It was as good a plan as any. And it was somewhat comforting to have Pru sound so confident. ABE led the way, his looking glass held before him. The glass provided some light, but the rough and uneven floor of the tunnel demanded their attention.

The tapping sound grew louder as they went. It wasn't as steady as ABE had first thought. It came in starts and stops.

"Hold on a second," Pru said, putting a hand on his shoulder.

"What is it?"

"Up ahead. I think there's another light."

"Maybe we should turn ours off and check."

Pru nodded her agreement and ABE whispered, "*Khvatit.*"

The tunnel instantly darkened. It didn't go pitch-black, though. Pru had been right. There was a faint light ahead of them. A way out?

"The tapping has stopped," Pru whispered.

ABE listened. He couldn't hear it anymore, either. In its place, though, came a new noise: a soft muttering sound.

"There's someone up ahead," he said.

They crept forward until ABE felt Pru's hand on his shoulder again. He stopped, and together they peered around a corner.

Ahead of them stood a short, stout man. His face and hands were black with dirt, and his leather tunic looked old and work worn. Oddly, though, and in stark contrast to his otherwise disheveled appearance, he wore necklaces and bracelets of gold inlaid with gems.

The man ran one hand along the rock of the tunnel wall. The gesture looked strangely like a caress. With his other hand, he lifted a pickax and began tapping the wall, pressing his ear close to the rock as he did. Other tools lay on the ground at his feet.

"What's he doing?" Pru asked in a whisper.

"He looks like he might be mining. Pru, I think he's a dwarf."

ABE had meant to whisper. In his enthusiasm, though, he spoke more loudly than he'd meant to. The dwarf dropped his small hammer immediately and drew a sword from his belt.

"Who's there?" the dwarf demanded.

"Nice, ABE," Pru hissed.

"Sorry."

"Step into the light so I can see you. Slowly, now."

They stepped around the corner. ABE raised his hands in the air until he realized that a Mythic from Niflheim would have no idea what the gesture meant.

"Children! What are children doing in the caverns of Niflheim?"

"Trying to get out, actually," ABE said.

"Out? Go out the same way you came in." The dwarf cocked his head and peered at them. "How *did* mortal children get in, hmm? You're not dead, are you? You don't look dead."

"No. We're not dead," Pru said.

"We're lost," ABE added.

"Lost?" The dwarf gave a hearty laugh. "Yes, I'd say you're very lost! Go on. Tell the truth. How *did* you come to be here?"

ABE had been excited about the prospect of meeting a dwarf. He'd always loved the stories of them toiling in their deep caverns, crafting magical items in their secret forges. All in all, though, he was finding his first actual encounter with a dwarf far less magical than he'd hoped. Judging by the guarded answer Pru gave to the dwarf's question, she felt the same way.

"We probably came in the same way you did," she said. "How did *you* get here?"

"Oh, that's good." The dwarf said. "You're clever, girl."

"Thanks," Pru said.

"I don't *like* clever." The dwarf jabbed his sword in their direction. "Mortals are clever when they're hiding things. What are you hiding, eh? What have you found? Is it gold? Is it gems?"

The dwarf's eyes began to shine with a manic light.

"No, we haven't found anything! We were just trying to get away from . . ." Pru bit her lip.

"Oho! Get away from who?"

ABE looked down at his feet. A quick glance out of the corner of his eye at Pru showed her doing the same.

"Go on," the dwarf urged. "Tell the tale true. We're all friends here. Aren't we?"

"Friends don't usually point swords at each other," ABE said.

The dwarf uttered a sound that was half grunt and half laugh. The covetous look that had taken over his face when he thought ABE and Pru were hiding treasure vanished at least, and he lowered his sword (but didn't sheath it).

"There. See? We're friends. I'm Fadir. Now, tell me. How did you get here?"

"I don't see that we have much choice," ABE said to Pru.

"Okay, fine. I'm Pru. My friend ABE and I came to Niflheim to talk to Baldur. He's dead. Did you know that?"

"What do I care for a god's death?"

"But Ragnarok is coming," ABE said.

Fair shrugged. "Ragnarok has always been coming. All things die. You still haven't told me who you're running from."

"The queen," Pru admitted. "She didn't want us to leave after we talked to Baldur."

"Fleeing the Dark Queen? The queen only keeps what is hers. You are thieves!" Fadir raised his sword again. "What did you steal, hmm? Something beautiful? Something precious? Show me!"

"No, we didn't take anything," ABE said.

"She said we had taken knowledge and that we couldn't leave," Pru added.

Fadir looked disappointed at first, but his eyes quickly lit with greed. "I bet the queen would pay a hefty ransom to see her pretties returned to her."

"No," Pru said. "Wait. Please. We can't go back. We have to get out and get home. Help us."

"And why should I help you?"

"Because . . ." Pru faltered.

"What if . . . what if we pay you?" ABE said.

"You said you hadn't found any gold," Fadir said suspiciously.

"No, no gold. But we have . . ." ABE did a quick inventory, but he knew he really only had one thing to offer. He took out his looking glass and held it out with a sigh. "I have this. It's magic."

"ABE, no!" Pru said as Fadir stepped forward and grabbed the device.

"We want to get out of here, right?"

Fadir ran his hands over ABE's looking glass, paying careful attention to the raven's head carved into its base and muttering all the while.

"Well crafted, yes. And strong enchantment . . . very strong . . . witch wrought!" Fadir's eyes lit up.

"Will that do?" ABE asked.

"All right, boy. Yes. This will do. For this prize, I will show you the way out."

"Great!" Pru said. "How long will it take?"

"Not so fast. The witch glass buys the boy's safe passage. What do *you* offer?"

"What? That's not fair. I don't have my looking glass anymore. I lost it."

Fadir shrugged. "No payment, no bargain."

Desperately, Pru began to dig through her satchel.

"What's that?" Fadir asked, suddenly alert. "Something metal. I can smell it."

Pru frowned. "There's nothing . . ."

Fadir dropped ABE's looking glass into a leather pouch and grabbed Pru's bag with the hand that wasn't holding his sword. He dropped her bag to the ground and reached inside. When he withdrew his hand, he held Pru's dad's badge.

"Hey!" Pru said, taking a step forward, "That's mine."

"This is valuable, is it?" Fadir clutched the badge to his chest.

"No. It's not even real gold. Now give it back!"

"No, not gold, but still valuable," Fadir said, studying Pru. "Or why would you want it so much, hmm? Yes, very valuable, I think. Give me this, and Old Fadir will return you both to Midgard, sure enough."

Pru opened her mouth to object but then closed it and held her tongue. ABE saw her inner struggle in her narrowed eyes and chewed lips.

"*Fine*," she said at last.

"Pru, are you sure?" ABE knew how important the badge was to her. Was she agreeing to give it up because it was her only choice? Or was she beginning to be influenced by their time in a World of Myth? Would she be able to live with her decision once they returned home?

"It's fine, ABE. So it's a deal? You'll get us out of here and return us to Midgard in return for our treasures?"

"Perhaps." Fadir studied them. He raised his sword again. "Or perhaps I'll just *take* the treasures."

"You don't want to do that," Pru said, backing away.

"No? Why?"

"Because . . ." Pru paused, then her eyes lit up, "because, like you said, the looking glass is witch wrought. We have magic. If you take our stuff, we'll put a curse on it *and* you."

Fadir hesitated. "You have no power."

"No? Show him, ABE."

ABE blinked in confusion. Show him? Show him what?

Pru gestured with her eyes to Fadir's bag.

"Oh!" ABE said. He raised his arm in what he thought looked like a wizardly gesture and said, "*Pokazhi.*"

ABE's looking glass flared to life and Fadir's pouch began to glow.

Cursing, the dwarf dropped the pouch and stepped away.

"Peace!" he said. "No need for that. It was a jest. We're friends, remember? I'll take you away from the queen."

"And take us to Midgard?" Pru pressed.

"Yes."

"We have your word?"

"Yes!" Fadir hissed.

Pru nodded to ABE.

He raised his hand again and waved it through the air.

"*Khvatit.*"

CHAPTER
24

THEY WALKED IN SILENCE. ABE DIDN'T MIND. THEY'D BEEN TRAVELING UPHILL almost from the start, and his muscles were beginning to ache. He wasn't sure he had the breath to spare to talk.

That thought gave him pause. He remembered his and Pru's journeys in Asgard. They'd never tired there. And he hadn't felt tired when they'd started their climb with Fadir. If traveling through Worlds of Myth didn't drain a person, did the fact that he was getting tired mean they were getting close to Midgard?

Maybe. He couldn't be sure, though. Anyhow, he had other concerns. Thirst and hunger soon outweighed the soreness in his legs. His lips felt dry. He passed the time as they walked seeing how long he could wait before moistening them with his tongue—and then how long it took for them to feel dry again.

When they came to a somewhat level and open area where the tunnel forked, Fadir said they would stop for a rest. ABE collapsed against a rock. Pru did the same a few feet away.

"You don't have any food, do you?" she asked ABE.

"No. I wish I did."

They both looked at Fadir.

"Not my job to feed you," he said as he stacked a few bits of kindling he'd pulled from his pack.

"You said you'd get us out," Pru said. "You're breaking the bargain if we starve to death."

"You're not going to starve to death." Fadir began striking two stones together. Sparks jumped from the stones to the kindling.

"No, but if we're weak from hunger and slip on the next climb, it's the same thing. So give us our stuff back if you're not going to feed us. Unless *you're* the thief."

Fadir glared at Pru over the blossoming fire. The lighting transformed his face into a mask as craggy as the rocky tunnels around them. Pru held his gaze. After a moment, Fadir reached into his pack once more and pulled out a large chunk of bread. He broke a piece off and threw it to Pru, who in turn broke some off and handed it to ABE.

"I suppose you'll be wanting water, too," the dwarf said.

"If you wouldn't mind," ABE said.

Fadir threw him a leather flask and ABE took a few swallows. He handed it to Pru without drinking as much as he would have liked. Pru didn't hesitate. She took a long swig before handing the skin back to Fadir.

Silence settled over the small camp at that point. ABE was tired, but he couldn't make himself comfortable enough to sleep. After a while, the silence became too heavy. Normally, he would have trusted Pru to break it. But one look at her made it clear that she was still angry with Fadir for taking her father's badge.

"So . . . I guess it's lucky we found you," ABE began.

"There's no luck, boy, no chance. Only fate."

"Right. So, um, what were you doing in the tunnels? Looking for gems? Not that I'm prying!" ABE quickly added. "I'm just trying, you know, to make conversation."

Fadir grunted and tended the fire. "There's treasure in the tunnels below. Most are too frightened of the queen to search for it."

"The other dwarves, you mean? Where are you from? Nidavellir?"

"So the human boy knows something of the dark fields?"

"Only from the stories I've read."

"And what do *you* know about stories, boy?"

It was an honest question, so ABE answered it honestly. "I know they change with the telling."

Apparently, the answer amused Fadir. He gave a bark of laughter.

"Well, then you know more than most. But you've only got it half right. They change with the telling, yes, but they change more with the teller."

"How so?"

The glow from the fire lit Fadir's face from below, casting him in an eerie light. His eyes glinted as he peered at ABE through a veil of smoke that rose from the flames. The smoke drifted up through one of the two tunnels that climbed steeply away from their camp.

"People tell the story they want you to hear, boy, true or not," the dwarf said.

ABE considered that.

"Enough talk," Fadir said. "It's been a long climb. We'll camp here tonight and go the rest of the way in the morning." The dwarf pulled a rolled blanket from his pack and placed it under his head. His snoring soon filled the cavern.

"Great. He snores, too. What a wonderful traveling companion." Pru pulled her knees to her chest and rested her forehead on them, eliminating the possibility of conversation with ABE.

ABE felt sad for Pru. He knew how much it hurt

her to lose her dad's badge. But he was also relieved to see that she was upset. It meant that they hadn't been in a World of Myth for so long that they'd lost their connection to home.

ABE rolled over. He didn't think he'd be able to sleep. But at some point in the unending, cavernous night, his eyes closed as exhaustion overtook him.

He wasn't sure how long he slept. When he woke up, the fire had mostly turned to ember and ash. It took long moments for his eyes to adjust to the dying light. When he could finally see, he jumped to his feet.

Fadir was gone.

They were alone in the caves.

Then the fire died, and all light vanished from the world.

CHAPTER
25

UNTIL THAT MOMENT, ABE HAD NEVER FELT CLAUSTROPHOBIC. HE KNEW WHAT the word meant, of course.

Claustrophobic: suffering from the fear of small, enclosed places

He'd been in small places before. It had never bothered him. But now he was in a cave somewhere between two worlds. There could be rocks for miles in every direction. He felt them all pressing in on him—crushing him.

His breath became slippery. He couldn't catch it. He began gasping. Hyperventilating? The definition swam through his dizzy mind.

Hyperventilate: to breathe at an excessively rapid rate, often brought on by fear or anxiety

Yes! He was definitely hyperventilating.

He felt a hand on his shoulder. He jumped.

"ABE, it's me!"

"Pru?" His breathing began to slow. It was still dark and he was still scared, but at least he wasn't alone.

"Yeah. ABE, Fadir's gone."

"I know. What are we going to do?"

"To Fadir? Something *really* unpleasant if I have anything to say about it. If we ever see him again, I mean."

"No, Pru, what are we going to *do*? We're alone. Fadir took our only light! We're basically buried alive!"

"I know, ABE. Don't you think I know?"

ABE could hear the fear in her voice. But he could also hear that she was trying to control it. He tried to follow her lead. He forced his breathing to slow even more and tried to think past the terror.

"Fadir said we would finish the climb today," he said aloud, remembering. "Maybe the exit is nearby."

"Maybe," Pru said. "Or maybe he was lying so he could run off on us and steal our stuff. But okay. Let's assume we're close. The tunnel splits in two directions from here. Which tunnel should we take? Fadir never told us."

ABE didn't even want to think about Fadir. He wished he could erase the memory of his last glimpse of the dwarf. Fadir had looked ghoulish in the firelight, wrapped in the rising smoke of the fire.

"Wait! Pru, that's it!" he said.

"What's it?"

"Before the fire went out, I saw the smoke rising up one of the tunnels. I remember it because I thought it made Fadir look creepy."

"Fadir *did* look creepy."

"Well, yeah. That's true. But I thought he looked creepier through the smoke. But the smoke—Pru, It was rising up the tunnel on the left."

"So?"

"It's like smoke going up a chimney in a fireplace. It might mean that there's some kind of ventilation that way."

"So you think that tunnel will take us outside?"

"I don't know. Maybe?"

"Maybe is better than anything else we have."

It wasn't easy making their way in the dark. They crawled so they could feel the ground ahead of them. The uneven floor of the tunnel threatened their hands and knees with sharp corners. Fortunately, the *domovye*-made pants and gloves proved more than durable and protected them as they groped their way through the dark.

ABE felt something tickle his cheek. He paused, waiting to see if it came again.

"Pru," he said, trying to contain his excitement. "I think I feel a breeze."

Pru was quiet a moment. "I feel it, too!"

They crawled more quickly, pulled by the promise of fresher air.

"ABE . . . am I crazy or is it getting brighter?"

He blinked, almost too afraid to trust his eyes. An excited giggle escaped his lips. It sounded ridiculous, but he didn't care!

"It is! It *is* getting brighter. Pru, I— OUCH!"

ABE's knee hit a rough piece of rock. Wincing from the pain, he reached out to find its edge. It rose up from the tunnel's floor and seemed to level off at about a ninety-degree angle. He gasped.

"Pru . . . I think these are steps!"

He heard Pru fumble in the dark. "You're right! They're rough, but they *are* steps. I think we found the exit!"

They clambered up the steps using their hands and feet. It was *definitely* brighter than it had been, and when ABE looked up, he saw a rectangular break in the darkness ahead, like an open entryway. They abandoned all caution and scrambled upward. ABE began to hear a roaring sound. In the dark, confined space of the tunnel, he couldn't tell if the sound was coming from somewhere nearby or if it was the sound of the blood rushing in his ears.

They burst, gasping for breath, through the opening at the top of the steps and emerged into an enormous cavern. Staggering into the wide-open space, they turned in a slow circle trying to figure out where they were.

Once on vacation, ABE's dad had taken ABE and his mom to a huge indoor football stadium. The circular cavern he and Pru discovered at the end of their climb out of Niflheim could have held two of those stadiums with room to spare. The domed ceiling was broken in the center by a large round opening, through which ABE could see both the moon and a heavenly assortment of stars.

Most of the cavern's light came from that opening far overhead, but not all. There were gems of various sizes visible in the walls throughout the cavern. The gems somehow captured and amplified the moon's light, filling the space with a magical silvery glow.

ABE lowered his gaze to the smooth floor of the cavern. With a start, he realized the roaring sound he had heard in the tunnel wasn't the blood rushing through his ears. A river cut through the center of the cavern, running from east to west.

"ABE, look!" Pru grabbed his arm and pointed to the eastern wall. ABE gaped in astonishment.

Two stone towers jutted out from the wall of the cavern. They rose from the floor to the ceiling, as tall as skyscrapers with a wide-open space between them. One tower stood on the north bank of the river, the other stood on the south bank, where he and Pru were. A number of bridges connected the structures, crossing the river at various heights along the towers.

"It's a dwarvish outpost!" ABE said. "It looks abandoned."

"Does it?" Pru pointed again, and ABE saw what he had missed. One of the windows near the bottom of the tower on the northern side of the river shone with light. It flickered like the open flame of a campfire.

"Do you think it's Fadir?" he asked.

"I don't know who else it could be. Let's find out!"

"What? Pru, no! We're almost out." ABE inhaled deeply. The cool, fresh air made him feel almost giddy. "I can see the sky!"

"I know, but unless you can fly, we have no way of getting up there. And look around. There are *dozens* of tunnels leading from this place. If we go the wrong way, we could end up more lost than before."

She was right. There had been so much else to see that he hadn't noticed the other tunnel entrances that dotted the walls of the cavern.

"We can do this, ABE," Pru said, placing a hand on each of his shoulders. "That has to be Fadir. Who else could it be? He'll know the way out. And even if he refuses to help us, we'll *still* be okay. That's the moon up there. *Our* moon. We're back on Midgard. That means that Mister Fox is on his way. I don't just want to stand around waiting for him."

He was so tired. But she was right. They were already exhausted and starving. They were probably dehydrated, too. Fadir had supplies, and he would know the way out. There was no telling how long it would take Mister Fox to find them.

"Okay," he said, taking a deep breath. "Let's go."

They followed the curve of the cavern wall to the tower, trying their best to stay out of sight. The bridge at ground level had crumbled, forcing them to enter the southern tower and climb to one of the bridges higher up. They found one that looked safe enough to cross on the third level. It was about as wide as a two-lane highway, and ABE stayed away from either edge as they crossed. He didn't much like heights.

"Wow," Pru said, stopping midway across the bridge. She pointed. "Look."

"Wow is right," he said, following Pru's direction. He'd assumed that the towers were the only structures in the cavern. They weren't. The gap that separated the towers stretched back into the wall, rising from the river to the ceiling to form a *huge* tunnel, large enough that the Statue of Liberty could have walked through it, if that were something she were inclined to do.

On either side of the gap, all along the north and

south walls of the tunnel, were more towers and spires. They stretched back as far as ABE could see.

"It's not a dwarvish outpost," he said in an awed voice. "It's a whole underground city."

"It's pretty amazing," Pru said, "but it's not what we're here for. Come on."

ABE pulled his eyes from the magnificent city of stone and followed Pru the rest of the way across the bridge.

The northern tower was in a much worse state than the southern. The ceiling of the first chamber they entered had caved in, covering its only other exit with a pile of rubble and timber. Fortunately, they were able to scramble up the pile to reach the level above, though they had to move carefully.

Their caution paid off. Had they been moving more quickly, they might not have heard the sound of a voice as it rose up through the floor of a nearby room. They crept into the adjoining space and found a narrow crack in the corner of the floor. Light shone through the crack. ABE and Pru moved closer and peered through the tiny opening. A figure crouched over a fire in the room below.

ABE had expected it to be Fadir. They both had.

It wasn't.

It was someone else ABE recognized, though, and perhaps the last person in the world he expected to see.

Loki.

CHAPTER 26

THE LAST TIME THEY'D SEEN HIM, LOKI HAD LOOKED PRINCELY. NOW his torn clothes hung loosely on a body covered with grime.

He was talking to himself. His mutterings echoed off the rock walls.

"Not long. Not long. They'll find me. He'll tell them how, when it suits him." He wrung his hands together over the fire. "Where to go? Where to run? Nowhere! I'm trapped. I can take any shape, but always Loki. Always the villain."

ABE felt a tap on his shoulder, and he looked up to see Pru gesturing toward the exit. Tiptoeing, ABE followed her to a spot a safe distance away.

"How is that even possible?" Pru said. "What are

the odds that we show up in the same cavern Loki is hiding out in?"

ABE tried to reason it out. "Maybe it does make sense—sort of, anyway. These caverns go down to Niflheim. The queen is Loki's daughter. Maybe he thought he could escape down there if he needed to. I wonder why he's stayed here, though. He looks like he's seen better days."

"He's going to see worse," Pru said, her lips set in a firm line.

"What do we do now? Should we—"

The room grew darker as the light coming from the cavern dimmed. Clouds must have covered the moon. A muffled wail rose up from below.

As quickly as they could manage while still being quiet, they returned to the spyhole and peered down. Loki had moved out of sight. Before they could decide what to do, he burst back into view, tugging his hair.

"Found! I'm found!" Loki stomped out his fire and disappeared into darkness. His voice remained, though, muttering over and over, "What to do?"

Pru and ABE tiptoed back to the next room to talk.

"It's Mister Fox," Pru said. "It has to be!"

"Do you think that he saw the fire? Do you think he's on his way?"

"I don't know. We have to get him here. Quick, go

back to the bridge. Get his attention in case he didn't see the light."

"I can't leave you here!"

"I'll be fine. I'm just going to keep an eye—or ear—on things. If Loki leaves, I might be able to see where he goes."

ABE didn't like it, but he agreed.

He found his way back to the bridge and stood in the middle of it. He scanned the cavern. His knees wobbled a bit as he saw three figures racing across floor. Not only had Mister Fox found them, he'd brought Thor and Hilde, too!

ABE waved his arms like a wild man. He resisted the urge to shout, and instead took his jacket off and began swinging it through the air. That seemed to work. He saw Mister Fox grab Thor's arm and point. They'd seen him!

ABE gestured toward the door in the southern tower where he and Pru had entered. Mister Fox and the others headed off in that direction, and ABE soon lost sight of them. He ran the rest of the way across the bridge to meet them, fighting back the urge to laugh. He couldn't believe it! They were rescued! And Loki was nearly caught.

Mister Fox appeared first. Hilde followed and Thor came last, a barely contained storm of energy.

"ABE! Thank goodness you're okay," Mister Fox said. "Where's Pru?"

"She's fine. She's back keeping an eye on Loki."

"Loki?" Thor exclaimed.

Hilde turned to shush him. "Can you take us to him, boy?"

ABE nodded. "Follow me."

They had nearly made it across the bridge when Pru poked her head out a window. Her short bob of hair framed her face.

"It's no use sneaking!" she called. "He saw you coming. He leapt into the river and shape-shifted into some kind of fish!"

"As my father foresaw!" Thor bellowed, turning on his heel. "To the river!"

ABE hesitated. Something was wrong. "Mister Fox, there's—"

"Not now, ABE. We have to catch him!" Mister Fox shouted. He grabbed ABE's sleeve and dragged him back across the bridge. When ABE tried to protest, the detective hissed in his ear, "Not here."

When they reentered the southern tower, Mister Fox called on the others to stop.

"There's no time!" Thor said.

"Wait!" Mister Fox insisted. "Go on ahead. But leave me a net."

"Why?" Hilde asked.

"A hunch," Mister Fox said.

"Give him what he wants," Thor said, already descending to the level below.

Hilde opened her shoulder pack and handed Mister Fox a folded up piece of mesh.

ABE paced, troubled.

"It was her hair," Mister Fox said as Hilde disappeared after Thor.

ABE stopped. Her hair? Of course!

"That wasn't Pru who poked her head out of the window," ABE said, catching on. "It was Loki. He took her shape, but he made his hair too short. He made it look like it did when he met Pru last year."

"Loki must be panicked. He wouldn't normally miss a detail like that. Let's make that work in our favor. Loki is going to be watching the river to see if we take the bait. He'll be focused on the others, especially Thor. If we're lucky, you and I can cross the bridge while he's distracted. Come on."

Keeping as low as possible, they raced across the bridge once more. ABE started to lead Mister Fox to where he'd left Pru, but Mister Fox stopped him. The detective was surveying their surroundings with his looking glass.

"This way," he said.

Mister Fox moved like his namesake. They wove their way through a labyrinth of rooms and corridors

ABE hadn't seen before. But Mister Fox's instincts were true. He paused when he reached a particular chamber and gestured that ABE should stop, too. They peered through a crack in the door.

Loki stood inside with his back to them. He was looking out a window, presumably watching Thor and Hilde. ABE couldn't see Pru anywhere.

Mister Fox pulled out the small piece of mesh Hilde had given him and began to unfold it. It was a finely woven net, so thin ABE doubted it could hold anything. He wondered if it was magic.

It certainly turned out to be larger than ABE had first thought. When Mister Fox was done, he and ABE held a net that was easily large enough to catch a man. Mister Fox mouthed, "Ready?"

ABE nodded.

"On the count of three." He paused. "One . . . two . . . three!"

They burst through the door. Loki spun around the moment they entered. He was fast. Feathers sprouted from his arms. His face narrowed and his nose became beak-like.

"Now, ABE, throw the net!" Mister Fox yelled.

ABE did. Mostly, he just released the net and let Mister Fox do the throwing. It settled on Loki before he could complete his transformation. Entangled, Loki fell to the ground with a thud and reverted to his true form.

ABE looked desperately around the room. He found Pru bound and gagged in a corner. He raced to her and crouched down to untie her.

"I was almost done!" she shouted as soon as her gag was removed.

Looking down, ABE saw Pru had found a sharp rock and begun to cut through the ropes on her own. He fell back to a sitting position. She was amazing.

"Are you okay?" Mister Fox asked, joining them. "Can you walk? Because we have to leave here. Now. Before it's too late."

CHAPTER
27

"WHAT DO YOU MEAN, 'BEFORE IT'S TOO LATE'? WE CAUGHT LOKI!" PRU SAID. "It's over."

ABE studied Mister Fox. A tightness remained around the detective's eyes.

"Yes, we caught Loki," Mister Fox said. "Now let's go fetch Thor and Hilde. The net was made by the goddess Ran. It will hold Loki and keep him from changing shape until they can collect him."

With the attention turned back to him, Loki ceased his struggles. "Do not do this to me. I beg you."

"Why, Loki?" Mister Fox crouched beside him. "Before we go, I have to understand. *Why?* The last time we crossed paths, you were trying to change your fate. Why did you surrender to it?"

"Surrender?" Loki cried. "I did not surrender to my fate. It conquered me!"

"That's not an answer!"

"I have no answers!"

Loki twisted so that he faced Pru.

"Pru," he pleaded. "We were friends once, when I was Fay."

"You were never Fay! You were lying to us the whole time."

"No! I was kind to you." Loki shifted to look at ABE. "Wasn't I always kind to you?"

"You were going to let Gristling kill us!"

"Only when I had no choice! I tried to let you go. Do you remember? Do you truly think I would have forgotten you in Asgard? I saw your escape. *I let you go!*" Loki writhed in desperation.

"Enough!" Mister Fox snapped. "This isn't about last year. This is about Baldur."

"And I am innocent! I did not kill Baldur! Listen to me. I beg you!"

"We don't have any more time for lies. Pru, ABE, we're leaving." Mister Fox gave Loki one last, inscrutable look. Then he rose and started for the door. Pru and ABE followed him. Loki shouted after them.

"Listen to me! I am innocent! *LISTEN TO ME!*"

It wasn't until they were across the bridge and halfway down the tower, with Loki's cries for mercy still echoing behind them, that Mister Fox said, "The sad part is, despite everything, a part of me still wants to believe him."

"Where's the Henhouse?" ABE asked, wanting to change the subject and spare Mister Fox the embarrassment of being wrong. "I didn't see it when you arrived with the others."

"It's hundreds of miles from here, in the nearest graveyard I could find. That's why I had to call on Thor and Hilde. I didn't have any choice. I needed their flying ship, *Skidbladnir*, to get here."

"They have a flying ship? Sweet!" Pru said.

"Where is here, anyway?" ABE asked. "I didn't think there were any caves around Middleton."

"What makes you think we're near Middleton? We're in Norway."

"Seriously?" Pru said.

"Become a Fibber," Mister Fox said. "Travel the world. Meet interesting deities. It's all part of the job description."

Pru gave a nervous but excited laugh. ABE wanted to be excited, too. But there was something beneath Mister Fox's humorous tone that worried him.

They reached the bottom of the tower and exited into the vast cavern. In the distance, Thor and Hilde walked along the river, searching the waters. Each held a net.

"Over here!" Mister Fox called to them, waving. "We caught him. *Hurry!*"

"What's the rush?" Pru asked. "You said the net would hold him."

"It's not the net I'm worried about." Mister Fox scanned the cavern as though expecting someone. "Where's Ratatosk, by the way?"

"Ratatosk never came back," Pru said. "ABE and I had to make our own way. We met a dwarf, Fadir. He led us here. Well, he led us most of the way here, the creep. ABE had to give him his looking glass, though. And I had to give him my dad's badge."

"You met a dwarf?" Mister Fox stopped his examination of the cavern long enough to look at them. "In all the vast expanse of the caverns around Niflheim, you found a dwarf who led you here, to this spot?"

Thor and Hilde arrived then, and Mister Fox, frowning, turned to them.

"Loki's caught, neat as you please, in a net in the north tower. Just follow the desperate screaming. You'll be getting my bill posthaste. All checks should be made out to *The Unbelievable FIB*. In the meantime, Thor, why don't you put those big, brawny shoulders to use and collect Loki *so we can leave.*"

Thoom . . . Thoom . . . Thoom.

Mister Fox stiffened.

ABE spun around, trying to discover the source of

the sound seeping into the cavern. A number of the tunnels leading to the space, all of which had been dark just a few moments before, now blazed with a fierce red light.

Thoom. Thoom! THOOM!

The sound didn't seep anymore—it poured into the chamber. It was a rhythmic banging, like that of a thousand drums beat in unison, or the sound of a marching army. Light shone in even more of the tunnels now, more than ABE could count. But it was the shadows newly visible in the lighted tunnels that sent ABE's voice soaring to its highest pitch. Shadows invaded the cavern, shadows of shapes huge and small, some with too many heads and arms.

"What's happening?" ABE cried.

"Mister Fox?" Pru said, pulling on the detective's sleeve.

"Too late," Mister Fox whispered, spinning in a slow circle. All the blood had drained from his face. He looked like a ghost. "They're here."

"Who's here?" ABE asked.

"Think about it," Mister Fox said, his voice uncharacteristically flat. "Some of these tunnels connect Earth and Niflheim. But there are other realms close to Niflheim, realms touched by Niflheim's cold and cruelty."

"What realms?" ABE asked, afraid he already knew the answer.

"The coldest reaches of Jotunheim," Hilde said.

"That means . . ." Pru didn't finish the sentence.

Thor did.

"Frost giants."

CHAPTER
28

"THIS IS LOKI'S DOING," HILDE SAID, DRAWING HER SWORD. "HE BAITED US and now the trap is sprung."

"Loki!" Thor roared, launching himself in the direction of the tower where Loki lay. "I must retrieve him!"

Pru started after him, but Mister Fox grabbed her arm.

"Let him go, Pru."

"What? But Loki . . ."

"Is Thor's problem. We're leaving! But which way?" Mister Fox scanned the cavern.

"Why don't we just leave the same way you came in?" ABE asked.

"There *has* to be another exit."

There wasn't. Every single tunnel now glowed red. They were surrounded.

"Here they come!" ABE cried, pointing.

The first frost giants charged into the cave through a tunnel on the other side of the river. They weren't alone. Trolls ran alongside them, like rabid dogs at the giants' heels, brandishing vicious spiked clubs. The frost giants wielded swords and axes that burned with the reflected light of their torches.

"We don't have any choice," Mister Fox said. He thrust his looking glass into Pru's hand. "Take this. You'll know what to do with it when the time comes. Now we have to move. There! See where the river exits the cavern? That's the way. Go!"

"Why are you giving me your looking glass?" Pru asked. But the detective ignored her question and pushed her into motion.

They ran. ABE and Pru did their best to keep up, but they were tired from their escape from Niflheim and Mister Fox had to adjust his pace. The distance stretched on forever as they ran toward the river's exit through the west wall of the tunnel.

More giants and trolls soon joined the first arrivals. An endless tide poured into the cavern, threatening to cut off their exit. The monsters' stampede sounded like thunder.

No. Wait.

That *was* thunder!

Thor had emerged from the tower with Loki slung over his shoulder. Seeing him, the swarming mass of monsters shifted course. ABE watched in astonishment as Thor grew in size and clashed with the first of his attackers.

Then ABE, Pru, and Mister Fox reached the west wall of the cave. There they found an ancient and narrow dwarvish road that ran alongside the river through a tunnel in the cavern wall. The road rested just below an embankment and only a few feet above the water level of the river.

The surface of the road was wet and slick. ABE barely managed to keep his footing as they raced along. The echo of the river's roar buffeted them in the enclosed space of the tunnel, blending with the clang of the battle that had begun behind them.

Theirs was the one tunnel from which no monsters had emerged. ABE soon saw why. This tunnel did not lead to a mythical realm. It led outside to fresh air and skies that had once been clear but that now roiled with the thunder god's battle rage.

"We're in the mountains!" ABE exclaimed, taking in the snowcapped peaks all around. Beside them, the river exploded out of the tunnel and plunged hundreds of feet down before disappearing into a cloud of misty spray.

They stood on a stone platform that had been built into the mountain by the dwarves, long ago. In addition to the road they'd followed from the cave, another path led to the southeast, back along the outside of the mountain.

ABE scrambled back from the precipice and pressed himself against the hard rock wall. A gust of wind threatened to rip him from his perch. His knees nearly buckled as he imagined it pulling him to the edge and over and down . . . and down and down.

"We have to keep moving," Mister Fox said. "We don't have any other choice. Maybe if we're fast enough . . . *come on!*"

The detective led the way along the stone path. ABE tried to keep his eyes fixed on Mister Fox's back. He looked over the edge of the path once, though—and immediately wished he hadn't. They were hundreds of feet up. A fall would mean certain death on the rocks below.

"*Travel the world*," Pru said behind him, repeating Mister Fox's words from earlier. "*Meet interesting deities . . . all part of the job description.*"

ABE nodded, swallowed, and fixed his gaze on Mister Fox's back once more.

The path gradually grew wider. They reached a stretch where they could easily have walked side by side with room to spare. Mister Fox hurried ahead, though. Pru followed next as ABE struggled to keep up.

CRACK!

The deafening sound tore through the air, and the whole mountain shook. ABE stumbled back a few paces and fell to all fours.

"What was that?" Pru cried, also on her hands and knees.

"The mountain!" Mister Fox said, leaning against its side for support. "The dwarves hollowed it out too much. It can't take the punishment Thor and the giants are dishing out. The mountainside might as well be an eggshell—it has about as much chance of holding up against the battle going on inside! We need to get out of here!"

ABE and Pru never even got the chance to stand up.

CRACK-A-BOOM!

The next tremor, ten times more powerful than the first, shook ABE's bones and rattled his teeth. He looked up just in time to see a huge boulder come crashing down from above. It was heading right for Pru!

"Pru!" he shouted, reaching for her. But he was too far away to help.

Pru couldn't scramble to her feet fast enough. She'd be crushed!

At the last moment, somehow, Mister Fox appeared.

He shoved Pru to safety, then staggered back as the boulder crashed down and came to rest on the ledge between them, blocking the detective from view.

"What was that?" Pru said, recovering. The detective's looking glass had slipped from her hand and skidded across the ground.

"It sounded like the whole mountain split in two. Actually, I think maybe it did," ABE said, pointing to the wall of rock above them. A vertical fissure had appeared in the side of the mountain, just next to the boulder that had nearly crushed Pru. The fissure was large enough to drive a tank through.

"It doesn't sound like it's stopped, either," Pru said. Rumbling continued to fill the air, sounding a little more removed than before. "It sounds like the whole cavern's collapsing. I bet that crack goes all the way back to—wait. Where's Mister Fox?"

"He's on the other side of the—*PRU, LOOK OUT!*"

ABE's warning came too late. A shape appeared in the crack in the wall, a fearsome and giant-sized shape that might have been conjured from ABE's worst nightmare. Gristling erupted from the fissure.

"At last!" Gristling bellowed. "He told me that if I brought my clan and my allies to this place that I would see both of you again. *Finally, I will have my vengeance!* And I shall begin with you, girl!"

Pru tried to get up and escape but cried out in pain

and fell back to the ground, grabbing her ankle. Roaring in triumph, Gristling reached for her.

"Gristling!" ABE shouted.

The giant lifted his head, and ABE locked eyes with the monster. Even with the bruises, even with the wound on his cheek that left the giant's wild beard caked with blood and grit, ABE knew Gristling's face. It had haunted his days and his dreams for the past year. It had been a burden of fear that ABE had carried for too long. He was sick of the burden. He was sick of Gristling's face. So he would banish it.

ABE lifted his arm. He held Mister Fox's looking glass.

"*NO!*" Gristling shouted as ABE caught the giant's reflection in the enchanted mirror and transported the monster back to the frozen reaches of Jotunheim.

"ABE!" Pru shouted. "You did it!"

ABE stumbled to her side. "Are you okay? Your ankle—"

"I'm fine," Pru said, standing. She winced, then leaned on his shoulder. "Well, mostly fine. I think I might have sprained my ankle. It's not bad. It just surprised me. Come on! We have to get to Mister Fox."

ABE returned the detective's looking glass to her and together they edged their way between the boulder and the mountain. ABE could feel the mountain still trembling beside him.

When they emerged on the other side of the boulder, they found the ledge empty.

"I don't understand," Pru said. "I thought you said he was over here."

"He was. I saw him. He stumbled back away from the boulder and . . ."

The same thought struck them both at the same time. They rushed to the edge of the ledge and looked over the side.

CHAPTER 29

ABOUT TEN FEET BELOW ABE AND PRU, MISTER FOX CLUNG TO THE MOUNTAIN. His hat was lost to the unforgiving ground hundreds of feet below, and his hair blew freely in the wind. One arm hung limply at his side.

"Mister Fox!" Pru cried.

"Are you okay?" ABE said, then felt instantly foolish.

"Climb up!" Pru said.

"I can't." Mister Fox's voice was laced with pain. "The boulder clipped my arm. My shoulder's dislocated. The arm may be broken."

"ABE, we have to save him!"

"I appreciate the sentiment," Mister Fox said, "but you have to go."

"Are you insane? We *will* save you," Pru said. She coughed, probably choking on all the dust created by the shuddering mountain. There were tears in her eyes, too, though ABE didn't think they were from the dust.

"There's no time. You have to go."

"I won't leave you!" Pru dropped to her chest and stretched her arm down as far as it would go. "I won't let you go!"

"Letting go. That always is the hardest part."

"ABE, find something," Pru cried. "Some rope—something! *Please!*"

ABE scrambled up and scanned the area for anything that could be of use. A vine, maybe. There was always a vine in the movies. Why couldn't this be the movies?

"What are you talking about?" Pru said, turning her attention back to Mister Fox.

"Letting go. Sending Fibbers out to Worlds of Myth. Wondering if it's right. Wondering if they're ready." The detective winced with pain. "Then, when you return, flying off in the Henhouse. It's never as easy as it seems, or as I make it sound."

"What does that even mean?" Pru was sobbing now. ABE hurried back to her.

"There's nothing, Pru," he said. "I'm sorry. I'm so sorry. I don't know what to do!"

A panicked chant rose from the back of ABE's

mind, a variation on what Alva had said to them: *Always tomorrow, never today. Always tomorrow, never today. Please! Never today!*

The mountain shook again.

"Pru, ABE, you two have to go! The cavern is collapsing. And it's going to take the whole mountain with it!"

ABE wondered how Mister Fox could know that.

"I won't leave you!" Pru shouted again. "*I won't!*"

"I know," Mister Fox said.

Then he did the only thing he could do, the hardest thing.

He let go.

CHAPTER
30

ABE LED THEM ACROSS THE TREMBLING GROUND AND THROUGH THE ROCKS that fell like crushing tears. He had to drag Pru at the start—she hadn't wanted to leave the spot where Mister Fox had fallen and vanished from their view, from their lives, forever.

The mountain continued to collapse until there was nowhere left to go. The ledge ahead crumbled before their eyes. They were trapped on the edge of a mountain that was decaying around them like an anthill in a hurricane.

"I'M SORRY, PRU," ABE shouted over the sound of the world falling apart around them. "I DON'T KNOW WHAT TO DO."

Pru clutched Mister Fox's looking glass to her chest

and stared with glassy eyes into the emptiness before them. ABE looked back at the mountain, wondering how much time they had left.

Something burst into view from beyond the mountain's crumbling peak. It flew almost straight up into the air. At first, ABE thought it was an enormous rock—but the mountain wasn't exploding, it was collapsing! It shouldn't be shooting anything into the air.

The object soared into the sky a short distance before its upward climb stopped. It hung in the air a moment, then circled back down. It looked like . . . it was! It was a Viking longship, not unlike the one they'd seen Baldur laid to rest in!

The ship sailed through the air and came to a stop next to the small ledge where ABE and Pru stood. Thor leapt from the vessel, scooped them up, one in each arm, and returned to the ship just as the ledge gave way beneath them.

"How?" It was all ABE could manage to say as Thor deposited them safely on the deck.

"*Skidbladnir!*" Thor said, gesturing to the ship. "A marvel of dwarvish construction. Once its sails catch wind, it can travel anywhere, over sea or land. The god Freyr loaned it to us for our search for Loki. Now, the gray shade, lad. The one you call Mister Fox. Where is he?"

"He . . . fell," ABE said, struggling with the words. "He's gone."

Thor placed a hand, surprisingly gentle, on ABE's shoulder. "Rest, lad. I will see to things."

The thunder god called out to Hilde as he set off across the deck of the ship, but ABE didn't hear what Thor said to her. Exhaustion and grief overwhelmed him, and he fell into a deep sleep. If he dreamt, he did not remember it.

He woke up to find himself wrapped in blankets on the deck of *Skidbladnir*. Pru lay beside him in blankets of her own, still sleeping. Not wanting to wake her, ABE rose carefully and quietly. Every muscle in his body felt stiff and sore. He walked to the stern of the ship, where he found Thor and Hilde.

"Ah, lad, you're awake. Good," Thor said. "How do you feel?"

"Thirsty mostly," ABE said.

Hilde tossed him a leather skin.

"Thank you," he said after a long drink. The water helped him feel more alert. "Where are we? How long have we been traveling?"

"We are near your town, lad. *Skidbladnir* travels fast. It is nearing the middle of night. Before we return you to your home, though, there is a matter we must discuss." Thor stepped aside and revealed Loki, still wrapped in Ran's net and now wearing a gag. "Loki's fate must be decided."

"Throw him overboard."

ABE turned, startled at the sound of Pru's voice. She stood behind them on shaky legs. Even in the moonlight, ABE could see her eyes were red.

"Pru!" ABE said, alarmed as much by her words as her appearance. "We can't . . ."

"It's his fault Mister Fox is dead! He brought those giants. He killed Baldur and Mister Fox. He is going to kill *everyone*. He needs to be punished!"

"You are not alone in thinking so," Hilde said with a grim nod.

"He cannot die," Thor said. "Even if there are those who think he deserves it."

"Why?" Pru demanded.

"Ah, now we get to the heart of things." Thor drew a hand across his face. His fingers traced through his long, unruly beard. "It is time you knew the truth. You see, my father first met Loki long ago, before he drank from the Well of Wisdom. My father prized Loki's clever mind. They became fast friends. Many were their trials and travels. In time, they took the Oath of Brotherhood. They shared blood and were bonded. On that day, Odin vowed that no one in Asgard would ever bring any harm to Loki. That is why, in part, Loki has never faced any consequences from the gods for his misdeeds. That blood oath my father gave protects Loki from all types of retribution."

"Wait—does that mean you can't punish him?" ABE asked. "Then what has this all been for? Why even bother to capture him?"

"You are correct, lad," Thor said. He hooked his thumbs in his belt and looked down at the deck of the ship. "We cannot pass judgment on him . . . but you can. Loki's actions on Midgard last year leave him vulnerable to your judgment."

"Great!" Pru said. "He's guilty!"

"I misspoke." Thor faced ABE. "*You*, lad, have the authority to pass judgment on Loki."

"What?" ABE staggered back. "Me? Why me?"

"Because Loki took you from your home last year. Prudence went to Asgard by choice to save you, her friend. A noble act. But you had no choice, lad. Loki took you. He trespassed into Midgard and stole you from your home. By rights, you can make claim against the trickster. You, and only you, can judge Loki guilty of evil acts. Doing so will give the gods the freedom to imprison and punish him on your behalf."

"But . . ." ABE didn't know what to say. He didn't want that power.

"It is a heavy burden," Thor said. "I wish it were not ours to place on you, or yours to bear."

A memory rose up in ABE's mind. "The day I met

you at Winterhaven house, you were shouting at someone before you came into the room. You were yelling at Odin, weren't you?"

Thor nodded. "I do not like that we gods cannot resolve this on our own."

"Wait," Pru said. "So the only reason you came back to Middleton was because you needed ABE?" Pru said. "You didn't think I—we—could help you find Loki. You just needed ABE here to pass judgment."

"None of this has any bearing on the here and now," Hilde said, interrupting. "We can wish forever that things were different. It changes nothing. Loki is caught. The boy must pass judgment."

All eyes turned to ABE.

He stared back at them, trembling. Why was he so scared? He knew Loki was guilty. Their investigation had proved it. But a lifetime of indecisiveness bore down on him. Why did *he* have to choose? What if he was wrong?

He shifted from foot to foot, and for once did not force himself to stop.

Could he refuse?

The thought came to him in a rush. What would that do to Odin's vision of the future? Would it change things? Maybe it would even stop Ragnarok!

As if he'd read ABE's mind, Thor spoke. "If we do not act, lad, the end will come now. You saw the giants and trolls rally to Loki's side. It was good fortune and the strength of Hilde's and my own arm that allowed us to escape with Loki from that cavern. If Loki goes free now, he will bring Ragnarok today."

"And if we imprison him?" ABE asked, seeking reassurance.

"The gods of Asgard existed for thousands of years before encountering your people in Midgard. Loki's imprisonment could last for thousands more. I do not know."

All they could hope for was time. *Always tomorrow. Never today.*

"Do it, ABE," Pru urged. "He's guilty. You know he is! Baldur said so. And think of what he did to you last year. He has to be stopped!"

"I know," ABE whispered.

"Then what say you, lad?" Thor asked in a low, somber voice, the last rumblings of a passing storm.

CHAPTER
31

"GUILTY."

ABE's judgment hung in the air. No other words were needed. Thor nodded, and ABE withdrew.

The rest of the journey passed in silence. Pru and ABE sat in the aft of the ship. They were too tired to talk.

Skidbladnir came to a rest against the cliffs alongside the Fort of the Fallen in Middleton. A walkway unfolded from its port side and settled on the grass outside the fort. Another time, ABE might have marveled at the ingenuity of the mechanism by which the walkway appeared. That night, he couldn't be bothered. He followed Pru off the ship. Grief left little room for long good-byes, and soon *Skidbladnir* sailed off into the night.

"It's done," ABE said.

Pru didn't say anything. She just limped toward home. ABE followed, thinking about how different things felt this time compared to their last homecoming. He soon learned how right he was.

They first realized something was wrong in the short stretch of road that connected the fort to the town. Pru walked with downcast eyes, so ABE was the first one to notice the flashlight beams crisscrossing through the woods. The voices came next, people calling his name and Pru's.

A flashlight blinded him, and he heard a voice he didn't recognize shouting "Here! Here, I've found them! Over here. They're okay!"

Almost instantly, he and Pru were surrounded by people asking if they'd been hurt. Someone put a blanket around ABE's shoulders and guided him and Pru to a fallen log, encouraging them to sit down.

Slowly, ABE's exhausted brain started to put together what had happened. Somewhere in their trek through the tunnels of Niflheim to the dwarvish city, they had crossed the boundary between Niflheim and Midgard. At that point, time had begun to pass normally. He and Pru had been gone from home all night and day. They'd returned somewhere in the early hours of the second night!

The town had organized a search to help find the two missing children. A part of ABE felt flattered. Mostly, though, he was embarrassed by all the attention.

More and more people gathered around them, checking on them and handing them water. ABE heard someone say they looked exhausted and dehydrated. He supposed they were. He found himself with a bottle of water in each hand and three more bottles on the ground at his feet. A drop of condensation rolled onto his hand from one of the bottles. It reminded him of standing before the windows at Winterhaven House. How many days ago had that been? Two? Three? So much had happened.

People stepped aside as a police car slowly pulled to a stop in front of them, its lights flashing but without the siren screeching. ABE thought he recognized the man who got out as Pru's dad's old partner. ABE's dad was with him.

"She's right here in front of me, Annie," Roger Lyons said in the cell phone he held to his ear. "ABE's with her. Yes, they both look fine. No, no. Don't come down. I'm going to bring them both to Middleton General, just to get checked out. Meet us there. Yes, I swear they look okay."

"ABE!" his dad said, grabbing him in a rough embrace. Was his dad crying? His dad never cried. ABE hadn't thought he knew how. "Are you okay?"

"I'm fine, Dad," ABE said. Somehow, his dad crying seemed more surreal than everything else that had happened since their journey to Niflheim.

People stepped back to give Mr. Lyons room to approach. ABE noticed Pru was still clutching Mister Fox's looking glass. He thought for a moment that perhaps he should hide it, but then realized that nobody except Pru and him could see it, anyway.

Mr. Lyons knelt down in front of them. "You two gave us a scare. Are you okay?"

ABE waited for Pru to answer. She just stared ahead.

"We're okay, sir," ABE said. "Sorry to scare you."

Mr. Lyons's worried eyes lingered on Pru a moment before focusing on ABE. "What happened, son? Did you get lost?"

Lost? It made as much sense as anything. Everyone knew he and Pru went for hikes in the woods.

"Yeah. We, um, we went out for a hike. We must have gotten turned around or something. We lost the trail. Then we just seemed to get farther and farther from town. I think Pru sprained her ankle." ABE looked at Pru, realizing that he needed to say something to explain how upset she was. "Pru realized at one point that she'd dropped her dad's badge. She got really upset. We tried to find it. We looked everywhere."

At the mention of her father's badge, Pru convulsed. ABE realized that she was crying silently.

"Oh . . . oh, hey, kiddo, it's okay. It's okay." Roger put his arms around Pru. "It's just a thing. Your dad is still with you. He'll always be with you."

ABE bowed his head. He wasn't sure he'd be able to explain why his eyes were also filled with tears.

CHAPTER
32

ABE'S PARENTS KEPT HIM HOME FROM SCHOOL THE NEXT DAY SO HE COULD rest. When he returned to class the day after, Pru was still absent. When school ended, he went to her house to check in on her.

Pru's mother answered the door when he knocked. She must have taken the day off work.

"Hi, Mrs. Potts. I don't mean to bother you. I just wanted to see how Pru was doing."

"No bother, ABE. I'm glad to see you. Come in." Mrs. Potts stepped aside so ABE could pass.

"Thanks."

"I was actually thinking about calling to see if you'd be willing to come by. Pru's been so upset since getting lost. She barely leaves her room. She hasn't cried like this since her dad. I didn't realize losing his badge would hit her so hard. I think it's just opening up old wounds."

"Yeah. I think loss is hard for Pru."

"You're a good friend, ABE." Mrs. Potts ruffled his hair. "Go on up. I don't know if she wants company. But if she'll see anyone, it will be you."

ABE nodded and made his way to Pru's door.

"I'm not really in the mood to talk right now, Mom," Pru said when he knocked.

"It's, uh, not your mom. It's me. ABE."

"Come in." Pru sat on her bed, propped up by pillows. Mister Fox's looking glass lay beside her. Next to it sat the card she'd received last year, the one that had begun their adventure. It seemed appropriate to have it there, now, at the adventure's end.

"Hey." ABE stood awkwardly by the door. For the past couple of days, he'd wished he'd had someone to talk to about Mister Fox's death. Now, though, he wasn't sure what to say. In the end, he said the only thing he could think of. "I miss him, too."

Pru turned to the window. ABE looked down at his feet. Neither of them spoke for a while.

"He knew it was going to happen, you know."

ABE looked up, startled. "What? Who?"

"Mister Fox. He knew he was going to die."

"*What?*"

"I kept thinking about what he said before the end. Remember? He gave me his looking glass and said I'd know what to do with it. I kept thinking about that. Then I realized I *did* know what to do with it."

Pru held the looking glass out so the mirrored side faced ABE. He stepped forward.

"*Pokazhi*," she said.

Mister Fox's face swam into view in the looking glass. He sat in the Henhouse's library, below the painting of Baba Yaga. For a startled, wonderful moment, ABE thought the detective was calling them, that he had cheated death and that the fox was in the Henhouse once more.

Then what Pru had said sank in. Mister Fox wasn't calling them. The detective had recorded a message on his looking glass the same way ABE had recorded an image of the torchlight. Pru had used the word to summon the image.

"Pru, ABE, if you're watching this, then that means I'm already dead." Mister Fox leaned back in his chair. He offered them his last lopsided grin. "Well, that's morbid, isn't it? Still, you can't say it's inappropriate. I mean, I do live in a house in a graveyard, surrounded by countless household spirits. Death has been waiting for me for a while, I think."

Pru choked back a sob. ABE wondered how many times she'd watched this.

"First things first," the memory of Mister Fox continued. "You two need an explanation. I suspect you're wondering how I could know to send you a message from beyond the grave. It was the Eye of Odin. Do you remember when ABE handed it to me in the cemetery last year? I made the mistake of looking at it. *Into it.* And it looked into me. It showed me the future, my future. It showed me my death.

"The images were quick—scattered flashes across my mind. I saw Loki, captured. I saw a battle in a cavern, an escape onto a ledge. I saw Pru, nearly getting crushed. And I saw . . . well, you know what I saw. If you're watching this, then you saw it, too. And I'm sorry for that. I truly am. I thought . . . I thought perhaps that I could change things. I thought . . .

"That doesn't matter now. What matters now is you two. My story is done, but yours is just starting. Make the stories of your lives be fantastic. Because you two, you're brilliant. It's been the joy of my life to work with Fibbers like you. Because there's one thing so many myths, so many stories get wrong. So often, they tell you that the heroes are special because they're born with some power or because they're from some special lineage. That's not so. True heroes are special because of what they *choose* to do, not what they were born to do. They're special because they're brave, and kind, and clever. You two are those things, and more. You're unbelievable."

In the image, Mister Fox stood, and ABE realized a *domovoi* must have been holding the looking glass, because the view followed Mister Fox as he donned his coat and hat.

"We've arrived in Norway, the *domovye* tell me. You two are miles away yet. Thor and Hilde are on their way to meet me with *Skidbladnir*. It's a flying ship. How fantastic is that?"

The childlike delight that showed in Mister Fox's eyes whenever he was exposed to magic shone brightly as he strode through the Henhouse, down the long hallway of doors that led from the inner courtyard to the exit.

"What's coming next will be hard for all of us. Don't worry about me. I've had a good life. A long one. I've seen wonders most people can't even imagine. And, one could argue, the greatest mystery lies before me. One last question to answer. So don't worry. Be strong. The monsters may be out there, they may be coming, but it's like I told you once before, Pru. There are things that make the monsters worth facing. Traveling houses. Talking squirrels. Brave companions."

Mister Fox paused before the final door of the Henhouse. He looked directly into the glass.

"And you two, Pru and ABE, are among the bravest and the best. Good-bye."

With that, the final door to the Henhouse opened, and Mister Fox stepped out into the light.

"He's gone," ABE said as the image in the glass faded. Tears rolled down his cheeks. "He's really gone."

"That's how come he didn't want to join the search for Loki," Pru said. "He knew what would happen if we found him."

"It explains why he was so desperate to believe Odin could be wrong, too. It wasn't about wanting Loki to be innocent, not really. Or at least not completely. It was about wanting to believe that he could change his fate."

"But he couldn't. And he *knew* that when he came to get us in Norway. But he came anyway."

"To save us," ABE said. Every moment he'd ever doubted the detective came crashing down on him. The guilt threatened to bury him.

"I think I'm going to lie down now," Pru said. "I'll talk to you later. Okay?"

"Yeah. Okay."

Pru returned the looking glass to its spot on the bed beside the card. The side of the card with Mister Fox's handwritten note lay faceup: *Be grave in your search, and avoid having stones in your head.*

That clue had led him and Pru to the cemetery. As he walked home alone, ABE hoped that, wherever he was, Mister Fox was resting in peace.

CHAPTER
33

THAT NIGHT ABE HAD A DREAM.

Or maybe it was a nightmare.

ABE stood once more in the hall of the Palace of the Dead. Baldur was gone. Only the queen remained, perched on her throne.

"You disappoint me, young hero," she said.

"Sorry." ABE ducked his head. Was this just a dream? Or was it another message?

"Are you? Then return to me."

"Um . . . I don't think I can do that."

The queen stood and vanished. ABE took a step back, startled. When he did, he backed into something—or *someone*.

The queen's shriveled right hand settled on his

shoulder from behind. Her dark fingers curled in a vise-like grip, and ABE's skin crawled at the frigid touch. Breath heavy with the scent of rotten things touched his left ear as the queen's voice—the awful, scuttling voice—whispered, "You cheated me. You *stole* from me."

ABE pressed his eyes closed.

"I know. And . . . I'm sorry. I really am. I mean, I know you tried to trick us and everything. But . . . but it was a good trick. And a fair one. We just *couldn't* stay." The funny thing was, he meant what he said. He hadn't liked the outcome, but he had to admire the way the queen had outsmarted them with words.

The pressure vanished from ABE's shoulder. He slowly opened his eyes. The queen sat on her throne once more. Her burning eye held his gaze.

"You speak the truth," she said in her honeyed voice.

ABE swallowed and nodded.

"What a curious thing." The queen folded her hands on her lap. "So be it. Your debt is paid."

"What?"

"I accept this truth as payment. Three truths given, three returned. You and your friend are free of any obligation to me."

"Really? That's . . . wow. Thank you!"

The queen inclined her head. "But you may still

return, if you wish. I would give you a place of honor here, young hero. I think it would surprise you to know that there are some who hunger for my attention."

ABE looked upon the two aspects of death, the beautiful and the terrible, and he felt fear, yes, but comfort, too.

"No. No, I don't think it would surprise me," he said.

The Queen of the Dead raised her eyebrow.

"Another truth. And a kindness. Two things that are rarely given freely, and two things I have known little of. Very well, young hero, I will not be found wanting. Let there be a balance. In kindness, I shall return to you something you lost while in my realm. For the truth you may ask me one question. I will answer it as best as I am able."

"That's very kind," ABE said. "But I'm not sure I have any questions left. Well, wait. Actually, there is one thing I still don't know. If Loki didn't give you the riddle to send to me . . . then who did?"

"Odin," the queen said.

"Odin? I don't understand. Why would Odin send me the message?"

The queen smiled. "I offered you a truth, young hero. I said nothing of the gift of understanding. One does have a reputation to maintain. Farewell."

CHAPTER
34

ABE WAS PLEASED WHEN PRU RETURNED TO SCHOOL THE NEXT DAY. SHE returned physically, anyway. Mentally, she still seemed absent as she went through the motions of the day, lost in her grief.

The other kids mostly avoided them as they walked through the halls. ABE was used to that, though. What he didn't expect were the glances people kept shooting them and the half-heard whispers that carried to his ears. Apparently, his and Pru's disappearance had been the subject of a fair amount of talk. He learned how true that was at the end of the day.

When the bell announced that language arts was over, Mr. Jeffries asked if he could have a word with ABE. Pru said she'd wait for him outside the school.

"ABE," Mr. Jeffries said after she'd left, "I just want to say first of all how glad I am that you and Pru are okay. We were all very worried about you here. Every teacher in the school was out looking for you two."

"I really appreciate that. I know Pru does, too."

"Actually, ABE, it's Pru I wanted to talk to you about. I know that Pru has had a difficult time the last few years. I heard the story about her father's death. It's no wonder that she's been in so much trouble in school. I'm sure she's a good kid. I don't think there are any bad kids. But you're a good kid, too, ABE. Everyone around here says so. Now, I don't know what you and Pru were doing out there in the woods the other day—"

"We just got lost—"

"I know, I know." Mr. Jeffries held up his hands in a placating gesture. "I'm just saying, I'd hate to see you get wrapped up in anything bad, ABE, just because your friends don't always make good decisions. I'm sure you know what I mean."

He did know what Mr. Jeffries meant. And he'd had enough.

"You're wrong," he said.

"Excuse me?"

"You're wrong. And . . ." ABE struggled for words. Pru always made defying authority look so easy. What would she say in his place? "And, sorry, but you're being a jerk."

"Excuse me?"

"Sorry!" ABE winced. "Well, mostly. I know you're not really a jerk. I actually think you're really nice most of the time. And I really like your class. But you're wrong about Pru."

Mr. Jeffries leaned back in his chair and studied ABE. "Okay. I'm listening, ABE. Tell me why you think I'm being unfair to Pru."

ABE took a deep breath. "Ever since school started, you've been suspicious of her. I've seen it. She's seen it. But you haven't really taken the time to get to know her. You made up your mind about her before you even spent time with her. You heard all Mrs. Edleman's stories about how she was a troublemaker, and you let that affect how you thought of her. So every time something bad happened, you assumed she did it and . . ."

ABE stopped, frowning.

"And?" Mr. Jeffries prompted.

"Huh?" ABE blinked. He'd forgotten for a moment that Mr. Jeffries was there. "Um, sorry, Mr. Jeffries, but can I go? I'm sorry I called you a jerk. I am. I'm just . . . it's been a hard week. But I do think you're not being fair to Pru."

Mr. Jeffries was quiet just long enough that ABE began to worry he'd gone too far.

"Okay, ABE. You can go. I accept your apology. And . . . I'll think about what you said."

"Thanks," ABE said. Then he left the room at a near run. He didn't slow down until he'd found Pru outside the school.

"Pru, we have to go to Winterhaven House."

"What? Why?"

"I'll explain when we get there. *Please*, Pru. It's important!"

CHAPTER
35

WINTERHAVEN HOUSE LAY IN RUINS WHEN ABE AND PRU ARRIVED A SHORT
time later. News reports after the trolls' attack had
claimed that the devastation was caused by a gas leak
and explosion. Reporters had celebrated the fact that
no one had been hurt or killed. Mister Fox would have
called it a reasonable explanation.

People saw what they wanted to see, and they didn't
see what they didn't want to.

They entered the remains of the mansion unchal-
lenged and made their way to the long room where
they'd twice met with Odin. The room was empty.
The table had been shattered. No fire burned in the
fireplace.

A huge hole gaped in the room's eastern wall, and

through it ABE saw a short scruff of land that ended in a cliff overlooking the ocean. A single figure stood on the cliff, leaning heavily against a staff. He wore a blue cloak and a broad-rimmed hat. Two ravens circled overhead.

"I've been expecting you," Odin said, staring out at the sea as they approached. "You have a question, boy, yes?"

"Well, yeah. Actually, I do. I've been thinking about Loki—"

"ABE," Pru interrupted, rousing herself from her grief. "I don't want to talk about Loki."

"I know, Pru, but we have to. *I* have to. I got into a little argument with Mr. Jeffries just now. I told him I thought it was so unfair that he made his mind up about you because of things Mrs. Edleman told him. It made me so angry that one person would judge another based on stories they'd heard. But then I realized something. That's just what I'd done—it's just what everyone's done—to Loki."

"Loki is, was, and must ever be evil," Odin said.

"But did it have to be that way?" ABE asked. "I know Loki did terrible things. But people saw him as the bad guy even before he did anything bad. They judged him because of the stories you told. You didn't just let the future happen. You nudged it along by making everyone hate Loki. He told us once how hard it was for him living in Asgard. I don't think he was lying about that. It's almost like you wanted to turn Loki into a villain. But why would you do that, unless . . ."

And, just like that, ABE knew the answer.

"You *wanted* this to happen. Didn't you?"

"What did I want to happen, boy?" Odin challenged.

"This, all of this. I don't know why . . . but it's the only thing that makes sense. You *want* Ragnarok to happen."

"ABE, that's nuts," Pru said. "He dies in Ragnarok. Everyone dies. Why would he want that?"

"Why wouldn't I?"

Slowly, Odin lifted his head enough to peer at them beneath the rim of his hat.

"You pitiful insects. You presume to understand the mind of a god?" Odin slammed his walking stick on the ground. "What do *you* know of the future? Do you think that because you glimpsed a vision in my Eye that you know something of what *I* know? Bah! Your mortal minds could not begin to understand! You saw a hint of the future. Moments. A blink of the Eye. I did not see *the* future. *I saw every future!*"

"What?" ABE asked, stunned.

"I saw *every* future. When I drank from the Well of Wisdom, every possible outcome of every event was laid before me like the infinite branching of Yggdrasil's roots. Each branch represented a different

271

possibility, a different future. *And I saw them all!* Can your tiny human mind begin to imagine what that meant to me, Odin—god of wisdom, seeker of knowledge—to suddenly know *all* things?"

"But . . . if you saw a lot of futures . . . then that means you chose which stories to tell," Pru said. "You chose the future you wanted. ABE was right. You wanted all of this to happen!"

"But you'll die," ABE repeated, staring at Odin. *"Everyone dies."*

"Yes! I will die. Finally! I will die leading the gods of the north in a final, triumphant battle in which evil will be vanquished from the world. They will sing songs of my sacrifice and my triumph until the end of time!"

"You're insane!" ABE said, shaking his head in disbelief.

"No, boy. *I'M BORED!* Your mortal mind cannot conceive my burden. You cannot imagine what it is to be a god of wisdom, always craving knowledge, always seeking answers . . . and then, in one moment, to have all knowledge given to you with one sip from an enchanted well. No more seeking, no more learning. No more questions. Just an eternity of days, *which you have already lived.* No more!"

Odin threw wide his cloak and stood at his full height. He towered above them, casting off the illusion of the tired, world-weary old man.

"Let the god of wisdom die. Let me be Odin, god of war! Father of battles! Odin, the Warrior! Odin, the Terrible! Let the ax age begin! The wolf age! Let the age of blood and battle and death begin!"

ABE and Pru staggered back, cowed by the awesome figure before them.

"You cannot imagine how long I have had to wait for this or how carefully I have planned. I have manipulated each choice and navigated each branch of the future with more skill than that miserable squirrel navigated the branches of Yggdrasil. It began with him, of course. I let him see me bury what you called the Middleton Stone. I knew the wretched rodent was so desperate for attention that he would tell Loki where it was hidden. I used Ratatosk and the stone as bait to lure Loki here to this town so he could meet the two of you."

"But why *us*?" ABE asked.

"When I drank from the Well of Wisdom and had my future—all my futures—stolen from me, I knew that my only redemption would be to die in honor and glory as befits a god of war. And I knew that the only villain worthy of me was Loki. So I turned everyone against him by sharing my visions of his evil deeds. But that was not enough. I knew that for Loki to become the villain I needed, I had to turn him against Asgard. To do that, I needed him to suffer. I needed him punished."

"But you couldn't punish him," Pru said. "Thor told us so. No one in Asgard could punish Loki because you and he were blood brothers."

"Yes. It was a foolish indiscretion of my youth, but it was also an oath I could not break. The magic was too strong. No one in Asgard could punish Loki. So I needed a judge who was not from Asgard. I scanned my memories of the futures I'd seen, searching for the right mortal pawns. They had to be clever enough to keep the Eye from Loki, but easy enough to manipulate into condemning him when the time came."

ABE expected outrage from Pru. Instead, she spoke in a monotone. "You used us," she said. Her shoulders slumped.

"And you both played your parts perfectly," Odin said. "I hid the so-called Middleton Stone here so Loki would follow and cross paths with you both. I saw that he would abduct the boy and that, when the time came, the boy would judge him guilty. Of course, to condemn Loki, you first had to find him."

Odin spun in place, sweeping his cloak about him. By the time he completed his spin, Odin, Allfather of the gods, did not stand before them.

Fadir did.

"It was you?" ABE said. He'd completely forgotten that Odin had the ability to change his shape, as he had in the myth about the Mead of Poetry.

"Of course. Did you truly think it was luck you met a dwarf in the caverns of Niflheim that led you, by chance, to Loki? There is no chance."

"Only fate," ABE said, finishing the now familiar refrain.

"Only *me*," Odin corrected.

Another spin and Odin stood before them once more.

"But take comfort, children. You may disagree with my actions and my motives, but in the end I was right. Perhaps I was hard on Loki. Still, he showed his true colors at the last. He committed an unforgivable act. He killed my son and proved himself the villain. And now you have ensured his just imprisonment. You are heroes."

Were they? ABE didn't feel like a hero. Did Loki's crime justify Odin's cruelty to him? Or did Odin's manipulations *make* Loki commit the crime? Who was the villain? And did it even matter anymore?

ABE had so many questions left in his head.

Pru, it seemed, just had one.

"Why?"

She appeared a bit more alert as ABE turned to look at her.

"Why what?" he asked.

"Nothing. It doesn't matter." Pru's eyes once more lost focus as she retreated.

"No, really. What did you mean?" ABE asked, eager to keep Pru present in the moment.

"I understand that Odin manipulated Loki. But Loki never wanted to be the villain. What changed his mind? *Why* did Loki kill Baldur? It's the one thing we never figured out. We were looking for motive and opportunity. We found out that Loki had the opportunity to kill Baldur. He was in the right place at the right time. But we never established a motive." She shook her head. "Never mind. Who cares? It doesn't matter now."

ABE frowned as Pru turned away.

Why *had* Loki done it? They knew he was guilty. Baldur had told them so.

Except he *hadn't* exactly. He'd said the trickster had killed him. Why had he phrased it like that? Things had been so crazy since their interview with Baldur that ABE hadn't given the god's choice of words any thought. But why hadn't he just indicated Loki by name?

He supposed Pru was right and it didn't matter. Everyone knew Loki was the trickster.

In short, avoid assumptions. They're just beliefs in different clothes. Mister Fox's words echoed in ABE's memory.

But Loki *was* the trickster. He fit the definition perfectly. ABE should know. He'd just defined the trickster figure for Pru a few days ago: Trickster figures are usually able to change their shape. They're also usually greedy. That greed can drive them to cause trouble, but sometimes their actions can bring about good things and be a boon to people, too.

ABE gasped!

Pru looked at him, but without any real interest. It was Odin who spoke.

"Have you figured it out at last? You were close before. I'll grant you that. You figured out that *truth-teller* referred to me. But you never quite got the answer to my riddle right. You see it now, though, don't you? *When is a truth-teller not telling the truth?*"

"When he's a trickster," ABE said as the truth delivered its crushing blow.

The definition of a trickster fit Loki perfectly. But it fit Odin, too. The clues to the riddle were in the myths. Odin had changed his shape in the myth about the Mead of Poetry. *And* he shared the mead with people and gods alike—so his greed also resulted in gifts for humankind.

"It was you. *You killed Baldur!*"

"I did what had to be done."

ABE paled as the horror of the act sank in. *Filicide*, the deliberate act of a parent killing her or his child. It was a definition ABE wished he didn't know.

"But . . . but I don't understand," ABE stammered. "We talked to Baldur. Why didn't he just tell us it was you?"

"My doing, I'm afraid. I foresaw your interview with my son in the Palace of the Dead. I knew you would ask him who killed him. So I whispered a charm in my son's ear at his funeral. It prevented him from naming me as his killer, even in death. Of course, your bargain with the queen forced him to answer your question truthfully. A difficult position. So my son gave the only answer he could. He spoke the truth, but not the complete truth. Not a lie, either. Something in between." Odin's eye shone wickedly. "A fib, shall we say?"

"Don't you *dare!*" Her fists clenched at her sides, Pru glared at Odin. "Don't you dare even talk about him!"

"No . . . but . . . this doesn't make sense!" ABE insisted, hands digging through his hair. He didn't want it to make sense! But it did—all of it, and more. ABE could see everything now. Odin hadn't just had motive—he'd had opportunity, too. He'd *created* opportunity. The myths had offered more clues. Odin had cast the charms that had made Breidablik a safe haven. Of course he was able to bypass them. And Odin had allowed mistletoe to be the one thing that could hurt Baldur. It had been such an obvious oversight! But no one had looked too closely at the holes in the myths because everyone had always assumed Loki was the villain of the story.

Still, ABE didn't understand one thing. "The riddle basically tells us you're the killer. But *you* sent the riddle. Why would you do that?"

"Because my one regret has always been that Loki would be remembered as the clever one. Evil, yes. But clever. But now we know the truth, don't we? You once boasted to Loki, child, that while he was the Lord of Lies, you were the better Fibber. Perhaps so. But now we three know the truth. I outsmarted you, your mentor, *and* clever Loki."

Odin stood straight and tall. All doubt had long since vanished from the god's face. He lifted his chin proudly and stared down at them with his one eye and singular vision.

"I tricked you all."

CHAPTER
36

"SO YOU TRICKED US," PRU SPAT. HER DETACHMENT WAS GONE. HER EYES burned with fury. "But you killed your son. *Your son!* And you're *proud* of it! *You're a monster!*"

"MY SON WAS ALREADY DEAD! He died the day I drank from the Well of Wisdom. I watched him die. I watched *everyone* die. Do you understand? *You're all already dead.*" Odin snorted with contempt. "You just don't know it yet."

"We'll stop you," ABE said. He wondered if the words sounded as clichéd and hollow to the others as they did to him.

"Will you?" Odin laughed. "And how will you do that?"

"We'll tell Thor," Pru said. "And the other gods."

"They would not believe you. Besides, you will not get the chance. The gods will no more return to Midgard. Even my errant son, Thor, has learned his place. And you have no means to get to Asgard. Your mentor is dead. So is the rodent you called friend."

"Ratatosk is dead?" Pru took a wounded step back.

"Garm's most recent prey."

"All these deaths," ABE said, trying not to imagine poor Ratatosk in Garm's jaws. "Pru's right. You *are* a monster."

"Worse," Pru said. "You're a coward!"

Odin swung his walking stick through the air. Midswing, it became a vicious-looking spear, its blade glinting in the sun. It hung in the air between them.

"I could kill you. Sometimes I do, you know." Odin's eye took on a faraway look. "But I think I will not be so kind. I will leave you with the greatest curse I know. You will live on with your knowledge of what is to come. Let us see if you bear that burden better than I."

Odin turned his back on them. He whispered something ABE didn't understand, and a curtain of light appeared before him—Bifrost, the rainbow bridge that led to Asgard.

"Your part in this is done, children. Be grateful that your lives have been so touched by greatness. Farewell."

Odin stepped into the light and vanished.

ABE dropped to his knees. "What have I done? I condemned Loki. He was innocent."

Pru spun to face the ocean and hugged her arms to her chest. Her shoulders shook.

"We have to do something," he said. "Pru?"

She remained silent.

"Pru!"

"What can we do, ABE?" Her face was wet with tears when she turned to look at him. "Mister Fox is dead. Ratatosk is dead. Odin's right. We lost."

"We could try . . ."

"*Try what?* He's seen the future, ABE. He's seen *every* future! He'd know everything we did before we did it. He's unstoppable."

He didn't want her to be right. He didn't want to be Odin's pawn. Mister Fox had said nothing was worse than letting someone else choose your role for you. But Odin had chosen everyone's roles—and he'd gotten away with it.

Now Ratatosk and Mister Fox were dead and gone forever, and nothing, *nothing* could ever change that.

Or so he thought.

"No, no, no!" a high-pitched voice behind him said.

ABE rose and spun around in one fluid motion, not quite daring to believe his ears. A small, rough-looking gray squirrel with a notch in his left ear sat on the ground a few feet away.

"Ratatosk!" Pru cried. She ran forward as the squirrel bounded to her. She skidded to her knees and Ratatosk jumped into her lap. "But . . . how? Odin said you were dead!"

"Almost was, yes! Might have been! Garm had me in his teeth. Everything went black. Then . . . I opened my eyes in the Queen of the Dead's palace. The queen gave me safe passage from Niflheim! Strange, yes? Bewildering! Incomprehensible!"

"A kindness," ABE whispered, remembering his dream and the queen's words. "She said she would return something we'd lost."

"What?" Pru said, glancing up at him.

"It's not important. I'll explain later. What matters now is that Ratatosk's back! But what I don't get is how."

"Who cares? It doesn't matter. All that matters is that he *is* back. He's not dead." Pru scratched Ratatosk's nose and the squirrel chittered happily.

ABE shook his head, though Pru wasn't paying any attention to him.

It did matter. Didn't it?

Odin could see the future. He should have known that Ratatosk would come back. Unless . . . What if he could see the future . . . but he wasn't *looking*?

"Pru, do you remember when Odin told us the story of how the Eye of Odin came to be? He said that when he went to the Well of Wisdom, he went in a disguise and the guardian didn't recognize him."

"I remember." Pru didn't look up. She merely shifted her attention from Ratatosk's nose to scratching behind his ear. "So what?"

"You joked that the guardian wasn't very good at his job if he was so easily fooled. I remember because Odin got defensive. He said the guardian was farseeing. He told *us* to try looking out at a beach sometime and seeing every grain of sand at once."

"So?"

"Well, maybe Odin got defensive because he has the same problem the guardian did. Odin saw so many futures. He's farseeing. But maybe he can't see every grain of sand at once. Maybe he can't keep all those futures straight in his head." ABE spoke quickly, unable to contain his excitement. "Don't you see? Ratatosk is alive. That means Odin can be wrong! He doesn't know everything."

Pru stopped scratching Ratatosk's head and chewed her lip. "Maybe . . ." she agreed.

Ratatosk cleared his throat and nudged Pru's hand. She smiled at the squirrel and stood, placing Ratatosk on her shoulder.

"Maybe you're right, ABE. And maybe it's important. But I don't want to think about it right now. Everything went so wrong. And Mister Fox . . . Look,

I'm tired. I just want to be glad Ratatosk is alive. I'm going to take him home and let him rest. Okay?"

ABE nodded. This wasn't the time to push Pru. She'd be ready to talk soon enough. Then he could explain why he was so excited. It could wait until tomorrow.

Tomorrow. It was such a simple word. But, really, it was the most important word.

We all hope for more time.

That's what Alva had said when she'd defended the gods and their failure to act on the day of Baldur's death. But the gods weren't the only ones guilty of taking tomorrow for granted. ABE had done it, too.

It had been the worst part about learning that Ragnarok was coming. Ragnarok meant an end to all tomorrows. But if Odin could be wrong about Ratatosk, maybe he could be wrong about Ragnarok, too.

Maybe. *Possibly.* It wasn't certain.

But that was the point, wasn't it?

ABE didn't know what would happen next. So many questions remained. Everything seemed so uncertain. But somehow, that uncertainty suddenly felt like a victory. Odin had wanted them to believe that he had all the answers, that the future was sure and set. That wasn't true. Uncertainty survived—and with it the magic of possibility.

They'd lost so much. Now, though, ABE felt like they had won back tomorrow.

ABE closed his eyes and pictured Mister Fox, knowing he'd never see the detective again, except perhaps as a ghost in the looking glass. He felt a rush of sorrow, but he also felt gratitude and a deeper appreciation for the detective as—for the first time—he truly understood why Mister Fox had been such a champion of uncertainty.

Sometimes it really was okay not to know.

And, with that realization, ABE discovered the answer to another question, one he had nearly forgotten. He had one last battle to fight that day.

CHAPTER
37

ABE FOUND HIS DAD TINKERING WITH THE LAWN MOWER WHEN HE RETURNED home.

"What happened?" ABE asked.

"The front wheel cracked," his dad said. "Must have been a rock or something. I pulled this replacement off the old mower in the shed. It's not a perfect fit, but I think it will do for now. Hand me that wrench?"

"Sure." ABE crouched down beside his dad. "Can we talk for a minute?"

"You bet." His dad gave a final twist to the bolt that secured the wheel, then settled back against the front step. "What's up?"

"I kind of wanted to talk to you about Danny. He's that kid who was on the bike the other day."

"I remember. What's wrong? Is he still giving you a hard time?"

"No. Well, actually, yeah. But that doesn't matter."

"It *does* matter, ABE. You can't just let people—"

"No, Dad, wait, okay? Just listen."

His dad opened his mouth, then closed it without saying a word. He nodded.

"Danny can be a jerk. But he's not the problem."

"He's not? Who is, then? Who's giving you a hard time?"

"That's just it. *You* are, Dad."

"Me?"

"Yeah. I mean, I know you're trying to help. I do. I know you don't like the idea that Danny is picking on me. But it's like I said. Danny can be a jerk. So why should I care what a jerk thinks of me? And the thing is, I don't. I do care what *you* think of me, though."

"ABE, you're my son. I love you."

"I know. But . . . but I want you to understand me, too. I heard you tell Mom that I don't stand up for myself."

"Oh, hey, ABE, I'm sorry." His dad blushed. "I didn't mean for you to hear that."

"No. It's okay. See, I've been thinking about it and you're right. I don't stand up for myself a lot. For a while, I wondered if it was because I was scared. But you know what, Dad? I'm not. I mean, I do get scared,

288

obviously. But I don't let that stop me. So I kept thinking about why I don't stand up for myself as much as I stand up for my friends."

"Oh? And did you come up with anything?"

"Yeah. Yeah, actually, I did. I think the reason I don't stand up for myself is because I'm still figuring *me* out. I mean, how do you stand up for yourself if you don't really know who you are yet? I'm still working on that. But that's okay. I mean, it's okay with me anyway. I've known a lot of people lately who have had other people tell them who they should be, or how they should act. That hasn't really worked too well for anyone."

ABE fell silent.

"I'll tell you this, ABE," his dad said. "Pru's mom got one thing right, that's for sure."

Were they talking about Pru now? ABE's shoulders sagged.

"You are one smart kid."

"Oh!" ABE smiled. "Ah, thanks."

"You're welcome." His dad grabbed a rag and began to wipe some grease from his hand. "So listen. I know you and Pru like to go hiking. I did a lot of hiking in college. I learned a few things about following trails and wilderness survival. I was thinking maybe this weekend you and I could go out. If you'd like that, I mean."

"Really? Yeah! I think that would be great."

"Great." His dad stood. "I'm going to head in and wash up. You should probably get started on homework. After all, tomorrow is another day."

ABE stood, too.

"Yeah," he said, smiling. "Yeah, it really is."

ACKNOWLEDGMENTS

I have to start by thanking the fantastic group at Algonquin Young Readers: my editors, Elise Howard and Krestyna Lypen; the amazing group of marketers and publicists I worked with, including Brooke Csuka, Eileen Lawrence, and Trevor Ingerson; and my copy editors, Robin Cruise and Brunson Hoole. Their knowledge of and delight in children's literature, and their passion for getting books in the hands of young readers, was inspiring every step along the way.

I'd also like to thank Tarana Akhmedova, Andrea Lanoux, and Irina Shchemeleva for their help with the Russian terms in the book. ABE and Pru would still be wandering around in the dark without their help (and so would I).

Finally, I'd like to thank my critique group—Jane LeGrow (who also plays the part of my wife), Frances Kelley Prescott, Joan Domin, and Karen Lindeborg— for their support. I would also like to thank (belatedly) Sara Neilson, who was a reader for book 1 that I failed to thank (despite being thankful!).

And, of course, I'm grateful to everyone who has read (and hopefully enjoyed!) the Unbelievable FIB books. You are all Fibbers of the highest caliber.

Adam Shaughnessy is an author and educator. He received his BA in English from Connecticut College and is currently pursuing his MA in children's literature from Hollins University. Adam lives in Waterford, Connecticut. *Over the Underworld* is the second book in the Unbelievable FIB series. Visit him online at adamshaughnessy.com, or on Facebook (Adam Shaughnessy—Author) or Twitter (@adamshaughnessy).

STAY UNTIL
TOMORROW

Other Books by Anne Maybury
in Thorndike Large Print

The Brides of Bellenmore
Falcon's Shadow
The House of Fand
Whisper in the Dark
Someone Waiting

STAY UNTIL
TOMORROW

I

Walking down the aircraft steps from the plane, Anna found herself clinging with her free hand to the rail as though it were her last link with her old life.

She glanced up at the racing, cumulus clouds of an April shower, then around at the straggling airport buildings, the distant lines of red brick villas.

Nothing is changed. It's just as I remember it when I was at school here! Just as I remember it – and yet I'm a stranger!

She turned quickly and glanced at the man by her side, meeting his fine, Indian-dark eyes, his reassuring smile. His hand touched her arm lightly:

"It's all right, Anna!"

Ever since she was a little girl, Aidan could give her back her confidence at times when she was most near losing it. Yet, just this once, he could not dispel the sudden icy premonition that shivered through her.

She said aloud to comfort herself:

"Martin will be wondering what happened to the plane. We're very late!"

Aidan laughed. "I doubt if he would expect a plane from Delhi to London to arrive at a split second's timing. It was a long journey."

"It was a *lovely* journey!"

"When we were last together here at London Airport, you'd left school and were going home. Remember?"

"Yes." She was walking quickly now towards the great building and the memory of her dismay those six years ago at the thought of saying goodbye to Aidan was still poignant. He had been remaining as house surgeon in a hospital; she was returning to India for good.

He had just asked, "Remember?" As though you ever forgot those heartbreaking moments of girlhood when you believed love was going out of your life forever!

Aidan had taken both her hands saying:

"Goodbye, Anna. We'll be meeting when I return to Delhi." And she had wanted to cry:

"Don't let any other woman take you away from me!"

But it would have been no use, for the love

8

was all on her side. Aidan had given her friendship and it had been a wonderful thing but she had slowly faced the fact that that was all she would ever receive from him. . . .

And now, walking by his side in a swinging, shaggy cream coat and no hat on her blue-black hair, Anna was going to meet the man she was to marry.

Somewhere in that vast airport building centered in a star pattern of runways, Martin would be waiting for her.

So why was she afraid?

Because she knew she had come expecting too much? Wanting everything perfect? Wanting Martin's family to love her, to merge herself into the English scene as though she belonged here? Well, her mother was English, so why be so afraid she would fail?

She glanced at Aidan and saw only his profile, strong and remote, unusually aesthetic for someone so young, and yet warmly familiar to her. . . .

She thought: *he's half Indian, and yet I'm closer to him than to anyone else . . . except, of course, Martin. . . .*

The difference of blood was, perhaps, less important than environment. She was all Western, with an English mother, an unknown French father and a wise and brilliant Hindu surgeon for her stepfather; India had been her home all her life and its peoples her people by virtue of her love and understanding of them.

But she was in England now, for good, and it would be easy, it *must* be easy, to adapt herself to people who were, after all, hers by the relationship of "blood." She had found it easy at school, so why be afraid now?

Because six years of life in Delhi and Kashmir lay between then and now!

She found herself suddenly swept into a throng of people and there was no longer space in her mind for nostalgia.

Officials and travelers surrounded her; questions and answers; the thud of luggage; the click of locks being snapped open and through the Customs at last. Then, beyond the airport barrier that divides the stateless zone of the skies from the passport-ridden earth, Anna saw Martin.

Her heart rose. She walked in a strange, winged dream towards him, not taking her eyes from his face. He had seen her and his expression lit up. Then he looked from her to the man by her side and she had time to note the shadow that drew his brows together.

He might have shouted his thoughts across to her, so clearly did she know them. Must he be by her side even here? That man, Aidan Narayan?

Anna went the last few yards towards Martin in a little rush, arms encumbered by fur coat, handbag, books, but hands reaching for him. He looked again at her and the frown cleared. She saw the steady flame in his eyes as his head bent to her.

"Anna!" He took both her hands and kissed her. "Oh, Anna, this is good!"

He held her a little away from him and looked at her as though he were corroborating the memory of her which he had been holding closely during the six months' absence. His eyes, his smiling lips said what his English reticence couldn't say in front of a third person. *You are as beautiful as I remember you!*

Then he turned to the man by Anna's side.

"This is a surprise!" he spoke the truth, politely, but with cool welcome.

"Aidan has been invited over here to work at St. Agnes Children's Hospital and we traveled together."

"That's an interesting step in your career! Congratulations! Are you over here for long?"

"For six months."

"You must come out to Dion House and see us."

"Thank you." The dark eyes smiled. "And now I'd better go and see about my luggage."

"Where are you staying?"

"With Sir Humphrey Gail. He's Dean of St. Agnes and is a friend of my father's." Aidan held out his hand. "Goodbye," he smiled at them and was gone, moving so lightly, so swiftly that almost at once he was invisible.

"We'd better get along, too, Anna. Where's your luggage?"

She indicated it. "The rest is coming by sea," she said, and watched Martin give directions for the three rawhide cases to be taken out to his car.

Then, turning her head, she saw Aidan again. He was far over by a huge plate glass window and she saw him turn and glance in her direction. She raised her hand, but if he saw her gesture across the crowded hall, he made no sign. It was as though he had already gone out of her life.

Seated behind the wheel of his car, Martin made no attempt to start the engine. Instead, he reached out his hand and his fingers closed over hers.

"It's been a long time, Anna!"

"Four months."

"Four months too long! That's love!" His face was alive with a physical urgency. "A man gets hungry for the touch of one woman. I want to kiss the breath out of you."

"You'd better leave enough to keep me alive,"

she laughed. "I'd hate to die of being kissed!"

A thin silver rain began to spatter the windshield.

"You've come to a gray country, sweet."

"I know England. You forget, I was educated here."

"I think of you only against a background of India. Do you remember how I always wanted you to wear a sari?"

"And I told you the only time I'd worn one was when my stepfather made me dress up one Christmas – we kept Christmas, but then you know that! – in one of those lovely ones of his mother's. Sometimes, with my background, I feel a bit like a salad – English tomatoes, French lettuce and garnished with Indian garlic!"

He laughed and leaned over and kissed her.

"You smell of jasmine as you always did! Oh lord, I'm reminiscing again! But I like it. It's a glorious indulgence after being so hungry for you. Do you remember the first time I came to Kashmir to stay with your family and I wanted to buy you some flowers and how I thought someone was pulling my leg when I was told that you bought jasmine by the yard?"

He had paid the old flower seller who wore a tattered *pheran* more than he had asked and twined the white garland around her throat like

13

ropes of petal-shaped pearls.

That was the first time Martin had said, "I love you, Anna."

She remembered the scene up near Dal Lake with the china trees giving them shade and the lotus flowers on the serene water and the Himalayas, like white headed gods looking down on their flowering love.

The car moved out of the airport purring beneath its long dark hood, heading south.

"Was I abrupt with Aidan?"

"You were, rather."

"That was jealousy. Childish, isn't it? But at least I admit it!"

"I've known Aidan all my life, Martin!"

"That doesn't make it any easier. Two babies can play together at three years old and fall in love at twenty!"

"But I'm in love with *you!*"

"I know, Anna, but there's almost all your life that I know nothing about! Although I lived in India for two years, the Indian world is totally strange to me — exciting, moving, but — I don't know —" He paused, searching for words. "Well, always somewhere beyond a golden gate, as it were. And there, in that place, was your life, Anna — the Indian way of life. I suppose that's why I resent Aidan, because you shared a world I can never understand."

She said quietly, "Whatever my life has been, please always try to remember that I'm Western —"

He lifted his head in a gesture of impatience.

"How did we get on to this topic, anyway? I'd love you even if you came from Outer Mongolia or the walled city of Karna where women go veiled. I think I'd rather like you to be veiled, then no other man would look at you."

"Oh, Martin!" She broke into helpless laughter.

"Jealousy is a very violent and primitive emotion, darling. Seeing you with Aidan started me off. So be careful!" He accelerated past a slow moving car. "But I've clamped down on the demon! Now let's talk of important things. How are you?"

"I'm fine."

"Was it a wrench leaving the Institute and all those test tubes and magnifying glasses?"

"It was," she admitted. "They were investigating a mysterious disease that has broken out in Sukh Lal's saffron gardens up near Pampur. I think we'd isolated the germ."

"You're going to miss your work, Anna."

"Well," she said matter-of-factly, "I'll just have to hope you'll let me in, on the conversation side, of the work you're doing in the laboratory at Lavernake. I won't mind how much shop you talk when you come home in the evenings!"

"That'll be quite a change," he laughed. "The family all contrive to look blank when I start to talk about progeny tests and chromosomes and they begin a counterattack about mutation in sweet peas."

"But," she queried, "it's all one, surely? Your work and theirs, I mean."

"Mine's too scientific for them – except Jaimie, but then he's the real expert. The rest have studied horticulture, but get by mostly because they've grown up in the nurseries. They've acquired a sort of native knowledge. And talking of families, when do your parents arrive?"

"In two months' time. Father can't get away earlier. That means we could be married in June."

"That's too long!" He gave a swift turn of his head towards her and then, eyes on the road again, said, "I've got an idea! Let's get married quietly and then have a church ceremony when your parents arrive."

"No," she said hastily. "Apart from the fact that I want them to be here for my real wedding, I need a few weeks to get acclimatized."

"And to be quite certain you haven't made a mistake?"

"It's a point to consider!" she darted back at him.

He said, seriously, "I think, up to the very last minute, I was so afraid you'd change your mind and not come, and it's made me edgy. You know how mothers get nightmares about some late child having been run over and then he turns up and mother, out of sheer nervous relief, slaps him. That's how *I* feel!"

"You're no anxious mother and I've no wish to be slapped! I'm here, and we're going to get married. It's all quite simple."

Martin narrowed his eyes at the traffic lights.

"Bet me I can't get through before they change." Hands steady on the steering wheel, he accelerated.

But Anna bet him nothing. She was thinking: *Is it all so simple?* The greatest upheaval of my life?

Pictures shimmered through her memory. She leaned back in her seat, hands folded over her large green leather handbag and saw, not the twisting road under the piled April clouds, nor the huddled lines of brick villas, but the beautiful, flower hung summer house in Kashmir with its spacious rooms . . . the Benares silk hangings, the Kirman rugs, the rich black walnut furniture, the lovely lamps, painted with delicate strokes by cat hair brushes, the flowers, always her mother's beloved flowers. . . .

Her family would be preparing to leave Kashmir after their brief holiday and return to Delhi where her father was senior surgeon at a hospital. She thought of her English mother who had been a pathologist in London and whose first mysterious marriage had been quickly over. Anna had been three months old when her mother had married Ram Kashinath. She thought of her half sisters, Rashti, already in her third year at Stanford University in California, and Sarojini, only eighteen but already noticed by critics in India for her lovely mature poetry. And David, her half brother.

To those who made didactic statements that such marriages could not last, her mother and this man she called "father" were a glowing denial. Anna could not remember a time when the harmony of her home had been broken by bickering; when there was not laughter, or the knowledge that all childish heartbreaks were cured, not by spoiling, but by reasoning.

"Cigarette?" Martin broke through her thoughts. "Light me one, too, sweet."

Flicking her lighter, she asked, "How's work?"

"The laboratory seemed quite glad to have me back. They've enlarged the place during the two years I've been away and my special pal, Robert Staines, has been sent to Mexico City. I

18

just got back in time to say 'hail and farewell' to him and to tell him that I'd rather he than me!"

"You wouldn't like to go to Mexico?"

"Oh, maybe some other time. But India was my second job abroad. I've had enough, for the time being, of being loaned out to foreign laboratories like some technical book at a public library! I want roots now."

"Sussex roots?"

"Of course," he lifted the cigarette in his left hand and drew deeply on it. "It's the call of the blood, I suppose."

Anna felt her heart twist. The call of the blood. . . . Or the call of environment? She had yet to find out how strong that latter was.

"Your family must be glad to have you back," she began.

"They almost killed the fatted calf!"

It was no use saying, "I hope they'll like me," because Martin's easy answer would be, "Of course they will." So she said nothing, but sat watching the light rain silver the lambent green fields as they flashed along the secondary road Martin had taken. There were cars in front of them, and cars passing, yet no dust: she thought of motoring in India. Of the swirls of it that rose, seeming to try to form a cloak over the fabulous country. The dust, and the hot violent beauty; carmine and violet skies; the prismatic lights at sunset over Malabar Hill. . . . Something, deep inside, choked a little.

Martin's closeness, his shoulder near hers, the occasional touch of his hand, the brief moments when, held up by traffic, he would turn and smile at her, all these things dispelled the chill feather of doubt that kept touching her as her plunging heart remembered.

Presently at the top of a hill Martin slowed down.

"Look, you can just see the house from here," he pointed to the right.

Anna saw a sprawling, dull red brick building surrounded by a great acreage of plantations; glasshouses gleamed like sheets of pewter and the spreading earth was carpeted with the white and blue and dazzling yellow of spring flowers.

"It's a monstrosity," Martin was laughing. "The house, I mean. But it's home."

There it is, she thought, Martin's home – the home of all the Claremondes standing with a kind of blank neatness among the nurseries which they worked for a living.

Many times during the past months Anna had tried to visualize Martin's family. Sapphira, the eldest, who managed the accounts, and ran the house; Eve, who, with her husband Jaimie, supervised the plantations and the hothouses. Bridget, a distant cousin, who had been trained in horticulture, had invested her money many years ago in the business and ran the flower shop in London.

The car coasted down the hill and turned in under an arched gateway that had the words "Dion House Nurseries" poised in wrought iron writing over it. The drive was neat and curved to the house between shrubs of laurel and ancient oaks. A wide path ran at an angle from the main drive towards the nurseries, past a huge garage open to reveal vans which a man was hosing, and a red brick office.

Seen close to, the house, at the head of the curving drive, still had the flat, cardboard look that had struck Anna when she first saw it from the top of the hill. Two identical pointed roofs topped it and bay windows, bare of curtains, gazed up the drive like square, expressionless moon faces.

It looked solid and safe and ugly.

One window was wide open and Anna saw that the room beyond seemed to stretch the depth of the house for she could see the light gray sky at the far end. High clear voices drifted out, raised in angry argument.

"*Can't* you understand?"

"I think, for once *you* could listen to *me!*"

"The whole thing is impossible. We can't let —"

Someone banged something down and the voice stopped halfway through the sentence.

Anna turned quickly as Martin joined her.

He laughed. "Introduction to the family! Don't look so alarmed, sweet! They're always quarreling among themselves; it doesn't mean anything. Given an outside dilemma they'll close their ranks and fight as one." He felt for his key and, turning it in the lock, flung open the heavy oak door.

Anna had an impression of solid oak furniture, age-dimmed pictures in gilded frames and a great deal of beaten brass looming from the cavernous darkness.

The absence of light in this large hall puzzled her until she glanced back and saw that the two hall windows had stained glass halfway down through which the light came, reds and blues and greens dulled by the lack of sunlight.

She saw one beautiful thing, however, as she crossed the hall by Martin's side. A huge bowl of flowers stood in the center of the refectory table; daffodils and narcissus and flowering cherry swung a little in the disturbed air through the open door and were like a spring song in that somber place.

The voices from the inner room which had risen to the crescendo of anger, now were still, silenced as though someone had bade them stop and listen: listen to the slam of a car door, and footsteps and a strange girl's approach.

The coming of Anna Kashinath.

Martin pushed open the door of a room to the left and Anna blinked at the vivid sunlight which suddenly broke from a cloud and poured through the bay window of the enormous room.

Four heads turned, eyes watched her as she stood in the doorway.

And in that moment there came to Anna one of those flashes of knowledge that had no explanation.

These three women and one man had been quarreling about her. Then, with her arrival, they had closed their ranks, as Martin had said, and they were there as one person to greet her.

In friendship. In enmity? She had no way of knowing in these first suspended moments. All she knew was that, alien among them, she felt like an untried actress making her first entry in a play of which she knew neither the plot nor the lines. A comedy? A tragedy? Straight and uncomplicated?

"This is Sapphira," Martin was saying. Paling auburn wings of hair, faintly touched with gray; cool, quiet eyes, an effort at warmth in the handshake.

"Welcome among us, Anna."

"And Bridget, my cousin."

Auburn hair again, but rich and red gold, smartly set by a hairdresser who knew his business; vivid carmine mouth, delicate small boned nose with flaring nostrils that could denote courage. A beautiful, insolent, defiant face.

"You arrived in rain, didn't you, Anna? I'm glad the sun's come out at last. You'd have had a very bad impression of our climate, otherwise." The greeting was social and polite enough, but the eyes watched her, saying silently: *So you're the girl from India Martin wants to marry!*

Anna turned away as Eve Claremonde held out her hand.

"You must be tired after that long flight halfway around the world!"

"I like flying," Anna said and adjudged Eve. She was red haired like the others and she would have been almost as striking as Bridget but for that faint, disintegrated look which many neurotic people had.

Jaimie, Eve's husband, was saying kindly, "It's good to see you at last, Anna. We've heard so much about you."

Martin looked around. "Where's Julie?"

"Eve put her to bed, she was running a bit of a temperature."

"Not again!" Martin frowned.

"You know she's not strong —"

"So you keep telling me!"

24

Sapphira said quickly, turning to Anna, "You'd like to go to your room, wouldn't you? Bridget, tell Amy we'll be ready for tea in about ten minutes. I'll take Anna upstairs."

Martin and Jaimie followed with her suitcases, climbing the dark, curving, highly polished staircase to the first floor.

It seemed that all the rooms in this house were large, Anna thought, passing half open doors.

Sapphira entered a room at the end of the corridor.

"You have beautiful large rooms here —"

"Oh, this house was built in the days when people had money. Now it's different. We own it, so we stay," she crossed to the window and looked out over the garden. "This room has a view partly over the nurseries. It's our land as far as that Christmas tree plantation. But it's hard work!"

"You love it?"

"It keeps us," Sapphira said shortly and continued to stare out.

Martin dumped down the two cases and took the third from Jaimie at the door.

"Sapphira brooding over her domain!" he laughed, straightening and watching her.

"It's beautiful land," she said without turning around.

"I wouldn't exactly say that. It's rich soil and there's a fine sea coast —"

"It's beautiful, valuable land," Sapphira said again.

"I don't think our investments in this business exactly bring us in a fortune," he said lightly, "but we get by!"

"One day," her voice slurred as though she were speaking to herself. "One day —" and then as though remembering that she had an audience, she broke off and turned to Anna. Her voice was formal again.

"I hope you have all you want. There are spare blankets in that closet. You'll probably feel the cold after India. The bathroom is right opposite and there's constant hot water, if you want a bath."

She walked out of the room as she spoke.

"Sapphira seems to love this place, Martin!"

"I've never been quite certain. Those few audible comments of hers weren't intended for us. She was answering some thought of her own. Don't ask me what! She does that. She may be in the room with us and then quite suddenly she seems to have moved right away! Her dreams take over. She's deep —"

"She could be terribly attractive."

"It's strange she never married. She's thirty-seven, but you should have seen her ten years ago. She was really lovely then. Men would ask her out once or twice and then never again. She was invited to parties, but it was the older women who sat and talked to her while her friends danced and found men friends and got married. Sometimes I think Sapphira's the most vulnerable of the lot of us, at other times —" He broke off and went to a bowl of daffodils and white carnations standing on the mahogany chest. "I feel they should have been crimson roses and Crown Imperials — Indian flowers — but I left the choice to Eve and we don't grow Crown Imperials, anyway."

"They're lovely!" Anna stood by Martin's side and touched the petals. "They came from the nurseries?"

"Eve had them picked this morning."

"Have she and Jaimie been married long?"

"About five years. Nice chap, Jaimie, a very clever horticulturalist but somehow a shadow. He never seems to come alive in the house, but in the nurseries he's a changed man. He's always winning prizes in big shows —"

A sudden flow of gleeful, childish laughter cascaded through the house. Martin's little daughter! Anna said, "That's Julie, isn't it? She doesn't sound as though her temperature worries her much!"

"Nothing ever gets Julie's spirits down! She's not strong, but there's no actual disease, and the doctor says she'll grow out of her slight chest weakness. Eve looks after her – she's a trained nurse, you know. Only when father died and left us this business, she threw up her hospital work and studied horticulture."

"Shall I see Julie tonight?"

"Of course. But I'll leave you now to pretty yourself up. Do your unpacking later. But first –" He held out his arms.

She went to him and he held her close.

"Happy to be here?" His lips were against her cheek.

"Of – course –"

"Mind you stay that way," he held her away and his face lost its laughter. "It's going to be hard for you to get acclimatized, but I'll understand. There's precious little glamor here –"

"There's also precious little of the poverty of India!" she said. "Where I live isn't important. It's who lives with me!"

"I never knew such a girl for saying the tactful thing!" His arms tightened around her and he kissed her. "I'd like to have tea with you up here, just the two of us, but that, I suppose, would offend the family."

"Of course it would. Go and tell them I'll be down in ten minutes."

"So the idea of tea for two up here doesn't appeal?"

"It appeals too much!" she cried, and waved

her hands at him, laughing.

When the door closed behind him, Anna opened a suitcase and took out a dress of dark green wool. Underneath it was a small tissue paper parcel. She unwrapped it and held in her hands the beautiful little wooden model of a tiger. Bihari Lal, the old servant who was caretaker in their Kashmir house, had carved it for her as a parting present. She stroked the highly polished wood for a moment or two before she set it on the table by the bowl of flowers.

When she had come to England to school, he had carved a little monkey for her. She had brought that with her too, in one of her suitcases, with Aidan's lovely gift of a small jade dragon. She set Bihari Lal's little gift on the chest beside the flowers and then stood for a moment, staring at the carved alabaster bowl which held the daffodils.

She had seen it before, in India, in Martin's house there.

Grim memory flowed over her. She remembered the one and only party there she had gone to; how Gillian, Martin's wife, had disgraced herself by a sudden violent burst of temper, how she had flung out her hand to sweep away everything within her reach but before she could complete her act of exhibitionism, someone had caught her arm and the lovely alabaster bowl — this very bowl — was safe.

How Martin dreaded those parties Gillian insisted on giving and which she always ruined! How he must have hated his life in those days! At the Institute, working in close contact with him, she had watched him growing more and more harassed; nerve and will torn by the tempers and nagging at home. He worked desperately hard, staying late most nights because he dreaded to go home. Sometimes he was embarrassed by Gillian's arrival at the Institute, her demand to see him, her accusations that his staying late was just an excuse for some secret affair. With whom? She would never accept that there was no one.

And then had come the tragedy. One day, while Martin was at the laboratory, Gillian took an overdose of barbiturate and killed herself. Anna had never lost her conviction that Gillian had only meant to frighten Martin, that this had been just another piece of exhibitionism but that this time it had gone wrong. She had been sinking more and more deeply into her world of demented jealousy, of screaming accusations, and in a mood of unbalance and hysteria she had taken a large dose of the drug, believing, Anna was certain, that Martin would come home and find her just in time. But on that particular night he had had to stay longer than usual in order to wait for the results of an important experiment and when he arrived at the house it was too late. As a final twisted gesture, he had found Gillian lying on a beautiful crimson Indian silk shawl wearing her wedding dress, so beautiful until he looked close and found that she was dead.

There was a suicide note, sweetly worded and deadly, saying that she laid no blame on him, that all men were inconstant; and loving one woman became a bore. And, by the very things she wrote, hoping to enslave him in remorse forever.

It was after Gillian's death that Anna came into Martin's life. The harassed years had taken their toll of him; he was on edge; moody, restless, and, save in his work, uncertain of his judgment and of himself.

For one thing, after the first lovely days of their romance, he grew doubts and tormented himself with them, unable to believe that Anna really loved him. It was to him as though he had reached out and touched the fringe of some forbidden dream; as though if he dared too much, it would all fade and leave him floundering again in the torment of those dark years. This deeply rooted self-doubt was Gillian's legacy to him, and Anna faced the fact that she would need all her patience and understanding to give him back his faith in himself. Now that she saw him again, she realized the tremendous change in him. In these past months he had learned to laugh more and to speak without fear that the most innocent remark might be misinterpreted.

II

When Anna went downstairs again, the family was waiting for her.

Sapphira sat at a small table on which stood the tea tray; Eve in jodhpurs lounged on the upholstered window seat; Bridget sat with a black cat on her knee, Jaimie and Martin stood by the imitation Adam fireplace looking at some flower photographs.

They asked her how she liked her tea, explained the cakes they offered her: "These are bath buns. They're delicious when they're fresh and gooey on top, but they do put inches on your waistline − not that you have to worry about that! Those long things are éclairs. Our local baker makes them."

As though, she thought with wry amusement, I didn't know! As though I sat on silk cushions in a harem and ate Halva and sugared almonds all day long!

They asked her questions about herself. Yes, her mother had been a pathologist in London before she married; no, she wasn't a Hindu she was a Christian. Yes, she played tennis and swam. She used to ride, but once some years ago a horse threw her rather badly and she had lost her nerve.

"We have some lovely rides here," Bridget said. "Don't we, Martin?"

"They go out together," Sapphira cut in, "for hours — over the hills and far away, they tell us when they get back."

Anna looked at Martin. He said, "We've got some stables near here — they have a few really good horses — I think you'll have to try one."

She said quickly, laughingly, "Oh no, I've had all the riding I want, thanks! Father told me when I had that fall that I should have got straight back into the saddle, but I didn't, I limped all the way home and ached for weeks, and felt every horse's hoof against me! I'll leave riding to you and Bridget." She glanced at her and saw the swift, bright look that seemed to flash Martin a message Anna could not interpret but which disturbed her vaguely like the proverbial cloud that was no bigger than a man's hand.

While she drank the strong tea and ate, not

the éclairs but tiny luscious macaroons, Anna glanced about her and wondered how three comparatively young women could live in such a jumble of rather shoddy Victoriana. Were they too busy with the nurseries to take any interest in the house in which they lived? Or did they cling to this cluttered ugliness out of sentiment for a house and its contents that had been their parents' and their grandparents' before them? Looking at them, at Sapphira's calm, withdrawn face, at Eve's thin, dissatisfied mouth, at Bridget's sophisticated grooming, she doubted whether sentiment entered into their scheme of things.

"Martin tells me," Sapphira was saying, "that your parents will be coming over for the wedding. We could, of course, put them up here —"

Anna was quick to notice the reticence. She explained that they had already booked a hotel room in London.

"It's very kind of you, but it would be much more practical for them to stay in London. You see, my stepfather will have to be at his old hospital quite a bit and they both have lots of friends over here to visit."

"Where are they staying?"

"At the Martignan; they usually do."

Is she rich? Martin didn't tell us, said their bright, inquisitive expressions.

"Anna's stepfather has been invited, while he's over here, to lecture at the Institute for Tropical Medicine —" Martin was collecting the used tea things and setting them on the tray. "I'll carry this out for you, Sapphira, and then Anna and I will go up and see Julie."

"She may be asleep —"

"Well, that's all right. We'll just look in and see —" He carried the tea tray out to the kitchen.

Bridget was watching Anna.

"I've only flown short distances. It must be very monotonous to do the long journey from India."

"Oh, we enjoyed it. A friend of Aidan's met us in Beirut and we had great fun."

"You had company?"

"Yes — Aidan Narayan. He's a very old friend of my family's. He has come over here to work on children's ailments."

Their silence held a concerted thought. An Indian! But then, of course, she's more used to them than to English people. . . .

"Come on, Anna," Martin called from the doorway. "Come and see your future stepdaughter."

They went up the dim, shallow staircase with the pretentious portraits of the heavy browed men and women staring down at them and the

36

sun burning through the leaded patchwork of violet and green and carmine window panes.

Julie's room was down a short flight of steps from the main passage. They paused at the half open door.

"It's not going to be easy for her —" Anna began.

"Don't you believe it! Julie makes nothing difficult for herself! She's no problem child, thank God!"

"She may be asleep." Why, she thought, be so scared of meeting Martin's little daughter, hoping for a postponement?

He put his hand to the door and it swung open.

Julie Claremonde wasn't even near sleep. She was sitting up in her bed by a window, a night light on the table by her side, and she was making strange, contorted movements with her fingers that threw giant shadows on the wall.

Martin stood frowning in the doorway.

"For Pete's sake, why do they give her that damned night light? Encouraging her to fear the dark? That's the worst of leaving your child to someone else's care. But Gillian didn't want her out in India with us and Eve, afraid she'd miss her mother, started her on this night light habit."

Julie looked over her shoulder.

"Hello, Daddy, guess what this is!"

"I'll lay a cabbage to an old shoe, I can answer that one!"

"Well, go on!"

"It's an elephant." He took Anna's hand, leading her to the pretty pink bed. "Now you guess who *this* is!"

"It's Anna," Julie said promptly. "You said she was coming to stay with us." She held out her hand. "How do you do? You've got an ordinary dress on!"

"What in the world did you expect her to wear? A bikini?" Martin laughed.

"Aunt Sapphira said —"

"What did she say?"

"That Anna would wear funny clothes, sort of wound around her."

"Saris!" Anna said quickly. "That's what we call them in India, Julie. But *I* don't wear them. You see, I'm European."

Julie looked disappointed; she leaned her cheek against the bed head, eyeing Anna obliquely.

"But Aunt Sapphira said —"

"What did she say?" Martin asked again.

"That Anna wasn't like us."

"Then Aunt Sapphira's talking out of her hat!" Martin began angrily.

"As a matter of fact," Anna broke in, her hand

on Martin's arm, "I *have* got two saris with me. They belonged to my stepfather's mother."

"Have you got a red one?"

"Julie's going through a red period," Martin explained, restored to good temper by the light pressure of Anna's hand. "She'll probably grow up to be a female matador."

"I've got a green silk one embroidered with real gold thread and a white one with silver edges. I'll show them to you some time."

"Some time, some time, never!" Julie chanted the words like a little parrot. "Aunt Sapphira says so. She said —"

"Martin, you really must stop talking to Julie!" Eve's voice from the doorway startled them. "You know how difficult she is when she gets excited."

"I'd have said she was the least excited of children," Martin observed. "But have it your own way."

Eve went across the room and pulled open a French window that led to a little balcony.

"And who shut this —"

"It blew to —" Julie said.

"You must get all the fresh air you can, darling." Eve looked around, found some books and used them as a door stop. "There, that's better."

Martin laid a hand on Julie's forehead. "It

doesn't feel to me as though you've got a temperature. You're cheating!"

"I don't want a temperature, Daddy, I want to get up and come downstairs with you!"

He bent and kissed her. "You do what you're told. Lie down and go to sleep and I'll see you tomorrow."

"Don't go –" She clung to him.

"No go tonight, no see tomorrow!" he said and disentangled her arms.

Back in her room again to complete her unpacking, Anna realized that Julie was certainly not going to present any difficulty. She liked the calm way the child accepted her, the healthy interest in this future stepmother from the East; the way she lifted her face, without shyness, for Anna's good night kiss. If she resembled either parent, thank heaven, she was more Martin's child than Gillian's!

Anna wondered which room along this wide corridor was Martin's, whether he had furnished it from some of his own pieces which had been stored while they were in India. Was there, in this house, anything that stood as a reminder of Gillian – a photograph, a painted portrait, a possession? Or had the family washed her out of their minds as completely as she knew Martin must do if he were to eradicate the harm she had done to his spirit?

40

She stood at the window and saw the sunlight and shadow chasing over the fields and woods that stretched away to the spires and skyscrapers of the busy town of Lavernake. When she had emptied her suitcases she went downstairs again.

The living room was empty but as she entered Martin came in silently from the French windows that led to the garden.

He slid an arm around her shoulders and she jumped.

He said, "There are doors everywhere in this house, Anna! Sapphira had all the old-fashioned windows on this side ripped out and glass doors put in so that it would be easy for them all to get to and· from the nurseries instead of always running around to the front door."

"I saw that there was even one – a French window – in Julie's room."

"Oh, her room was built on to the house years ago as a dayroom for my grandfather's brood. Eve chose it for Julie because the doctor said she must have as much fresh air as possible."

"But there was an iron staircase to the garden. Isn't anyone scared that some prowler might get in?"

"Good gracious, no! This village is a backwater – a place, thank heaven, that the town planners of Lavernake have forgotten. We live the old way here, no doors locked, no windows barred. Nobody would want to burgle us, anyway. There's precious little of value to take! Funny old place, isn't it?"

She said guardedly, "The rooms are beautifully proportioned."

"They were built in an age of leisure and cheap labor. Nowadays our mainstay, Amy, and the village woman who does the rough work occasionally, stir themselves up into a hymn of hate about the impracticability of the house. They stage a strike, then get over it, shake hands and all is sunshine and goodwill again!"

Anna glanced around her and saw the picture over the mantelpiece.

"Is that an original?" She walked over and looked up at it.

"Sapphira painted it. She's got a hut at the far end of the garden, right behind that knoll you see in the distance. All that part of the garden is wild — we leave it to itself; nobody ever goes there, not even Julie, because it's full of brambles and stinging nettles. So Sapphira has her isolated hut there which she calls a studio, and she won't let anyone go into it; it's her domain. She hides herself down there and paints when the mood moves her. I believe it's her way of getting something out of her system. She seems to enjoy it, though I'm afraid she's no artist."

The painted irises stood stiffly out of their green vase, their colors harsh, their lines without grace. They seemed, to Anna, to have something of Sapphira herself in their unyielding strength.

Anna turned away and looked up at the high, molded ceiling, and then at the fine proportions of the long windows.

"It could be made so lovely, Martin. I can just see this room, decorated in beige and a touch of gold, with lovely antiques and —"

"I'm afraid our tastes don't coincide, Anna. But then they can't be expected to, can they?" Sapphira's voice broke in from the doorway.

Anna swung around, dismayed. "I'm sorry. I didn't mean —"

"Oh, that's all right! I think I understand that you can't be expected to have our tastes —"

"Anna was voicing an opinion I'd asked for," Martin broke in.

"I'm sorry." The apology came stiffly and insincerely from Sapphira. She lifted an ash tray and tipped the cigarette butts into a blue-painted bin. "We've been thinking, Martin, the house is far too large for us and the west wing could be converted into a home for you both."

Martin caught Anna's swift, dismayed reaction.

He said, quietly, "It's something we'll have to think about, Sapphira."

"It would solve your house hunting problem."

"Yes —" he said doubtfully.

"Of course, it's early days to make plans, isn't it? I see that — Eve and Jaimie and Bridget are very keen on the idea but we'll have to discuss it later. After all, Anna has only just come —"

The telephone bell shrilled and Sapphira went to answer it. A moment later she called Martin.

"Now what?" he said, dismayed, gave Anna a little pat and called, "Coming!"

She wandered out of the empty room into the garden and stood looking over the lawns and the tall bordering trees. There was a smell of damp earth in the air, but the sun, clear now of cloud, still had warmth in it.

And then, as she stood there, Anna heard voices coming from a room farther along the terrace.

Bridget was saying, "But, Martin, it would be so lovely if we could go! It would be like old times!"

"Of course we'll go. We'll make up a party for it. Anna would enjoy seeing one of these small town festivals."

There was a pause.

"So it won't be like old times, after all!"

"It will! We'll all be together."

"You and I used to go on our own, Martin. Have you forgotten? And we had such fun, and –"

"– and we were very young!" Anna could hear his cool, matter-of-fact voice. "A whole ocean has passed underneath the proverbial bridge since then."

"If only things could have been different for – for both of us!"

"If only fortunes hung on trees!" he retorted lightly. "If only a charming millionaire would walk into your shop and sweep you away to a white yacht in the Aegean Sea, and I could be hailed as a genius with a microscope – and be paid accordingly! Nice dreams, Bridget!"

"But not mine!" she cried. "Mine are simpler and, it seems, even more impossible!"

There was a swift rush of high heels fading as Bridget ran across a polished floor.

It was nothing, of course! Just a conversation between cousins, wishing for the moon, as people did! And yet something hung there, significant and yet unexplained. Bridget saying *"If only things could have been different for both of us."* She pushed aside an urge to puzzle it out. Flights of conjecture and imagination did no one any good.

She crossed the lawn and climbed to the top

of the little knoll between rhododendron bushes and found a wooden seat facing south.

It was very quiet. On the far side, below the hillock, she saw a stretch of wild garden and in it Sapphira's wooden hut. Beyond it was a fence and a cart track that led to a farm. Around her, the laurel leaves shone in the sun like silver flowers, a robin swung on a branch of the oak and watched her inquisitively. From somewhere far away she heard the squawking of agitated geese and then the bells of the village church began evening practice. The sound, coming across the quiet fields, had a deep, moving sadness and she felt a swift urge to run towards the sound, to go into the little church hidden down there among the trees, and try to exorcise, in its dim peace, the unknown fear that had swept her the very moment of setting foot on English soil. What have I to fear? Nothing! Nothing! I love and am loved — who and what has power against that? And immediately she had her answer. The family — Martin's womenfolk.

Then I must make them like me!

Fair enough that they should be cautious about her! She was a stranger, yet there was more than caution in their manner, more than a watching interest. What then? Perhaps it was summed up in those overheard words — Bridget's words again.

So it won't be like old times after all!

A girl from another world had come among them and they had automatically closed their ranks.

III

As her glance moved, she caught sight of something brightly colored poised up like a great round flower in the laurel bushes. Reaching forward, she saw that it was a ball, colored with squares of red and yellow and blue. Julie must have been playing with it and either lost it or grown bored with it and left it where it was. She held it in her hand.

"You should have bells on your wrists, and then I'd know where to find you!"

She swung around, startled, and saw Martin smiling down at her. She had a sensation of her blood melting and of her heart pausing, as though poised on wings, waiting. This was their first really isolated moment since her arrival. Here they were hidden from the house with no fear that someone might walk in upon them.

Martin had the same thought. He reached out and drew her to her feet. Julie's bright ball fell, bouncing, to the ground.

"So you've been playing ball!" he teased.

"I found it in the laurel bushes."

He tossed it up and caught it, and then laid it on the seat.

She felt herself trembling, and said, matter-of-factly, "The sea is over there, isn't it?"

"That's right. We'll go there, perhaps, tomorrow. And there's the village, Blakesford, such as it is, and Lavernake away over there."

"Is that Sapphira's studio?" She pointed to the dark, isolated hut.

"Yes —"

"It looks a bit — grim!"

"It is, but there are roof windows on the north side," he laughed. "Don't ask me to show it to you! She keeps it locked. I think she must have a witch's cauldron bubbling in there, and books on magic —"

It looked, from where they stood, dark and sinister enough with the evening shadows flung across it.

Martin was playing with her hair, reaching out as the little wind stirred a strand across her face.

She squinted at it.

He said, "It's like black gold in the sunlight,

49

Anna. How much an ounce do you charge for a nugget?"

She turned and laughed at him. "It's yours," she said, "with love."

A sudden burst of twittering and fluttering came from a nearby bush, startling her.

"What's that?"

"That," he answered lightly, "is a good old-fashioned family quarrel among the blackbirds. They squabble over everything; the choicest insect, the juiciest berry, the most comfortable branch for the night. Anything is an excuse for blackbirds to argue over."

And only two hours ago she had stood on the steps of Dion House and heard angry argument from the Claremondes' living room . . . like the blackbirds.

She shivered.

"You're cold! We'll go in. But first —" He held open his arms and, stepping towards her, closed them around her, holding her fast. "First — this," he said and kissed her.

It was the loveliest moment since her arrival. She felt herself enclosed and safe and loved. . . . Then suddenly somebody laughed, loudly and raucously and the spell broke.

The sound came from the other side of the bushes, down in the cart track, and it cut through the beautiful, intimate moment like the lance of a demon king.

In a flash Anna broke away.

"It's all right," Martin reassured her. "They're not laughing at us. They can't even see us. It's only farm workers going home and seeing the funny side of something!"

And yet she was in the mood to read portent in everything; even in passing laughter that seemed to mock at the beautiful security of Martin's arms. . . .

"Come on," he said, "I'll play ball with you to the house," and tossed it to her and began running down the little hill.

The dark moment had passed. Laughing they ran across the lawn, the harlequin ball curving backwards and forwards between them.

From the lawn, Anna could see that there were three doors leading from the house to the garden. Bridget was standing at one of them, watching.

"I've been looking for you, Martin. You're wanted on the phone."

"Oh, not again! Must people love me so much?"

"It's the lab!"

He shot her a wry look. "I can't even take an afternoon off to meet my girl!" and went into the house.

Bridget remained in the doorway. Her eyes

caught sight of the ball which had dropped to the path.

"Julie lost that this afternoon."

"I found it up on that little knoll."

"Sapphira was wondering where you were. We always meet for drinks in the living room at six o'clock. It's now nearly twenty past."

"I'm so sorry. I didn't know —"

"Oh, it's not your fault, but Martin should have told you. Sapphira makes a kind of ritual of it." She stood, beautiful in a dress of olive silk, her hair blazing in the sunset. She was eyeing Anna strangely, as though trying to make up her mind whether to say something or not.

"You knew Gillian, didn't you?"

The unexpected question jolted Anna. "Very slightly."

"She was my friend, did you know that too?"

"No."

Bridget put forward one slender foot shod in a bronze leather pump and traced a pattern on the gravel.

"Gillian and I used to write to each other often. She was so terribly lonely in India that she had to pour it all out to someone."

"She should have been happy," Anna defended quickly. "People were prepared to be friendly."

"And sometimes *too* friendly — that was the

trouble!" Bridget's light eyes looked directly at Anna. She opened her mouth to say something more, hesitated again, and then asked:

"Who was it, Anna? Who was the woman who finally broke Gillian? She told me in her last letter that there was someone. She said: 'How could she bear to build her happiness on someone else's tragedy?' "

Anna put out her hand in a swift, denying gesture.

"There was no one. Gillian thought because Martin stayed late to work at the lab that a woman must have been the reason," her voice sounded hollow. "But it wasn't like that! He stayed because he dreaded to go home."

Bridget shook her head and Anna said quickly, "Anyway, I can't discuss it —" and made a move to pass along the terrace to the living room. But Bridget's voice checked her.

"Gillian was the kind of woman who would never admit to the outside world that she couldn't hold her husband! And when she found she couldn't, it broke her and she killed herself."

Anna spun around, stung to retort.

"I don't believe Gillian ever meant to do that! I think she hoped to frighten Martin, only he arrived home unexpectedly late — too late to save her. Now please, don't let's talk about it

53

any more. It's not for you and me —"

"To blame Martin? Oh, but I don't. I'm not criticizing him, if that's why you don't like discussing it! Gillian could be very difficult. I know that, and I believe the strain of it was so great that Martin scarcely knew what he was doing. He's a normal man; he wanted love and harmony so he tried to find it with some other woman. I don't believe for a moment it was love — men rush into things when they're blindly unhappy and sometimes they mistake the relief of loneliness for love. I know Martin so well — he's the kind who likes known, familiar things. He would be attracted and perhaps momentarily carried away by someone's — er — kindness, but that wouldn't last with him. Martin's the type who has to take his time, to grow into things — even love —"

Anna should have treated the pronouncement with sure disbelief; should have laughed, "That's all *you* know!"

Instead she evaded a reply, dissembled, saying:

"Sapphira will be wondering where we are —"

"Look, Anna, if you're going to be one of the family, you'll have to get used to our plain speaking. Maybe you don't do things like that in India — maybe women out there are more — reticent and don't probe. But we're different, we like to know the truth about things."

"I'm English, too, Bridget, and I like to know the truth about *things that concern me.*"

"This does."

"Concern me? I think it concerns Martin. Ask him what you want to know."

"But I can't! You must see that! I would be resurrecting the whole awful business when he was trying to forget!"

"Exactly!"

"That's why I had to ask you."

"But why do *you* want to resurrect the past?"

The tawny eyes lifted and fell before Anna's steady gaze.

"Gillian was my friend, I've told you, and I believe that Martin would never have hurt her unless there was some woman stronger, more ruthless than he who — well — shall we say, broke down his moral will power."

"You can rest assured there was no one."

"How *can* you be so certain?"

Anna said quietly, "I know Martin, that's why!"

"I know Martin, too. I've known him for many years, much longer than you, Anna!"

"We're going around in circles. Let's have just one thing clear now and for always. Martin gave Gillian no reason to take her life. And now, I think I left my gloves in the car. I'll go and fetch them and join you in the living room. Tell Sapphira."

She began to walk quickly away around the side of the house, towards the garage. She was afraid Bridget would call her back again. But there was no sound.

The dying sunlight dazzled her eyes.

Who was the woman in Martin's life during Gillian's lifetime? Bridget had asked. The woman stronger than he, more ruthless? And Anna could have gone on and on saying with growing vehemence: *There was no one! There was only I — after Gillian died. . . .*

Men mistake the relief of loneliness for love, Bridget had said.

Martin has to grow into things — even love!

But love had sprung from him, suddenly like a phoenix flaming from dead ashes. From a bruised and dead heart Martin had found feeling and vibrant life again there in the Vale of Kashmir among the lotus blossoms and the mountains.

A lonely man wanting consolation; wanting to rehabilitate himself in the world of normal men and women? Relief of loneliness, mistaken for love?

What am I thinking about? I was no straw clutched by a drowning man!

Why had Bridget chosen to have that conversation with her? Because Gillian was her friend and she had to know the truth? Or because she had to sow the first seed of doubt in Anna's mind . . . the girl from India, brought here to marry our Martin. . . . *Our* Martin — *Bridget's* Martin? Was that it?

IV

"We must have a party," Martin said. "I want Anna to meet my friends. I thought I might ask Diana and Paul Armstrong from London – I was at school with Paul and he's my oldest buddy –" he explained to Anna.

"It's much too far for them to come just for cocktails," Sapphira protested.

"Then we'll invite a few people for the afternoon and those living close can come in later for drinks."

"If you ask them for the afternoon, what do you propose to do with them?"

"Oh, swim perhaps!"

Eve said, shuddering, "The sea will be like ice! You'll all get pneumonia or something."

Sapphira, who had been frowning, brightened. "We'll organize something, Martin, leave it to me, will you?"

He grinned at her. "I hate organizing social events. Over to you, Sapphira! And thanks."

"You'll have to tell me who you want."

He ticked off names. First on his list was Michael Dare, who had come as assistant to Dr. March in Blakesford, and Michael's wife, Lynne. "Then I think, we'll have the Macpeads from Lavernake. Anna will like them — he's an architect and his wife is a sculptress. And the Wilsons. Those will do for the afternoon. Then perhaps we can assemble the rest for cocktails."

"Make a list of the people and then leave it to me."

Martin turned to Anna with relief.

"Sapphira's a master organizer — she always arranges any parties we have. By the way, sweet, is there anyone you'd like to ask down?"

She said easily, "I think I'd like Aidan to come," and immediately saw that she had made a mistake.

Martin said quickly, without thinking, "Aidan, again!"

"Of course, if you'd rather not," she went on, "then forget it. Only he is my oldest friend and somehow it would be nice for him to meet everyone."

"Of course he shall come!" Sapphira said quickly. "It's a party for Anna, so she must

59

have her friends. Is there anyone else you'd like?"

Anna shook her head. She looked up and met Martin's glance and suddenly he laughed.

"*Touché!*" he said. "You're right, Sapphira! Snap me out of my Victorian scruples! Ask Aidan by all means," he went to the big communal desk in the living room and wrote down a list of names and handed it to Sapphira. "Here are the people I'd like to come. Now, I'll leave it all to you. Anna, come and let's look around the nurseries."

When they were outside, he said, apologetically:

"Whenever I show jealousy, Anna, hit me over the head good and hard."

"I might even do that," she laughed, "because there's no need, Martin!"

He said, "Jealousy has no logic about it! If you were in love with Aidan, you wouldn't have chosen to marry me! Would you?"

"Does that even need an answer?"

He looked away. "Of course it doesn't! Let's change the subject, shall we?" He stopped. "Doesn't that tulip field look beautiful? Like a red sea!"

At the end of the nurseries they found a low wall, spanning the grounds, and there, sitting on the slightly warm stone, they talked about themselves and forgot Aidan and the party on Saturday.

Sapphira was arranging everything and no one questioned or asked her plans. All Anna knew was that Aidan had written that he would like to come and that everyone else had accepted the invitation.

Eight people arrived for lunch. The Dares, the Macpeads, the Wilsons, and the Armstrongs from London, bringing laughter into the gloomy hall of Dion House, tossing down tennis rackets, riding things.

Tennis . . . Riding . . . So that was what Sapphira had organized! Anna thought swiftly.

"But my tennis clothes are in a suitcase in the attic and they'll be terribly creased. And I don't ride —"

Aidan came last. He had been delayed at the hospital and he walked in while they were drinking sherry. Anna greeted him. He hadn't brought tennis racket or riding things; but she knew that he quite a good tennis player and probably the finest horseman of them all.

Sapphira outlined her plans. It was a lovely day, but she said too cool for bathing. She had booked six horses, the Wilsons and the Macpeads had agreed in a letter to Sapphira that they would enjoy a ride over the hills. That left two spare horses. The Dares and the Armstrongs had elected in their letters to Sapphira to play tennis. "I could only manage to book one court," she said apologetically, "but you won't mind a doubles match, will you?"

Anna looked at Martin. He was frowning.

"As you don't ride, Anna —" he began.

Sapphira's shocked voice cut in. "Oh! Oh heavens, what have I done? Aidan, I forgot to ask you in my letter which you would like to do. I'm so sorry." she glanced at Martin. He said, "Aidan can ride."

"In these?" Aidan looked down at his flannels and laughed. "Please don't apologize. It's a lovely day and I'd like a walk."

"Anna doesn't ride," Sapphira said, looking at her with thoughtful, narrowed eyes, "so perhaps —"

"*I'll* take Aidan for a walk over the cliffs," she said quickly. "We both love walking, anyway."

Michael Dare and his wife began to protest that they would walk and Anna and Aidan could play tennis in their place.

"Oh, but I haven't got my tennis clothes out of my suitcase. Please, everything's arranged — everything's fine! Martin, you must ride —"

"And Bridget can have the other horse. I actually booked Comus, the one she usually rides," Sapphira finished with satisfaction.

Anna caught Martin's angry gaze and moved over to his side, touching his hand.

"There's nothing to be done but accept the arrangements, darling," she insisted quietly. "Don't worry!"

"It's unforgivable of Sapphire to muddle things! I've never known her to do that before."

"It doesn't matter! It's a lovely day and we'll enjoy a walk."

Bridget called across delightedly, "Oh, Martin, they've sent the gray. Don't you dare let anyone else ride him, he's tricky! But it means we'll get a lovely gallop together."

"I could perhaps lend Aidan some jodphurs," Martin began. "Only he's slimmer than I am."

"Leave things, Martin – please!" Anna begged again.

He looked down at her and his eyes softened.

"Go on," she said. "They're waiting for you," and gave him a little push.

She saw the Dares and the Armstrongs come out of the house with coats thrown over tennis outfits, heard the laughter, the comments: "Rather you than me on that horse!"

"Don't hit over the side nets or you'll never find your balls again. They have a way of flying into the river."

"Your horse is dancing, Martin! Did he once do a circus act?"

"Bridget, on that gorgeous horse you should wear a dark green habit and have a feather in your hat!"

Bridget laughed happily, swinging herself astride Comus, her hair gleaming red gold in the sun.

And then they all moved away. Sunlight rippled on the shifting muscles of the horses; glossy necks strained forward eager to gallop up there on the cliffs in the crisp and shining air.

Bridget rode with Martin and Anna watched with honest admiration how she sat, beautiful and effortless on her chestnut, Comus.

Aidan was talking to Eve. Sapphira's voice from behind Anna said softly, "They make a wonderful pair, don't they?"

"Yes."

"You mustn't mind, Anna —"

"*Mind?*" She felt a little dense.

"Martin going off with Bridget —"

"But you know I don't! I've urged them to ride when they want to. Why not, anyway? It would be dog-in-the-manger if I tried to stop him just because I didn't ride, wouldn't it?"

"I'm glad you're not — jealous!" Her face was near Anna's, her light eyes held the dark ones steadily. "But you'll have a lovely walk with Aidan, I'm sure. You must have so much to talk about — so much in common."

She moved a little, putting up her hand to shade her eyes and watch the riders as they appeared again in the lane that led to the cliffs. Anna began to move away.

"Of course," said Sapphira, still staring after them, "I shan't tell Martin, so don't worry!"

"Tell Martin what?"

"That I asked *you* to drop a note to Aidan and find out which he wanted to do, ride or play tennis."

Anna swung around, in blank astonishment.

"You didn't ask me any such thing! You said you would write."

"But after Aidan had accepted and I was making up the numbers for tennis and riding, I asked you to find out what Aidan wanted to do."

For a moment the sheer lying effrontery rendered Anna speechless. Then Sapphira dropped her hand and turned with a faint gesture of impatience.

"It's all right, Anna! I've told you, I wouldn't dream of telling Martin — unless he goes for me about it, of course! But I don't think he will. Martin isn't one to rake up trouble."

"If you really thought you told me any such thing then you're quite mistaken!" Anna said firmly. "You asked for Aidan's address and then told me to leave all the arranging to you. You didn't mention it again, except to tell me that Aidan was coming."

Sapphira's face was devoid of expression, like a mask.

"Then leave it at that, my dear," she said with finality. "Oh, Aidan," she turned and her voice breathed sudden charm, "you and Anna will be going for your walk now, I suppose. Show him our monastery ruins out at Janis Hill, Anna. They say Cromwell sacked the place which was full of treasures. It's still a very romantic spot, so enjoy yourselves."

"Thank you," Anna said calmly. "I'm sure we will."

She was aware that Sapphira stood watching them walk together down the drive and that Eve had probably joined her.

She wanted to forget her anger so that she wouldn't spoil the afternoon for Aidan, but for the first five minutes of the walk she found herself striding, silent and resentful, by his side.

Anna reckoned without Aidan's help, however. Whether he sensed her annoyance or not she did not know, but after their minutes of silence, he took the last dozen or so steps to the top of the cliff at a run and then turned and held out his hand to help her up, laughing, as she slid a little on the dry, slippery grass.

"You never were very sure-footed, were you, Anna?"

"I'd make a rotten mountaineer!" She looked up into his face and saw in it a compete enjoyment of the moment. Immediately Sapphira, Bridget, Eve, none of them mattered. "But I'll match you in walking," she challenged, "so come on. We're going to find the monastery Cromwell sacked."

Once, in a fold in the hills, they caught a glimpse of the riders. Two were ahead of the others, galloping over the bare down. Bridget and Martin? It didn't matter; nothing did, but Aidan's company and the lovely, shining afternoon.

It was while they sat in the ruins of Janis, watching the swallows wheel and dart across the broken walls, that Aidan said:

"I'm glad to have met your future family-in-law, Anna."

"When we get back I expect Jaimie will want to show you around the nurseries."

"I'll enjoy that. Are you going to study horticulture and join up with them?"

"No. They'd hate me to, anyway."

"I'd have thought, as one of the family –"

"I'll never be one of the family," she said gravely. "They don't want it, Aidan!" Suddenly, talking about the Claremondes seemed sacrilege on such a lovely day. She said vehemently, "I want to forget them – I want to enjoy this afternoon with you."

"All right, Anna. Come, let's go and see if we can find a tea shop in the village."

Back at Dion House, riders and tennis players had returned and Martin's friends from the Industrial Laboratory and from Lavernake were arriving. Anna, the reason for the party, had not returned. Restlessly, Martin went into the office from where he could see the lane beyond the drive.

"Don't worry," came Sapphira's voice from the doorway. "I expect Anna and Aidan have misjudged the time — after all, she's new to this part of the world."

He swung around. Against the background of the chatter from the living room — his voice was low and angry.

"Why did you muddle things, Sapphira?"

"Muddle things? I?"

"You admitted it. You planned pretty badly, didn't you, leaving Anna and Aidan at a loose end."

"They haven't been at a loose end, Martin! My guess is that they're having a lovely time together. I watched them start off, like two people with wings to their feet. It was most touching!" Her long lips curved into a smile.

"And that isn't funny!" he snapped.

Her amusement vanished; her eyes flashed.

"You don't have to be angry with me, Martin! *I* didn't make the mistake!"

"But you said —"

"Oh, I *said!* That was because I didn't want an argument in front of guests! I took the blame, but I really am blameless, you know! You see, I asked Anna to write to Aidan —"

Martin lowered his cigarette slowly and looked at her, eyes narrowed over the coil of smoke.

"I suppose," Sapphira went on, "she forgot, or —"

"Or — what?"

"Well, perhaps she thought it would be nice for them both to have a little time together — a walk. They made such a fine couple, Martin, both so dark and so good-looking."

He made an impatient gesture with his hand.

"And you didn't ask her if she'd written? You didn't remind her?"

"I'm sorry, I'm afraid I didn't."

He walked past her to the door and she called after him.

"Martin —"

"Well?"

"Don't be angry with her! Let it go. I'm sure it was just an oversight —" Her voice held no conviction.

Martin said, "It's done now, and the party's

on. We'll forget it."

"Here they are!" Sapphira turned to the window. "Look, they're coming down the drive —"

But Martin had walked across the hall and joined his guests in the living room.

When she heard the sounds of the party, Anna flew into the house and up the stairs to her room, she washed, changed swiftly into a silk dress and sought Martin out.

"I'm so sorry we were late. I didn't know it would take so long to get back from Janis Monastery."

He looked at her and thought, "How radiant she is tonight!" and asked aloud, "You enjoyed yourself?"

"Oh yes. It was lovely. Did you enjoy your ride?"

He nodded briefly, and heard her say, honestly and generously, "I'm so glad, Martin! It's very good for you with your sort of job to get the exercise riding gives you. Ride as much as you like, I'll enjoy the thought of you enjoying it."

Martin looked at her and felt ashamed of his own resentment.

When all the guests had finally left, Anna wondered if she should speak to Martin about the muddled arrangements and decided against it. If Sapphira said anything to Martin he would tell her and she would defend herself. But if he said nothing, she knew better than to stir up trouble. It was over — everyone had enjoyed themselves, and if Sapphira thought she had left Anna to write to Aidan and she was equally certain that she hadn't, then let it rest. The afternoon had been happy.

Anna thought no more about it. She did not see this, too, as the cloud no bigger than a man's hand that would grow until it threatened her safety and her life.

V

Village life at Blakesford, Anna supposed, was not so different from anywhere else. Everyone knew everyone else; a number of the villagers worked at the nurseries and local gossip topped the poll, even ousting television as a favorite subject in kitchen and bar and over garden fences.

Anna took the lingering glances when "Good morning" was said as natural curiosity; when she went into a shop, people stopped talking but they smiled at her and were friendly.

Anna flung herself into any job she was given, filling her days because she realized from that first evening that Martin's family were not going to make any attempt either to understand her or to see her as anything but a girl from a world they did not know nor want to know.

For her, these weeks were just a marking time

until she was married. There was plenty to be done, shopping in London for her wedding and, jointly, the search for a small house in the neighborhood.

The agents sent lists of possible properties and she and Martin went to see them. Sometimes they were quite impossible, either too ramshackle or too large, but the one or two places that Anna liked, Martin found fault with.

One early evening they went to see a house which lay four miles from the village. It was a small Georgian-style house, beautifully proportioned and set in an acre of ground. Inside it was light and airy and whoever had lived there before had obviously loved it to have kept it in such perfect condition.

"Martin, it's lovely!" she cried, standing at the window that looked over a walled garden, with a vine and a walnut tree.

He made no response and she turned to him. "You like it, don't you?"

"I suppose so," he admitted reluctantly.

"But not enough to live here!"

There was a fractional pause.

"Let's say, rather, that I don't want to pay the high price they're asking."

"But it's not *that* high, Martin, and you could make them an offer."

"I know," he admitted uncomfortably, "but the fact is, Anna, I've just lent the family some more money."

"They're doing well, surely?"

"They bought those extra acres from Seth Lowther's farm for a Christmas tree plantation. They had to have bulldozers to clear tree roots and shrubs. It cost quite a bit of money, so I haven't any available cash to lay down for — this —" He nodded at the house.

"But why didn't you tell me before we started house hunting?" she cried.

She felt him fold away from her, armoring himself against her indignation.

"I was a coward, I suppose. I can't forget the terrible scene with Gillian when she found I'd sunk so much capital in the business."

"But I'm not Gillian," she said gently.

He laid an arm around her shoulder. "When Father left us the nurseries, it was on the understanding that I, as the man of the family, would see that it was maintained to a standard that would give the family a good living. I've tried to do that."

She had been staring at the light paneled wall, thinking. He can't quite trust me, even now! Gillian's legacy to him isn't spent yet! Poor Martin, still afraid of a woman's tongue!

"Let's go," she said as quietly as she could.

"We'll forget this house and look for something really small. A cottage —"

"Do you think there's one to be had for miles around?" he asked wryly. "Now that Lavernake has been developed into an important industrial town, everything of reasonable price has been snapped up long ago!"

"Then what do you suggest?"

His troubled eyes met hers. "I thought perhaps we could do what the family suggest and take over the wing of the house. We could be absolutely on our own there, and then in a year or so's time we could look for a house."

"Oh, no, not that! Martin, no!"

She saw his look of startled surprise.

"But, Anna, it would at least be a home and you would have perfect freedom to decorate and furnish it exactly as you like."

"We can't begin our married life living with the family."

"It wouldn't be like that! I'd have a door put in the passage to divide the house properly so that no one would be able to trespass on us unless we asked them. Anna — do you really mind so much? It would only be for a year!"

"But don't you see? I'd find in the end that it wasn't temporary," she protested. "Once we'd made the west wing habitable, you wouldn't want to move again."

"I would if you wanted it. I'd do whatever you said after I'd had a chance to get over this next twelve months. This money is only a loan, anyway. I haven't put it into the business for good. It will be paid back some time in the New Year when the Christmas tree plantation has paid its way."

"You could borrow from the bank for our house —"

"And start my marriage with a millstone around my neck? No, Anna."

"Then let my stepfather help you. He would, and so graciously, too, that you'd never mind taking it."

Martin said, "No," again, sharply. "I have no intention of borrowing from my future wife's family."

"That sounds pompous! Why refuse without giving it a thought? Marriage is a joint affair and Father would love to help us."

"Isn't it enough for you, Anna, that we're going to be together?" he asked her. "Does it matter so much *where* we live?"

The argument that could finalize all argument!

She walked away from him, staring out at the charming garden she would have so loved to tend and watch through the seasons.

"Martin, why did you agree to look at houses

if you had no intention of buying one?"

"In the mad hope, I suppose, that we'd find one ridiculously cheap — as though we would, these days! And, as I told you, cowardice," he continued in a flat, hopeless voice. "When I let them have that money, I was so certain you'd understand. But when Sapphira suggested the other day that we use the west wing, I saw your expression and I knew that you'd hate it. I suppose I hoped for a miracle — a house given away with a box of detergent!"

"It's no use staying here. We'll take the keys back to the agent and forget it."

But she knew quite well as she sat by his side in the car that they were both walking, one blindly, the other with clear sight, into an impossible situation. . . .

There were always piles of letters for the family at breakfast. Anna read her letter from her mother and then, folding it, heard Jaimie say:

"We've got another big order for herbs. We'll have to expand."

"You know," Bridget looked around the table, "I could perhaps sell them at the shop. People in this country are getting far more food conscious. If we did them up attractively, customers would buy them for little presents. We could experiment with new ones. Origanum, for instance. It's lovely for salads in summer or stews in winter. Then there's fennel, and basil."

Jaimie's eyes brightened. "There's all that ground beyond the knoll down at the far end of the garden. It's so much waste. We could utilize that for more herb growing."

"Yes. Yes," Sapphira said vaguely. She was only half aware that, as usual, they were deferring to her on this matter. She was reading a letter and her expression held a curious, muted triumph.

"Anything interesting in your mail this morning, Sapphira?" Bridget asked softly, her eyes flicking from the letterhead, which was all she would be able to see from where she sat, to Sapphira's face.

"Interesting? In my mail?" She looked up, blankly. "Oh, no! Not in the least." She folded the letter, slid it back into its envelope and seemed to be making an effort to recall what had been said. "You were talking about herbs —"

"Funny thing!" Bridget observed, "we never heard again from those land development people, did we? You remember they made us an offer and then when we turned it down —"

"When *you* turned it down," Sapphira said equally softly.

"When we all, except you, Sapphira, said 'No,' " Bridget amended, "they said they'd be approaching us again. But they haven't, have they?"

"You'd know if they had."

"We'd all have to know, wouldn't we?" Bridget said softly and her eyes met Sapphira's and dropped first.

Martin asked, folding his newspaper, "What's this about land development?"

"Oh, Masters and Stewartson made us an offer for all the land, plus this house," Eve explained.

"No one wrote to me about it —"

"It was at the time when Gillian — died. We couldn't have worried you with it," Sapphira said quickly. "Anyway it was solved between us —"

"After an almighty row that I should think they could have heard in Lavernake!" Bridget commented. "Eve and I didn't see why, having built up our business with damned hard work we should throw it all away and have to start again —"

"You'd have had capital to start," Sapphira retorted, and stirred her coffee with quick, angry flips of her wrist.

"And what did Jaimie think about it?" Martin asked quietly.

"Oh, Jaimie agreed with me," Eve put in quickly.

"Not quite," he said hesitantly. "I thought —"

"You thought *our* way when I explained it all to you."

"And Sapphira?" Martin asked, waiting, watching them.

"Sapphira wanted the lovely money. She saw herself investing and living well on her stocks and bonds. But you know that we have to go by the majority in this business. And it was one to three —"

"I — see — but I think I should have been consulted."

"Oh, but we knew you'd agree to keep the nurseries on, Martin," Eve said. "And as you were coming home — alone and well, it was awful, and —"

"What Eve is trying to say," Bridget cut in, "is that Gillian was dead and we couldn't bear for you to have no home to come to."

"That was *your* argument," Eve retorted. "Mine was that this was Jaimie's and my living. We'd never get sufficient capital to start really well on and we've done more than any of you to build this business up. The offer from the land developers has been turned down and now the matter is closed."

"Is it?" Bridget asked, ignoring Eve and turning to Sapphira.

Again their eyes met in that secret spark of enmity and again Sapphira outstared Bridget.

Chairs were pushed back, plates were stacked on the trolley. Bridget lit a cigarette and hummed an old Irish folk tune.

"I know where I'm going,
And I know who's going with me —"

Did she? Anna wondered, collecting the Pyrex dishes from the hotplate.

On Saturday, while Martin was at the laboratory, Anna found Julie in the garden. Two village children were with her and they had played ball, skipped, ridden up and down the paths on a green tricycle, and were now swinging idly on the branches of a tree, their attention wandering.

When Julie saw Anna she ran towards her. "We want a new game."

"It's beginning to rain so you'll have to find something indoors, I'm afraid."

Julie clung to her hand.

"It's more fun out here."

"It won't be when you get wet and uncomfortable," Anna said practically. "Come on, run for it, it's going to come down really hard! Why don't you choose a story from one of your books and dress up and act it?" she called after them.

"You choose a story, Anna," they turned inside

the doorway, and watched her.

"Very well."

"And you did promise – to dress up like an Indian –"

"In a sari? All right, I'll put one on for you. Go up to the attic. There's an old trunk of clothes up there, isn't there, that Aunt Eve lets you play with."

"Yes, lots of silly old curtains and broken bits of flowers," Julie said disgustedly, "but I suppose they'll have to do!"

Anna chose the brilliant green sari with the golden embroidery. She thought as she struggled with it, tucking it into the long petticoat band, how difficult they were for people unused to arranging them and yet how graceful if you had the knack.

She found the long gold earrings and two gold bracelets and put them on. She changed her hairstyle, parting it in the middle and drawing it down, Madonna-like on either side of her face. For slippers, the best she could do was to put on her flat heeled sandals.

The silken underskirt swished a little as she walked down the corridor and up the narrow attic stairs.

The children were delighted. They came, reaching out small inquisitive fingers, to touch the bracelets, the silk, the rich embroidery.

"Is it real gold?"

"Yes."

"Why don't you always wear it, it's so pretty," Julie said.

"Because I'm not Eastern."

"But Aunt Sapphira said —"

"What did she say?"

"That you really are an Indian lady."

"That's not true," Anna said patiently. "I've lived there all my life, except for coming to school here in England, and my stepfather is Indian, but *I'm* not." She turned, releasing herself from their hands. "Now, have you chosen a story you want to act?"

But the children were no longer interested in books they had already read. They wanted Anna to tell them stories. India was, to them, like the pictures in old books, a place of crimson trappings on elephants and jeweled and ospreyed turbans, and tigers.

> "Tyger, tyger burning bright
> In the forests of the night,"

Julie sing-songed in a small high voice, without meaning.

Anna, however, told them about the children of Kashmir: of the boy goatherds and the children who helped their families to weave rugs on latticed balconies in Srinagar, of the silver ornaments the children wore and the odd songs they sang. She kept the more tragic facts from them — the poverty, the tattered veils of the little girls, the wild unkempt hair and dirty clothes of the herd boys. She made it all sound like a fairy tale but then, she thought, for all their poverty, the Kashmiris were happy people.

None of them heard a light step outside.

"What are you doing?" Sapphira's voice demanded.

Glancing up, laughingly, Anna said, "Julie wanted me to dress up. And now I'm telling them stories about India."

"They'd be much better off playing some game of their own! Just sitting around listening to you isn't giving them their necessary exercise."

"I had no intention of letting them sit around the whole morning, Sapphira. It was just for a few minutes. They've been playing in the garden, you know, only it began to rain."

"And I don't think you should wear your Indian clothes here."

The color drained from Anna's face at the barely veiled insolence in Sapphira's tone.

"They aren't 'my Indian clothes.' They belonged to my father's mother."

"Your grandmother —"

"No! She was no relation."

"You said your father's mother. So I thought –"

"You know that he's my stepfather, only I've got used to calling him father," Anna said quietly. "I dressed up because Julie asked me to. She wanted to see what a sari looked like."

"Well, I should take it off now," Sapphira said briskly. "It wouldn't do, I'm afraid, to have the children telling everyone in the village that you go about the house dressed like that."

"You should know by now that I don't dress like this! I am Western –"

"Of course –" Sapphira gave her a long, thoughtful look. "But you have absorbed a great deal that is Indian, haven't you, Anna?"

"Have I? Yes, I suppose so. I grew to love it, like my own country –"

"Your own country!"

"Yes."

Sapphira was still staring at her. "How strange," she said slowly. "How very strange! Perhaps if you look at yourself in the mirror, Anna, you will see what I mean."

Anna rose, and moved past Sapphira. "I have worn this to amuse the children on a wet morning, that's all. Perhaps I'm obtuse, but I can't think what you see strange. This dress is so natural and beautiful on the women in India." At the door she paused, and said to the children,

"Pick out a story from one of your books to act and I'll come and help you when I've changed."

Sapphira's insolence had shaken her. She closed the door of her bedroom and leaned against it and caught sight of herself in the old-fashioned cheval mirror against the far wall.

And saw what Sapphira saw . . .

With the lovely silken folds draping her head and falling to her feet, the long earrings, the bracelets and the golden sandals, her raven black hair parted classically, she looked as though she had strayed from a picture of India.

An Indian girl! Was that what Sapphira had seen – what she had believed? That Anna had lied when she told them she was all Western? That she was in very truth a Hindu?

But Martin knew her family and he would have told the Claremondes all about it. Or, the thought froze her, what more could he have told them since she herself knew nothing about her real father save that he had been French. Perhaps they thought her an adventuress, determined, with the connivance of her family, to marry an Englishman. Then she could prove them wrong: she could write to her mother. . . . Write and ask, "Who was my real father? I am not half Indian, am I? The Claremondes – Martin's family – seem to doubt me –" An inner sensitiveness checked her.

Let them believe what they liked. The fact that she could tell them nothing about her real birth was unimportant to Martin — and that was all that mattered.

Anna dragged off the earrings with such force that the lobes burned and irritated for minutes afterwards; she pulled off the bangles and combed her hair back to its original style. She chose a parma violet sweater and black skirt and high heeled shoes.

And all the time she fought with her anger against Sapphira.

I shall live this down . . . I won't let Sapphira's insolence drive me away so that they can say to Martin, "She's not for you, she can't settle down here!" And so, perhaps, lose him.

She wasn't going to lose Martin by running out.

VI

On the following day, Sunday, Martin took Anna to the yacht club down in the Bay. He himself had no boat, but he very often crewed for his friends.

It was a deep blue day and when they had climbed down the steep path to the shore they crossed to the hard sand and walked as near as they could to the sea.

Away from the shadow of the old house, Anna was happy. They linked hands and dared the waves, leaping aside as one hurled itself at them with clouds of lovely, flying foam. In the distance she could see the club house, low and white against the cobalt sky, with the yachts drifting out on the light west wind, sails of white and russet against the shimmering sea.

Anna wore a green and gold striped skirt and a green blouse, her black hair blew free, weaving in the breeze.

Walking along, with their footsteps making deep imprints behind them, they gradually neared the yacht club.

I'm going to meet Martin's friends, she thought, and I want them to like me —

Immediately she entered the large lounge with its picture windows looking out over the Bay and saw people turn and greet Martin and include her in their smile, she knew it would be all right.

Everyone was dressed for yachting, the girls in slacks or shorts and sweaters, the men casual or jaunty or bearded and heartily untidy. There was a rich smell of rope, and sand and tar and the sea which permeated through the open windows.

Anna made friends with a blind bull terrier which, she was told, always stood between people's legs as though for comfort, leaning against them, trusting, his head turning as his quick ears heard a familiar voice, letting them pat his heavy thighs, loving everybody.

Presently Martin and Anna wandered out onto the jetty to watch one or two of the boats get under way.

A colleague of Martin's at the laboratory, owner of the bull terrier, joined her at the jetty rail. Martin was at the far end talking to two men and packing stores in a boat.

"I hear Martin has just renewed his club subscription. That means he won't be taking the Argentine job."

Anna repeated bewilderedly, "The Argentine job?"

"Didn't you know? Oh well, I suppose he didn't want to tell you because he guessed as you'd made this long journey to settle down here, you wouldn't want to be uprooted again. The boss is very disappointed because Martin is the best man to send, and the knowledge he can give out there and bring back to us would have been invaluable. Still, I guess it's your lives. And I'm glad in a way. Martin's nice to have around — we'd miss him."

Martin called, "Hey, Jim, you're going to be lassoed if you don't watch out! Catch!"

The man by her side leaned over and caught a rope deftly. A motor launch was sidling alongside. Anna watched it.

So Martin had been offered a job abroad again and he wasn't taking it; he wasn't even telling her about it. . . .

"Know anything about boats, Miss Kashinath?"

She shook her head. "Only houseboats in Kashmir, and one just lazes on them and if you want to change your mooring place, the boys do that for you."

"It must be very beautiful up there."

"It is beautiful."

"I hope you'll be very happy here. It's not a bad place —"

"What are you two in a huddle about?" Martin came towards them smiling, confident. She thought, as Jim was explaining that he was merely envying Martin his good fortune, how changed he was from the grave, harassed man who used to come every morning to the laboratories in New Delhi looking as though half his night had been spent sleepless by the side of a nagging, tempestuous wife.

"I *am* lucky," Martin was saying, looking at Anna with clear, unembarrassed love. "But we won't be popular at home if we don't get going. Come, Anna, the good old roast beef and Yorkshire is waiting!"

They took the short cut home, up onto the cliffs, and through the woods. The great roots of the trees made arabesques of reddish brown on the dark earth: above them a few birds sang and the sun broke through in patches where a tree bent a little away from its neighbors as though weighted sideways with its own rich leafiness.

"Martin —"

He had paused to touch a beautiful pink fungus with his foot.

"Yes?"

"I've just heard that you were offered a job in the Argentine —"

"In Buenos Aires. That's right. I suppose Jim told you."

"Yes."

"Well," he half turned, smiling at her. "Why so grave about it?"

"I wondered why you didn't tell me."

"There was no need, as I'm not going to accept it."

"What would it mean — if you did?"

"Two years in the Argentine at triple the salary I'm getting now, an apartment found for us —"

"South America would be lovely, Martin."

"I had a year in Kenya, and two years in India. Now I want to settle down. I want roots again, Anna —"

He waited and then turned to her, surprised at her silence. "You don't want to go, do you?"

"Not if you don't."

"You mean you'd like to?"

She nodded.

He stared away from her. "I'm sorry. I suppose England is strange for you — after India. I must have been too blind to see. Sapphira told me —"

"Told you what, Martin?"

"That I was expecting rather a lot to hope

that you'd be happy in this one-eyed village, and English rains and our simple lives after —"

"Martin, stop!" She stood quite still and faced him, the wind blowing her hair and her skirt back, cutting with cool fingers through her silk blouse.

"What have I said?"

"Everything that's wrong," she cried. "Or at least, Sapphira has! I've told you, I don't care where we live so long as we're happy together."

"Here? With roots?"

She looked away and he understood.

"But *not* here, Anna, that's it, isn't it? Anywhere — but not here!"

She stood, silent and helpless.

"*Why?*" he insisted.

She leaned against a tree, watching him. "Because," she said as steadily as she could, "I want our marriage to have a chance. And it won't if we stay here."

"But why not — if as you say you like England —"

"Your family will never accept me!"

It was as though she had struck him.

"But they welcomed you! It was their idea that you should stay here with them until the wedding —"

To assess me — to make me feel my difference

to them . . . perhaps. She remembered her presentiment at London Airport. *Perhaps to break something they disapproved. . . .*

"Anna!" He seemed to be unable to bear her silence.

She forced herself to meet his gaze, and suddenly the bitter things that rushed to her mind could not be said. Fear of a scene was in his eyes, and hurt and doubt made his face look drawn.

She said gently, "Let's not talk any more about it, Martin."

Her quiet voice, when he had steeled himself to expect upbraiding and reproach, had the effect of a spell. His love for her rushed over him in a great wave. In this moment of relief, she became magical and he could refuse her nothing. He put out his hands and touched her face with a curious reverence.

"Anna — don't you see, if they've shown you anything — any moment's unkindness, it's because you have much more than they have — you're beautiful and that beauty is in more than just *my* eyes! I heard Sapphira say so. And you've got an inner serenity and you're loved — that's a whole heap for them to have to swallow! Don't take any notice of their sharp tongues — it's a Claremonde characteristic, like their directness — I'm the only one

94

who had escaped that — it doesn't mean anything." He was pleading hard for them. "Even their quarreling is some necessary form of self-expression and it doesn't really affect their deeper feelings for one another."

When some tragedy happens that affects them all, they close their ranks like great allies . . . and I'm the tragedy . . . She held her peace.

"Darling —" He drew her close and kissed her. "I'll accept that Argentine offer," he held her away from him. "We'll go and begin our lives together there." He paused as she was silent. "Happy now?"

She had to say "Yes" because she loved him too much to hurt him with further argument.

She saw that he was giving in about South America because, still scared, he fled from trouble. Gillian's screaming, hysterical ghost hovered in the background of his mind.

The promise that they would go to South America was an uneasy triumph for Anna. She knew that the solution would not be resolved smoothly. She had won but she had yet to pay the price of her victory. That thought was with her when, at the end of supper that evening, Sapphira told Martin that she had been in touch with the builders over the alterations necessary to the west wing of the house.

Martin reached for the cheese platter.

"Thanks, Sapphira, but it won't be necessary."

"But you can't have the place as it is, there's no bathroom and —"

"I've decided to accept the South American offer."

"Martin, no!" It was Bridget who cried out almost before he had finished speaking. "Oh no. You'll hate it."

"I don't see why, since I'll still be doing the sort of job I like! And Anna and I have decided that we'd like to go, after all."

Their eyes were on her. *So Anna is at the bottom of this!*

"But Martin, you've always said your plan was to come home and settle down. You said —"

"Never mind that now," he interrupted sharply. "Anna and I have discussed it and I've made my decision."

"You're making a terrible mistake!"

He said quietly, "If I am, the responsibility for it is mine."

"It's going to be so hard on Julie, losing you again —" Eve began.

"Oh, she'll come with us, of course."

Eve nearly sprang out of her chair.

"Martin, you can't possibly take her to *that* place!"

"You talk as though we're going to live in

darkest Africa! B.A. is extremely civilized."

"It isn't that, it's her health. Dr. Varley says she must be very carefully watched for the next few years."

"I think Anna and I are quite capable of that!"

"But, Martin, we *know* her, we understand her and she's used to us. This is her home," Eve's pleading gave way to anger. "You left her with us when you went to India. You didn't worry then!"

"Gillian left her," he corrected. "I never wanted it that way."

"The fact remains she was in our charge and we grew to love her. Now you're snatching her away!"

"Put it any way you like," Martin said hotly. "The fact remains, I have made my decision. When Anna and I are married, the three of us go to South America. Have you finished Anna?" He glanced at her and then at Sapphira. "We're going into Lavernake to see the new film at the Regal."

"I'll just help clear away first."

"Thanks," Sapphira said, "but go along. We don't need you, Anna!"

They didn't. She felt their anger wrap around her like a choking fog; she saw their eyes follow her as she crossed the room, sliding away when she turned once to glance at the clock.

She knew that directly the door closed behind herself and Martin, they would begin to talk. They would whip themselves into a fury of argument, but this time there would be no dissension between them. They were of one mind. She was the alien. . . .

The evening was spoiled for Anna. She was only vaguely aware of the speed and fury of the drama on the screen; aware with a curious detachment, of Martin seated next to her, his arm touching hers, his hand reaching for hers.

She felt afraid and powerless before a united force. She knew that if she left Dion House she would be playing into their hands, that to do so could well be the first step towards losing Martin. . . .

VII

Anna was in her room after breakfast the next morning making her bed. Amy had a "Music While You Work" program jigging away in the kitchen, but above the rise and fall of the catchy tunes, Anna heard high voices. After a minute or two she realized that Sapphira and Bridget were arguing in the room below.

Anna stood, holding a corner of the thick green candlewick quilt. "They could be talking about me!" And then she pulled herself together and assessed herself with dismay. What's happening to me? I never used to be suspicious like this — crammed full of doubt. They've got a hundred things to argue about, why imagine it is me?

Swift, high heeled footsteps beat across the floor below, a door slammed. She heard a car rev up and drive away.

Later, as Anna passed the office on her way through the hall, Sapphira called her and she went into the small, neat room with its steel files and the two desks.

Sapphira was tall. She was standing, staring out of the window, and seemed to dominate it. She had a cigarette between her fingers, which was unusual for her, and she appeared to sense Anna's entry, for she spoke without turning around to make certain she was there.

"I want you to help us, Anna."

"Of course, if I can."

"You're the only one who can. That is, unless things have to get unpleasant."

"I don't understand."

Sapphira swung around. She tapped her cigarette on her nail and Anna saw that it was unlit.

"I'll come to the point." Her eyes were like cold amber. "You must prevent Martin from taking Julie to South America."

"If he says she is to go, how can I stop him? And I think Julie should be with her father —"

"And with *you*?"

"Yes, and with me."

Desperately she decided that reasoning might help them to understand. She said earnestly:

"I know what it's like to have harmony in the home, and I think I know how to bring it about. Julie will be happy with us — I'll see she is —"

Suddenly Sapphira's composure snapped. She shook with released anger.

"You plan well, Anna! First you get Martin and then, not only do you persuade him away from his home, his country even, but you rob us of Julie!"

"You say I 'planned' —"

"Well, didn't you?"

"As you weren't in India when I met Martin, as you know nothing of what happened out there —"

"But I do! Gillian was a faithful correspondent. She often wrote to Bridget."

"If you had known Gillian's state of mind out there, you wouldn't take much notice of what she said in letters."

"We had to take notice, Anna. The last letter of hers was full of — searing tragedy."

"I told Bridget, and now I tell you," Anna was gripping the edge of a desk. "I know! I was there and saw it all! Gillian wrote to you out of the hell of her own imagination!"

"As she's dead, there is only your word for that now!"

"There's Martin, too! You'd believe him, surely!"

"He's my brother, but that doesn't mean he'd admit to failing Gillian. He wants to forget the past, anyway, not to have it raked up!"

"But *you* want to rake it up, with me! Just as Bridget did. Why? Why?" She heard her own low, violent voice and thought: This isn't me talking!

"I'm senior in this house, that's why I feel I must speak to you. You've got to see, Anna, that you can't arrange everything your way. First Martin —"

"First Martin!" Anna's control snapped. With a rush of blinding clarity she saw what Bridget and now Sapphira was hinting at. "You think *I* was the woman Gillian wrote about, don't you?"

"Weren't you, Anna? While Martin was in that bewildered, unhappy state of mind, didn't you make every effort to win him away from his wife?"

The small room seemed to swim around Anna; she had a fainting sense of unreality. Words rushed into her mind — the words Bridget had quoted from Gillian's letter. "How could she bear to build her happiness on someone else's tragedy?"

So that's why they hate me . . . then did they love Gillian so much? So much that they haven't even a photograph of hers, a possession of hers in their house?

She heard her own voice forced out of her: "You all think I set out to steal Martin."

" 'Steal' is a horrid word, and as far as I am concerned it isn't important. For some reason of your own, you wanted to marry an Englishman and get to England and now you're here you don't like it!"

"For – some – reason – of – my – own? What do you mean?"

The thin shoulders lifted and dropped.

"Either you know, in which case, Anna, you don't want me to tell you, or you don't know, in which case it's still unimportant. I'm only interested in Julie's welfare at the moment and I am not going to stand aside and let you arrange even a child's life to suit yourself."

"You seem to forget that Julie is Martin's child. It's for him to say, not me."

"Martin will say what you put into his mind to say –"

"That's ludicrous!" Anna's rare temper broke through. She forced a kind of panic strength into herself.

"All I want is to marry Martin whom I happen to love and to be given a chance to live happily with him."

"He'd never be happy without Julie and she can't go. Even if we were all willing, no doctor would allow her to leave England until her strength is built up again after those two doses of pneumonia she had last winter."

"Then the sunshine will be good for her."

"The heat would tax her strength too much. It is quite out of the question for her to leave England."

"That's something you'll have to argue out with Martin," Anna said wearily. Her anger and her vitality had gone out of her like a light and she felt too tired to whip up any more resentment, too drained to stand arraigned any longer before this cold, accusing woman. What was the use? They had their narrow, preconceived ideas, and not even proof would convince them of her utter innocence in the tragedy of Gillian Claremonde. They wanted to accuse her. Because they had loved Gillian? Or because for hidden reasons of their own they did not want her in the family. What reason? What had she done, or not done; said, or not said? She had been walking without realizing it, to the door.

Sapphira was speaking again, and she thought how harsh her voice was when she was angry!

"Anna, please understand! It's best for us to be honest with one another. I'm not accusing you so far as Gillian is concerned. If you and Martin chose to have an affair, that's your business. But you've got what you wanted – *Martin*. Now try to compromise, for his sake!"

"If Martin insisted on staying here, then of course I would stay."

"My dear Anna, those are fine words! You know perfectly well that, at the moment, Martin will do whatever you want. It's one of the recognized weaknesses of a man during an infatuation – oh well, never mind that –"

"If you think that this is just an infatuation –" Sapphira's voice cut in loudly.

"Please understand, this is Martin's home. *You* may hate it, but he loves it; he has a very strongly developed sense of roots. You want to go to South America; he doesn't and yet he has given in. At least, that's how it seems at the moment, but many things can change. For instance, he will want to take Julie – *and we shall never let her go!*"

Burning indignation flared up in Anna.

"You dared to call Martin's feeling for me an infatuation! You stand there, making it clear that you will never accept me or even try to like me –"

"I happen to love my brother and want his happiness."

"His happiness – *your* way!" Fury blazed in her, yet something cautioned her that anger must not be her weapon. Her strength must be in her control, because she knew well that if she quarreled it would be she, Anna, who would suffer in the end.

Without a word she turned and walked across the room and out of the door, leaving it open. She went out of the house and across the lawn to the little knoll at the far end of the garden. There she sat on the wooden seat where she had sat on her first evening, and felt the cool east breeze shiver through her.

If you love Martin you will stay here . . . stay here and watch your fate move from your own mastery to theirs? Watch your happiness being slowly torn away? Because somehow, by a concerted effort, they'd win and you'd lose everything. Even a man's love can be worn down – Martin must have loved Gillian once. . . .

I've got to get away. But if I do, perhaps I'll lose Martin. Surely not if she explained and made him understand. Understand what? That they resented her here? He might even tackle them and they'd say the obvious thing. "We only want your happiness. Of course we're prepared to love Anna!" They would infer that it was she who was so different, that by upbringing and environment she was more close to the East than the West. They could also make him see that from a dissatisfied fiancée would grow a carping wife . . . another Gillian. . . .

Suppose she told him about the letter from

Gillian to Bridget. What good would it do? For Martin, it could only rake up the tormented past at this moment when he was at last shaking himself from the effects of the tortured years.

One thing was certain. She loved Martin and she would fight to keep him. She had only to hold on here for another few weeks, regardless of what was said or done. And, after that, she would be free of the Claremondes.

There came to her the memory of something her stepfather had said to just after her engagement. "You must understand him, Anna, as well as love him. What he has gone through will have left its mark on him for some time to come. It won't be easy for you."

And Anna had said, "I love Martin." As though in that were all!

One thing puzzled her. Bridget had revealed no particular love for Julie and Sapphira had never once shown more than a practical concern for her. Only the childless Eve doted on her; only Eve would really know a void in her life if Julie went with her father to South America. Then why should Sapphira fight so fiercely for Eve's sake? Looking at that withdrawn face, one did not associate such unselfish efforts with Martin's older sister. Then what was at the back of it all? What was Sapphira really trying to do? *Send me away? Is that it? Force me to realize that*

I am tearing Martin in two; that I can never make him happy?

Some days had passed since Anna's scene with Sapphira and she knew that, in spite of the family's outward courtesy and consideration, she was their potential enemy. She was taking Martin from them and now she was scheming to take Julie. Nobody mentioned the subject again but Anna noticed how the little girl was coddled, more indulged than ever as though they were working hard through Julie herself, to cement their claim on her.

Except when Martin was home and the family made fierce, concerted efforts to create a happy atmosphere, Anna was left fairly alone. Sapphira was usually at her desk or in the kitchen; Eve was always out supervising the workers with Jaimie. When the jobs she could do to help about the house were over, Anna would go for walks.

Her favorite took her over the hill and across the slopes of the rough grass to the sea.

One mild afternoon, she walked down to the shore and saw the English Channel lying still under a mist of pale pink pearl. The waveless beauty of it lured her down the steep path to the water's edge.

Two people were paddling among the rocks,

peering into tiny pools, laughing and slithering over the tangy brown seaweed.

They looked up, saw her and she immediately recognized a young married couple Martin had introduced her to at the yacht club. They called:

"Come and join us. We're on our way to tea at the club."

Anna ran over the sands, joined them and climbed and slithered with them over the rocks.

It was a slow journey to the yacht club for every tiny pool left by the receding sea held something to make them stop and look. A starfish lay quiescent in its own minute lake; infinitesimal tadpole life darted in and out of half submerged sugar-white rocks; tufted brown seaweed sunned itself.

And in that happy atmosphere of sea and companionship Anna forgot the Claremondes.

When, at last, she left the club, the evening was already closing in and the late burnished light brushed the countryside with amber and turned the rising moon into a ball of burnt sugar.

As she neared Dion House she saw that the lights were already turned on and seen like this, in the gentle light, the forbidding old house became almost benign.

As she turned the arc of the drive she heard

music. Someone in the living room had put on a record of Beethoven's Eighth Symphony and the sonorous music poured out into the misty evening.

The front door was closed and there was a note pinned to it.

She thought: The bell is out of order. And went up the steps and read it, with difficulty, by the light that came from the hall through the stained glass transom window.

The words were printed in childish, un-formed letters:

There is no place like home. So go back, Indian girl!

Anna stared at it... Had Julie and the village children been playing some game? *Red* Indian − *West* Indian − *East* Indian? And then the truth ripped through her. She felt as though a wall of ice had hit her. This thing, the kind that a child might chalk on a wall in a school playground, was meant for her; it was crude, but it was intended to be in order to disguise the adult mind behind it. No child could have reached up to pin it so high on the door. . . . Go home. Anna Kashinath − *Indian girl!*

She stood on the top step rooted in horror at the realization of someone's mounting hatred of her. For whoever had pinned it there knew that she would be the first to see it. She looked back at the hill over which the narrow lane snaked. When she had come along there a few minutes earlier, before the dip down to the gates of the house, she had had a glimpse of the doorway. Her eyesight was good enough to be certain that there was no white blob standing out against the dark wood of that door.

So, someone had watched for her to come down that long drive, then before she had reached the curve that brought her face to face with the house, had pinned the note there and slipped away.

Or were they hiding somewhere near, watching her reaction?

She swung around, glancing about her. Nothing stirred in the misty amethyst afterglow; there was no wind to bend the slender branches of the bushes, nothing to disturb the sable shadows and reveal a watcher. If anyone was there, they remained in utter, immovable silence. Even the music in the house had ceased. She stared again at the note. In the swiftly fading light the words were now almost invisible. On the face of it, it was childish and ignorant. Fundamentally, it had the taste of evil. . . .

VIII

Anna reached up and took the note down, and her shaking hands dropped the pin that held it. She didn't bother to grope for it in the dark but turning the handle of the door, and finding it, as usual, unlocked, walked in.

Sapphira sat alone in the living room reading a newspaper.

Anna crossed the room and laid the piece of paper in front of her.

"What's this?"

"Read it!"

Sapphira peered at it, frowning.

"But I don't understand. Where did you get it? Whose is it?"

"I found it pinned to the front door. It was meant for me, Sapphira. Someone watched me come up the drive and made quite certain that I should see it."

112

Sapphira's face was still a study of puzzled bewilderment.

"I'm sorry, Anna, but I still don't understand —"

"It's all horribly simple," she heard her own voice explaining with frozen clarity. "Someone hates me and wants me to leave here. Whoever wrote it calls me 'Indian'; the inference is clear, isn't it, Sapphira?"

The light, narrow eyes regarded Anna. "I think you are making too much of it! Calling you" — her gaze dropped to the paper — " 'Indian girl' is obviously just a manner of speaking, because you are very dark and came from India. One of the village children, of course —"

"I don't believe a village child wrote that! Whoever thought it out, believes —"

"Believes — what?" Sapphira asked softly, watching her.

"That I only pretend I'm English — that I — I really have got Indian blood."

Sapphira's hand shot out and snatched at the piece of paper.

"Then whoever did this can't be in his right senses." Her wrist moved but before she could fling the crumpled paper into the fire, Anna whipped it from her.

"Whoever wrote that *was* in his right senses; his right, malicious, meddling senses," she began to smooth the paper.

"Throw it away, Anna!"

"I'm going to show it to Martin."

"Don't do that!"

"He should know — what people think about me, what *someone* is whispering."

"What good will that do? He has met your family, he must know — the truth —"

Something in the way Sapphira said those last two words quickened Anna's perceptions. "Why do you say it like that —"

"Like what?"

Their eyes tried to out-stare one another. Sapphira's dropped first.

And Anna said, "Do *you* doubt whether I'm European, too? *Do* you —"

"Of course I don't. Martin told us that you had a French father — that you never knew him; that he died before you were born — that's it, isn't it?"

"Yes."

"Where *were* you born, Anna?" It was lightly asked, but every part of Sapphira's body seemed to hold attention.

"In India. My mother went there after — after my father died. She had cousins in Bombay — they thought it would be better for her if she could get right away —"

"Of course. Did your father have a

long illness, or —"

"I don't know. I don't know anything about him — Mother never talked to me of him."

"Strange. Your own father —"

"Whom I never set eyes on!"

"But you have photographs of him —"

"No."

"How very odd!"

"Why?" Anna's voice was hard. "I don't seem to see any photographs of Gillian *here*."

Sapphira leaned back in her chair, her lids dropping over her eyes. "We thought it better to put them away — in the circumstances —"

"Perhaps my mother —" Anna began and then stopped abruptly. It was not for her to tell this comparative stranger that her mother might have reasons, too, for keeping no photographs of Anna's father. Because she didn't know . . . she knew nothing about him . . . she didn't even bear his name, and suddenly she saw how significant that would seem, not to Martin, for he loved her, but to Martin's family. And she could tell them nothing. They must take her birth on trust.

But someone didn't. . . .

Suddenly she asked, "Where's Bridget?"

"In town. She rang up a little while ago to say she'd be late home. She's having drinks with friends."

"And Eve?"

"In Lavernake."

"Then there's only you and Jaimie in the house?"

"Jaimie's doing the rounds outside. I've been here for the past half hour — it's the only chance I get to read the newspapers. So, as it was most certainly not Jaimie or I who wrote the note, it must have been one of the villagers."

"Why should anyone so completely disinterested in this family do such a thing?"

"Interference! It's often the major pastime of a small rather ignorant community, Anna."

"Who in the village could possibly know — or care — enough?" Anna demanded.

Sapphira was standing at the old-fashioned marble mantelpiece, her hands pressed down on the shelf. She asked softly:

"Won't you tear that note up, Anna, and forget it?"

"Words take root like seeds. I can't forget it — you know that! Perhaps when I've shown it to Martin."

Sapphira wheeled around. "You'd be so unwise!"

"I think the time has come to — let him in on the — the gossip —"

She saw Sapphira stiffen. She turned her head away and looked directly, challengingly at

Anna's reflection in the ornate gilt mirror. "I haven't a clue what you're talking about!"

"I think you have, Sapphira. Gillian's letter. You and Bridget taking such pains to tell me about it — I kept that from Martin because, in a way, I saw your point. Because I happen to love him, I didn't want him to be harrowed all over again any more than you did."

"Doesn't it dawn on you that this could also trouble him, that someone — someone —"

"Doubts my European birth?" Anna supplemented and was surprised at her own calm. "Since you were frank with me over Gillian's letter, Sapphira, let me be equally frank. You didn't tell Martin about it because you couldn't bear to hurt him, but you could tell me! And now, you don't really mind my having received this note, but Martin mustn't know! As though feelings are the prerogative of the few! I'm angry and indignant, but I feel hurt, too! Hurt that someone isn't even trying to like me for myself; she wants to fester doubts, trouble —"

"She —" Sapphira whipped around.

"Of course. No man printed those words! So, *she* wants to break up everything between Martin and me — to kill his faith in me! The adventuress from India, aided and abetted by her family, no doubt, passing herself off as entirely European in order to catch an English

husband! Those are the horrible inferences behind this!" She flicked at the crumpled note.
"Perhaps she wants me to show it to Martin and
raise doubt in *his* mind! Well, I *shall* show it to
him — because I know there are no doubts!"

"You must do as you think best!" Sapphira
said stiffly and went to a drawer and took out
the vivid satin patchwork she was working on.
She returned to her chair and opened her little
needlework box. Anna watched her, saw the
calm finality, the inferred closing of the subject,
and furious indignation ran through her.

"You have never met my stepfather, Sapphira.
He is a Hindu, but he is the greatest man I have
ever met; great in character — he was educated
and studied medicine here in England and he is
a brilliant surgeon. He's the only father I ever
knew and nobody could have had a more wonderful one, nor a happier home life — I'd be
proud, yes, proud, Sapphira, if he were really
my father! My mother must have loved him
very much to let me bear his name —"

"I'm quite sure your parents are charming,"
Sapphira said politely, selecting a small square
of ruby satin, and reaching to tilt the lampshade
a little so that it fell on the gleaming colors of
her work.

"Draw the curtains, will you please, Anna?"
In silence, she crossed the room and drew

the heavy blue Italian brocade curtains across the window.

Drop the subject . . . forget it . . . that was Sapphira's attitude.

Well, why not? Why let such an act of furtive malice have power over her?

"You don't like us, do you, Anna?" The sudden change in the conversation disconcerted her.

"Why do you say that?"

Sapphira's fine eyes were resigned.

"I don't blame you! How can you expect to understand us, brought up in India as you were, in such different surroundings?"

"It works both ways. If people tried more to understand, everyone would be happier, you and I — and all the world."

"The world!" Sapphira made a gesture of impatience. "What's that to me? This is my world!" She made a light sweeping movement with one hand. The flash of ruby silk in her fingers gleamed as it crossed the arc of lamplight. "And that's all we must concern ourselves with — our own, personal little world. If I went into your life in India, I'd probably hate it as much as you hate ours."

"You're so wrong! I don't hate your world!"

Sapphira looked at her in cool disbelief.

"My dear Anna, you don't have to pretend

with me! I know and that's why I'm worried about you and Martin."

Anna tore her eyes away from Sapphira's. She felt in the pocket of her coat, found a packet of cigarettes and lit one. The smoke soothed her ragged impatience with Martin's sister. She said at last, "You don't have to worry, Sapphira – Martin and I love one another and that's the important thing."

She saw Sapphira's expression harden, saw the long, thin lips draw in.

"You are ten years younger than I, Anna. That's a decade and in that time one learns wisdom." She paused, and then she continued, her voice a soft hiss. "Don't think I haven't had my emotional experiences, too! And I've learned my bitter lessons. Love? What is it? A passing attraction of the senses. Infatuation? Or – imagination run riot? What else is it – ever?"

"Real love," Anna said quietly, "Is just that – love! It's how I feel for Martin and he for me."

"I'm glad you're so sure. But if it were really that, wouldn't you be happy with him wherever he chose to live? Have you faced that? Have you asked yourself why you want to uproot him again? For his sake, Anna? Or because you want him absolutely on your terms?"

Anna sat down slowly on the arm of a chair. "Why keep on? I am doing what I honestly believe is best for both of us."

"If it were what you so nobly call love, being with him would be enough, wherever he chose to live." Sapphira was leaning forward, her eyes brilliant with an almost hypnotic stare. "How can you hope to keep Martin's love for you alive when you tear him from his roots and his child?"

Suddenly Anna could bear the stare and the repetitive insistence no longer. She turned and fled from Sapphira and reached the sanctuary of her own room in a few breathless moments.

Down in the hall, the grandfather clock struck six. Martin should have been home by now.

Anna wandered to the window and stared out at the sky, lying dusty indigo above the mist.

Martin's working late, she thought, vaguely.

She turned her head and saw the note lying on the dressing table where she had dropped it. She would show it to Martin tonight. Or would she? She almost heard Sapphira's voice cut in on her thoughts. "If you love him, you would want to keep this piece of village gossip from him!" Just village gossip. . . .

"Stay but till tomorrow and your present sorrow will be weary and lie down to rest."

The words, read somewhere, crept into her mind. *Everything passes*, so stay. In seven weeks' time all this would be over — just seven weeks out of a lifetime. . . .

Through her own absorbed and troubled reasoning, Anna heard Sapphira calling her.

She opened the door and listened.

"There's someone on the telephone for you. From London."

She flew down the stairs, her eyes registering the fact that the living room door was ajar. She picked up the receiver and a familiar voice said, "Hello, Anna?"

"Aidan!" Her heart was beating hard so that her voice came a little breathlessly. "This is a lovely surprise!"

"Hold on a minute." She heard him speaking to someone in the room and felt backwards with her foot for a chair, dragged it forward and sat down a little weakly.

"I'm sorry about that," she heard him back on the wire, "but someone came in with some letters. I rang to know if you're coming to London at all."

"Yes, I am." She'd have said "Yes" if she had been a thousand miles away!

"Good; because the Trusloves in Bombay have asked me to buy you a wedding present from them. They want me to take you to Hannigan's to choose a tea service. When can you manage to get up to London?"

"Any time, Aidan. Tomorrow?"

She heard him laugh. "Of course, if you like. I've got a fairly free afternoon. Lunch with me."

"That would be wonderful!"

"Not very early, though. I shall be at the hospital until one o'clock. Say half past one? The Franciscan —"

"That's where you used to take me when I came up to London for a day from school," she said happily. "It would be lovely to go there again."

Behind her as she replaced the receiver, she was aware of Sapphira's light, smooth step passing from the living room into the kitchen and she knew that she had been listening.

On the chest of drawers Anna saw, as she returned on wings to her room, the little green jade dragon. She wanted to touch it, to say to it, "I'm seeing Aidan tomorrow!" as though to a friend. She turned and caught sight of the horrible printed note. As though that telephone call had been a signal, she walked over to the dressing table, picked the crumpled piece of paper up and tore it into little pieces.

IX

Because Martin arrived home late that evening bringing two friends to dinner and afterwards ran them back to Lavernake, Anna did not have a chance to tell him that she was lunching with Aidan.

At breakfast the next morning, the family were in full battle over the growing of orchids and Martin pushed back his chair, chuckling, saying:

"Fight it out, girls! I've got some nice specimens of plant disease lying waiting for me under the microscope," and went quickly out of the room.

Sapphira rose, too, and Anna, collecting a pile of plates, followed her out.

In the hall Martin was picking up his brief case. Sapphira, halfway to the kitchen, paused and turned.

"Oh, by the way, Martin, Anna could use the Ford today, couldn't she? We shan't be needing it."

"Of course," he said in surprise. "She knows that if it isn't wanted here, she can take it."

"She's going to London, I believe, and I thought —" Sapphira was addressing Martin, but her eyes watched Anna.

Martin was at the door, asking in a hurried, preoccupied way, "You thought what?"

"That she could take up an order for that lime sulphur; McGee's want a written order from us and it would save time if she handed it in —"

"That's your domain, Sapphira. I know nothing about your requirements." He was running down the steps.

"But as Anna has shopping to do and a luncheon date, I thought —" Her voice trailed into silence. Martin was completely out of hearing. Anna said clearly:

"I'll have plenty of time to take whatever order you want. My shopping can be done in the afternoon and my lunch date with Aidan isn't until half past one." Then she turned, running out of the door and down the steps. "Oh, Martin, I didn't tell you —"

At the same moment Bridget flew past her, yellow coat swirling, wafting Guerlain's *L'Heure Bleu*.

"Oh – Martin –" she called, like an echo.

He turned in the driving seat and saw Bridget first. She ducked her head in at the window.

"Drop me at the top of the lane, will you? I want to slip into the stables and book our horses for tomorrow morning – you did say you'd ride, didn't you?"

"Sure, I need exercise. But if I take you, you'll have to walk back, I won't have time to run you home. Why don't you use your car, or telephone them?"

"Because, Martin dear, I'd like a walk back. It's a lovely morning." She opened the door by the passenger seat and slipped in with a single swinging movement of her legs.

Martin leaned over her, peering out.

"Can't I lure you into riding with us, Anna?"

"No thanks," she managed a laugh. "I told you, when I'm near horses, I like to be able to look them straight in the eye – you can't do that from their backs! By the way, Martin –" Her voice was drowned in the leaping roar of the engine.

Anna almost jumped when Sapphira's voice sounded on the steps behind her.

"You should have asked Martin if you could use the Ford when you told him of your date in town and he'd have got the car out for you. It's a difficult garage. Never mind, Jaimie will do it."

Anna said quietly, "Thank you, Sapphira, but I'll manage."

Whether she used the car or went by train was of no consequence to Sapphira. The important thing was that she had not been certain if Anna had told Martin about her date with Aidan and she intended him to know. Only Martin had been in a hurry and when she herself was about to tell him Bridget had got there first.

By half past eleven Anna was on her way. She wore a sapphire blue suit and small hat. Her only jewelry was a garnet star lying against the narrow single mink skin around her neck.

There was no question of guilt about this meeting; Aidan was her friend and Martin knew it, and tonight she would tell him.

Aidan was waiting for her in the foyer of the Franciscan.

As a schoolgirl she used to think: Nobody is as good-looking as Aidan. The thought still held.

They lunched at a table in a corner by a wall of glass that gave onto a little courtyard where potted plants grew in profusion against a painted yellow wall.

Anna sat back, relaxed against the deep upholstery of the *banquette* and let Aidan order lunch for her.

She watched his quiet courtesy with the waiter, the obvious pleasure the thin sardonic man took in serving him.

Aidan made no reference to the Claremondes. He talked easily about general things; London again after six years in India; hospital work; mutual friends he had looked up.

He chose a fine white wine with the chicken, and through the main course and the hothouse peaches that followed, he continued to keep the conversation on a light, impersonal level.

Later, when black coffee had been poured from a slender, gleaming copper pot into their cups, Aidan asked quietly: "What is the matter, Anna?"

She wasn't surprised by the sudden question. Aidan knew every light and shade of her expression, her manner even, and she had no intention of dissembling with him.

"Things have happened — rather horrible things," and then she told him about Gillian's letter to Bridget and the note she had found on the front door.

"I wasn't the cause of Gillian's death!" she said in distress. "When she was alive, Martin was only a colleague in the laboratories — I never thought of him as anything more than that. I liked him but that was all."

"We all knew that. Gillian was on the razor's

edge of mental sickness; she had to fasten on someone as the scapegoat for her imagined tragedy, and I suppose it happened to be you."

"Martin knew so many women – friends of both of them. Why me?" she demanded.

"Gillian's death was due to her own inability to accept reality. People who live in an illusionary world are ill-equipped for compromise. Gillian was responsible for her own death. But what you have to face is not that, but that someone in the house chose to tell you about it."

"Bridget told me. She pretended that out of her friendship for Gillian she had to know who the woman was. She didn't accuse me and I was too dumb to realize until Sapphira made it clearer, that that was what they all thought!"

"People jump to wild conclusions –"

"The awful thing is, Aidan, that although one sees the danger of what is happening, it isn't a case of being forewarned! I should be able to say they don't want this marriage to take place, and be prepared to defy them all. I *can't*. The seed of doubt has taken root."

"What is your doubt, Anna?"

"To wonder whether love is enough, whether I can make Martin happy . . . I told you, I'm urging him to take this job in South America when he wants roots here – that's wrong of me, isn't it? Sapphira said as much, and if I'm honest I know she's right. Yet, if I don't persuade him to take that job I know there'll be no happiness for us here. Even if we had our own house away from the family, they'd manage to encroach. The very fact that Martin's money is tied up in the business would be excuse enough."

"So what do you want?" His voice was light, but his eyes were gentle.

"Tell me if I'm being selfish in wanting Martin to go to South America."

"How can I? I'm not Martin. I'm not you. It's always easy to give advice according to one's own lights — but —"

"Aidan —" She leaned forward, her fingers touched his arm. "This is terribly important to me! Don't you see, on what you tell me, perhaps my whole life, and Martin's, could depend? I always used to ask for your help, Aidan."

He said, "You've learned to think for yourself since then! And that, I'm afraid, is what you have to do now. No man is God, my dear, to tell another human being what to do in an issue as big as one which dominates their lives."

"You're passing it all back to me!" she cried disappointedly.

"Of course. You're the only one who can answer your own question." His fingers curved around the twisted stem of his liqueur glass. He looked down into the golden liquid. "You have the strength in you to solve your own problems, Anna."

"Strength? *Me?*"

"Yes, you have inherited it from your mother. Do you think it was easy for her in the beginning? Don't you think she had a lot to overcome? Prejudice most of all! Yet, she built a very highly civilized and happy home."

"But I'm not surrounded by that happiness and understanding now. The Claremondes —"

"Are you marrying the Claremonde family — or Martin?"

"If I stay in England, I'll be marrying the family! That's just it!"

Aidan looked at her and then at her untouched glass of *Grand Marnier*. "Drink up, Anna."

She obeyed and felt the amber liquid run warm and tingling down her throat. He wasn't going to help her. . . .

She had driven to town, singing aloud! Aidan could solve her problem for her, she had told herself. Solve it, how? Her way! "Of course you must go to South America . . . get right away from them, Anna," she had expected him to say, and she had a vague sense of being let down.

She looked across at him and — while he gestured to attract the waiter for more coffee — she looked at the fine, sensitive face and suddenly understood.

But of course he didn't condemn even the Claremondes! *That's Aidan's way to understand all things, even the supposedly evil! To know that wrong is done because the doer honestly thinks it right. Ignorance isn't a sin, it's a level of being. That's why Aidan won't help me — because he has compassion even for Martin's family.*

Their coffee cups had been filled again and the waiter was gone.

Suddenly Aidan laughed.

"You know, there's an old Arab saying: 'Nobody but God and I know what is in my heart.' Well, what *is* in your heart, Anna? Enough love for Martin to fight for him? Go home and answer that and every other question will fall into place like the pieces of a jigsaw puzzle. Now let's talk of other things." He consulted his watch. "I've got another hour to spare so we'll get a taxi to Hannigan's and choose your tea service."

"It's a princely present, Aidan."

"They're princely people. And they're coming to England soon so we'll have a grand reunion."

Perhaps it was the warmth of the place, the

good food and the wine that relaxed her, but quite suddenly her problem was no problem at all. Something would resolve itself. Something – but she had no idea what. . . .

They took a taxi to Hannigan's and Anna chose a tea service in blue and gold. When they left the store and walked into the spring sunlight Aidan glanced about him for a taxi, but Anna wanted to look at the shops.

"I'm going up to Oxford Street."

"Then I'll walk a little way with you."

They took a short cut through Berkeley Square and when they reached the far end Aidan paused. "I'll have to get a taxi from here or I'll be late." He took her hand. "Goodbye, Anna. You'll be all right."

"It was lovely being with you, Aidan!"

"It has always been lovely being together." The sunlight caught his eyes and she saw behind the smiling reflected light, something that turned her heart over. For a moment the little world of Berkeley Square swung dizzily around her. If Aidan had, in the past, ever looked at her like that she would have known without any word being spoken that he loved her. It was there in his eyes, deep and burning and undeniable. Aidan loved her. . . .

"Aidan! . . ." The spinning sensation continued around her. She closed her eyes for a brief moment and felt, for the first time ever, his lips touch her cheek lightly and swiftly. She opened her eyes and said his name again.

But no one was there, only two men jostling past her, half blocking the view of the slim, quiet Indian walking swiftly away from her.

X

Aidan loved her! She would have given all she had in the world for that to have happened barely a year ago. No word had been spoken . . . no word could be spoken now, because the chance was gone and she loved Martin. . . . She swung around and began, nearly at a run, to go the way she had come. The sun dazzled her eyes, the din of the traffic throbbed against her eardrums.

Had he always loved her? If so, why leave it until now to let her know? Or hadn't he reckoned that she could read his heart in his eyes? Didn't people know how their eyes gave them away?

She walked, looked in shops, made a few purchases as in a dream, and kept saying, over and over again to herself: He never told me he loved me, For some reason best known to himself, he never told me. . . .

When Anna arrived home that evening, Martin was sitting with the family in the living room.

Anna knew, by the sudden silence that fell as she entered, that something was wrong. Then they began a quick, nervous conversation.

"– Sapphira, we really must order some more packing boxes –"

"– Julie's running a temperature again –"

"– That brown dog of the Lowthers' was prowling around the nurseries. I wish someone would speak to them."

A jumble of words, all spoken at once, the first things that came into their minds, in order to cover up the silence.

Then Sapphira asked, "Did you have time to see McGee's?"

"They're sending the lime sulphur immediately." She turned in the doorway. "I've put the car away. I'll just go and clean up."

Upstairs, while she changed, she could hear the burr of voices from the living room. A deep listlessness had fallen on her and she thought, smoothing the skirt of the dark green dress she had put on: It's the strain of driving through so much traffic. I'm not used to it.

She picked up heavy gold bracelets and slid one over each wrist, clipped on topaz earrings and told herself that a drink would cheer her out of her heavy mood.

Martin was waiting for her in the hall.

"Come and walk around the garden with me a bit, Anna. It's a fairly warm evening, but slip your coat on." He fetched the thick gray coat which she kept in the downstairs closet and put it around her shoulders.

Outside it was nearly dark, but an aureoled moon was rising over the trees like the top of a domed temple. Anna drew a long breath.

"The air's so fresh here after London!"

Martin made no response. She reached out her hand to take his and felt his fingers react without the usual enthusiasm at her touch.

"Anna, why did you go to London?"

She might have guessed that was the trouble!

"I wanted to go shopping and while I was up there I lunched with Aidan."

"Thank you, at least, for being honest!"

"I'd no reason for being anything else. I was going to tell you tonight —"

"But you knew yesterday, didn't you, and yet you said nothing."

"I suppose Sapphira told you Aidan rang me." She went on without waiting for an answer. "I would have told you last night, only it was very late when you ran your friends home and I was in bed by the time you returned."

"Fair enough! They asked me in for a drink and we started yarning. But there was this morning. You didn't say anything."

"The family was arguing non-stop over orchids – you know, you were laughing at them – I didn't get a chance! And then later, Bridget was there asking for a lift and you drove off before I could say anything."

It had been real and reasonable at the time; it didn't seem to ring quite like that now!

"Why?" she asked. "Was it so terribly important that I should tell you before rather than after I'd seen Aidan?"

Martin's silence was not reassuring. She urged: "Martin, *was* it? Important, I mean?"

"Yes, Anna, I think it was."

She stopped dead along the path made luminous by moonlight.

"I can't believe that you mind!"

"But I think I do!"

His head was bent a little towards her with the moonlight behind him so that he was in shadow and she faced the relentless, revealing light. He must, then, have seen her dismay.

"But you always knew we were great friends –"

"In India, yes. You're in England now and –"

"And what?"

He turned away slowly as though giving himself time to answer. There was an old sundial on the lawn and he reached out and laid his hands flat upon it. Watching him, Anna had the queer feeling that he needed the comfort of the old familiar stone.

"I wonder what nostalgia made you go to lunch with Aidan?"

This is a moment, she thought, where there are two ways – and I can take either. Tell him that her only reason was because Aidan had to take her to choose a wedding present on behalf of some friends in India. That, at least, was partially true. Or tell him the more urgent truth. She chose that.

"I went to see Aidan because I had a problem and I needed help."

He turned in genuine surprise.

"But *I'm* here, Anna. If there's anything –"

"I know. I know. But you see, darling, *you* were the problem."

"What's troubling you about me?" She felt, though his face was half turned from her, that he was frowning.

She looked down and saw that she was standing by a wooden seat and leaned against it, needing support.

"Ever since I urged you to accept the South American post, I've had it on my conscience that I've been unfair to you."

"It's all settled, Anna," he said sharply. "I've told Manson that I'll go —"

"But nothing is — finalized?"

"That's merely a formality," he said a little impatiently. "The main thing —"

"The main thing, Martin, is that you don't really want to go abroad again, do you?"

"No. I'm not one to like changes. But there are two of us to be considered and I think I understand how you feel." He took his hands from the sundial and reached out for hers. She felt the ice cold touch after contact with the stone. "You don't like England, Anna. You wouldn't be really happy here —"

"I —"

"Oh, don't let's dissemble! We're adults, let's be honest. I know you were at school here, but you were a child then, and much more malleable. Now it's different. You've had six adult years in India. So you see," he finished, "I have a problem too!"

She lowered her eyes from the grave, narrow face caught in the moonlight.

He dropped her hands. "I'm beginning to wonder," he continued bluntly, "if I've made a terrible mistake in persuading you away from your own surroundings."

Anna's eyes flashed open, her body tensed, sharply aware of a danger point.

"What have I done to give you the idea that I am not happy here?"

"Nothing," he said, "nothing at all, Anna. But then you wouldn't. You'd keep it from me because you wouldn't want me to be hurt."

"Then – the family –!"

"They see so much more of you than I do. I'm away all day. I suppose that's the testing time. The time I mean when we're not together. And, after all, a man's working hours are a devil of a lot out of a day for a woman to be unhappy in!"

"If I thought I would neither be happy with you nor give you happiness, don't you think I'd break off the engagement? Really, Martin," she added angrily, "what in the world has it to do with your family?"

He appeared to accept her indignation. He said, in defense, "I suppose because of what happened with Gillian they want everything to be right for me the second time."

"And so they think by bringing me over from India, wanting to marry me, you've committed some grave mistake! They interpret my feelings as they choose!"

"It wasn't like that, Anna. Sapphira –"

"Yes, you told me before! Is she so knowledgable about the feelings of others?" she demanded bitterly.

He shook his head. "If you want to know, all I did was to ask her how she felt you were settling into the family."

"And Sapphira said, 'Not at all.' Is that it?"

"Whatever Sapphira had said wouldn't have worried me, Anna, if I hadn't known that today you went to lunch with Aidan — to talk to him, tell him how you felt and thought — things you should be discussing with me!"

"Jealousy, Martin?"

"Not entirely, just a realization that a woman in love doesn't confide in another man."

"Oh, doesn't she? That's all you know! Sometimes the last person one *can* confide in is the one nearest!"

"But not Aidan!"

"Why? He's my closest friend."

"A friend? Or is he in love with you?"

She knew he couldn't feel the sudden leap her heart gave.

"If he had been," she said loudly, "there was no earthly reason why he couldn't have asked me to marry him ages ago."

"In the East time is nothing and patience is second nature. He might have been waiting —"

"For what?"

"To see how things would develop. Perhaps he hesitated because you are Western."

"The question of what Aidan felt doesn't enter into it, Martin," she cut in a little wildly. "This is a discussion about *us* – you and me!"

"Very well, then, let's get back to us. Why aren't you happy here, Anna?"

"You haven't worded the question quite rightly, Martin! If you asked: Why haven't I a sense of 'home' here, then the answer is because your family doesn't want me to."

"That's not true! They've all talked to me about you – Sapphira, Bridget, Eve – they've all said they want to make you welcome and happy –"

"Then why did Bridget and then Sapphira make a point of telling me about Gillian's letter?"

It was out; the thing she had made up her mind she would never tell him. . . .

A small sick feeling swept her and she closed her eyes against Martin's violent reaction.

"What in sweet heaven's name are you talking about?"

"Gillian's last letter to Bridget – perhaps – the last one she ever wrote in her life –"

"What about it?"

She said wearily, "You'd better ask one of them!"

"I'm asking *you!*"

"Very well," she faced him squarely. "I'll tell you. Bridget was apparently a friend of Gillian's and wrote often to her. I haven't seen the letter in question but two people made it their business to tell me about it. I gather it was hysterical, full of self-pity. But there was one line in it which they both quoted to me; it concerned an unnamed woman. Gillian wrote, 'How could she bear to build her happiness on someone else's tragedy?' "

"My God!"

"And Bridget tried to find out from me who the woman was — at least that's what I thought she was doing! Sapphira enlightened me. She believed, and I'm sure Bridget really thought so, too, that I was the cause of Gillian's suicide."

"This is monstrous!"

"It is, but I have a feeling I haven't been able to convince your family so."

"Why didn't you tell me this before?"

"I hoped I could keep it to myself! I meant to, Martin —" She waited, sensing his withdrawal — from shock — or guilt? She had to know! "Martin, if there was someone before me — someone you — knew — when Gillian was alive, then tell me so — make them stop — accusing me among themselves." Her words dropped into a long silence. Only the trees rustled where their tops caught the wind.

"Martin, I want an answer!"

He said at last, wearily, "There was no one, Anna."

"Then Gillian must have meant me! But why did she link our names? She scarcely knew me —?"

He brushed a hand over his forehead and it seemed to shake a little. Somewhere a lonely dog started to bark.

"I scarcely ever talked to Gillian about the lab and the people I knew there. I think occasionally I mentioned you — but always casually, in connection with the work. I must have praised you, some time." He was searching his memory. "I believe I said that it was a pity you didn't come to England and take a degree in science because you had a flair. I also believe I once said that you were beautiful."

"And Gillian added together those few complimentary remarks and made a love affair out of it! Oh, Martin!"

"But she can't have! The whole thing's ludicrous!"

"Nothing is ludicrous to an unbalanced mind! Did she ever mention me, Martin?"

"I believe so — occasionally. But then every woman we knew, from the age of eighteen to eighty, came in at some time or other for her frenzy. I had long ago ceased to take notice. And now Bridget has to bring it up —

for God's sake, *why?*"

"Because she says she was Gillian's friend and she wanted to know who it was in your life who sent – Gillian – over the – edge –"

"Can't it be forgotten?"

How violently, she thought, hearing the sharp note in his voice, he rejected anything that risked a scene! But it couldn't be forgotten – now that the story was half told.

She said steadily, "Two nights ago someone pinned a piece of paper to the front door. It just said, 'There is no place like home! So go back, Indian girl!' "

She saw his hands jerk involuntarily. He drew a long harsh breath.

"Go on – go *on* –"

"There's nothing – more –"

"Whose writing?"

"I don't know –"

"And you didn't tell me!"

"No – I told Sapphira and she and I didn't want to distress you."

"What in the name of heaven am I supposed to be?" he nearly shouted. "A wax doll to be wrapped in cotton wool away from things that might melt and burn me up? Distress me! That's an understatement! It maddens me, and I'll find out who! These damned villagers!"

"Villagers?"

"Who else? We may be only seventy miles from London, but it's a small enclosed world. What do they care, or know, of anything outside their scrubbed doorsteps, what interest do they take in anything beyond their own hills?"

She wanted to cry, You're including your own family, Martin! What she actually said was, "There's nothing to be done now."

"You bet there is! I'm going to the police. I'm going to get punishment for that evil piece of anonymity. Let me have that note and see what I'll do!"

"I destroyed it."

"You – *what?*" His voice rose again.

"After I'd talked with Sapphira, I decided to tear it up and forget it." She saw him catch his breath. In the moonlight his eyes were luminous sparks of anger.

"You – did – that? Heaven give me strength!" He seemed to check his violent emotion and when he spoke again his voice was controlled. "Do you realize, that note was evidence? *Now* what do we do?"

"Forget it!"

"Oh no, I'll probe it in my own way! I'll find a way of testing every single person in this village. I'll get at whoever thought they'd hound you from the village. Oh, Anna –" His voice broke. "Darling, I'm sorry – I'm apologizing for them

147

– for my village. I –" The anger went out of him and he buried his face in her hair, whispering, "How evil can people be? Or is it just blind ignorance, morality gone wrong?"

"I've told you. Now let's forget it," she said shakenly, thinking: He doesn't even stop to wonder if it was one of the family – Sapphira or Eve or Bridget. . . .

"I'm glad now that we're going to the Argentine," Martin was saying. "But if anything else like this happens, promise you'll tell me first – do you hear?"

"Yes."

She leaned her face against him and felt his body like a rock against her weight.

"It won't be long now, Anna," he whispered against her hair, "and then we'll all three be away from it. You and Julie and I."

She said, "But perhaps she won't be able to go. If she's not strong and the climate would be bad for her."

"Rubbish! Fresh air and sunlight will do her a world of good. She's coming, anyway. She's my child. She's been bundled about from aunts to grandmother and back to aunts again, and now I've no intention of leaving her. Whatever happens, Julie shall be with me."

Whatever happens! But what if Julie couldn't go – what if the doctor said "No"? Then Martin wouldn't go either, and would stay here after all. And I? How strong *is* love? Is it all that's necessary between two people, after all?

While he held her close, she tried to think clearly and couldn't. Aidan — a quiver ran through her body. Aidan would have known the answer; but he wouldn't give it to her . . . she had to find her own way, because that was the only real answer.

When they reached the house dinner was on the table and Sapphira was looking cross.

"Your meal is being spoiled, Martin! You knew we were almost ready to start."

"I'm sorry. I wanted to talk to Anna."

Sapphira's lips tightened. "Don't blame me if the meat is dry."

Anna sat down in the chair Jaimie held out for her and involuntarily glanced at Bridget. She was watching Martin, her eyes hungry and questioning.

Amy brought in heated dishes and Martin served himself and Anna from the side table.

Bridget reached for the butter. "My car's giving trouble. I wonder if you'd have a look at it some time this evening."

"Of course. Though I'm no mechanic."

"But it may be just a loose plug or screw or whatever they use under the hoods," she said vaguely. "I wouldn't know. And I don't want to take it to the garage, if it's just something that wants tightening."

"It's high time you exchanged it for a new one with all the mileage you do," Martin grinned across at her.

She said softly, "I suppose it is, but I'm particularly fond of it. Women are sentimental about cars, you know. Do you remember, you came with me to choose it?"

"So I did."

"And I said I wanted a yellow one and you said, 'Just like a woman. Give her pretty upholstery and nice colored paintwork, something she thinks suits her type, and she doesn't care if the engine's a crock!' "

Bridget smiled. The aquamarine ring on her finger glittered in the lights as she buttered toast. "We went for my first long drive in it too. Remember? We went out to Branswood Point and lay in the sun — it was a beautiful afternoon —"

"Sure I remember. We used to have real summers in those far-off days!" he said lightly.

"They were such lovely days," Bridget said softly.

Words overheard between them came out of the immediate past. Bridget saying with aching regret, "So it won't be like old times, after all."

After the meal was cleared away and washed

up, Anna went upstairs and, passing Julie's room, heard her small voice singing softly to herself.

She went to the door and looked in. Julie was sitting up in bed, twisting her small clever hand so that grotesque shapes appeared on the wall.

"You like making shadow pictures, don't you?"

Julie glanced around and nodded. "I saw a man do it in a pantomime once. He made a cat laugh and he made elephants. Look" – she manipulated her small, supple hands – "what's this?"

Anna looked at the swift, twisting, turning shadow.

"It's very clever –" she said vaguely.

"It's a squirrel running after its own tail. I saw it this morning on the lawn. I see lots of things from here." Her eyes turned to the window by her bed.

"Should you have your curtains back like that?" Anna asked.

Julie nodded. "Aunt Eve comes in later and draws them again. But I like looking out."

The French window stood propped open. They give her an unnecessary night light, Anna thought, but they leave the French windows open so that anything, from a stray cat to a prowler, could walk up that twisted iron staircase from the garden into Julie's room. . . .

But then in this village front doors were left unlocked, windows kept open — nobody ever seemed to call the village policeman because a burglar had stolen the family silver; nothing like that ever happened in Blakesford. Nothing? Only a note pinned to a door. . . .

Julie called, "Look, Anna."

Anna saw on the wall a figure bent over something, and the lifting and falling of a hand.

"That's Aunt Sapphira sewing," Julie said.

The neat bent head, the quiet rhythmic movement of the needle in shadow play was so characteristic that Anna laughed.

"You don't like Aunt Sapphira, do you?"

"What on earth makes you say that?"

The large eyes under the falling cloud of fair hair regarded Anna with interest.

"Aunt Bridget says you don't."

"Then Aunt Bridget has made a mistake," Anna said briefly.

"But Aunt Eve said so, too," Julie's eyes were bright with curiosity. "She says you come from a funny country and we aren't like you, so you don't like us."

"Julie, that's not true," she went quickly to the bed. Anger welled up in her and then fell away as she saw the honest puzzlement in the child's eyes. "I do like you, Julie, and I'm going to love you a whole heap more. I come from India, you know that, but I'm English, too." She sat down on the side of the bed. "My stepfather and mother have a lovely house right up at the foot of the highest mountains in the world, the Himalayas. And there the little girls don't dress like you, they wear white pantaloons." She sketched them with her hands. "And they go hunting for crystal in the mountains — lovely shining pieces — I wish I'd brought you some!"

"Anna, what are you doing, keeping Julie up like this?"

"I wasn't asleep, Aunt Eve. I was making pictures on the wall."

"Then lie down and go to sleep at once."

"You can't go to sleep just because somebody tells you to," Julie said logically.

"You can make yourself."

"But Anna was telling me lovely stories — the little girls in *her* country keep goats. I'd like a goat —"

"Beastly, primitive things! You shall have a pony when you're a bit older."

"But I want a goat — with a little bell."

"People like us don't keep goats —"

"What's people like us?"

"Oh, don't keep asking questions!" Eve snapped, and then immediately regretting it went across and put her arms around her.

"Ponies are so pretty. You'll love one of your own, darling." She looked across at Anna. "Now, please, leave her and let me get her to sleep. You've over-excited her —"

Anna said quietly, "I'm sorry," and went out of the room perfectly well aware that Julie wasn't in the least over-excited. The whole conversation, from the time Eve had appeared in the doorway, was redolent of one thing.

Whatever happens, Julie mustn't be allowed to love you. Julie is ours — mine mostly. . . . And whenever she went to the little girl's room, one or the other of them came in and sent her away.

Anna went slowly down the stairs, forgetting what she had originally come up for.

If they had their way, Martin will lose Julie if he goes to South America. . . . But she was his child, his only child — yet!

She walked to the end of the passage and paused by the long window. Suddenly, startlingly, there came out of the silent night the demon cry of a vixen in the woods. Anna heard it without knowing what it was, and shivered.

Martin was standing by the window in the small office which was chiefly Sapphira's domain. He had been unable to find the opportunity to speak to her the previous night and rather than quote Anna in front of all of them, he had sought Sapphira alone in her office the following morning on his way out of the house to work. He came straight to the point.

"I think you should know that Anna has told me about Gillian's letter and about the note pinned to the door —"

Sapphira rose slowly, she crossed her arms and her fingers clutched her elbows.

"So she came running to you after all!"

"On the contrary, she was blazing angry with me about — well, about something else and it all came out. Anyway, it's obvious that we've got to get away."

"You think that's the answer?"

He looked at his sister. "I think it should be clear to you! Someone in the village sent her that horrible note, and you, Sapphira, chose to upset her by telling her about Gillian's letter."

"Blame Bridget —"

"Bridget told Anna, but she didn't accuse her of being the woman in the case. *You* did. Why?"

"Anna caught on quickly!"

She looked at him without rancor, head high, arms still folded, plucking at the red cardigan which did not suit her. "I did it for Bridget. It was on her mind so dreadfully."

"You had to find out whether Anna and I were having an *affair* before Gillian died because a letter from Gillian was harrowing Bridget?" he asked unbelievingly. "Oh, no, Sapphira! Don't give me that!"

"But I tell you, it's true! I see so much, Martin — I'm not involved in people like the rest — like Eve with Julie, Bridget with —" She broke off and Martin chose not to press the point.

"And if Anna or I had admitted that she was my mistress before Gillian died, what good would it have done any of you?"

Sapphira shrugged her shoulders. On her breast a paste brooch gleamed as it caught the light with the movement of her breathing.

"At least we would have known —"

"And so justified your dislike of Anna, is that it?"

"We don't dislike her!"

"She thinks you do."

"She's quite determined to think anything that will give her a right to get you away from us," Sapphira said waspishly.

"How little you know Anna!"

"Do *you* know her, Martin?"

"Of course," he continued impatiently. "But we're getting away from the subject! I just wanted to warn you that if there's any more of this hounding of Anna, I'll marry her immediately by special license, even if I have to dose her with drugs to get her to the registrar's, and when you go to the village you'd better spread it around that next time a note is pinned to the door, it goes to the police. And Bridget can stop asking Anna about Gillian —"

"Bridget has done nothing wrong," Sapphira cried heatedly. "She can't help —"

He paused halfway to the door. "Can't help what? Being inquisitive about my private life, and Anna's? Why the devil was she, anyway? I might have suspected it of some women — but not her." He heard his own vehemence and for the life of him couldn't help it. It was unreasonable to mind, but there it was — he did. And then with a jolt — he heard Sapphira say:

"But you must realize, surely, that Bridget loves you!" She saw Martin's look of stupefaction, and pressed home her point. "Before you married Gillian, we all thought it would be Bridget. You were always taking her dancing and swimming and playing tennis. You were her constant companion so that everyone looked upon her — as — well — as your girl!"

"Bridget had the capacity for being a good friend," he heard his own voice, stiff and unreal. "We enjoyed one another's company. That's all it ever was between us."

"You must be remarkably innocent, Martin, if you think that women like Bridget are ever content to remain just friends with a man!"

"Very well then, I'm sorry, but I *was* remarkably innocent. After all, she took my engagement to Gillian pretty well!"

"Because she never believed it would last. She gave you five years and then she said you'd be heartily sick of each other."

"Did she now? And I suppose you're suggesting that, when it broke up, she would be there, waiting for me —"

"She was, Martin. It took a little longer than she prophesied, but she *was* there — only you fell in love with Anna before you even came home to give Bridget a chance."

"Why are you carrying on for Bridget so strongly?" he asked with a sudden flash of suspicion.

Her handsome face became a mask; her eyes, which would be hooded when she grew older and thinner, dropped.

"You grow fond of people when you live together as we do here."

A glimmer of sardonic amusement shone in Martin's eyes. He had a suspicion that there was something more behind all this — Sapphira's seeming concern for Eve over Julie; Bridget over himself — a wheel within a wheel — but he'd had enough of atmosphere. In a few weeks' time it would all be over. He tried not to listen to that lurking whisper that stirred in the corners of his brain. *But would it be over in the way he wanted it?*

He said, reasonably, "I'm sorry if Bridget really does feel like that, though I have an idea you're adding your own little touch of romance to it, Sapphira! Bridget meets too many people in London to play the Victorian game of the Faithful Heart!"

"You can sneer —"

"I'm not, but I'm afraid I don't take this seriously."

"If you knew Bridget loved you like that, would it make any difference?"

"You mean," he met her eyes blandly, "would I send Anna packing and marry Bridget? No, of course I wouldn't."

"But if Anna left *you*," Sapphira said softly, "it would be another story, wouldn't it?"

Martin made a gesture of helplessness.

"I'm taking that as an honest question, Sapphira, and I'll answer it that way. I love Anna and I hope she'll never grow out of loving me."

The jewel at Sapphira's breast remained with just one facet gleaming as though she were being very still, holding her breath.

Martin had lit a cigarette and was gazing down at it, and his face had a deep sadness. His voice, when he spoke, was of a man thinking aloud, unaware of a hearer.

"I took her from a lovely and happy life; I took her from a beautiful house and everything she wanted. And because of all those things, I'm never quite sure of her. There *is* a man who could take her from me — the fear is always inside me that he will beckon her just once and she will go to him."

"Then you'd let her go, Martin, wouldn't you?"

He had been so engrossed in his own thoughts that her voice startled him. "I'm sorry — what was that you said?"

"You're talking of Aidan, the Indian, aren't you? They are two of a kind, Martin! If she went to him, you'd have to let her go, there'd be no point in fighting — the dice would be too heavily loaded against you." Sapphira drew an audible breath; she put out her hand and laid it on her desk, leaning against it. "Martin. I must ask you."

"Well?"

"Are you sure you aren't making a terrible mistake?"

He raised his head and looked at her.

"Watch us together, Sapphira," he said, "and you'll have your answer. Just watch the way we look at one another," and strode out of the room.

160

XI

Anna didn't know what cut through her sleep, but she found herself suddenly starting up in bed trembling with the sudden exertion, and listening.

Moonlight flooded in from the parted curtains and in the stillness only her heart beats sounded, thudding from her sudden startled energy. Such stillness . . .

And then it came again, the thing that must have awakened her. A child's high scream.

Anna shot out of bed, switching on the light, and reached for her dressing gown.

Julie must have been having a nightmare! As Anna thrust her feet into slippers she thought she heard a rush of sound, like padding footsteps, but when she tore open her door there was no one there. She ran down the passage and the short flight of steps to Julie's little room.

It was in darkness.

"Julie —"

She heard a faint answering whimper from the bed.

She felt for the light switch, and the room glowed softly pink.

Julie lay shuddering and sobbing under the bedclothes.

"What is it, darling? Did you have a nightmare?"

Anna crossed the room to her side. And then she saw it! On the floor by the open French window, half on the balcony, lay a mound of luminous silk — white and silver. . . . Anna bent to pick it up. It was her own white sari with the silver embroidery.

She moved to the bed. "Darling, what happened? Julie, tell me what happened? Where did you get this?"

"I — I — didn't —" Julie shuddered.

"What are you doing here, Anna?" Sapphira's voice sounded from the doorway, cutting across Julie's crying.

Anna swung around. An edge of the silken sari lay in her hands, the rest was coiled on the floor.

"I heard a scream and I came to see what was the matter. I found this on the floor."

"What is it?" Sapphira wore a blue-black embossed velvet housecoat. With its flowing folds and wide sleeves and the hood which was draped to cover her carefully pinned hair, she looked like a nun.

"What in the world is going on?"

There was a flash of scarlet behind her. Bridget, in flowing satin, pushed past Sapphira.

"Is Julie all right?"

"Why do you ask?" Sapphira wheeled around.

"I heard footsteps running this way. I think something woke me —"

Anna said, "Julie screamed three times."

The little girl had wriggled into a sitting position. She was still frightened, but the grownups gave her security and she was also curious. But she couldn't stop shaking. Words came stammering out of her. "I s-saw it. I s-saw it, horrible and white like that story of a ghost. It s-stood over t-there" — she pointed to the French window — "and it just stood still and looked at me. It was long and white —"

There was a flurry at the door. Eve, bedraggled in a washed-out cotton dressing gown, her hair standing out like a red witch's, pushed past them with Jaimie behind her. She reached the bed, elbowing Anna away.

"Darling Julie, darling." She gathered the child to her. "I heard! You thought you saw a ghost. But there aren't such things! Someone

163

must have been playing a horrible joke." Julie suffered herself to be rocked in Eve's thin arms. "Who was it, Julie? Who did this thing?"

"There wasn't a face," the little girl began to hiccough.

"Where's Martin?" Sapphira swung around.

"You know he sleeps like the dead —" Bridget began.

"Then, go and wake him, someone."

"Everything's all right now," Jaimie began, "so why —"

"Do as I say. Get Martin. There's an explanation to this that he must hear. What's that you're holding, Anna?"

"Someone must have dressed up in my sari and frightened Julie."

"Your night light isn't on —" Eve cried.

"It was out w-when I w-woke up. I saw the t-thing there in front of the big moon."

Anna's eyes flashed to the window. The moon *was* outsize tonight.

"It went down the steps," Julie pointed.

The outside steps to the garden. . . .

"I've always said it was mad to keep that door open at night time," Bridget began. "The window is quite sufficient fresh air for her!"

"The doctor says Julie must have as much as possible. She's not strong —"

"She's a darned sight stronger than you let her be!"

"Be quiet both of you!" Sapphira's voice broke in. Then she turned to Anna. "How could anyone have taken your sari?"

"I took it downstairs because some of the silver threads opened and I was going to mend it."

"And so —"

"What is all this?" Martin strode, tousled and impatient, into the room.

"Julie has had a bad fright," Eve said. "Someone dressed up in Anna's sari and frightened her."

Martin looked at her as though she'd gone a little mad.

"And we want to know who!" she added.

"I heard a scream," Anna said, "and I came to see what had happened."

Bridget was peering at the night light. "It couldn't possibly have gone out by itself, there's plenty of wick left."

"Then someone blew it out and then went to the French windows and woke Julie."

"Someone — who?" Jaimie blinked tired eyes.

"I think," Martin looked at Julie, "we'd better continue this conversation outside."

"I'll get her to sleep," Eve said. "You're all right, darling, now. We won't leave you. Bridget, will you warm some milk?"

"Of course."

Martin was at the bed. He put his arms around his little daughter and kissed her.

"Look, sweetie, there aren't such things as ghosts, only stupid people playing a game with you. You go to sleep — and I'm going to shut this door and lock it. That window lets in quite enough air —"

"But," Eve began, "the doctor said —"

"She's my daughter," Martin said quietly, "and *I* say we're not going to risk anything more." He was deliberately keeping calm in front of Julie, but Anna saw the bright anger in his eyes.

Where the staircase divided, one part going up to the main passage and the other leading down to Julie's small room, was a wide landing. On this was a settee and a small oval table with a Dresden figurine simpering on the polished surface.

Bridget flew downstairs to fetch warm milk, and Martin stood by the landing window. He pulled a packet of cigarettes from his pocket, lit one and looked at them through a smoke haze.

Jaimie began nervously, "It's inconceivable that anyone would do a thing like this. People don't —"

"Let's not philosophize," Martin said curtly. "Nor ask who did it, because nobody's going to own up."

"It must have been someone from the village."

Anna's heart thudded. The same one who pinned that note to the door? Another piece of malice directed at me? *My* sari? But why? Why?

She was aware of everyone talking at once, repeating the facts, mulling them over, protesting that it could only have been some outsider.

"I suppose we'll never know. I'm no detective and I can't very well go to the police and say, 'Someone tried to frighten my daughter by playing ghosts.' But one thing I can do, and that is to take Julie — and Anna — away from here. Julie can go to her grandmother —"

"Martin, no! *No!*" Eve stood, harassed and untidy, rooted at the top of the short flight of stairs. "You can't do that! You —"

"What do you suggest I do, then? Leave them both here to be scared and intimidated by someone who's too much of a coward to say openly what his, or her, grievance is?"

"Julie would hate it so!" Eve's eyes slid around to Anna and their expression said, "*You* can do what you like, go where you like —"

"On the contrary, when Julie was allowed to visit her grandmother, she had a whale of a time."

Sapphira lifted her head a little, looking at Martin.

"You would be very unwise to uproot Julie

again, Martin. Ever since she was born she has been handed around from her grandmother to us and back again just because Gillian couldn't be bothered with her when you traveled."

"It won't happen again, Martin." Eve looked thin and pinched as though it was she who had seen the ghost. "I'll sleep in her room tonight. Jaimie can get out the camp bed from the attic. And I really will keep that glass door shut, now!"

Bridget came upstairs, one hand gracefully lifting her beautiful scarlet housecoat, the other holding a little tray on which was a cup of milk.

Eve saw her. "Oh, I managed to get her to sleep quite easily, so we won't wake her."

Bridget looked about her. "Anyone want this milk?"

Nobody took any notice of her. She set the tray down on the table and shook back her hair. She looked so much softer, so much more beautiful with her hair loose and she had stopped to put on a little lipstick.

Martin was saying abruptly, "Has anyone looked to see if the front door is open?"

"It often is —"

"I know, that's why I'm asking. Which means that whoever scared Julie could have slipped down the iron staircase and back into the house!"

"But nobody here would do such a thing. We love Julie —"

We love Julie! We, the family! But I, Anna, I am the outsider — the suspect? But this was unthinkable. Or was it? Perhaps one of them had done this thing hoping she would be blamed. . . .

"Well, there's nothing more we can do tonight —"

Sapphira had turned to the landing window. "There's a full moon tonight and there are people who go strange at such times. Perhaps one of the villagers —"

"We've known them all our lives," Bridget said. "None of them has shown any signs of being bewitched. And there's no one new in the village who might be — peculiar." Their eyes evaded Anna as though they all had the same thought in their minds.

Then Eve began to cry. "I couldn't bear it if Julie was taken away —"

"Do you think *I* can bear having my child frightened by some half wit who likes to dress up? It's a child's trick, not a grownup's — but no child did this tonight!"

Sapphira folded her arms slowly across her breast. She stood quite still looking over their heads at the far, shadowed walls.

"There's evil in this house —" Her voice was

slurred and dreamy. "Can't any of you *see?*"

"No," snapped Bridget. "We can't! And nor can you, Sapphira. You're just playing at dramatics."

"I'm telling you! No good can ever come from here now —"

"Stop it, Sapphira!" Martin's voice ordered. "And go back to bed. Eve, is Julie asleep?"

"Of course. I wouldn't have left her if she hadn't been. And I'm going back there now if Jaimie will get the camp bed."

The group scattered silently. Slippered feet padded along the passage, doors opened and closed. No one said, "Good night."

Anna carried the sari over her arm and Martin walked by her side.

At her door he bent and kissed her. She clung to him for a moment, fingers feeling the firmness of his arms through his dressing gown.

"Martin, *I* didn't do this thing!"

"I never for a moment thought you did."

"Then who —" she whispered.

He shook his head. "It's incredible that anyone in this house should have such a twisted mind that they'd frighten a child. Thank God Julie's the resilient kind! If she were highly strung I hate to think what a scare like that could have done to her."

"It couldn't have been anyone in this house,

Martin. Perhaps someone in the village hates the family for some reason or other. Have they dismissed anyone lately, has there been any trouble among the workers?"

He shook his head thoughtfully. "The workers are well paid, their jobs are guaranteed except for a few who volunteer for casual work at busy times of the year. They all get free fruit and vegetables. No, I can't think of anyone in the village."

"But someone wanted to cause trouble by pinning that note on the door and it couldn't have been anyone in the house. Sapphira wouldn't — it would have been too obvious — and certainly not Jaimie. The others weren't even in the neighborhood."

He said, "I've a feeling I may go to the police tomorrow."

"But what would they have to go on? Someone pinned a note to the door, and I've destroyed it; someone frightened a little girl —"

"Someone is a little mad," he said gravely. "I may be quite wrong, but I have a feeling that this is only the beginning —"

"What could the police do?"

"Wait!" he said. "Be ready just in case I need them."

She leaned tiredly against the door post.

"Perhaps it's me they're hitting at. The

note certainly was —"

"If only you'd kept it!"

"— and tonight it was my sari." She lifted her face. "Perhaps I ought to leave here —"

"And stay at some hotel in Lavernake?"

"I've got friends in London."

Before even the shadow crossed his face she knew she had made a mistake. London was synonymous in his mind with Aidan and in spite of all that had happened tonight, he couldn't forget that.

He was saying, "You have friends here, Anna. There's only one person antagonistic. One person — perhaps here in this house —"

"I can't believe —"

"God help me, *I* do!"

"Then if I left?"

"I don't believe it would solve anything. Whoever is doing these childish macabre things must be found, and the only way for that is for the reason for them to remain."

"Me?"

A smile touched his face fleetingly.

"Perhaps. I don't know." He caught her arms and drew her to him. "Anyway, *I* want you here, Anna. I want you near me, now and always. . . . If you left" — he drew in a sharp breath and then kissed her with a violent hunger. "Anna," his voice was a ragged whisper. "Don't go! Nobody will really harm you here, whoever is responsible wouldn't go to those terrible lengths. If you left here, I have a dreadful fear I might lose you."

"But Martin, you wouldn't. How could you?"

"I don't know," he said slowly. "I just don't know. . . . Call it a hunch."

"Nothing can part two people who are in love!"

"Oh, yes it can! There are other forces —" He broke off and then in a different voice said, "Go to bed now, Anna. Good night, my darling."

Fatigue, depression, fear, all fell from her as he kissed her again.

When he let go she stood for a moment watching him. Then she opened her door. Somewhere, way down the passage, long before Martin reached his room, she heard another door close softly.

There was a muted atmosphere about the house the following morning and in the afternoon Anna went in to Lavernake making shopping an excuse.

She spent her time wandering around the big new stores built on the vast gaping spaces left by the bombing raids of 1944. She bought a few things — a pair of garnet earrings for herself, a book of Norwegian fairy tales for Julie, a ball point pen for Martin who was always mislaying his. She had tea in the roof restaurant and then went for a walk by the river.

She didn't want to get back to the house until she knew Martin had returned. Nobody had accused her of having been concerned with last night's episode, nobody this morning had referred to it other than to inquire of Eve, who always supervised Julie's dressing, how the little girl was that morning. She was fine: she had decided, with the shrewdness of a child, that something important enough to rouse the family had happened to her and she was going to cash in on it at school. She had seen a ghost and the family had all come to her in the middle of the night. The ghost had left its clothes behind. It was a ghost, it *was* a ghost – dressed in Anna's sari.

The walk did Anna good. She felt the soft wind at her face and looked up at the sky, saw the way the high clouds were racing and thought:

It's blowing from the east! From how far away? Where were winds born? In the mountains of eastern France? Farther away, in the wild Caucasus? Or still farther, where the gaunt red rocks of Afghanistan guarded India. . . .

India. How Eastern am I? Not in birth, not in religion. And yet, something was there, cemented by environment, something that made her suddenly homesick. The rushes rustled in the wind and the Avon flowed, gray and swift, turning in a beautiful angle through fields to run at last into Southampton Water. . . . And she found herself wishing Aidan were with her.

The thought shook her, and she tried to rationalize it. It was Martin she loved, yet Aidan whom sometimes she wanted. . . . Why? Could one love two people in different ways — just as you chose your friends for different qualities you liked in them? She thought: When I'm happy, I want Martin. But when things go wrong I know that it is Aidan who can give me strength. He had those rare qualities of complete understanding and compassion; he had a strong sense of religion, one that was all his own, embracing Christianity, Hinduism and Buddhism, taking the essentials from each and making them the fundamentals on which he lived his life.

When she returned to Dion House, she found Martin playing with Julie. She hailed them from the car, hooting lightly on the horn, and then got out and crossed the grass towards them.

Martin looked up.

Julie, clutching a huge new ball, glanced at Anna over the top of it.

A black kitten, a new acquisition, played with a leaf.

"Hello, Julie. Did you have a nice day at school?"

There was no answer.

"Anna asked you a question," Martin said.

"Yes, thank you, I had a nice day at school," she said stiffly, and deliberately turned her back.

"Shall we ask Anna to join us? Three makes a good game."

"No," the child said firmly, and bounced the huge yellow ball and ran after it.

"I know a lovely new game —" Anna began.

Julie's small straight back was rigid.

"*Julie.*"

"Yes, Daddy?"

"You don't turn your back when you are spoken to."

The child swung around, her eyes large and dark and angry.

"Anna pretended to be a ghost last night and frightened me."

"Who told you she did?" He took three striding steps towards her. Julie stood her ground.

"Martin, don't!" Anna cried

He might not have heard her. He stood frowning over Julie.

"Last night you said you didn't know who

it was who had frightened you. You said there was no face."

"It *was* Anna. I know it was!"

"You aren't speaking the truth, are you? You know nothing of the kind!"

"I *do*. I *do!*"

"Stamping your foot won't help. Why did you say one thing last night and now contradict it? Oh, and don't look so puzzled, you know perfectly well what I mean!"

"I told you, I saw her." Suddenly Julie lost her temper. *"I saw her!"* she shouted, tears of anger in her eyes, her body tensed against her father. "I know it was Anna and not even God can make me say it wasn't!"

Martin looked up and his eyes caught Anna's gaze. She shook her head and her lips framed one word silently.

"Don't!"

He crouched on his heels so that his eyes were on a level with Julie's, and laid his hands on her arms.

"Look, Julie. It was a horrible experience for you and we know it and we're all very sorry. But you know, honey, you mustn't lie about it. It wasn't Anna who was in your room last night, it was someone who stole her sari and played a trick on you. Perhaps someone did it just to test you and see how brave you are. And you *were* brave. You screamed because you were startled, but then you were wise and told us about it and then went to sleep. That was my good girl! Now, I don't know who it was who was in your room, but it wasn't Anna. She loves you. One day soon we're all going to be together, you and Anna and I."

"I don't want ever to live with her," Julie tried to wrench herself out of his arms.

Anna half turned to go. Martin saw her.

"Stay," he called. "Let's hear this out together. Julie, why this sudden change towards Anna?"

"You believe *her*, you don't believe me!"

"If you mean 'Anna,' say her name, don't say 'her.' "

"It's because you love her more than you love me. You won't ever love me again like you used to."

"When Anna first came and I told you I was going to marry her, you were quite happy about it. What's changed you. *Who?*"

"She — Anna! She wants to frighten me so that I don't want to live here any more."

"And you didn't think *that* one up by yourself!" Martin said bitterly.

"It's true, Daddy! Send her away back to that black place —"

"If you mean Kashmir, then it's not black! And when you talk of countries you know nothing about, don't pull that face." He laughed suddenly. "If you could see yourself, Julie!"

She burst into angry tears. He hugged her. "I'm sorry, but I seem to be seeing a new Julie, and one I don't like much."

"Daddy, you *must* like me!"

"I will if you'll be yourself. All this isn't you. I do love you, Julie, of course I'll always love you. Loving Anna won't ever make any difference to how I feel for you."

"But Aunt Eve said —"

"Eve said! So that's it!"

"She wants me for her little girl. And so does Aunt Bridget and so does —"

"You're quite in demand, aren't you?" His face became gentle and smiling. "Stop being such a baby, Julie! You and Anna and I are going to have a lovely life together. And now, go and get hold of that kitten of yours. It's wandering out of the gates."

He watched her run off, his face shadowed and thoughtful.

Anna said quietly, "It'll be all right, Martin."

"Of course." His manner was preoccupied.

"You're worried?"

"Not really. It'll all blow over. The trouble is that there have been too many women adoring her." He turned. "I'd better go and rescue the kitten."

He wasn't going to discuss his thoughts with

her; he hadn't even kissed her as he'd always done at their meeting at the end of the day. Well, what of it? Was she going to be childish about a kiss?

Anna turned slowly towards the house. So last night's incident was closed. Whatever Martin thought about it, he had decided not to discuss it any further. Perhaps because, like all men, he hated trouble and knew that soon they would be free from it all. Yet doubt lingered. If she married Martin, would she ever be free of the Claremondes? And was her sin that, in spite of her denials, they believed her to have been the real cause of Gillian's death? Or was there some deeper wrong they felt she had done Martin?

XII

Anna's twenty-sixth birthday came a few days later.

When she went down to breakfast that morning, Martin was waiting for her in the hall.

He held out his hands, smiling, and drew her close.

"What does it feel like to be twenty-six?"

"Lovely," she said, "like this!" and lifted her face to be kissed.

Dimly she could hear the family's voices in the dining room, but that was a world away. Martin released one arm and keeping the other tight around her, felt in his pocket.

Then he held out a small jewel box, took her hand, palm upwards and laid the case into it.

"I hope you'll like it."

She undid the tiny, old-fashioned clasp of the box and found inside a large dark purple ame-

181

thyst pendant set in small diamonds sparkling in the muted, jeweled sunlight that came through the stained glass windows.

"Oh, Martin!" Anna lifted it out by its slender platinum chain. "It's quite lovely!"

"Put it on. Or no, let me!"

He fastened it around her throat and then stood her back and looked at it. She glanced down, seeing the glint in the large central stone of graduated lights, from palest violet to reddish purple.

"It's the family heirloom," he said with a laugh. "No, I mean it. Most families, even ordinary ones like ours, have something or other that great-grandmother wore. Well, this is ours. It's been in the family for about a hundred and fifty years and it is always given to the wife of the eldest son for her lifetime. That will be your position, soon, and I so wanted you to have it."

Anna had gone to the oval mirror on the wall and put up her hand to touch the pendant.

"It shouldn't be worn with an ordinary sweater," she said softly. "It should be lying against a bare throat."

"It will be. One day you must have a white evening dress and I'll buy you earrings to match the pendant and we will save up and go to grand places where I'll be so jealous because men will look at you and you'll laugh and enjoy it all!"

"Oh, Martin!" There were moments even in such a prosaic, coffee-and-toast smelling hallway, that brought tears to eyes and throat. This was one.

She put up her hands to take the pendant off, but Martin stopped her.

"Wear it, just for a little while. Then you can put it away for gay occasions."

"I feel rather like someone wearing a tiara to breakfast!" and her laughter shook a little.

Martin felt for her hand and they went together into the dining room. Eyes turned to her; voices said politely:

"Happy birthday, Anna."

And then they saw the pendant.

She felt rather than heard the astounded "Oh!" that shivered through the room. Martin sauntered to the hotplate on the side table.

"Bacon and eggs, Anna?" He peered into the dish. "Oh, there's tomato —"

"No thanks. Toast, as usual —"

"But this is your birthday and you should feast!" he coaxed. "Come on, never mind the waistline!"

"Then egg and tomato," she gave in.

"Anna probably doesn't eat pig," Eve said, eyes still riveted on the pendant. "You forget, Martin, they don't eat it in India."

"You've got your facts muddled." Martin's voice was ice cold. "But anyway, Anna is Western. You know that, so don't make silly statements!"

"I'm sorry! I —" Eve sought for words.

"Let it rest!" Martin retorted and brought a plate to Anna. "Eat that up, sweet. Mind, it's hot!" His eye caught sight of a pile of parcels by her plate. "Goodness, birthday presents! Open them and let's see what lovely loot you've got!" He was determined to eradicate Eve's stupid remark.

Anna reached for the nearest parcel.

"That came two days ago, but we held it up until today," Martin said.

Inside were two lovely Thai silk scarves from Rashti, one in red and gold and the other pale blue and petunia and peacock green; there were tiny earrings of exquisite Chinese translucent jewel jade from Sarojini, a glass paperweight shaped like a lotus flower in luminous white and green from a cousin, and a little Mogul water color of pale parrot greens and carmines from her brother. Her parents had sent her a check and the Claremondes had clubbed together to buy her three beautifully illustrated books on the English scene. Julie, off to school, handed her a present politely, saying, "Many happy returns of the day," but refusing to meet Anna's eyes.

The family remained very silent as Anna undid her parcels. When she had seen them and shown them around, she took them all to an arm chair by the window, out of the way. She had returned to the table and was passing her cup to Sapphira for more coffee when Bridget walked in.

"Heavens, I'm late this morning. Eve, you hell cat, why didn't you call me?" She rushed across to her chair, angry and beautiful in a gray suit. "By the way, Anna," she glanced up. "Many happy –" Her voice froze. Her eyes flew to the pendant.

"Who gave you that?"

Martin said clearly, "I did. Why?"

"But you can't! Martin, it isn't – it isn't yours –"

"Be quiet, Bridget," Sapphira commanded. "Here's your coffee."

"I don't want it! I don't want anything." She pushed back her chair and fled from the room.

"Good gracious, what's the matter with Bridget?" Jaimie asked.

"Leave her alone and let's get on with breakfast," Sapphira snapped.

Anna put her hands up and unclasped the pendant and laid it back in its little black box.

"It really doesn't go with a sweater,"

she said quietly.

They heard Bridget's high heels tapping towards the living room, but nobody said anything. Jaimie and Martin rustled newspapers, Sapphira went on reading letters, passing one to Eve, saying:

"This is from the Masons in Knightsbridge. They want us to supply them with any new herbs we can get hold of."

"There you are. What did I tell you, herbs are going to be good sellers. People are far more taste-conscious in this country!" Eve cried triumphantly.

Martin pushed back his chair and lit a cigarette.

"I'll be home as early as I can tonight, Anna. We'll go out somewhere and celebrate." He flashed a smile at her and went out of the room.

The door of the living room was open and as he passed Bridget called to him.

She was standing by the French window, and as she heard him enter she swung around.

"Martin, how *could* you?"

"How could I what?"

"Give Anna that pendant! It belongs to the family."

"Anna belongs to the family," he said shortly.

He thought she whispered, "Not yet," but he couldn't be sure because a van passed up the drive branching towards the nurseries. He leaned towards an ash tray, tipping ash from his cigarette.

"I must go or I'll be late."

"Martin, remember that my father —"

"Was the eldest son and your mother had the pendant for her lifetime. Yes. But your parents didn't have a son did they? So it went to me when your mother died."

"She always said that ritual was outdated and that it should be mine when she died."

He said quietly, "You haven't got the facts quite right! It was left in your father's will to me, but the arrangement we made between us was that if you married before I did, then you should have it. But you aren't married, Bridget!"

"That's cruel!"

"Why?" he asked in genuine surprise. "You're objecting to something I did, and so I'm explaining why I had every right to do it!"

"Martin, I'm sorry," her tone changed, softened. "I shouldn't have behaved like that in front of Anna, but it was such a shock seeing something I thought of as mine. I — I've been waiting for you to pass it to me. But you're right, if I'd stopped to think —"

"Let's forget it." He was about to turn away, the whole affair over and done with, and glancing at Bridget saw to his amazement that there were tears in her eyes.

"Bridget, don't let a piece of jewelry upset you so. It's not worth it!"

"You don't understand, do you, Martin?" Her lovely face was tilted, no longer masked in sophistication, but raw with love. Martin would have been blind in that moment not to have understood. All he knew was that he would have given anything for this moment not to have happened. He felt caught in an unwanted web of emotion, embarrassed and inept. He wanted to glance at his watch, say "I'm late," and beat it. But something deeper, some compassion, some memory of their once lovely friendship, made him stay, saying:

"Don't be harrowed like this! Bridget — please —"

Her hands moved blindly towards him.

"Nothing will ever be the same again!"

"Nothing goes back; only forward. That's life!"

"For me it's like death!" She closed her eyes and he felt that her distress was genuine. He laid a hand gently on her arm.

"*You* talk like that! You're young and beautiful — you know that! Everything is beginning for you."

The tawny eyes opened and regarded him,

tears wet on her cheeks. He had dropped his hand but immediately she sought his fingers, clinging to them.

"I've always believed that there's no room for pride in love! You have to be honest. Martin — I've loved you for so long."

"Oh God!" he writhed under her touch. "I'm sorry, Bridget. I don't know what else I can say."

"I always believed," she went on as though he hadn't spoken, "that one day we would be together. Then you married Gillian. I somehow knew that wouldn't last and I waited. Then she died — and you brought Anna back with you from India."

"I never led you to believe there was anything more than friendship between us. We were very young —" He moved his hands gently from under hers. "People change, Bridget. Young romance dies — ours did."

She shook her head. "Not for me."

"I really must go."

"Martin, please understand if I say something," she cried. "You see, it's because I love you that I'm so afraid for you, *really* afraid. I can't bear to see you make a second terrible mistake."

He stiffened. "That's my affair."

"It's not Anna's fault," she cried softly. "Perhaps a kind of malevolent fate mishandles your life for you, Martin."

"I don't feel very mishandled at the moment."

"But suppose, after a short time, you realize how wrong you were to take Anna out of her setting, away from her own people —"

"Why won't you all realize that Anna is entirely Western?" he cried impatiently.

"Because she has lived most of her life in India, her stepfather is a Hindu — environment must have played a tremendous part in her way of life."

"You're talking about something of which you know nothing," he said sharply.

"If you're really so sure of her, why be in such a hurry to marry her? You bring her over to England for barely seven weeks —"

"Because I know I love her."

"Or because you're afraid if you don't marry her quickly she'll go to one of her own people?" Bridget asked softly. "Is that it? Are you afraid of some man — her friend Aidan perhaps —"

He froze. "Why should I be? She's choosing to marry me."

"She promised to marry you when you were both in India, *her* country. Now you've taken her away from all that, don't you ever ask yourself whether she feels quite the same —"

"Whatever I ask myself is my affair! And now, I must go."

"Anyone's life is the affair of the people who love him."

"You've always got an answer, haven't you, Bridget?" he said bitterly. "But answers can be wrong. Neither Anna nor I are holding up a daisy and picking off its petals. 'Is it love? Isn't it?'" he added sharply. "We're adults, you know! And let's stop needling each other!"

Without warning, Bridget went close to Martin and kissed him. Her lips, warm and ardent on his, brought the blood thudding through his heart. His hands went up to push her away from him, but she moved first. Tears were streaming down her face.

"Go," she said, and turned her back on him. "Oh, Martin, *go!*"

He turned without a word and went out of the room.

In the hall he picked up a briefcase from the big center table. Then, as he strode out, the doorbell rang.

Martin was nearest and pulled open the door. A messenger stood there and in his arms was a great cellophane-packed sheaf of flowers.

"Miss Kashinath?"

Martin said yes, signed for the flowers and gave the boy a shilling. Through the wrapping the flowers glowed — yellow roses and sprays of while lilac, golden tulips, and plum blossom.

There was a tiny envelope pinned inside the cellophane and Martin could just see the writing, recognizing it from the time when Aidan had written congratulating him on his engagement.

Of course, he thought, stilling the wave of jealousy that washed over him, Aidan would know Anna's birth date, would have for years remembered it with a gift. . . .

Sapphira, coming across the hall, said, "I thought I heard a bell."

"You did. Flowers have arrived for Anna."

"Oh —" She took them and her eyes searched curiously for the customary little envelope. "Who —"

"How should I know? It's Anna's gift." He spoke too sharply and a small smile curved Sapphira's long, thin lips. . . .

Flowers from Aidan! Martin slammed the door of his car, let in the clutch too quickly and jerked forward. For Pete's sake, did that gift look nearly as suspicious as Bridget kissing him? Suppose Anna had walked in at that moment!

What do I do now? Get away from Dion House because I distress Bridget? But this was the first indication of it! It was probably all said in an outburst of pique and temper over the amethyst pendant! And then he felt mean. He shook himself and tried to concentrate on the lovely morning, the coming of summer over the hills, the winging of a bird high up in the shimmering, aquamarine sky.

They would be away soon, and then Bridget would settle down and wonder why she ever thought twice about him. She was too attractive to be alone all her life, and she was warm and vital underneath all that sophistication! He remembered her kiss and shook the thought away, only to replace it by a more troubling one.

Fair enough that Aidan should send flowers to Anna! But that they should be yellow roses. . . .

Unwillingly there came the sharp memory of an evening in the Nishat Gardens in Kashmir. They had been looking at the terraces of roses and Anna had quoted softly:

"If you find me fair,
    Bring me white roses:
Should passion be all,
    Red blooms bring me.
But should you love me
    Then lay yellow roses at my feet."

He had said at the time, laughing, hand touching hers, "I will bring you the white and the red and the yellow!"

And now Aidan had given her yellow roses. Laying them, with his love, at her feet?

Oh, sweet heaven, was this the effect of all the emotion of this morning? He forced himself to stop thinking of anything but the work ahead of him and was thankful when the great gates of the laboratory came into view and behind them he saw the solid, red brick building where for hours he would be too busy to think of personal problems.

Aidan's note had just said: "Many happy returns of the day."

Anna slipped it into her handbag, went to the little room off the hall where the flower vases were kept and arranged Aidan's lovely gift. There were no flowers in the living room and she thought how much more perfect they would look in that big room than in her bedroom. She put them on a mat on the mahogany chest, pausing and touching the delicate plum blossom, thinking how like Aidan not just to order two dozen carnations and leave it at that! Then she went upstairs to her room to make her bed and dust.

On the table by the window, her tiny transistor radio played a Haydn Symphony, so that she was only vaguely aware of a tap on her door.

194

"Anna?"

She heard Eve's voice.

"Come in."

Eve entered, carrying the vase of flowers.

"You left these downstairs."

"Yes, I meant to. I thought we'd share them."

"Thanks, but we don't need them. I'm sure you appreciate your gift far more than we would!"

Anna met Eve's smoldering eyes.

"Yes, I do appreciate them. It's lovely when one's friends remember a birthday," and thought: Why does she have to be jealous?

Eve set the vase down on the chest of drawers.

Anna, a blue duster in her hand, waited for Eve to go. But she hung about, her eyes curious.

"If you're going to town today, you'll let Sapphira know because of lunch, won't you?"

"I hadn't thought of going to town."

"As it's your birthday —"

"But Martin couldn't get enough time for us to go to town to lunch. We —"

"No, no of course, Martin can't!" There was only the faintest emphasis on the name, although the inference was clear. *But Aidan can.*

Anna chose to ignore it. "Martin and I are

going to celebrate tonight. We're going to a show."

Eve had something else on her mind. She hovered.

"About Julie —" she began. "I'm afraid it will be quite impossible to take her to South America with you. She's not strong —"

"So you tell me. I haven't noticed much wrong with her."

"That's because you aren't used to children —"

"Oh, but in India I did a certain amount of work in a children's clinic —"

"That's not the same thing at all. I happen to be a trained nurse. And if you don't believe what I say about Julie, you'd better ask her doctor."

"I believe that Julie isn't robust. But I'm sure that the sunshine and fresh air in South America —"

"*She's not going, Anna.*" Suddenly Eve was changed. She seemed taller, her eyes lost their fretted look and took on an amber brown depth, regarding Anna with hot defiance, her mouth tightened, strengthened. The effect of her inner emotion on her looks was startling. "We will move heaven and earth — and hell — to keep Julie with us!"

"You'll have to defeat her father's wishes. That will be even a greater miracle!" Anna retorted dryly.

Eve took a step forward. "Anna, why did you deliberately frighten Julie the other night?"

"I – frighten – Julie?" Her heart dropped with each word. So that's what they thought; what they would perhaps manage to persuade Martin to believe!

She recoiled from the tall, auburn haired woman fascinated by the transformation from weakness to strength of the face thrust so near her.

"Don't ever dare say that again." She spoke slowly, each word a thrust. "Do you hear? *Don't ever suggest that I dressed up to frighten a child!*"

"We hated – to think it – of course." The power was disintegrating before Anna's anger; the fret of neurosis showing in the puckered face. "It's all very well for you to be angry, but there was no one else –"

"On the contrary, you had a choice of four people."

"The family? Oh, no, it couldn't have been one of them!"

"But it could. Did someone want Julie to fear me so that it would be impossible to take her to the Argentine with us? Did someone mean to make me the scapegoat? Who?"

"Not one of us! How *can* you?" and then suddenly her eyes opened wide; she clapped her hand to her mouth. "Oh no! No!"

"What's struck you, Eve?"

"Nothing." The closed look that made Eve on occasions seem so like Sapphira came back. She turned towards the door.

Anna was after her. She seized her arm and tried to swing her around, but Eve's body resisted her.

"What is it, Eve?" she cried.

"I don't know what you mean. Let me go, I've got things to do. I'm busy —"

"Not too busy to tell me what you suddenly remembered. It was something that points to whoever has done these things — Eve, tell me, who frightened Julie? Who wrote that note pinned to the front door? *Who?*"

Eve wrenched her arm away and tore at the door handle.

"I don't know! I don't know —" She was repeating the three frantic words as she fled down the passage.

But she *did* know, and it meant that Eve, as a suspect, could be eliminated. That left Sapphira and Bridget and Jaimie . . . idiotic to include that mild young man but she had to do so because sometimes, behind the stillest face, the fires raged wildest . . .

Anna knew she would not tell Martin of her conversation with Eve. This was her birthday, a gala, their first celebration together in England, and she had no intention of spoiling it.

Martin took her to London to see a musical show that promised a long run. Afterwards they had supper and danced. Over her shoulder she could see her reflection in the mirrors. Black wings of hair, smooth forehead, dark crimson folds of chiffon falling from the high-breasted dress, and the pendant which Martin had asked her to wear gleaming against her skin.

Dion House and the Claremondes were a world away; she and Martin were close and happy and gay. This, she thought, was what it would be like in seven weeks' time. When they were free of Dion House. They toasted each other in champagne; the music seeped around the room, making people remember, making people forget.

"Happy?"

"So very happy, Martin!"

It happened that Martin was nearest the telephone the following day when Aidan called Anna.

He handed the receiver to her. "For you."

Aidan's quiet voice asked her if she'd had a happy birthday and then said:

"The Graysons are over here from Bombay. They looked me up and said they'd like to see you, but I never like to give private addresses without permission —"

"I'd love them to contact me!" Anna said happily. "I'll write and ask them down here."

"Ask Aidan, too," came Martin's voice from behind her.

She wheeled around, receiver still at her ear.

"I mean it! Ask Aidan. Let's make a party of it. Ask them all for next Saturday," he went on. "The weather looks fairly settled. We could picnic down in the cove."

"Martin, what a lovely idea," she turned happily to the telephone. "You're all to come down on Saturday to lunch — Martin's special invitation."

When she hung up, she turned to him.

"Thank you! You're sure Sapphira won't mind —"

"Why should I mind?" She had been there all the time, quietly in the background of the dark hall, feeling down the side of a tapestry chair. She glanced over her shoulder. "I'm glad your friends are coming down. Have either of you seen Jaimie's sun glasses? He says he left them on the arm of this chair when he went to see about the parrot tulip order. Ah" — she unearthed them from deep in the back of the upholstery and crossing the hall with her almost nun-like serenity of tread, continued, "Did I hear you say the name of your friends was Grayson? Does that mean they're English?"

"Yes."

"Oh!" Her eyes flickered over Anna. Then she moved towards the office. "Martin, glance through some accounts for me, will you?"

"Of course. Now?"

"Yes, please. Then I can get them paid and out of the way."

He said, grinning at Anna, "Sapphira's determined to make an accountant of me!" opened the office door and closed it behind him.

Immediately they were alone, Sapphira faced him.

"Are you wise to ask Anna's Indian friend down here?"

"Why not?"

Her shrewd eyes rested on Martin's averted head.

"I'd have said it was risky throwing them together! Or perhaps you mean it to be? Is that it, Martin?"

He jerked his head up, saying vehemently, "I don't know what you mean! Now let's drop the subject. Where are those accounts?"

But while he sat at her desk checking them he was aware of her standing still and impassive at the window. She can't know, unless she's a witch, she can't *possibly* know why I want Aidan here ... Want him? He didn't. He wished him a thousand miles away! But he had to watch them together, just once more. Anna and Aidan. He scratched out a line of figures with a violent gesture, and then almost laughed at himself. All right, so Anna lunched with Aidan in town without telling me first . . . she had flowers from him, yellow roses! . . . So what? What was he, man or mouse, that he must suspect secret emotions behind everything that concerned the two of them? Anna was adult. If she found she didn't love him, she'd say so.

What's happened to me? I never used to be seized with jealousy like this! It's the atmosphere in this house. It's charged with a new force . . . and something that could be interpreted as sinister. Yet where did it come from — *or from whom?*

"You've crossed that out three times," came Sapphira's voice. "Here, let me do them —"

Martin got up, turning so that the eyes of brother and sister were on a level.

She said quietly, "There's something wrong, isn't there? I feel it, Martin, too!"

He stared at her, startled by her perception.

"Something wrong," she went on, "that pervades the whole house — in fact ever since Anna came here."

"*Not* from Anna —"

"From something she has done — perhaps quite innocently — to us all!"

"Then the sooner I take her away from here the better."

"Running away won't help you!"

"I won't be running away," he defended hotly. "I'll be making a home with Anna and —"

"Have you noticed," Sapphira cut in, "that Julie is afraid of her?"

He frowned. "Because someone here has worked on the child! Well, that's going to stop! I can work on Julie, too!"

"But, Martin, you know your daughter. No one could make Julie afraid unless she herself had good reason. There's something —"

Martin strode to the door, dragged it open, flung over his shoulder at his sister:

"There's *someone* here who wants to break up my happiness for her own purpose! Or, it could be that someone here has a secret axe to grind and is using Anna as a vehicle. Well — think it over, Sapphira. Which? And who?" He slammed the door.

Sapphira just stood there, and looked with blank, light eyes at the empty room.

XIII

The Graysons arrived about twelve o'clock on Saturday morning. They tumbled out of Aidan's long dark car, greeting Anna with hugs of joy. They had been married five years and were still wholeheartedly and uninhibitedly in love. Barbara was a young Juno of a girl, fair and tanned and statuesque; she abounded with health and vitality in spite of five years in the energy draining climate of Bombay. She was wonderful with her witty but quite impractical husband and in his eyes she was ravishing, lovely.

The Claremondes, when they put themselves out, could be both amusing and intelligent. In spite of the fact that the day was very beautiful, there was a cool wind so that lunch was prepared at home, and in the afternoon Martin suggested they might find the cove warm enough to lie in for an hour or so before going to the Yacht Club for tea.

Eve wanted the family car to take Julie to tea with some friends in Silchester, so Martin's car and Aidan's were to be used. Sapphira went with them.

Bridget went to see friends and Jaimie stayed behind to do some work in one of the glasshouses.

The road to the sea climbed a bare hill. On either side, cliffs rose whitely, gulls wheeled and the grass on the cliff top trembled in the light wind.

They found the cove sheltered from the wind and Barbara flung out her splendid young arms and started to run across the beach, stumbled and fell and lay laughing on the white shell sand.

Anna went with Nick to the edge of the sea. The lacy edges of the waves darted at their feet with little rushing sounds.

"Well, how do you like England?" Nick asked.

Anna's hair streamed back from her face; her eyes were dazzled with sunlight. She said, "I always loved it, Nick."

"And this particular bit where you'll make your home?"

"Oh, but we shan't be living here for a long time — if ever."

He turned to her in surprise. She explained, "Martin has a job offered him in South America —"

"Oh lord, poor chap! Off again?"

She said "Yes" and fell silent as the others joined them. She watched the waves, sucking at the pebbles.

Poor chap! That's what others, besides the family, thought. Poor Martin, robbed of roots . . .

She turned quickly away from the green, dancing sea and caught Aidan's glance. He smiled at her, and then was whirled around by Barbara and given some flat stones and told to play ducks and drakes on the sea with her.

Presently they flopped down in the shelter of the cliffs and lifted the fine sand and let it sift through their fingers; rolled over and hid drowsy faces on their arms; the wind, rippling the sea, made it too cold for bathing, but they were content. At least, on the surface, they seemed to be. If occasionally Martin lay, chin on elbow, and looked from Anna to Aidan and back again to Anna, nobody could guess his thoughts.

They had tea at the yacht club and much later decided to return home by a different route.

Martin drove Sapphira and Nick. Barbara chose to go with Aidan and Anna went with them to direct him in case they lost sight of the car in front.

The drive through the evening sunlight was very beautiful. It was the golden era of the day, with field and wood, cliff and sky bathed with rich, mature light.

They planned to meet at an inn for drinks and just as Anna had indicated the old sixteenth century coaching inn, her eye caught something else. "What's that?" She craned back.

"What's what, Anna?"

"Stop the car, please."

Aidan drew the powerful engine to a halt and Anna was out of the car, running back along the road. Here, where the hedge came down sheer to the roadside, she heard a soft whimpering and saw a movement. The next moment a small boy half crawled into sight.

"What's the matter?" Anna asked gently.

"I've hurt my foot," he whimpered a little, face puckered.

"Let me see, will you?"

He stuck out one foot and she saw the twisted, swollen ankle.

"You certainly have! How did you do it?"

"I fell on that bank the other side of the hedge —"

"Well, we must do something about this, musn't we?"

Barbara called, "Hey, what's this? A casualty?"

Aidan moved past her and said to the little freckled boy, "I'm not going to hurt you, but just let me have a look at that ankle."

His hands were gentle and exploratory. "I know, old chap, it hurts, doesn't it? I'm sorry. Look, I think we'd better take you home. Where do you live?"

"In the village."

"Which one?"

"There," said the boy and pointed the way they had come. "Manning Wood."

"But that's four miles back!" Anna cried.

"I know and I want to go home," he whimpered again.

"All right, we'll take you. Don't worry! But first of all, Anna, get my first-aid kit out of the car, will you? It's in the trunk at the back. Take the ignition key, the second on the ring opens the trunk."

She ran back, found the first-aid kit and brought it to Aidan.

When he had bound the foot he said, "There, that'll make it easier. Now for home. You'll have to tell us exactly where your house is, because we're strangers."

Aidan was slim and light himself but he picked the boy up as though he had been no more weight than a little pile of books and carried him to the car.

"The others haven't passed us, have they, Anna?"

"They must have stopped the car somewhere to look at the view."

"Then we'll take Barbara to the inn – leave her to explain to the rest. Then you and I will take – what's your name?" he asked the small boy, sitting him by his side in the front passenger seat.

"Tommy –"

"Well, then, we'll take Tommy home. Do you mind, Barbara, being left at the inn?" he asked, looking at her doubtfully. "I'll need Anna to show me the road again."

"I'll be one cocktail ahead of all of you. But don't take me there – I can walk. It's only a hundred yards," she slammed the car door and waved at them and was off down the road with a swing of a white pleated skirt.

It took them barely five minutes to reach the tiny cottage where Tommy lived, but when they arrived there was no one at home.

The door opened direct into a living room, which was neat enough and comfortable although so dark that they blinked a little after the evening radiance outside.

"Where do you think your mother is, Tommy?"

"She's gone out to find a job."

"On a late Saturday afternoon? Where is she likely to be?"

"I dunno." Now that he was home and comfortable on the shabby settee he was at ease and unworried. "She didn't say. She just said she'd get some work. Father died last month."

"Have you any brothers or sisters?"

"Nope," said Tommy, who had an ear for American jargon, and then he wriggled. "I'm hungry."

"Do you think I might raid a strange larder and get him some food?"

"Yes, if he really means he's hungry," Aidan laughed. "And I guess he does! What's your last name, Tommy?"

"Calshott."

"Well, Tommy Calshott," Anna said briskly, "I'm going to raid your larder for some food and I hope your mother won't think I'm taking liberties in her house!"

He gave her a quick freckled grin. "Mum won't."

Anna went into the small dark kitchen and found some stewed fruit, a triangle of cheese, biscuits and a bottle of milk.

Bringing them back into the living room, she asked, "Do you think we can leave him now, Aidan?"

"I'd like to have a word with his mother. You see, she probably won't think that, as the ankle is bandaged, it's worth calling in the doctor. But it is. Also, I don't want him to walk about and he might if there's no one here. You take the car and go back to the inn and then I'll find a telephone somewhere and ring you when I want to be picked up. You pass this way, don't you?"

She was pouring milk into a tall glass. "There you are, Tommy," she said, "drink that up." Then she turned and walked across to join Aidan at the window.

"We'll stay together," she said firmly.

He smiled. "You're missing drinks in what Martin tells us is a bar lounge that used to be a meeting place of smugglers!"

"The atmosphere will keep!" she laughed.

Aidan was looking on to the tangle of greenery and budding plants in the stretch of garden that seemed to be communal to the whole row of cottages.

"Isn't it strange how history repeats itself? Do you remember, that morning in Srinagar how we went riding and found the small boy lying hurt on the rocks by the gorge?"

She said slowly, "His name was Nana Ram — I even remember that!"

"And we took him back to his village and his

father hung jasmine flowers around your neck."

"That," she said slowly, staring into the garden, "was my last real ride. The next day I had the accident."

"You were riding alone that time!"

She nodded. "And the horse became frightened by that stupid prancing goat and threw me —"

"Do you ride here?"

She shook her head. "I've never ridden again. I know I should have got back on the horse at once and saved my nerve, but I thought she was hurt and I walked her back." She could recall so clearly that early morning, the smell of spices, the incredible, beautiful background of mountains, like a painting on a backcloth and only herself in that lonely place, with the gorge and the rocks that here and there glittered with crystal chips. Her back had stabbed with every step she took and the horse limped a little by her side. Two sad living things in a beautiful world. And all because of a demoniac prancing goat!

"Martin loves riding, doesn't he?"

"Oh, yes. He often goes out with Bridget. My courage has quite failed me, I'm afraid."

He said softly, kindly chiding, "Coward!"

"I know. I've had plenty of falls in my time, but this one was different. I can never get over the horror of seeing, as I fell, that awful chasm looming up with the water roaring and tearing over the rocks, and being terrified I couldn't stop myself falling into it; and knowing there was no one, not even the goat boy at hand, to go for help if I did. I think I died a little in that moment before I stopped my fall just before I reached the edge. That's something you perhaps can't ever get over." She turned, her tone changing. "How are you getting on, Tommy? Good heavens, you've got an appetite! There's an English nursery rhyme about licking the platter clean, isn't there?" She saw the grin come back on his little freckled face.

He said, "Honestly, I'm all right now. I was listening to what you were saying about horses. I like horses. I ain't scared of anything 'cept – well – like getting hurt today!" he added sheepishly. Then to Aidan, "Say, you a doctor?"

"Why do you ask?"

"The way you did things, like doctors do – sort of knew."

Aidan laughed. "You're a bright boy, Tommy! Yes, I'm a doctor."

"We had a doctor like you when we lived in Silchester. He was an Indian, too."

"I hope he was a good doctor."

"So-so," said the boy and peered into the biscuit tin.

Between then and when a small, scurrying, skinny woman came up the path, Aidan and Anna told the little boy stories about India.

Tommy's mother stood on the threshold of her room and gaped at them.

"You looking for me?" she began uncompromisingly.

"Mrs. Calshott. Please don't think we're intruders," Aidan said in his gentle voice. "We found Tommy by the road. He'd hurt his foot so we brought him back. That's all."

"You mean you hit him? That car I saw outside —" Her eyes flashed big and brave in her small face; she shot across the room to her son.

"We found him at the side of the road. He'd hurt his foot falling down a bank," Aidan explained, "so we brought him home. I've bandaged his foot for him, but his own doctor should see him."

"Is it very bad?" She glanced at the strong, grave face anxiously.

Aidan laughed.

"Good heavens, no! Only there's just a chance a small bone might be broken and he shouldn't walk about until your doctor has examined it. We stayed because it would have been too much to have expected Tommy to lie still alone until you came home."

"For one thing," Anna put in, "he was hungry, so I raided your larder. I hope you don't mind. I'd better explain. I'm not a casual passer-by; I live at the Dion House nurseries."

"Thank you for being so kind. Please, won't you stay and have a cup of tea?"

"No, thanks, we have to meet some friends." Aidan looked at her with interest. "I hear you were out after a job. Did you get it?"

"Yes, cleaner and general help at the pub — the Red Lion. But I don't drink, sir!" she hastened to add.

Aidan smiled, his eyes on the white, tired face.

"I think you might try it. Drink in moderation is no vice, Mrs. Calshott, so don't be too hard on it."

Anna was at the door, ready to go; Tommy had an eye again on the biscuit tin. Mrs. Calshott was opening the door, and no one, save Anna, saw the quick movement of Aidan's fingers as a pound note was slipped under the hideous red pottery dog on the mantelshelf.

The gold had faded from the hills as they got back into the car and the twilight had come and gone. Now both hills and woods lay in darkness.

"Shall I telephone the inn to see if the others are still there?"

"It might take us just as long to find somewhere to telephone from as to get to the inn; it looks that sort of village."

"Scorning neon lights and telephone booths!" he agreed. "All right, then. Let's go."

They drove in silence for a few minutes, the headlights of the car shooting a golden ribbon along the nearly deserted road.

Then Aidan broke the quiet. "I overheard you telling Nick that you are going to South America."

"Yes."

"Whose decision was it, Anna?" he asked gently.

"Martin's," she said honestly. "But only because he wants to please me. He doesn't like the idea of going, but then neither do I, much."

"Then why go?"

"I see it as the only solution."

"Suppose you found a house of your own, away from the family?"

"It wouldn't work. I know! Martin would have to be fairly near the laboratories and he's now so involved with the family business that they would always be calling him over or coming to our house."

Aidan made no comment and suddenly she knew she had to make him see why she was doing this seemingly selfish thing.

"There's an undercurrent in that house,

216

Aidan. Someone is working against me; they don't want me to marry Martin. It could be Eve because she adores Julie and dreads the fact that we shall take her with us to South America. Or it could be Sapphira because —"

"Because — what?"

Anna said quietly, "She doesn't really believe I love Martin. She thinks I want to free myself from all my Indian environment and contacts. She's narrow and bigoted — she can't see how proud I am of my stepfather, of my whole family."

"It's understandable enough! She's lived a narrow life, Anna. She has brains, she has intelligence and vitality and she should never have shut herself up in a village for half her life."

"There's Bridget, too. She could be causing this atmosphere, this feeling that someone is working to break up my life."

"But what has Bridget got against you?"

"Martin," she said simply. "She's in love with him."

"But, Anna, Bridget gave me the impression of being a woman of the world. She might be in love with someone who didn't love her, but she wouldn't go to extremes. She'd be philosophical about it."

"Can one ever be philosophical about love?"

"Sometimes it's the only thing we can do!"

She wanted to ask, "We? *You?*" but she didn't dare open the subject. Now that she believed Aidan loved her, but would not tell her so, it would only distress them both to probe.

She heard herself saying, despairingly, "You know I'm not overimaginative. But I'm quite certain that something — someone — is forcing a climax and that I'm the center of it."

"Crossing bridges, Anna?" he asked gently.

"Preparing myself," she retorted.

"Don't dwell too much on it, so that you draw to yourself the thing you dread. You're going to marry Martin. Prepare for *that!*"

"You're right, of course." Aidan was always right! She sat back, staring ahead of her at the black caverns the night made of the woods. "It's not so very long now to bear it; just a little over two weeks. Aidan," she turned to him. "You'll come and see us often when we're married, won't you?"

He laughed.

"When planes fly at five thousand miles an hour, I'll drop in on you in Buenos Aires for lunch!"

"And we'll kill the fatted calf. Oh, Aidan, what fun that would be!" She, too, laughed and, still laughing, saw the ancient lamplit inn come into view where the road curved. Aidan turned the nose of the car into the courtyard.

Inside they could hear the rise and fall of voices, and the clink of glasses; a cloud of smoke from heaven knew how many cigarettes blurred the vision of the little bar as Anna and Aidan passed by the diamond paned windows.

"Come along. You'll have to catch up on your cocktails," he said and took her arm.

At the doorway, hung with a ship's lantern, Aidan paused and said quietly, "Fight for what you want, Anna. Always providing you know what that is! That's my only advice!"

Always providing you know what that is. She felt Aidan's hand slip from her arm as he let her go ahead of him into the bar.

They were all there, sitting in a far corner that looked out onto the vast indigo void that was the sea. Their eyes watched the two weave their way between the tables. Barbara said brightly:

"Here come the knight errants!"

Sapphira looked from one to the other. "The child must have been badly injured —"

"No. Just a sprained and twisted foot."

"You were gone so long, we thought you must have taken him to a hospital."

Martin made a space for Anna on an old high backed settle. She sat down, explaining, "Tommy's mother was out and so we stayed because

Aidan said he was afraid the boy might try to walk if there was no one there and he wanted to tell his mother to get the doctor to him."

She didn't know why, as she spoke, she looked at Sapphira and saw her eyes grow veiled. "That's your story!" said that significant drop of white eyelids.

Quickly Anna turned to Martin. "I'm so sorry about all this, but we *had* to stay —"

"Of course," he said quickly. "Now, what are you going to drink, Anna?"

She chose a Martini and the conversation became general. Nick and Barbara thought they ought to get straight back to town but Martin managed to persuade them to come back to Dion House for supper.

Reminded of the time, they began to make movements to leave.

"Anna, you go with Martin this time, and I'll go in Aidan's car," Nick suggested. "We'll follow you, so we won't lose our way."

Anna standing close to Sapphira as they moved forward between the tables, heard her low chuckle. She turned quickly, ready to join in a joke, and saw Sapphira with lips parted in a smile that was without kindness.

"That was a mean suggestion of Nick's, wasn't it, Anna?" Sapphira said softly. Silent and angry, Anna swung back, pressing her way between the tables. The chuckles, the insinuation had been obvious.

She believes our stay with Tommy was a ruse! She is certain we worked it all out in order to be alone together. . . .

She knew Sapphira was close behind her as she went along the inn passage with its old prints and stags' heads; but she did not pause or turn until she was out of the door with Martin and Aidan at their cars.

A little mist clung to the trees and the moon was like a golden apple.

It was, however, Sapphira who was persuaded by Martin to go with Aidan in case he lost sight of the leading car in the darkness. "Sapphira knows this part blindfolded!"

When they reached Dion House, Bridget and Eve had a cold supper ready.

They were arguing about the merits of the various cheeses, Wensleydale and Cheddar, Double Gloucester and Danish Blue, when the telephone rang. Bridget answered it, returning to say:

"It's a Mrs. Calshott for Anna or for Aidan. She says 'either the lady or her husband left a cigarette case behind.' "

There was a moment's dead silence, then Eve began to giggle.

Anna said clearly, "It must be mine. I remember taking it out when I was in the kitchen looking for food for Tommy. I must have left it on the table – I'll speak to Mrs. Calshott," and walked unhurriedly out of the room.

She thanked Mrs. Calshott for telephoning and asked her how she knew where to find her.

"You mentioned the Dion House nurseries and I had a sister who worked there once."

Anna asked about Tommy, was told that the doctor would call next morning. "But I got worried about this cigarette case, ma'am. It looked valuable."

"I'll fetch it tomorrow, if I may."

When she replaced the receiver, she stood, making an effort to pull herself together. It was a natural mistake. "You and your husband." She was a simple woman, agitated by these strangers in the house, worried over Tommy, she wouldn't bother to look to see if Anna wore a wedding ring under her engagement ring. "Your husband" – Aidan! Ironic that she should have voiced her conclusion into Bridget's ear!

Anna forced herself into steadiness and re-entered the dining room.

"I'm going over to fetch the cigarette case tomorrow," she said quietly and sat down and reached for the cheese biscuits.

No one made any further mention of the telephone call. At half past nine Barbara and Nick stood by Aidan's car with demands that Anna and Martin should come to London and dine with them.

Aidan made his general farewells and spoke his thanks to them all. Then, from the dark depths of the car, he looked at Anna. It was a silent message just for her. Just "Goodbye" again? Or more? With all the family's eyes watching and the porch light illuminating her face, she did not dare do anything but smile back briefly.

Barbara's arm reached out and encircled Anna.

"You're slipping, dear! You always used to kiss Nicky goodnight. And Aidan, too. Come on — finish your job!"

Nick wheeled around.

"I'll take up that challenge!" He swept her into a hug and kissed her soundly.

"Now Aidan," Barbara called.

Anna blew one, laughingly, into the car window.

"Cheat!" said Barbara and tucked her beautiful legs in the back of the car. Aidan started the engine and looked ahead along the golden ribbon of the curved drive.

With the rest, Anna stood there, waving the

car away, laughing, calling "Goodbye."

As the rear lights disappeared around the curve of the drive, Martin said, "It's a lovely night. Come and walk around the garden."

He took her arm as they went around the side of the house. As they passed the short iron staircase that led to Julie's little room, Anna glanced up. The glass door was now kept shut, but the curtains were back and she saw Julie's face at the window.

She lifted her hand to wave and the curtain shot back.

So Julie hadn't forgiven her for what she was supposed to have done! She sighed a little.

"Tired?" Martin asked.

"Not really. It's been a lovely day."

"Has it?"

"Of course. You've enjoyed it —"

He stopped walking and turned and took her violently in his arms.

"Yes, I have. And no, I haven't! For heaven's sake, Anna, why is it always such 'a lovely day' when Aidan's around?"

She saw, as his face bent to hers, the angry glitter of his eyes. The lights streaming from the uncurtained windows of the house lit up the stark doubt and hunger of his face.

"You're just imagining," she tried to keep her voice calm. "Aidan has only been here twice, anyway, and both times it was a party where I think we all enjoyed ourselves." She pushed with her hands against his chest to free herself. "Can't you see I'm happy with *you!*"

He dropped his arms from about her and felt for his cigarette case. When Anna refused to smoke, he lit his own, blew a coil of smoke into the still air, and said:

"You were so gay, just as though you had wings. It was like those old days in Kashmir."

"But I've been gay at other times here, with you —"

He shook his head. "Not in the same way, Anna. Today you had Aidan and the Graysons — they were all part of your old life in India."

"Must you torment yourself with seeing me as someone separate from your world, someone from the East? Oh, Martin, *must* you?"

"Don't you see, Anna, why I sometimes ask myself, 'Is love enough?' "

"What else do two people want?" she demanded despairingly.

"I've a feeling that love can die like a seed sown in the wrong soil."

She thought: this is the Martin Gillian made! Full of doubts, torn with questioning. . . .

She said patiently, "*This* is my soil, Martin, where you are —"

"But you want to get away from it, Anna!

225

You're proving my point, the *place* matters, the *circumstances* matter — and love is *not* enough."

(And I was so happy — so at peace . . . now Martin shatters it all — questioning, doubting. . . .)

"Anna!"

Martin reached out and swept her close with a fierce violence. He reached up and held her head with one hand so that she could not move, then kissed her with such passion that pain shot through her lips. She couldn't cry out, she couldn't move! His fingers, his arms, his body imprisoned her. This was hunger, need, passion — all those things! And love? His interpretation of love? If so, in very truth — *was* love enough?

XIV

Back from that strange violence in the garden, Anna wanted to see or speak to no one.

On the way upstairs she heard a sound from Julie's little room and crept down the short flight of stairs.

She entered the room before she realized that Eve was there.

"What do you want, Anna?" Eve was pulling at a curtain.

"I heard a sound and wondered if Julie was all right."

"Quite, thanks. Only she seems to have been disturbed by something she saw in the garden," Eve said shortly. "She should have been asleep long ago."

Julie had been crying. Someone has been trying to frighten her again, Anna thought in alarm, and asked, "What disturbed her in the garden?"

Eve straightened herself. Her lips remained tightly closed, but her eyes flashed her answer – "*You* should know!" they said.

I – know? But what? And then she remembered the curtain shooting back as she had looked up when she and Martin had passed Julie's window. And later, that curtain would have parted again and Julie would have seen them – her father holding Anna close, kissing her; the two of them faintly visible in the glow of the downstairs windows – a man and a woman; with a child, shut away in a lonely room, like a small love locked out.

She turned sickly away, knowing that there was nothing she could say to make things right – not with Eve there, wanting them to be wrong!

When they had all gone to bed and the house was quiet, Anna sat in her room, too restless for sleep. It was not a cold night, but she was shivering and a sudden longing overcame her for the comfort of a light woolen housecoat she had left in a suitcase which Martin had stacked out of the way in the attic for her.

She rose, tied the sash of her blue silk dressing gown more tightly around her and opened her door silently. A dim light burned in the passage lighting the narrow, curving staircase that led to the attic. Although she trod lightly, the stairs creaked. Once she thought she heard a door open softly, but she didn't turn around to see.

When she switched on the single light, the room lay, untidy and dusty, full of discarded tables, chairs, oddments of sports equipment and piles of suitcases. While she stood locating hers, she realized suddenly that she was over Sapphira's bedroom and that there was someone there with her. The bare floorboards, some of them broken and gaping, and the wide old chimney all conducted the sound of voices – raised in anger.

Anna padded across in her slippers to her cases and opened one. The soft cream wool dressing gown lay folded on top. As she pulled it out she heard quite clearly what was being said in the room below.

"It's three to one!" Sapphira was saying. "Eve will do what I suggest, and Jaimie will follow anything she says. So that leaves just you –"

"This is a form of blackmail."

"How can you be so stupid? Just for your signature to a piece of paper, I am promising you what, on your own admission, you want most in the world – Martin! But you aren't prepared to pay the price, are you?"

"You talk of price! You talk of promising me

what I want! You're mad!"

"My dear Bridget, you're being melodramatic! I'm being the sane one. Martin isn't married yet!"

The conversation came, cut by the inflections; by the rise and fall of the voices. But the implication was clear to Anna, crouched and listening. Do something that I want and I will get you Martin. Martin to be bartered for Sapphira's will. . . .

Then Bridget's voice came sharp and shrill. "You talk big! You always did. But what do you think you can do?"

Anna sat, frozen limbed on the bare boards, her warm dressing gown dragged from the suitcase and clutched in her hands.

"Martin . . ." Bridget's voice was becoming hysterical, "he's not a man walking in a kind of paradise garden. He's in love with Anna – you won't shake him and you know you won't. You're just promising a miracle to get your own way with me!"

"If you think that, then you're a fool –"

"How – how could you – part them?"

"That's my business. Will you sign?"

"No," said Bridget. "You can promise the sun and the moon and the stars, Sapphira, but you're no miracle worker. No, I won't sign.

"You will, you know. In the end,

you'll do just that."

"I said – you must be mad!"

"On the contrary, I'm the sanest and by far the most intelligent of the lot of you. Eve's a hysteric, Jaimie's weak and you're a fool to have let Martin slip through your fingers –"

"That's fine coming from you! When could you ever hold a man, you everlasting spinster –"

There was a movement and a sharp cry of pain.

"Sapphira, you –"

"I hit you. Yes – now get out. Get out of my room!"

Anna waited and heard the opening and the closing of a door, then swift, running footsteps, light over the thick carpet.

When the house was quiet again, she turned out the light and crept down the stairs. There was no sound from Sapphira's room but a light showed underneath the door. Farther along the passage, as she turned the corner, she heard soft sobbing coming from Bridget's room. . . .

She wrapped her white dressing gown, made from the wool of the mountain sheep, around her and crouched by the fire in her room.

Sapphira had a scheme! And for its purpose, she wanted something of them all – Bridget and Eve and Jaimie.

Through her window no wind blew; it was a mild night, but Anna rubbed her cold hands. Like pawns on a chessboard, she and Bridget and Martin were to be moved according to Sapphira's will.

But the whole idea was crazy. Nothing would part them because she would see that it didn't. She knew quite well that if she told Bridget what she had overheard, she would deny it all. So, of course, would Sapphira. The whole thing would be turned against her, the girl from India, trying to make trouble in a family. . . . Divided among themselves, they would close their ranks if Anna interfered.

But because of that and those overheard snaps of conversation, she was forewarned. And forearmed? She sat there on the deep pile of the rug and knew that her only armor was her love. And heaven knew how much use that would be against a power she could not assess. . . . What was Sapphira planning to do? Get rid of her? How? Sapphira must have some knowledge that could break up everything between her and Martin! She was not the kind of woman to promise blindly. But what could she do? What did she know?

Perhaps if I could have heard everything that was said; perhaps a missed word here or there changed the whole meaning. . . .

I've got to get away until the wedding, she thought. Explain to Martin. Explain what? That Sapphira was plotting against her. Martin might say "You heard too much or too little, sweet! Never take any notice of half a conversation. Its meaning is changed." Or, "Sapphira can't do such a crazy thing!" Or again, "I'll ask her what was said." Whatever his reaction, telling him wouldn't help.

And if I leave, I'm playing into Sapphira's hands. I shall make it so much easier for her to say, "You see? Anna can't be happy now, when she's just engaged to you! What will it be like when you're married?"

I've been here for just over four weeks; I can manage another three, surely. I've got to! And yet, even as she crouched there gathering her strength, something warned her that courage wasn't enough.

Bridget flew into the dining room while they were having breakfast. She wore a bright yellow coat with a lynx collar and a tiny black hat. She looked towny and elegant and beautifully groomed.

"Martin, that car of mine!"

"What's wrong with it this time?"

"I don't know. I believe the garage puts one thing right and secretly puts another thing wrong —"

Jaimie said lightly, "Perhaps they're giving you a reason for coming back to them! It can't be often they see Bond Street come to Blakesford!"

Eve said sharply, "Really, Jaimie, Bridget's had that coat for ages —"

"If you had it half that time it would be a rag!"

"Why would it be a rag?" Julie, washed and brushed and neat, stuck her corn flakes spoon up like a weapon and gazed at her aunts.

"Eat up your breakfast. You'll be late for school," Eve said, scarlet with anger.

Martin was at the door. "I'll have a look at the engine, Bridget."

"Thank you, if you would —"

Their "daily," Amy, entered with the tray and Sapphira rose to clear away. Eve fussed over Julie, saying she would miss the school bus if she didn't hurry.

Anna piled plates.

"Leave them," Sapphira said. "We can manage here. You go and get yourself ready — you are going to London today, aren't you?"

"Yes, I thought I'd get some shopping done."

When she had made her bed, Anna went to the window with its angled view of the drive. Martin was doing something to a nut of

Bridget's car engine. She was leaning close to him, peering in. Martin's arm reached out for part of the engine farthest away from him, and he lost his balance a little and put out a hand to Bridget to steady himself. For a moment, laughing, they remained like that. Then, Martin drew away and was obviously telling Bridget to switch on. She got in and tried the self-starter. Nothing happened. Then Bridget switched off the engine and slammed her fist furiously down on the car door. It must have hurt her for she put her fingers quickly to her mouth with a wry look at Martin, got out and slammed the door. Again they looked at one another and began to laugh.

Anna drew back from the window, and turned to the mirror, picking up her lipstick.

If I hadn't come, Martin would have married her and they would have been happy — and the family would have been glad. Everything would have been fine, everyone would have been happy. Only Martin chose me. . . .

"Anna," Bridget was outside her door.

"Come in."

She stood there in her lovely yellow coat.

"What time are you going to town?"

"Quite soon —"

"Then will you give me a lift?"

"Of course —"

"I've just missed the fast train —"

"I can be ready in about ten minutes."

"Thank you. That dratted car of mine has really let me down this time!" She turned to go downstairs again and through the open door Anna heard Sapphira call "Bridget! Come in here, will you?"

The office door opened and closed. Anna went to the tall, old-fashioned wardrobe and took out her sapphire suit. She pinned a garnet star to the lapel, put on garnet earrings and ten minutes later ran down the stairs; Bridget was still shut in the office with Sapphira. She heard their voices, low and violent, cutting in on one another. Any odd word she might have heard as she crossed the hall was drowned by the noise of the Hoover in Amy's vigorous hands. The front door was open and Anna went out and across the gravel drive to the garage to get the family car. By the time she had brought it around to the front door, Bridget had come out and was standing on the steps. She looked beautiful and agitated and her eyes were overbright.

"Would you like to drive, Bridget?"

"No thanks. I hate this old bus."

She got into the passenger seat and took out her cigarettes and lit one, while Anna restarted the car.

"I hope you won't be too late at the shop."

"The girls can carry on if I am." She pulled at her cigarette, blew a great cloud of smoke into the car and then asked, "I suppose you're going to lunch with your friend, Aidan?"

"No."

"But I thought —"

"You thought what?"

"That that's what you were going to town for."

"What gave you that idea?"

"I took it for granted, I suppose. You and he must have so much in common —"

Anna let it past. She steered the car between two stationary trucks and then stepped on the accelerator. If this was going to be the trend of the conversation, then the sooner they reached London the better.

Bridget pitched her half smoked cigarette out of the car and immediately lit another. She played with the clasp of her beautiful leather bag with its gilt monogram in one corner; she crossed and uncrossed her legs and kept looking at her watch.

"When we get through Lavernake," Anna promised, "I'll speed!"

"Oh, that's all right. I'm not thinking of the shop — I told you, they can carry on."

But something was agitating her, and when they reached the crossroads at Lavernake High Street, the lights changed to red. Bridget turned quickly, hand on the handle of the door.

"I'm getting out here —"

"But —"

"It's all right. I — I have some things to do. I'll catch a fast train to town later."

"Would you like me to wait in the car lot? I'm in no hurry."

"No, get on," said Bridget sharply, and was out of the car as the amber light changed to green.

There was nothing to do but to go on. She gave a swift puzzled glance in the rear mirror and saw Bridget dart across the side road and wave for a taxi.

She could, of course, be going back to Dion House because she had forgotten something. But if she had, surely she would have said so. Whatever made her decide to turn back was something she did not want to discuss with Anna. Then what? Martin? Was she going back to see Martin at the lab?

She had involuntarily slowed the car and a truck, too close behind her, hooted at her. She increased her speed, unable to drag her mind away from Bridget's inexplicable act.

Presently, however, Anna reached the beautiful road over the Downs and Bridget was forgotten. The spring sun poured down brightly, the woods lay like pools of new, glowing green in the hollows and the villages she passed through were bustling with their little activities.

Anna's day in London was busy. She went first of all to the Martignan Hotel and asked about her parents' suite. They were so well known there that Anna was taken to see it. She then arranged with the florist in the foyer to send flowers to them immediately on their arrival. She had thought about ordering them from Bridget and decided against visiting the shop, since Bridget had never invited her to see it. She visited the bank and drew out more money than she had meant and spent it in a few hours' spree. Useless, of course, to buy anything for the home – they would have to settle between themselves when they reached Buenos Aires whether they would furnish their own place or rent one already furnished. But she did buy clothes for herself, the kind of clothes she knew she would want in such a country. Martin had said when he gave her the amethyst pendant:

"You must have a white evening dress," and she found a lovely one of silk chiffon with a swathed bodice and full skirt. She also bought high heeled dance slippers that were just thin ribbons of criss-cross amethyst kid. She bought herself a housecoat of dusky pink lace over deeper satin, tailored so that it was both neat and yet feminine. She hesitated over a hat and decided against it, bought a slender gold bracelet for Julie with a St. Christopher charm hanging from it, and a box of handmade cigarettes for Martin. She wanted to buy something collectively for the family and decided at last on pale green embroidered table napkins monogrammed with a "C" in darker green, with a cloth to match. Deep down, she knew her extravagance that day to be part of a desire to reassure herself that everything was all right and only her own imagination made portent out of harmless shadows.

When she had finished her shopping and had arranged for everything to be sent to Dion House, she had lunch and then went to the London Planetarium and sat looking at the wonder of the moving universe and remembered how in India the stars had hung low over the Dal Lake when Martin and she had sat there and talked about their future together.

"You could almost pluck them like silver fruit," Martin had said and had kissed her throat as she had reached up laughingly to the blue-black sky.

When she reached home everyone except Bridget was gathered in the living room and Julie was saying "good night." Politely, as Anna came in, she went to her and gave her cheek to be kissed, but the friendly warmth with which she had first accepted her was quite gone.

"Good night, Anna," she said with an eye on her father for his approval.

Sapphira looked at the clock. "Did Bridget mention to anyone that she was staying in town tonight?"

Everyone said, "No."

"She didn't say so to me either, but she's very late."

"She's probably met some friends and is having a drink with them," Eve said resentfully. "You know what Bridget is — she thinks cocktails at the Savoy is high society!" She shepherded Julie out of the room and up to bed.

Sapphira lifted her drink. "Eve feels waspish tonight."

"She's not been quite herself lately," Jaimie frowned out of the window. "Something's worrying her, but she won't tell me what it is!"

"My dear Jaimie, something's always worrying Eve!" Sapphira said unkindly. "She loves and cherishes her grievances."

"Sapphira, stop needling!" Martin intervened quietly. "Do you want any more sherry?"

"Yes, please, I think I will."

When Eve came back into the room she said: "I wish Julie had never started this shadow picture craze. She just won't lie quietly when I put her to bed. As soon as my back's turned she's sitting up wriggling her fingers —"

"Leave her alone; children soon get tired of their crazes."

"I hope she'll get tired of *this* one! I think we'll have to find her other interests to keep her mind more occupied during the day."

Martin laughed. "She seems pretty occupied to me! That child collects friends like a candle flame collects moths! There's always someone calling to ask her out to play!"

"I'm glad," Eve said. "Being an only child would be dull for her otherwise. I thought, though, that we might get her a pony in the summer."

"It's a good idea, but she won't be here in the summer."

Eve, who had picked up her drink, made a violent gesture and spilled it on the carpet.

"Oh, do be careful. Now look what you've done!" Sapphira snapped.

Eve took no notice. She was staring at Martin as if he had suddenly become her archenemy.

"But, Martin," she burst out, "of course Julie will be here! Now that you've dropped this idea of taking her to South America with you —"

"Who said I had?"

"Why, Sapphira —" She turned and looked

across at her sister.

The older woman's eyes met hers serenely: the long thin lips smiled faintly, but behind the smile Anna caught a shadow of something else, a flicker in the eyes, a faint drawing down of the lips. Sapphira was smiling calmly for them all to see; but she was sending a message of warning to Eve. . . . *Be careful* said that flicker of expression, *and hold your tongue!*

Eve was on her feet. Caution was her last consideration.

"Sapphira, *you* said —" she began.

But Martin wasn't listening. "I don't know what Sapphira told you — but the fact has never changed. We both want Julie out in the Argentine with us and she's coming and there's no more to be said!"

Jaimie was rubbing at the spots on the carpet. Eve stared down at him as though he were in another world. She was shaking, and her voice was tense and brittle.

"How *could* you! Martin, after the way we've looked after her — how *could* you take her away!"

"I'm sorry," he said more gently. "But we've had all this out! Julie *is* my daughter and when Gillian and I went to India it was you who insisted that she should come here rather than go to her grandmother's. I seem to remember there was rather a scene over *that!*"

"But of course. She belongs here."

"You know, I think she belongs just as much to her grandmother," Martin said gravely. "But let's not argue about that now."

He got up and handed his cigarette case to Anna. As she leaned forward for a light, her eyes glanced for a moment beyond his shoulder. She saw Eve turn to Sapphira; she saw the two women, one seated, one standing, confront each other like antagonists. Then Sapphira's eyes dropped. She picked up her glass again, saying:

"Leave things, Eve. Leave everything —"

"To you? To —"

Sapphira did two things simultaneously. She rose to her feet and her hand went up sharply as though to slap her sister.

Eve stepped back quickly and Sapphira said in a quick, low voice, "Haven't you learned yet, Eve, that patience is an ally?" Then she turned to the rest. "I'm going to help Amy serve. Go on into the dining room all of you."

Eve stood for a moment and watched Sapphira close the door. Then she wrenched it open and flew after her, her feet hammering on the parquet flooring of the hall.

Jaimie stood, cloth in hand, staring after her. "What in the world was all that about?"

Martin, leaning in a bored manner by the

window, asked, without turning around:

"All what?"

"That odd remark of Sapphira's about patience being an ally."

"Don't ask me. She probably thought it was time Eve stopped fussing about things she couldn't help and realized that instead of flying off the handle, if she only had a bit of patience things would work out. After all, Anna and I will only be in South America for two years. Then we'll be back and she'll be able to see Julie again. . . .

Anna's heart slumped. In two years they would be here again. Not in this house, please, dear heaven, not in this house! But somewhere near Martin's job — near enough to Dion House for the old pattern to reappear; the pattern that wove the Claremondes so unhappily into her life. . . .

Another thought stirred restlessly underneath that, a thought that perhaps Martin had misinterpreted Sapphira's seemingly out of context remark. Patience is an ally. *Patience. . . . Eve! Patience . . . wait and things will be as you want them.* Was that what she meant? *Julie will not go to South America.*

How could any of them stop it? Anna remembered Eve's startled reference. "Sapphira *you* said —" The silent message that flashed from her eyes . . . the moment's antagonism as though Sapphira had somehow let her down. . . .

Something was working in this house . . . like a subterranean tunnel undermining the foundations of a structure — the structure of her happiness with Martin? For the first time for many years, Anna felt real fear. She looked across at Martin, standing by the window, and could not get comfort from his slender, withdrawn figure staring away over the cloud dappled garden.

When they filed into the dining room Sapphira called out to Martin to ring up Bridget's apartment in London.

"Find out if she's there or whether the porter knows where she is?"

He went down the hall and picked up the telephone receiver and dialed. He spoke too quietly into the receiver for them to hear what he was saying, but when he came into the dining room he told them:

"She's not at her London apartment and the porter has no idea where she could be. He says she hasn't been at her apartment at all today. It's no use calling the shop, it'll be closed." He sat down next to Anna. "Why worry? She's just gone out with friends and has forgotten to let you know she won't be here for dinner." He turned and smiled at Anna. "Fair enough?"

She thought how easily Martin dismissed things, how he let words, gestures, ideas that might cause complications slip over him. He listened to things and accepted them only with his superficial self and she understood so well why. He had learned the trick of avoiding argument or interpreting trouble from his unhappy years with Gillian, he had armored himself so that his sensitiveness was locked up deep inside him. Once you are invulnerable, the gods give you everything. Martin had learned, through the terrible years, to be invulnerable.

She thought: If he hadn't, he'd see the tension-charged atmosphere here; he'd drag it into the open and make something concrete and tangible of it. Poor Martin, how he must have suffered in the past to have forced himself to this rejection of pointers towards danger!

Or perhaps I'm veering the other way, towards being too sensitive to it all. Perhaps it's only family tensions, and there's no real danger. . . .

Bridget did not come home that night. Sapphira rang her apartment three times and then gave up.

"She's probably gone to an unexpected party. We'll leave it."

But Anna could not forget Bridget's agitation

in the car that morning, nor her unexpected flight at the traffic lights.

She waited until she found herself alone with Martin, much later that evening, and told him about it.

"I thought perhaps she took the taxi out to the lab to see you."

Instead of denying her suggestion, Martin played with his lighter. Then he threw it down on the coffee table and said, "As a matter of fact, Anna, she did try to see me this morning."

"Oh —"

He shook his head. "But I couldn't spare the time. She came when I was in the middle of some rather tricky experiment, and she went away again. After that, I don't know what happened."

"But Martin, didn't she leave a message?"

"No. The porter at the gates said she just asked for me. When she heard that I couldn't come, she thanked him and left. She had a taxi waiting."

"Then there was something important she wanted to talk to you about — something she couldn't talk about here!"

Martin looked unhappy. He said evasively:

"She probably wanted to ask me something about her car — she's not pleased with the garage which services it at the moment. And tonight, I'll make a guess she's having a riotous time with friends. Bridget's not like Eve, you know! She doesn't spend every moment of her waking life here at Dion House!" He bent forward and kissed her. "I like you in blue," he said softly.

Sapphira opened the door at that moment. Her eyes flicked over them both.

"Where's Eve?"

"How would I know?"

"She's been missing for the past hour and I want her to tell me what she wants ordered for the greenhouses."

"She may be out there with Jaimie. I believe he's gone on his final rounds."

"I've been out to see. Heavens, what's the matter with this family?" She pulled aside the heavy brocade curtains. Suddenly she stiffened. Without a word she unlocked the French window and stepped through them into the night. A wind blew the curtains out and Martin shivered.

"My family never bother to shut doors!" he complained, and went to the window. In the beam of light that shone out they saw Sapphira hurrying down the path.

"She's probably seen a stray dog," he said, and laughed and closed the window. "We won't lock it, then she can get back," he stretched out his arms. "Come here, woman."

With a sweep of her wide blue skirt, Anna went to him and he enfolded her in his arms.

"Love me?"

"It's an idea! I'll think about it." She tried to catch his mood, teasing him.

"Oh, Anna!" He bent his head and kissed her. "Everything's all right, isn't it?"

Fear, uncertainty, the atmosphere of the house communicating itself!

"Of course everything's all right," she said, helpless to put her heart into her words.

XV

Nobody saw or heard from Bridget for the whole of the next day.

Calls were put through to her apartment and to her shop. Then the head assistant at the shop rang up to say that a card had been received from her by second post. "It bore only the name of the town "Brighton," and it explained that Bridget would be away a few days and would they carry on?

"But I don't understand!" Eve cried. "Neither the day nor the night porter at her apartment have seen her, so who carried her luggage down?"

"If she had just a light case she would have done it herself," Sapphira said.

"Bridget? Carry a suitcase?" Eve mocked. "Why, she won't even carry a box of flowers out to the car!"

"Well, just this once the porter must have been busy and she did it! Perhaps she's taken very little with her."

"But why Brighton?"

"The Dorrits live there — don't you remember?" Jaimie said. "We could find their number and ring them."

Sapphira corrected. "They left ages ago, and went to Scotland."

"She always liked the place very much and has probably gone to a hotel for a few days. But I fail to see why she's being so mysterious about it!"

"Bridget's dramatics!" Sapphira snapped.

"Or perhaps she's terribly unhappy over something —" Eve began, and then folded her mouth in and walked out of the room.

Martin was taking the following day off, and he and Anna were going to town together.

A card came for Sapphira by the second post and she called out to Jaimie and Martin, who were in the hall together, that it was from Bridget.

"She's staying a few days in Brighton. I told you it's like her to be dramatic and make a vanishing trick of it," she said.

Anna going up the stairs to get her hat and coat, turned. "I'm so glad she's all right!"

Sapphira looked up at her. "All — right? Oh no, it's not *that* for Bridget. But then, it's not for any of us any more —"

"You talk as though the sheriff were around the corner," Martin said lightly and went to the door. "You're as bad as the farmers! Nothing is ever quite right with your world!"

Sapphira looked after him and went into her office.

When Martin had brought the car around, he went into the office — Sapphira was on the telephone extension there, ordering groceries. He waited and catching sight of Bridget's card, picked it up and read it.

But that wasn't Bridget's writing! There were certain letters formed as she formed them — the exaggeratedly rounded "S," the squirl she always made of a "G." But the basic line was too tight, too ill-formed to be her writing. He turned to Sapphira as she replaced the telephone receiver.

"Bridget didn't write this card!"

Sapphira crossed to the desk and took it from his hands.

"Don't be silly, Martin! It's signed by her —"

"But it *isn't* Bridget's writing!"

"It's a pretty bad scrawl for anyone's writing!" Sapphira observed. "She probably wrote it on her knee in some promenade shelter —"

"Or didn't write it at all!"

Sapphira's hands straightened and the card dropped on to her desk, lying with the picture of the Old Steine fountains uppermost.

"If she didn't send it, who did? Martin, why should anyone send us a card purporting to come from Bridget? Unless it's some ridiculous hoax. But again, *why?*"

"I don't know," he frowned. "And I don't like it."

"Do you think *I* do?"

"No," he surveyed her slowly. "But something's got to be done."

"Something? What?"

He said steadily, "I'm going to the police."

"But, Martin, you can't! Bridget would loathe you to do such a thing. It would make her look such a complete fool when she turned up —"

"If she turned up —"

"I don't know any more than you what I think! I only know that someone wrote this card pretending to be Bridget."

Sapphira picked it up and twisted it, trying to read the post mark.

"It's terribly blurred."

"Perhaps the one the assistants received at the shop won't be so blurred."

"You mean it mightn't have come from Brighton at all?"

"Exactly."

Suddenly Sapphira cried, "Martin, stop this! You're making me as imaginative as yourself. There's an obvious explanation if only you'll face it."

"Why shouldn't I face it? What in heaven's name has it to do with me?"

"Everything," Sapphira blazed. "Even this" — she slapped her hand down on the card — "this writing you're so suspicious of! Bridget has gone away, she intended to go away that day — because of you."

"Oh, for Pete's sake —"

"You won't look at the truth squarely, will you?"

Martin said quietly, "I've had to look at pretty ugly truths in my life, Sapphira!"

"I know. I'm sorry." She put her hands to her face, "And now — this! So much unhappiness; so much muddle; so many lives being upset because —"

"Because what?"

Sapphira looked at him levelly and met his eyes without flinching.

"Because you are marrying Anna."

Martin pulled out his cigarette case.

"For God's sake, do we have to go through that again?" The fingers flicking the cigarette lighter were taut.

"I would never have brought it up but for the

fact that you're talking so glibly about going to the police. Don't you see that Bridget wants to be left alone, left to hide quietly away until after you are married? What do you think it's like for her here?"

"She had her apartment in London to go to."

"Perhaps there are memories of you there, too, Martin."

He thrust his hand through his hair.

"She's managed to seem quite happy all this time —"

"Bridget doesn't wear her heart on her sleeve. And those are the people who break. Besides, until you actually brought Anna here, I think she always felt there was a chance —"

"We'll skip that!" he said shortly. "The fact remains, this is *not* Bridget's writing!"

"Don't you know what it's like to have to write something in a state of acute distress?" Sapphira demanded. "It's even worse for a woman because they cry more easily — she might have been crying when she wrote this."

Suddenly Sapphira covered her face with her hands. The gesture of weakness from his strong older sister shook Martin. He put out his hand to steady her as she swayed a little.

"You know, you're taking Bridget's feeling for me far too seriously."

"I'm taking your happiness seriously! If I

thought you were going to be happy with Anna, I wouldn't mind. I'd even say 'leave Bridget alone to get over it.' But Anna isn't of your world – and she won't ever try to be –"

"I don't want to listen." He moved to the door.

"Martin," Sapphira was pleading. Her voice soft, changed. "I'm your sister. I half brought you up – please listen."

"I will not discuss Anna with you."

He heard her sharp intake of breath. Then her voice came, strong and ringing.

"You're committing another living suicide for yourself! Martin!"

He stopped quite still, without turning his head.

"Is that all you have to say?"

"No. Martin, listen to me. Why do you think Bridget is so upset?"

"You've made that pretty clear."

"She's an intelligent woman and she really loves you. She wouldn't have behaved in this desperate way if she hadn't felt beside herself – *for you*. If you had a chance of being happy, it would have been different; Bridget would have accepted it – she told me so. But this – Martin, how can you believe Anna loves you when she is prepared to uproot you again because she doesn't like it in England? Will she like it any better out in the Argentine? Ask yourself, before you marry her, *ask* yourself, Martin. If she's behaving like this now, what will she be like when you've married her? You took her out of her country, away from her people — all right, so she's half English, but that's a poor half in her, Martin! And the French half — if it *is* really a French half — isn't *that* strong either. What's strong in her is the environment of India. I wonder why she never married that Indian doctor, Aidan?"

"For an obvious reason," he snapped.

"It's strange, Martin, that no one knows about Anna's father! Don't *you* find it odd?"

"I haven't thought anything about it one way or another. Why should I? It's Anna I'm concerned with."

"We know nothing about her," Sapphira said thoughtfully. "Nor, I'm beginning to suspect, do you!"

"I'm not asking for her family tree, if that's what you're suggesting."

"No, Martin, just facts about her father — if she'll ever tell. Maybe Aidan knows — I've a feeling he knows quite a lot about her! For heaven's sake, Martin, watch them when they're together — *that* isn't just friendship —"

"Be quiet!" he strode to the door.

Her words followed him.

"But she won't marry him because she wants

an English husband. She wants to try and wipe out all traces of India. So she's marrying you. A convenient marriage for her; a choice of head, not heart."

Martin took a long breath; his hand went in a quick, nervous gesture to his hair, and brushed across it.

"Think what you like, but if you ever dare speak like this again to me, I shall never have anything more to do with you. That doesn't sound much in words, but by God it means a hell of a lot! One more hint, one more insinuation and you could be dying for all I'd come to you."

"Martin!" Her voice broke. "Don't say such things. All I've said is for your sake, to make you see the truth."

"Then remember the words of Pilate about truth and think about it and try to be ashamed —"

"You're angry because something inside you knows that what I'm saying, all I'm risking, is for your sake — for *your* sake, Martin!"

But the door had slammed and Sapphira was alone.

For a moment or two she stood where she was, staring at the closed door, trembling so much that she had to lean against her desk for support.

Martin ran down the steps to Anna. "Sorry to have kept you."

She saw his angry eyes and caught back her question. He started the car and roared down the drive and onto the main road.

They maintained their silence until they reached Lavernake and drew up at traffic lights. Anna could bear the silence no longer.

"What's the matter, Martin?"

He maintained silence.

"If you don't want to tell me —"

He said, "All right, Anna. I've seen that post-card Bridget is supposed to have written, and I don't believe she sent it."

Anna glanced quickly at him.

"I've been arguing with Sapphira about it, that's why I was such a long time. She believes it really was from Bridget."

"The family believe she has run away because she loves you and can't bear to face our wedding — that's it, isn't it?"

She flashed him a look of surprise and dismay. "And it could be, you know, Martin!"

"She's got her London apartment to stay in if she really feels that way." The indifference in his tone was out of character. She looked at him and was sure that it was a mask for her benefit.

He took one hand off the wheel and laid it over hers. "And now, let's forget trouble — just for a few hours. Have a cigarette and light me one, sweet, will you?"

Anna sat watching the fields flash by, feeling the cold finger of despair at her heart. She had been so determined to fight for Martin; to stay because she knew they wanted to drive her away; knew, too, that by going, she was weakening the tie between herself and this man she loved. She heard herself say thinly:

"It would be better if I went away — until the wedding."

"You want to go, Anna?"

"I want harmony in my life!" she cried. "I want to go to my wedding feeling that everything is right with my world!"

"And it isn't —"

"No, Martin, it obviously isn't! I'm upsetting the family because I'm taking you away."

"That's my concern — and my life!"

"I'm making Eve miserable over Julie, and Bridget —"

"You and I fell in love in India, and you knew nothing of my family then. The fact that they happen to be so interwoven in my life is a misfortune — but it's not your fault. Try to understand if they ever, unthinkingly, hurt you. For my sake, Anna!"

Unthinkingly?

Did he still believe the note on the door; the

attempt to frighten Julie in order to implicate Anna, the stranger, the girl from India, were the works of villagers? Could he be so blind? She sat without speaking. He misinterpreted her stricken look.

"I'm not succeeding in making you happy, am I, Anna?"

"Do *I* make you happy?"

"I love you," he said as though that were answer enough.

It was as though, with that, argument was over, at any rate while part of Martin's attention was forced upon his driving.

I love you, he had said.

And *I* love you, Martin! Yet for either of us, is that enough? Aren't there other things; things like understanding, like trust, that become the essentials, the things that remain when all passion is spent . . . the things that were there in her relationship with Aidan?

When they reached London, they went first to Bridget's shop. The window was a blaze of late spring flowers, of iris and parrot tulips in lovely shaded colorings of green to mauve, pink to green, with deep serrated petal edges. Posies and single orchids from the Claremonde hothouses lay on beds of velvet, tall sprays of late blossom formed great fans and Bridget's name was written in golden lettering across the window.

There were three assistants in the shop, all young and pretty. The head assistant had had to go to a house to decorate it for a wedding reception.

Martin spoke to the girl who came forward recognizing him. "Good morning, Miss Orion, I've called to ask if you still have the card which I believe Miss Claremonde sent you."

"Oh, yes, it's in the office at the back."

"May I see it, please?"

The girl looked puzzled but said "Of course," patted her sleek fair hair and led the way into the small back room.

The postcard was on a shelf. It was short and to the point and as scrawled as the one Sapphira had received. It just said:

"I have been called out of town for a few days. Please carry on," and was initialed B.L.C.

Martin peered at the postmark.

"It looks very much like 'Lavernake', to me."

"Then Bridget wrote them some time after she left the car the other morning!"

"I doubt if she could buy a postcard of the Palace Pier, Brighton, in Lavernake. I think these cards were somewhere in the house."

Martin gave the card back to the startled girl.

"And you've heard no word since?"

"No."

Martin made a gesture of frustration. "All right. Thank you, Miss Orion. Come, Anna, let's go."

"Hopeless," he said when they were outside standing in the busy street. "Absolutely hopeless." He frowned at a man who brushed past him. "I don't know what to think. Let's get along to her apartment and see what we can find there."

But when they arrived the porter would not let them in. He stood behind the highly polished semicircular desk in the lobby and shook his head.

"I'm sorry, sir, I have no instructions to let you into Miss Claremonde's apartment."

"But this is urgent. Miss Claremonde is my cousin. She lives with my family and she's disappeared."

The words made no impression on the tall, lugubrious man.

"Sorry, sir, but you'll have to get permission from the authorities."

"You mean the police?"

"Yes, sir."

Martin gave him one look from under his dark brows. "It might even come to that!" he said shortly. "Very well. Thanks."

Outside he said, restarting the car:

"Now to find a parking lot for the car while we go shopping."

"You really want to, Martin? You aren't too worried?"

"Of course I'm worried, but on the other hand, I refuse to believe in melodrama. There's nothing more I can do without the family's permission. Sapphira's probably quite right. Bridget has just chosen to disappear. Now, as I say, let's go shopping. What first? I know. We'll make a plan. We'll go in search of that summer evening coat you want – then we'll pay a visit to the tailors for my tropical suit. I'd be a dog in a white tuxedo and a red cummerbund, wouldn't I?" he grinned. "After that to Hatchards – I want some books on Buenos Aires – we may as well know beforehand a bit of what we're going to! Then to the Dorchester for a drink and lunch. This afternoon we might go to a matinée."

But although the day was full and they did not once mention Bridget's name, her shadow lay over them with the beginnings of a sinister query.

XVI

When Anna reached home she found that Eve had gone to bed with one of her migraine headaches. Sapphira was busy helping Amy with preparations for dinner, and so Anna offered to see that Julie was bathed and put to bed.

Julie herself suffered this with politeness and an avid curiosity as to where Aunt Bridget had gone.

When she was in bed at last, Anna lit the night light, and kissed the warm cheek.

Julie reached forward and pulled back one of the curtains.

"You've got enough fresh air, darling, with that other window open."

"I don't want this window open, I just like to see out."

"But it'll soon be dark."

Julie looked at her meaningly. "I see lots of things, even when it's dark," she said mysteriously.

"Do you? What things?"

"Oh — things to make shadow pictures of."

Anna laughed. "I know. You see Uncle Jaimie doing his nightly rounds and your kitten sitting on the steps mewing to come in."

Julie nodded. In spite of her suspicion of Anna, she could not resist showing off. "I see funny things, too, when it's really dark!" She pulled the curtain over the window again and made the room dark, then she raised her hands, twisted them, changed her mind and twisted them another way.

"Watch," she said.

Slowly the hands joined and bent and moved across the pale pink wall.

"What's that?" Anna said. "Someone walking? She looks very bent."

"She is." Julie's little fingers stuck up to make a topknot. "And she's got a big bulge in front, like *that*." She bent a knuckle.

"But where do you see her?"

"I think she's a witch," Julie said, perfecting her shadow picture with intense concentration. "She comes every night. Well," in an effort to be honest, "last night and the night before *and* the night before —"

"Comes to this house?" Anna watched the little girl.

Julie nodded. "And someone gives her something and then she goes away —"

"But Julie, we don't have old beggars around here at night time!"

"She's *not* an old beggar, she's a witch and if she doesn't get her basket filled she'll put an awful spell on the house."

Julie watched the bent shadow cross and recross the wall. "Once she dropped something from her basket, and her head bobby-de-bobbed up and down as she tried to find it in the dark!"

"But where does she come from and where does she go?"

"I don't know. I just see her go. She's funny. Once she looked up at my window and I hid behind the curtain. I was afraid she'd put a spell on me."

The child's eyes were widening, she was growing enthralled by her own story and that meant she might not sleep. Her mind must be eased off imaginary witches. Anna sat down on the edge of the bed and laughed.

"Do you know what she reminds me of?"

"No."

"In Kashmir, where my father has a house, in winter the people all have little fire pots in wicker baskets and inside them there are hot charcoal embers. It's very cold up there in the mountains, and when they go for walks they hug their baskets close to them to keep warm. Your old lady looks as though she had one of those, doesn't she?"

"Do they have lovely big flames like a fire?"

"No, if they did, they burn themselves terribly. They're just glowing pieces like coal." She omitted to tell the child that sometimes they did burn themselves terribly, by holding the fire pots too near to their shivering stomachs.

"Now, go to sleep and forget the old witch. Don't look for her tonight."

"Perhaps she is an old witch from your country," Julie said thoughtfully. "Perhaps she's come to put a spell on us."

"Of course she hasn't! We don't have witches any more than they do here."

"Then perhaps that black man who came the other day brought her —"

"Who do you mean?"

"That man Aunt Eve said you ought to marry!"

Anna went cold. She said, "If you mean a great friend of mine, Aidan, he's one of the kindest men in the world, Julie. Children love him. And now, go to sleep and forget about witches; they belong in fairy tales." She couldn't trust herself to say anything more. She went out of the room shaking with anger that even a child should be drawn into the family's dislike of her.

When she was calmer, she went in search of Martin and told him of Julie's old witch.

"You know what children's imaginations are like. It's probably a tree shadow waving in the wind —"

"It may be —"

"Anyway, it's rained this past three nights and we've all been in and nobody has rung either the front or back door bell."

After supper, when they had cleared away, Sapphira always remained in the kitchen to do a few last minute jobs and would send them in to turn on the television.

Tonight, however, it seemed that no one could settle down. Martin was preoccupied and troubled; Jaimie kept creeping up to Eve's room to see how she was. Sapphira, crossing the hall as he came down the stairs for about the third time since supper, almost screamed at him to go into the living room and stop fussing.

"She's just got a headache; she's not dying!"

Martin went to his room to look for some old papers he had mislaid, and Jaimie went out at last to take a final look around the orchid house.

Only Anna remained in the living room. But she could not rest, either. She turned on the television but after a few minutes she told herself that she must see if Julie was tucked down and sleeping. For this one night the little girl was her responsibility.

As she opened the living room door, the front door closed softly. But Jaimie had gone out of the house by the back door some time ago! By the clock, it was just after eight — the time when Julie's witch walked up the garden path!

Anna ran across the hall and made for the window of the dark, empty office. Outside was all wet blackness and nothing else. Nothing? As her eyes grew accustomed to the dark, she saw someone bent and hurrying go down the path, pushing past the thick rhododendron bushes, cowering against the rain. She was not taking the path to the left which led to the drive, and she was carrying in front of her something that might have been a basket. On her head was a scarf, tied in a top knot.

Anna's first thought was that she might be some old woman from the village, creeping in each night to steal vegetables. But this woman had taken the path from the house, this strange, huddled figure like the witch from Hansel and Gretel.

She flew to the small cloakroom next to the office and snatched at her coat. Flinging it around her shoulders she let herself out of the front door. She made her way down the dark path, brushing the dripping leaves, rain on her hair.

This was the way the old woman had taken. But it led nowhere! It was a path that wandered aimlessly towards the hedge and stopped. Hugging her coat around her, her hair flattened damply against her head, Anna followed. She passed the little knoll and saw in front of her, the high, looming black hedge. The total blackness of the night made everything strange, unrecognizable.

Anna paused, looking left and right. In the distance, huddled away from everything between the high hedge and the knoll, was Sapphira's hut retreat where she painted her indifferent pictures.

The tall, wet grass slapped against her legs, her feet were already soaked in her thin, impractical shoes. And there stood the hut, like a black void, isolated from the world and silent.

There was a sense of intense loneliness with the rhododendrons and laurels shutting in the wild, neglected place. She turned and a nettle dragged at her nylon. She paused to pick it off gingerly and as she did so she heard a sound. It was like a muffled cry.

Anna stood quite still, trying to place the sound. Someone must be there beyond the hedge, in the lane that was a cul-de-sac ending in the long mud track to Mark Ferrier's farm. . . . Someone was hurt. . . . She began to make her way to the hedge, stepping through the vicious tangle of nettle and bramble.

The sound came again, more clearly this time. Anna turned her head and a shower of raindrops, blown by the wind, pricked her skin. She put up her hand to her wet hair, every nerve sharpened with fear, wanting to run back to the safety of the house, yet impelled to find out who was crying in that streaming, blustering night.

Then suddenly she knew where the sound came from.

Sapphira's hut.

Thick curtains had been drawn across the window so that no light showed. Cautiously, wet to the knees, Anna crept to the window. But she could hear nothing except the spatter of rain falling on the blackly shining laurel leaves.

But she had heard those two cries, so sound must be coming from somewhere! She crept around the hut and found, on the far side, the high window.

It was curtained, too, so that no light showed, but it was open. Anna moved carefully until she was directly underneath it and then she stopped, leaning against the wet log wall.

Like that, straining her ears, she could hear voices – or rather, a voice. Low and hard and threatening, Sapphira was talking to someone.

". . . and if you scream again, back goes the gag. You idiot, Bridget. . ." The wind took the rest of the sentence ". . . and nobody uses this lane after dark. . . ." The wind again rustling the leaves, smothering the words. Anna craned her neck upwards towards the high window.

I've found Bridget . . . she thought in fear rather than relief.

"Now look what you've done to yourself, trying to wriggle free. You'll really hurt yourself if you don't stop, and I don't want that – I really don't, you know!"

There was a stir in the hut, the sound of a chair scraping bare boards. Then Sapphira resumed her monologue.

"Eve will sign, she's paying that price for Julie. And Jaimie, poor sap, will do anything she wants. I'm not even bothering with Martin, he can be faced with the *fait accompli*. I'll have a majority signature without him. Now, will you talk sensibly, or do I have to make it a little tougher for you before you sign?"

Trees and wind defeated Anna again. She clenched her hands, straining to hear.

Then came Bridget's voice, high and hysterical: "You promise – what you can't possibly fulfill. Martin will marry Anna."

"My dear Bridget, don't you know the old saying about there being many a slip 'twixt cup and lip? Well then —" Sapphira chuckled.

"This is all talk. You can do nothing —"

"Listen. I *know* I can break up that engagement! *I know!* Have you grasped that? Within three days of your signature, I shall have proof that will send Anna flying back to India where she belongs!"

"If only it weren't Anna —"

"What on earth do you mean?"

"I can't help liking her — in spite of everything —"

"In spite of the fact that she has got your man? In spite of the fact that she schemed to get Martin while Gillian was alive —"

"We don't know!"

"Well, what does it matter now, anyway? I'm not concerned with the past, only with the future, *my* future! I've laid my plans, all you have to do is to sign —"

There was a long pause. Anna stood, immovable, feeling every limb frozen against the wooden wall.

Sapphira had said she had proof that would send her back to India. Proof of what? What monstrous thing had Sapphira got against her? What did she know? *What could she know?*

She tried to move, to force her legs to take her to the door of the hut, to fling it open against the wind and the rain and confront Sapphira with this outrageous promise.

Move! Move! she urged herself, and was transfixed.

Through spinning dizziness, she heard Sapphira say:

"When I tell Martin what I know, Anna will be out of this house in a few hours. Out – forever."

"And what do you think you know?" There was a flash of spirit in Bridget's voice.

"That's something *you'll* know when you sign this paper. I'll tell you this, though. I've already got someone working on it."

"On – what? You're mad to think anything you could find out about Anna would stop Martin marrying her."

"Wait and see –"

"You're mad!"

"Oh, do stop saying that! As though you don't know that everyone tries to get what they want in this world! I'm just having to try a little more desperately than most!"

"Just for money!"

"That's fine coming from you! You love it enough! And anyway, I'm fighting for money and freedom – *freedom from you all!*"

"But, Sapphira —" Again the words were lost to the listening Anna. Drenched, she leaned, waiting, against the sodden wall.

"I hate you all! You have your London life, your apartment there, your friends, your clothes. Eve has a husband. I — what have I got out of life? Nothing — *not yet!*"

There was a sudden commotion, then a cry and the sound of a struggle. "You asked for it!" came Sapphira's voice. "I warned you if you made another sound I'd gag you again. And you've scarcely eaten any of the food I brought. That's silly of you! You don't want to be any skinnier than you are!"

Crouched against the wooden wall, Anna listened, losing some sentences, catching others. So all this time Bridget had been here, in this place that was a joke among them all. Sapphira's "studio"!

Suddenly there was only one urgency; one panic impulse. Find Martin and let him walk in on the scene. . . .

She turned and stumbled on shaking legs through the sodden bracken, trying to find the path and not finding it, tripping over a tree stump; finding herself idiotically climbing the knoll and running down it, blindly across the lawn; out of breath; running, dry throated and gasping towards the dark house.

She turned the handle of the front door and almost fell into the hall.

"Martin!"

The television sounds drowned her voice.

She went forward, flinging open the living room door. He was sitting back in a corner of the settee, Jaimie in the other corner, watching the bright screen.

"Martin!"

He turned, startled, and saw her. "For God's sake, Anna —"

He crossed the room in a stride and flicked on the main lighting. Then he put his arms out to steady her.

"What's happened?"

"Bridget." She was shivering, still holding her bedraggled coat around her as though she were not aware she was inside out of the rain.

"Bridget," she said again. "I've found her. She's down there in Sapphira's hut and — she's hurt."

"Sapphira's hut? But Sapphira was down there today, painting."

"Not painting — terrifying Bridget into doing something — something — she — wants. I think she's tied up — a prisoner."

Martin ripped Anna's coat from her and pushed her into a chair by the fire. "Take off your shoes and stockings. Jaimie, get a towel

278

from the cloakroom and let her rub her hair. We'll go down."

"Be careful —" She was shivering. "Martin, be careful! I think she — she must be — mad."

But Martin was out of the room. He came back throwing Jaimie a mackintosh and flinging his own over his shoulders.

"Come on."

Anna heard the footsteps cross the hall, heard them crunch on the gravel, running. . . .

Anna took the towel and slowly wiped the worst of the wet from her hair. Her hands were shaking. The television was droning on. She leaned over and turned it off. Then she began to drag off her shoes and stockings, her hands shaking, fumbling. The house was very silent. Nothing stirred.

Nothing?

And then she heard it. A light footstep entering, someone going past the living room towards the kitchen.

Eve, feeling better and bored with bed? But the footsteps hadn't come down the stairs.

Sapphira, then. *Sapphira.* . . .

Had she seen the men and dodged them? Had she escaped back into the house and would she be quietly doing some small job in the kitchen when they returned? And would she raise her cool, serene eyes to their faces and say:

"Someone did this! But it wasn't I!"

But it was too late to fence with them. Bridget could tell. And if Sapphira said, "She's mad! She's making up a melodrama for herself!" then she, Anna, could testify.

She began to rub her hair again and slowly, through her movements, saw the living room door open. She stared at it, frozen, and dropped the towel.

XVII

Sapphira walked in.

"Oh, Anna, all alone?"

The normality of the question was almost terrifying.

"Why —" Sapphira's eyes flashed over Anna. "You're all wet! Don't tell me you've been walking in this rain!"

"I've — been out — yes —"

"You'll catch your death of cold! And you wouldn't want that, would you, just before your wedding?"

She came with her quiet step into the room, closing the door behind her. "Where are the men?"

"Out."

"Where?"

"I — I think they've gone down the garden."

"In this rain! Why?"

Anna was trying to give no sign of fear; she was sitting very straight and tense with her wet hair falling back from her face. But she knew that her eyes gave her away. She could not check their blaze of terror.

"Did *you* send them out, Anna?" Sapphira's voice was soft.

"Why – should – I?"

"Did you wander around the garden, Anna dear?"

Suddenly Anna started up. She thrust her feet into her soaking shoes, and turned, grabbing her coat.

"Where are you going?"

"To – find – Martin –"

"Oh, no, you don't!" Sapphira's hand shot out and gripped Anna's arm, fingers that had suddenly become like claws dug into her skin. "No, dear – you'll stay here in the warm and get. nicely dry and tell me all about it."

Eve was upstairs; at any moment Martin and Jaimie would be back, hot on Sapphira's mad trail. She was quite safe. Sapphira wouldn't really harm her. She met the light amber eyes and said: "I have found Bridget."

"You have?" But she had known that from the moment she looked into Anna's eyes! "Well now, isn't that a relief to us all! Stupid girl, Bridget! *I* found her, really, you know, in my hut. That's where you've sent Martin and Jaimie to look, isn't it. She planned this disappearing act because frustration has sent her a little over the edge — frustration over Martin, you see! I've just had a tussle with her. Anna — why don't you help her?"

"I — I?"

Sapphira nodded. She had taken off the knotted head scarf and her hair was flat and damp to her head. "Why don't you go back to India — marry one of your own kind?"

"But Martin *is* my kind!"

"You know he's not, don't you, Anna? In your heart, you *know!*"

Anna backed a little from the thrust forward face, the soft insinuating voice.

"Why did you come here, Anna, lying to us all?"

"I don't know what you're talking about. I haven't lied."

"Oh, but you have — about that mythical French father. Go back to India." Her eyes gleamed, golden as a tiger's in the lamplight. "You'll have to go back eventually! Martin won't marry you when he knows —"

"Knows — what?"

"That you are an Indian. That's why you're so friendly with Aidan, only Martin won't see it — it's the call of the blood!"

"You are mad! Or just — evil!"

"I see the truth others are too dense to recognize. You are not of our blood, Anna. You are Indian. I can prove it! Kashinath is your name; your real father's name."

"My father was French."

"Then tell me about him. What was his name? Where in France did he come from? You don't know, you see!" she cried in soft triumph. "Because there is no French father! And now I've found you out and I'll prove it. There will be records —"

"My father was French!" Anna cried to this tall, softly menacing woman.

"And when Martin hears the truth, Anna Kashinath, he will hate you for your deception!"

Suddenly Anna's spinning brain could take no more. She gave one violent wrench to the arm that had clutched her and fled to the door. In her mad scramble to turn the handle Sapphira caught up with her.

"Go back," she whispered. "Go back to India and leave Martin alone. Do you hear?" Her hands gripped Anna's shoulders from behind, dragging at her. "Go back — or something dreadful will happen. I'm warning you —"

"Let me go!" Anna reached up and thrust at Sapphira with such force that she staggered.

The door opened, Anna shot across the hall.

At the same moment Eve appeared on the stairs in a long blue linen housecoat.

"What's happening?"

"Don't go into the living room. Eve — stay out!"

"For goodness' sake," she came down the rest of the stairs, "why? Is there a fire in there or —"

"Anna is a little hysterical," came Sapphira's voice from the door. "Don't take any notice."

There were footsteps outside and the front door opened. Jaimie came in first with Martin behind him, and between them they half carried Bridget.

At that moment Sapphira began to laugh, quietly, lightly, as though by her undramatics, proving her sanity.

"Well! Well! Our lost cousin!"

Bridget looked at her, eyes large with fear. Then she cried:

"Martin, get Anna out of the house. *Get her out!*"

"I'm sorry, but I'm not going."

"Get her out." Bridget gasped again and then began to cry.

Eve went to her, holding the damaged wrists and looking down at them. "For the love of heaven, what have you done to yourself?"

"She tied me — with rope. She got me to the

hut because she said — we could talk — more easily there. Then she gagged me —" Bridget looked as though she would faint.

"I'll call the doctor —" Jaimie began.

Their attention had been on Bridget and Sapphira had an advantage. Suddenly she moved. In a flash she was up the stairs, skirts flying. Jaimie was after her, but she had too much start. A door slammed; Jaimie hammered on it.

Sapphira had locked herself in her room.

Martin said with quiet authority, "Anna, go up and change out of those wet things. Pack a bag and get down here as quickly as you can."

"But —"

"You're leaving right away," he cut in on her protest. "Jaimie will take you to London and while you're on your way I'll fix up a room for you at the Malton in King's Square."

Anna stood her ground. "Why do you want me to leave?"

It was Bridget who answered. Still clinging to Martin, she cried hoarsely, "Sapphira's mad and you're in danger. Anyway, there's been enough trouble — enough —" She stopped, swayed a little, turning in Martin's arms. "Oh, darling!" she whimpered.

"It's all right," he said and held her close.

Anna turned without another word of protest and went up the stairs to her room. She packed a small case, tied her hair up in a scarf and put on a thick coat. Every movement was automatic. She wasn't even shaking any longer, she was dreadfully steady.

One could stand so much, so much and no more. . . .

This is the end, she thought. *This terrible, desperate thing that Sapphira has done has frightened even Martin!* He can't take it after Gillian . . . he'll capitulate to the family. . . .

And Bridget — the picture was still there of Bridget in Martin's arms. . . .

If I had never seen Julie's shadow picture, I'd never have followed Sapphira . . . and if I hadn't. . . . She stood, dazedly, in the center of the room and looked about her. On the chest was Aidan's little green jade dragon. She took it in her hands, then, opening her case, laid it inside. Martin is sending me away. . . .

"Anna?" Martin stood in the doorway. "Is that your case?" He picked it up. Then he paused and looked at her.

"I'm sorry, Anna, but this is best. It's safest for you."

"Safest?"

"I'll send for the doctor. And if I must, the police. But it's better that you're out of the way." He looked white and preoccupied. "I'll be ringing you, sweet, in the morning. And I'll get in touch with Aidan."

"*Aidan!*"

"Yes," he scarcely noticed her surprise and dismay. "He'll look after you in London." He turned. "Come now, Jaimie's waiting."

"Why can't you take me to London, Martin?"

"I've got to stay here."

"But now you know — about Sapphira — what's the danger to me — if I stay?"

He led her firmly to the head of the stairs. "God knows what will happen next!"

She walked, feeling like a mechanical doll, down the stairs. In the hall she paused. "Martin —"

"Go," he said. "Go, Anna. Jaimie's in the car waiting," and glanced over her shoulder at the clock. "You should be in London by half past nine."

From the living room came a sharp, distressed call, Martin raised his head.

"Bridget's calling. I must go to her. Here, Jaimie, you'd better get away now."

Bridget was calling and Martin must go to her. He must send Anna away and call Aidan to look after her. . . .

Jaimie tucked a rug around her. "We'll keep the window nearly closed," he said, "in case you get cold with that wet hair."

She scarcely heard him. She just sat there, numb and shocked and understanding nothing except that this seemed to be the end. She was vaguely aware of a commotion in the house; of Eve running across the hall. And then Jaimie started the car and Martin remained inside, in the living room with Bridget.

On the journey to London, Anna scarcely said a word. Jaimie let her be quiet.

When they reached the outskirts of the city, Anna came slightly to life.

"What's the answer to all this? Do you know, Jaimie?"

"Possessions," he said unhappily. "The land. Sapphira wanted to sell, but none of the rest of us did."

"You mean sell the nurseries?"

"Yes. Life has soured Sapphira. She was envious of us all. Bridget had her looks, her shop, her London life; Eve had me, for what I'm worth. But at least I was a man. I believe it all started years ago by her being sorry for herself and it grew into frustration, and then into an obsession."

"But why this fantastic plan to hide Bridget?"

"I can only guess that it was because she wouldn't sign. Sapphira had already worked on Eve. The land was our joint possession, you see, and there had to be a majority signature before it could be sold."

"And for the price of that, Sapphira promised Eve something — someone — Julie?"

He said, "That was madness. But Eve believed her — she wanted to believe, you see."

"How could Sapphira promise?"

"Let's not talk about it."

"I may as well know, Jaimie. I'll have to in the end."

"I can't tell you, yet, what Sapphira really meant to do. All she'd say was that she had a plan."

Julie for Eve; Martin for Bridget. *Two things she could promise only by getting rid of Anna.*

Get rid of me! But how?

Her blood ran cold. Of course, that's just what she has succeeded in doing! In a way she didn't bargain for, Sapphira had won! Anna had been sent away, "for her safety," Martin said. But taken by Jaimie — while Martin stayed with Bridget — and delivered into Aidan's keeping.

"Are you cold?"

"Only right inside where nothing will warm me!"

Jaimie laid a hand over hers. "I'm sorry about all this, Anna. You see, I like you, and I believe Eve and Bridget would have, too. It was Sapphira who kindled mistrust, who flung out hints, warnings, fanned fires that could easily have died if she'd left things alone."

Sapphira working for her own ends; for the price of land; the price of her freedom; the triumph over her own monstrous self-pity.

When they reached the hotel, Anna walked into the bright foyer and felt desperately alone. She signed the register, took her key with its heavy brass tab and then hesitated, looking at Jaimie.

"I'm seeing you get something hot to drink before you go to bed," he said. "Come, let's find the lounge."

They turned and at the same moment someone said Anna's name.

"*Aidan!*" she cried, and he put out a hand and steadied her.

"It's all right, Anna. Everything's all right! Let's go and sit down somewhere. Martin rang me."

They found a corner table in the bar and ordered brandy for her. Anna felt it run warmly, richly down her throat. But there was a cold it could not touch, an ice cold of the heart that knew everything was over; that her determination to stay and fight for Martin had been doomed from the beginning.

What had been said by Bridget when Martin found her in the hut, she had no idea; what exactly Jaimie knew she had no idea either, for he wasn't telling all. But when he walked into that hut and saw Bridget, something seemed to have changed in Martin.

She heard Jaimie saying to Aidan:

"My sister's a difficult character. She always has been, and I think she has bottled everything up until it has burst like a volcano."

"You're talking of Sapphira —"

Jaimie laughed shortly.

"On her eighteenth birthday, she walked in on us all and announced that from then on nobody was ever again to call her by her name, Madge. She was to be Sapphira. And Sapphira she insisted on until we got into the habit of it."

"She's ill —"

"I suppose in a way she is."

Jaimie finished the coffee which was all he would let Aidan order for him, and lit a cigarette.

"I'd better get back to help Martin. God knows what's happened there this past couple of hours! You're all right now, Anna, aren't you?"

She took his hand and said quietly, "I'm all right, Jaimie, and thank you for everything."

As she watched him go she said brokenly to Aidan, "Would you think that I could have caused so much trouble, so much — near-tragedy?"

"You?"

"Of course. If I had never met Martin, he would have married Bridget, and would have stayed at Dion House and everyone would have been happy."

"But that wouldn't have solved Sapphira's problem of the land. Don't you see, Anna, you were heaven-sent to Sapphira — you made the price she could pay for what she wanted — their signatures on the land deal!"

"And all the time Sapphira didn't want me to leave. I was important to her scheme. She just wanted the others to — to hate me — to build up something which she could use. Oh, Aidan!"

"And now," he said, "it's all over!"

"It is," she said from the dead hollow place inside herself. "A man can take so much and no more. Martin had had more than enough of domestic trouble when I met him. He was bruised and hurt and full of doubts and he had no time to recover before all this happened. He — couldn't take it! How *could* he?"

She turned away, feeling as weak as though she had just emerged from a severe illness. "I'm going to bed now."

She heard Aidan say, "Try to sleep, Anna, and

if you can't, don't worry! Just lie and relax. Things will seem different in the morning."

He could give her no more comfort than that and, being wise, he didn't try. But at the door of the elevator he bent and kissed her.

"Goodnight."

Again she saw the strange new light in his eyes and thought with a sad, twisted irony: Aidan does love me. . . .

XVIII

She lay in bed that night and heard the unfamiliar noises of the London streets. The room was high up over the entrance and she heard the taxis and the cars draw up, and doors slam; she heard the swish of tires on the wet streets and a little spatter of rain brush the windows lightly.

I shall never sleep, she thought, the whole long night will be like this, with everything going around and around in my mind . . . Bridget bound in Sapphira's hut . . . Sapphira promising that she had a way to get rid of me. A way? But how? The memory of those light amber eyes fixed on her from the doorway earlier this evening brought a shudder of horror. What would Sapphira have done to her? Her mind repelled the wild thoughts that leaped in. Sapphira wasn't mad. She wouldn't have staged an accident to frighten her away. Such an accident could misfire and prove fatal. . . . She wouldn't have dared, or would she, in final desperation?

I'll never sleep! . . . she tossed in the big bed, threw a blanket off and immediately felt cold. Somewhere nearby a door slammed and two people laughed. . . .

Sapphira would never have harmed me! Then how was she going to get rid of me! The voice came, soft and infinitely menacing. "You are not of our blood, Anna. You are Indian. I can prove it!"

But if that was her weapon, then it must turn to straw in her hands, for how could she prove what wasn't true?

Anna lay, staring at the ceiling. My mother is English; my father was French. French? Where did he come from? What was his name? What was he like? She closed her eyes, trying to recall if there was anything, just one tiny fact she had ever been told about him.

But there was nothing. She had been content all these years to know nothing because once, when she had been a little girl, she had asked her mother about him, and she had said:

"He's dead, darling, and you never knew him. You never even set eyes on him. You have your stepfather's name. He loves you — try to think of him as your father."

When she was a little older she had accepted the fact that for reasons of her own, her mother wanted to forget him. Anna had respected that wish; and time and love and environment had at last made her almost forget that she wasn't the daughter of the man whose name she bore.

She twisted and turned in the strange bed and in the lonely early hours of the morning, her jumbled thoughts snowballed and became fearful. Who was my father? *Who am I?* Has Sapphira found out something – but what? And how? In her office, at her desk, what secret letters had she written, what telephone calls had she made to search for the truth about Anna?

At last she must have slept for when she opened her eyes again the sun poured light through the drawn green curtains.

As Aidan said, "things seem different in the morning," and she bathed and dressed with a lighter heart, certain that Martin would call her.

So that she wouldn't miss him, she stayed in after breakfast, reading newspapers, forcing herself to write a few letters, glancing up with an expression of bright hope every time the page put his head around the door. But the calls were never for her.

By half past twelve she gave up, put on her

coat and went out. She was standing on the semicircular steps, wondering which way to go when she heard her name.

"Miss Kashinath? A call for Miss Kashinath."

Anna swung around and darted back into the hotel. She sped into a telephone booth and picked up the receiver.

But it wasn't Martin. She heard Aidan saying:

"I've been at the hospital all morning, Anna. But now I'm free. Have you heard from Martin?"

"No."

"Then will you have lunch with me? I'll pick you up at a quarter to one."

She said gratefully that she would, heard him name a time and place and went back into the lounge to wait.

The second call came about ten minutes later. Anna lifted the receiver, thinking: Martin! Oh, Martin. . . .

But it was Eve asking in her high, agitated voice:

"Is that Miss Kashinath? Oh, Anna, I'm glad I caught you. A cable has come for you and I opened it – I hope you didn't mind but I thought it would be quicker than sending it on to you. Your parents are arriving this afternoon."

"Oh, thank you. I'll get in touch with them."

She clung to the receiver. "Is — is Martin there?"

"No, he's at the lab." She sounded surprised at the question. "By the way, Sapphira has been taken to a nursing home — the doctor calls it a severe breakdown. She fought like a wild cat! Bridget is better this morning —"

"Did — did Martin say if he was coming to town?"

There was a pause. Then Eve said:

"No, he didn't say, Anna. He just went off as usual this morning."

"I — see. Well, thank you, Eve, for telling me about the cable."

"That's all right."

"Goodbye."

There was nothing more to say; nothing more to ask. . . . Anna thought that Eve said, "Oh, Anna —" as she hung up, but for the life of her she couldn't have listened to any more. The faintness of despair swam around her; she felt as though her whole body was dissolved, and there was nothing left of the real, vital Anna.

Martin wasn't coming to town today to see her . . . Martin wasn't even telephoning her. . . . Turning, she pushed her hands against the door of the booth and found it wouldn't give. Then, dimly, she saw that it folded back but it needed all her strength to make even that small effort.

She walked as in a dream back to the lounge and sat waiting for Aidan.

When he came, she told him in a faint, far-away voice that didn't seem to belong to her that her parents were arriving that afternoon.

"Then after lunch I'll take you along to the Martignan to see them."

"Thank you."

She walked out into the sunshine with Aidan. Felt him take her arm and pilot her into a taxi. Soon she would face her mother and her stepfather. She would say:

"Oh, Father, I'm so glad you had meetings and things over here; it makes your journey worth while. You see, there isn't going to be a wedding . . . I'm not going to marry Martin. . . ."

Her planned words shook her whole being. It was the first time she had dared to let the truth creep into her mind. And it was absurd! Nobody had broken off an engagement. She loved Martin. And he? Face it! Remember how he held Bridget; how he looked at her; remember that he never came out to the car to say goodbye when he sent you to London so peremptorily. Your father always taught you to face things. The Claremondes had sent her to London for her own sake certainly, but also for all their sakes. . . .

The delicious food set before her nearly choked her. She smoked too much, emptying her own small silver case and taking more cigarettes from Aidan's. She drank Nuit-Saint-Georges without even tasting its richness; she made conversation as though in a dream and she blessed Aidan that he did not fuss her.

As the wide, white door of Suite No. 45 at the Martignan opened, she saw the sun streaming into the room. A pile of opened telegrams lay on the table; late spring flowers were everywhere in vases and baskets and bowls. And amid these signs of welcome stood her mother and her stepfather, filling the room with vitality and warmth.

"Anna!" Her mother kissed her.

Her father held her for a moment closely and then set her down in a chair and said, with a wave of his hand towards a suitcase that had not been taken into the bedroom, "That case contains wedding presents for you."

All the joy went flat. Anna opened her mouth to speak. She took a breath and then, at the last minute, decided on silence, knowing that this was not the moment to tell them that there was not going to be a wedding. . . .

Anna looked at her mother and once again thought: How wonderful she is! In spite of the climate of India, she had kept her good looks and her luxuriant chestnut hair. She seemed so young to be the mother of grownup children and there was a kind of suppressed excitement about her as though arriving in England was a great adventure.

Anna's stepfather was a slim man, as delicately built as Aidan. His forehead was his most arresting feature — fine and broad and strong — until you looked at his eyes, and then you realized that they, with their depth and their wisdom, were what you would always remember about him. Now, the eyes were smiling.

"This is the same suite that we had last time, Marian. Do you remember?"

Anna's mother laughed. "We've had it more than once. I seem to recall — oh — years ago, we brought Anna to this very room on a school holiday and she was cross because she hadn't won the poetry prize."

"Yes, of course!" Anna cried. "I wrote a poem about a goat. And, you, Father, said, 'Let me see a copy and I'll tell you what I think of it.' I found one and you read it. You said, 'You rhyme "Shaggy" with "Haggard"? Oh, Anna!' And then we all laughed and I felt better."

Anna's mother went to the window and looked out.

"You know, I scarcely recognize London with all these changes! Skyscraper buildings and new roads!" She glanced at her daughter. "Take your coat off, darling."

But Anna wouldn't stay. "You've only just arrived. I think I'd better let you get settled in now."

"Perhaps you had. Come back in a couple of hours, when your father has had a chance to make some telephone calls, and then have tea with us."

But before she left, she had to find out something that had become suddenly terribly important.

She said, "Please, can I talk to you for a moment?"

Her mother's charming face glanced across at her stepfather.

"I'll start my telephoning now," he said. "I'll do it in the bedroom," and closed the door softly between them.

"Well?" The eyes smiled a little, waiting.

Now that the moment had come, it was dreadfully difficult to say.

"Mother, I don't want to ask this, and I wish I could get out of it, but I can't!"

"Then ask." Her mother's face was serene and

unsmiling now. She was sitting back in her chair, watching Anna.

"It's about my father — my *real* father, I mean —"

"Why do you ask?"

"Didn't you think I would, sooner or later?"

"Yes, but I've been ready for it for such a long time that I'd ceased to think you were even interested. When you were a little girl, Anna, I used to lead you up to your stepfather and say, 'This is your father,' and you were perfectly happy about it. When you were older I often wondered if I should tell you the truth, but you were so happy as you were that I didn't want to do anything to spoil it or, selfishly, remember it myself!"

"And now I've brought it all back —"

"You have a right to ask, darling, if you really need to know."

"Was he — French?"

"Oh, yes." Her mother sat for a moment looking down at her broad hands. "His name was Lafeuille — that was your name, Anna, until we had it changed legally."

She repeated it slowly, thinking: How very French! Sapphira could have made nothing out of that!

"Who was he, Mother? What did he do? Where did he come from?"

304

"He came from Lyons and he was a writer of sorts, an intellectual. I was very young, Anna, and his bright brain attracted me. I didn't see where it was leading him, where it *had* led him –"

Anna waited, at ease now.

"It's all such old history," her mother took a long breath, "and ugly. You see, Anna, he was a spy for the Nazis before the war. The French caught him but somehow one night he managed to escape. He came to our home and he told me about it – desperation made him honest at last! He said I was his wife and I must hide him. He found that I was going to have a child – you – and he" – her voice became unsteady – "he knocked me down in anger. He never wanted you and he would never have loved you, Anna. He threatened my life, and yours, if I didn't hide him. But the authorities came for him and he was shot escaping from the house. He died immediately. Three months later you were born. Now you know."

The picture of her father was brief and stark. Anna said shakenly:

"The fact that he harmed you and never wanted me makes it easier to forget him." She wanted to know more about him, but her mother rose, took a cigarette from the silver case on the table and lit it, saying briskly:

"Now that you know, don't ever let's talk of it again. But of course, tell Martin if you wish."

Tell Martin! But it was too late now.

"I'm going out for a walk," Anna said gently, "and I'll see you later."

"Yes, darling, of course." She smiled. "And thank you for these lovely flowers."

"I didn't send all those." Anna looked around at the vases. "You and father have so many friends!"

She put her head around the bedroom door and her stepfather said, "I'll come to the elevator with you."

Arm around her shoulder, he walked down the corridor with her.

"Have you seen much of Aidan?" He saw Anna shake her head. "You know, there was a time when your mother and I worried for you. We were afraid you were in love with him."

"But I was – I think I still am – or, rather, I *love* him, which is different, isn't it? But why have minded, Father?

He said, "Aidan has a vocation – he will always be primarily and completely a healer of sick children. Don't you see that for yourself, Anna?"

"No –"

"He is of the stuff that priests are made – the man with a calling; the perfect celibate."

The elevator glided to a halt, and the gilded door swung back.

"We'll see you later, Anna," said her stepfather and smiled and the door closed between them.

She leaned against the wall. So, out of a chance remark in a hotel corridor, had come the truth that all along she had really known! Aidan was nearer loving her than any woman; but his life was vocational, "like a priest's." No woman would ever own Aidan Narayan — only the children would do that; the children of India to whom he was returning to give his whole life.

Anna sat for a long time on a park bench. Around her people walked and talked; dogs barked and played and pigeons strutted. The sun made arabesques of gold and sable as its light danced through the leaves. It was a laughing day; but Anna felt like a shell that no longer even held an echo. Drained of feeling, she was not even comforted by the thought that the two people who loved her selflessly were here in London, and that she could go to them and tell them everything. She *must* tell them! And yet she dreaded to put into words, even to them, this final chapter to her doomed love for Martin.

Presently she began to think about the Claremondes. Eve, childless, clinging to Martin's little daughter. Bridget refusing to believe that

Sapphira could move men and women like pawns in a game, *her* way: refusing to have faith in Sapphira's mysterious promise. *I will get rid of Anna!* How ... how? What mad scheme dominated her? Perhaps something that started by being a dream, had grown more beautiful in her mind until it became an obsession. Soured into evil, and yet hiding behind such self-control that it fooled them all!

When it was four o'clock, she went back to the hotel. Outside her parents' suite she paused.

Tell them! Get it over! Say, "There isn't going to be a wedding."

She lifted her finger and pressed the little bell and as though someone had been waiting on the other side of the door, it opened at once.

Anna walked in. The sun still shone on the vases of flowers, the cool green brocade upholstery, the blank face of the television. She turned and thought she swayed a little, saying a name.

"Martin!"

"I came as soon as I could, Anna."

A miracle was happening. His arms were around her, holding her close. "Your father left me here to wait for you. They've gone downstairs to tea and we are to join them."

She said, a little dazed, like a child not believing a story she had heard, "I don't quite understand why you're here —"

"Because *you* are! That's right, isn't it?" He was laughing. "Oh, Anna, don't look so hurt! It's all right — everything's all right. Come here, close again — let me show you just how all right everything is!"

And then the miracle was manifested.

Presently, while she still had breath left with which to speak, she asked, "The family — Sapphira! Eve said on the telephone this morning that she was in a nursing home."

"That's right."

"Last night you let Jaimie take me to town," she accused shakenly.

"I didn't dare leave, but you had to for your own safety. I didn't know then just how close Sapphira was to — madness. I couldn't assess anything clearly till the doctor came and I was afraid she would do you harm. I *had* to get you away, because you were the focus of it all in her sick mind."

"What did I *do*, Martin, for her to hate me so?"

"Nothing. She just saw, through you, a way of getting what she wanted. Money for the land. I've been on to the land development people — she was offered a percentage if she could induce a majority of the family to sell. And so she promised —"

"Julie to Eve, you to Bridget. But Bridget wouldn't sign —"

"Because she has courage, and she knew perfectly well that Sapphira's plan was merely a flight of obsessive fancy."

"Her plan to get rid of me! Martin, how?"

"The workings of a mind on the razor's edge aren't even plausible to us!"

She heard the evasive note in his voice.

"What was her plan, Martin?" she asked again, half knowing it.

"Does it matter now?"

"Yes, to me. *You* know, don't you? And since I am the one concerned, I want to know too!"

He said reluctantly:

"Very well. Eve told me. I'm afraid wishful thinking made her believe that Sapphira would work her mad miracle."

"What?"

He said, "Don't you think it would be best not to bring it into the open? It's over now —"

"I've never been an ostrich! What did Sapphira have against me that made her first try to send me away by that note and then by trying to make me suspected of frightening Julie — because she did those things, didn't she?"

His arm was around her as he led her to the window. Together they looked out over the snaking traffic of Park Lane, over the bright new spring green of the trees, to the sunny distances.

Martin was finding it hard to tell her, but he saw that she had to know.

"Yes, she did those things, Anna. She thought she had hit upon a way to break our engagement. Since the moment she heard that you had never known your father, she brooded and imagined and at last persuaded herself that she had found the truth."

"And what – did she think – that was?" Anna kept her eyes averted from Martin's face, sensing his distress in having to tell her what she demanded to know.

"She made herself believe that you were not half French."

"She more or less told *me* that!"

He said unhappily, "Do you want to hear any more?"

"Yes, please."

"Sapphira whipped herself up into a kind of frenzy of conviction that you were the child of your stepfather and a Eurasian woman he may have married before he married your mother. You see, she *wanted* to believe that, and she became so obsessed with her idea that she was planning to have inquiries made –"

"So she thought if I could be proved half Indian, you wouldn't marry me!"

"What she didn't know, my darling, is that you could have been a Hottentot for all I'd care! I'd have married you whatever the color of your parents' skin!"

She felt his arm around her tighten and she leaned a little against him, blinking into the sunlight.

"But if she had made inquiries, she'd have found out how wrong she was!"

"By that time, it wouldn't matter. She would have had Eve and Bridget and Jaimie's signatures for the sale of the land — *they* were to pay in advance with their agreement to sign. If she were proved wrong about you, then it would be too late for the family to withdraw. She would have the land development company's signature, a promise of her share of the sale of the nurseries plus the big commission they had promised her if she managed to put the deal through for them. She couldn't lose, you see."

"So I — as a person — didn't matter to her!"

"You were just the vehicle she was using for her own ends, I'm afraid. I was blind; but then one is when one is very close to people, and since the others thought they would gain what they wanted — *who* they wanted — by Sapphira's scheme, they were careful to keep me ignorant of what was going on. But I had my own anxiety, Anna —"

She looked at him. "What?"

"Aidan," he said. "That was something I had to fight. Only suddenly I saw how mad it was to mind your friendship. A woman wouldn't love one man and marry another — so what was I worrying about?" He turned her around to face him, hands on her shoulders. "There's one thing I want you to do before we go to South America."

"We aren't going, Martin!"

"Oh, but we are! We'll put two years between the past and the future, Anna. After what's happened, it's best that way. Darling," he chided, laughing, "you look all set to argue. Don't! I *want* to go — and I mean that. I've talked to your parents and you're going to stay here with them until the wedding. But what I want you to do, if you will, is to come down to Dion House again, just for a weekend."

"Oh, Martin!" she just managed not to shudder.

"I know. But it will be different now. Sapphira won't be there — she'll be away for a long time. The others are beaten and ashamed. Sapphira always ruled them and she worked on them too hard and they weren't strong enough to resist her. *She* mixed the poison; they just swallowed it because it was forced on them. Their fault was their weakness. Only Bridget tried to fight her. But Anna, forgive them, will you?"

"Of course. Oh, Martin!" she cried impulsively. "Loving you, knowing what you went through with Gillian, I didn't want to harass you any more. I wanted to try and sail through it. I told myself 'it's only for a few weeks. I can stand it.' But it nearly broke me."

"Don't ever 'stand anything' for me again! I should have been aware of what was happening, only I was too used to Sapphira to notice the subtle change in her."

"The one thing they all tried to do was to keep their behavior towards me separate from you. But it's all over – I've got to remember that – to forget –"

"And forgive?" He cupped her face and kissed her. "Tonight we're going to celebrate your parents' arrival. We're going to dance."

She looked down at herself. "In a suit and black walking shoes?"

"Oh, I've brought your evening things with me. Your new white evening dress arrived and Eve has repacked it. Bridget found your sandals, and the amethyst pendant and nylons. They've thought of everything you'll need."

Gestures of friendship . . . pleas for forgiveness. In that moment she would have forgiven the whole world!

THORNDIKE PRESS HOPES you
have enjoyed this Large Print
book. All our Large Print titles
are designed for the easiest
reading, and all our books are
made to last. Other Thorndike
Press Large Print books are
available at your library,
through selected bookstores, or
directly from the publisher. For
more information about our
current and upcoming Large
Print titles, please send your
name and address to:

THORNDIKE PRESS
ONE MILE ROAD
P.O. Box 157
THORNDIKE, MAINE 04986

There is no obligation, of course.